CW00540794

SEEING THINGS

SUZANNE LINSEY-MITELLAS

Matador
9 Priory Business Park,
Wistow Road, Kibworth Beauchamp,
Leicestershire. LE8 0RX
Tel: 0116 279 2299
Email: books@troubador.co.uk
Web: www.troubador.co.uk/matador
Twitter: @matadorbooks

ISBN 978 1800460 300

British Library Cataloguing in Publication Data.
A catalogue record for this book is available from the British Library.

Typeset in 11pt Baskerville by Troubador Publishing Ltd, Leicester, UK

Matador is an imprint of Troubador Publishing Ltd

ACKNOWLEDGEMENTS:

Thank you to my family, both the living and the dead, who supported and encouraged me through the toughest of times, without them I would not be here now.

I would especially like to thank:

My husband and best friend Alan, for his love and devotion, and for the many hours he spent editing and improving my novel. Without his support 'Seeing Things' would never have made it to publication.

My eldest son Lewis, who has grown into a strong, intelligent and wonderful young man that any mum would be proud of.

My youngest son Trent, for his interesting plot and character ideas.

My late mother and father, Maureen and Peter Linsey, for their love, support and strong values that shaped me into the person I am today.

Last, but certainly not least, a special thanks to my late grandmother, Alice Whitfield, for her strength of character, and her fascinating stories and experiences of the paranormal which were the basis for this book.

Let no one be found among you who consigns his son or daughter to the fire, or who is an augur, a soothsayer, a diviner, a sorcerer, one who casts spells, or one who consults ghosts or familiar spirits, or one who inquires of the dead.

Deuteronomy 18:10-11

Behold, I set before you this day a blessing and a curse.

Deuteronomy 11:26

PROLOGUE

The boy walked down the middle of the magnificent room and sat beside the old rabbi. Being dressed mostly in black, with a white shirt, skull cap and ringlets, the boy looked much the same as his fellows whom he had left playing and cat-calling to each other on the synagogue steps.

"I must speak to you, Rabbi. It is a matter of importance," he declared.

The old man, who had been deep in prayer, frowned. He removed his small horn-rimmed spectacles, rubbed them on his sleeve and replaced them on his nose before looking slowly at the child. "Unless you have something important to say, Adam, you should not be talking in the shul." He dropped his head back down to resume his devotions.

"It is most urgent; it is about a vision I had, about something to come. I must tell you so that you may act upon it."

The rabbi made a low, grumbling noise and turned to the child. "Visions... fortune telling... it is not permitted. I am aware that your family knows more about this than most, but you must refrain from entering the darkened path of the soothsayers."

The boy looked into the distance. "I was allowed to see this vision by our Creator, so we might be saved... *all* humanity might be saved from an evil coming to this world. I was instructed to find you, Rabbi Lieberman, and tell you about this, so you could stop it."

The old man turned sharply. "Immodesty is wrong, Adam. You believe He would speak to you about a matter such as this, even though there are older and more righteous men walking the earth, who are far better placed to take on such a message of importance? Why would He choose a young boy? How old are you?"

"I am nine, Rabbi."

"A nine-year-old child, chosen by Him, to speak of the coming of evil. It would not be right."

"Let me tell you my vision. He asks I share it with you, so I must."

The old man went to open his mouth, then closed it again. Looking to his right, he saw the child's father with the other men, standing deep in conversation, forming a mass of black coats and hats. Should he listen to this transgression? If he didn't, Adam would no doubt disturb his prayer further. He rather hoped that there was nothing substantial in what the child was about to say, but, knowing Adam's lineage, anything the boy said should at least be heard out. "To me, it sounds like a load of baloney," he said. "But if you must speak, make it brief."

"Yes, Rabbi." Adam settled down, and spoke slowly and deliberately. "His voice came to me in a vision. It was not a dream; I was not asleep but was walking to my room when I saw, through my own eyes, what may come to pass…"

"Continue."

"There was a woman, who was maybe thirty, walking slowly across a bridge that was like one of those rope bridges you see in jungles, which sway in the wind. It was suspended between two sheer cliffs: one in sunlight, warmed by the sun, and the other one in front of her, darkened and cold, as if in shade…" Adam hesitated, looking intently at the rabbi, before saying, "*He* spoke to me and told me about this woman and her importance."

"Is she a Jew?" broke in the rabbi.

"No… but she had some kind of misfortune, which means she can see the dead and *shedim*, but without ailing or her sight being robbed from her. She is powerful, but is unaware of the importance of the treasure she commands. He told me that, unless it is stopped by good men, evil will use her for its own ends. The creatures that live in darkness will see this power and use it against the righteous."

"Is that it?" asked Rabbi Lieberman.

"No, there is another woman, who is young… She also has the same powers as the first, but is not manipulated by the creatures of the darkness. She may be our ally."

"Is *she* a Jew?"

"No, but she wears something across her face, like a curtain." To demonstrate, Adam held his sleeve helpfully across his own face, so only his eyes showed.

"Harrumph… So what your so-called vision tells us is that an evil is coming to wreak havoc, and the only two people who can stop it are non-Jews and, what's more, are *women?*"

"Yes, Rabbi."

"This is all preposterous. I believe none of it."

"He told me that you would one day witness the first woman and that it would be up to you to assemble brothers to drive the *shedim* from her, or if that fails, to make sure she does not remain in this world or the next."

"Do you mean *murder* her? Go to your father, Adam. I wish to hear no more."

"Only you can stop it. This is why I have spoken of my vision. He has entrusted the future of all of humanity to you."

The old man turned angrily to the boy. Pointing to an older man in robes who was speaking to Adam's father, he spat, "Why not tell this hokum to your own rabbi? See, him there... Tell him this tale of evil about to assail all mankind, and the ridiculous idea of women... and me... saving the world from darkness. Why tell me when he stands before you?"

Adam stood up on seeing his father approach. "Because he is no use, Rabbi Lieberman. Like me, he is alive, but you are dead, and we need someone on your side of the veil to be effective."

With that, he walked away, leaving his perplexed father to stare at the completely empty seat his son had just been speaking to moments ago.

CHAPTER 1

Sitting in the classroom alone and listening to the children playing outside, she knew there was about two hours' worth of work to do in about thirty minutes. She had got so behind, and she knew why, but playing on her mind more and more was how she was going to catch up and get her life back on track.

The children could be heard outside, screaming and laughing distantly; they were so carefree. Looking back down at her lesson plan, which had been due two days before, her mind immediately went blank. Her head had been pounding recently, worse than normal, and she had been doing everything possible to try to stop the pain so she could get on with her life and—

"Cough."

The noise made her turn around, only to see the headteacher, Mr Andrews, filling the doorway. To his right, the wall was decorated with a poster, showing a rough drawing of a bird with the words 'Penguins need love' in a child's writing over the top. Some said Mr Andrews resembled a fat bird; more specifically, a turkey.

"Miss Holloway, have you got the lesson plans for next week?" he enquired.

She hadn't done them; the pain in her head twisted like a corkscrew. *What shall I say? Shall I admit I haven't done them or lie?* "I have started them," she said, "but I thought they needed some fine tuning, which is what I am doing now. They will be ready on Monday, without fail."

"They should have been on my desk today."

"I know, Mr Andrews. Apologies for that, but I wanted to make some last-minute changes."

"Monday; last chance, Rachel."

Somewhere in the distance, a bell went, and the school began to rumble at once with the feet of hundreds of children, as if it had instantly stirred itself to life. Mr Andrews jumped at the sound, like an antelope hearing the growl of a tiger, and rushed away.

Monday. I need to get it sorted for Monday, mused Rachel. Her head ached again. She checked the clock on the wall, clipping time away gently; there was approximately three minutes before her next class came in.

Rachel closed her papers in front of her, reached into her bag and pulled out the shiny, small wrapper that contained her migraine medication: her magic – or not so magic – bullet. She popped a pill out frantically and swallowed it with a small mouthful of water from the bottle on her desk. *Please let this kill the migraine*, she thought.

Before putting away her bag, she pulled out the textbook needed for the next class. As she stood up ready for the children's arrival, she saw a small movement out of the very corner of her eye; it was almost imperceptible, but it was there. A flicker, then it was gone. *A mouse? Please, God, not mice again.* She would have to tell the maintenance staff.

★

Rachel had woken up worried. Everything had felt different, but she didn't know why. She had been feeling unwell since yesterday and her migraines had been growing steadily worse during the last three weeks or so. Her vision had also become increasingly blurred, and she had felt dizzy a few times as well. The doctor had said her blood pressure was extremely high, so had increased her medication. She knew what the problem was: stress. That little word that creeps up on everyone. That modern plague of stress. But what was she supposed to do about it?

Her job as a primary school teacher, which had been her profession since leaving university, had given her a lot of pleasure; however, as the years had passed, the work had become more and more bureaucratic. There had been more paperwork, more and more difficult parents (or so it seemed) and more incidents where her teaching ability had been called into question. There were also longer hours now and more classes to deal with.

It appeared that the children coming through the gates were becoming more challenging. Some even arrived at school in nappies, unable to read or write, or without the slightest grasp of basic life skills or manners. Rachel thought a lot about the children. She had gone into teaching to help young people, and now, more than ever, she felt she was making less and less of a difference. Less of her time was spent working with the children in the classroom, and more and more of her time was spent fighting for equipment, resources and help for her increasingly vulnerable pupils. It had taken its toll on her.

She had felt so ill recently, what with the blood pressure and the migraines that were barely held back by this dam of pills that she kept popping – a dam of pills that was constantly springing leaks.

Rachel got out of bed slowly, as she always did. After getting ready, she decided to finish the lesson preparation notes, which would at least be one less thing to worry about on Monday.

With papers and pen at the ready, sitting in the room, she forced her mind back to the lesson and being back in the empty classroom. Then she felt it; it was as if someone was gently pressing a finger into the side of her head. It was an odd feeling, like a hand that wasn't there, pressing into her left temple. Then the familiar pain began, increasing slowly with each heartbeat. She went to get her bag again. It was time to pop another pill.

CHAPTER 2

The fact that all the lights were off in their flat should have been taken as a sign, but then John was never very good at heeding subtle signs. He always said it would need to be a six-foot-high sign, embellished with lights, before he would notice it; it was a joke he always said in pubs or at birthday parties. It wasn't clever or funny, but that didn't stop him saying it.

He let himself in, dropped his bag by the door, switched on the light and walked past the table, which was strewn with school books. He glanced at them, then went to the fridge and pulled out a beer. He frowned to himself, thinking, *Rachel? Where the hell is she?*

He went to the bedroom. Rachel was in bed. *She's probably ill again or maybe suffering another headache. Which one? I'd better show sympathy.* "Are you OK?" he asked, and then he sat down by the bed. He couldn't see her, just a shape.

"No, I've got a bad head… I'm really ill. It's a bad one; my eyes are hurting too now," Rachel explained.

"Oh, have you taken your pills?"

"Yeah, they're not working."

It's best to leave her to it when she's like this. In the two years that John had been with Rachel, he had noticed her health had got worse. She had her good days and bad days, but now she was sick more times than she was well. "I don't suppose you want to do anything tonight?" he murmured, already knowing what the answer would be.

"No, sorry; I really don't feel well at all."

Well, that's that then. Another Saturday night blown out. He felt himself caught between going out, and therefore making himself resemble 'the uncaring boyfriend', or playing safe by staying in and falling asleep in front of the TV. He felt like an old man, and he was only thirty. *Screw this.* "OK," he said.

Rachel felt his upset, but what could she do? She had worries of her own, and the pain was terrible, as if someone had put a power drill to her head, and was drilling slowly right into her skull and brain. She could feel the pulsing of the drill and the scraping of the bit. She lay on her left-hand side, where the pain was, hoping that might help. It didn't.

She went off to sleep eventually, but her dreams were plagued with nightmares. She saw dark figures, flashing back and forth, then the dream cleared, and she found herself on a flimsy rope bridge, strung between two cliffs. Standing in the middle, being buffeted by the wind, she saw both of the cliff edges: the one behind her was in sunlight, and she could see people standing there, watching and calling to her. She turned to what lay in front of her, where the bridge was tethered. Here, the cliff was in dusk. Figures were standing there as well, but they were silent and in darkness. They were not calling, just watching; watching her…

On Monday morning, Rachel felt a whole lot better. She had been unwell most of Sunday, but she had slept it off and was pleasantly surprised to find that the pain had gone. She was almost back to her normal self, and she was grateful about that because she was going to be very busy at school that day. The inspectors were coming in later in the week, so everyone had to be on top form. Rachel felt good; nothing was going to stop her now.

Rachel had noticed John had left earlier than usual that morning. She was sorry she had messed up his plans for the weekend, but she had been so ill and was sure that he would understand.

On arriving at the school, Rachel saw everyone rushing around, getting ready for the inspectors on Thursday. The building had been cleaned, the paperwork had been audited, the staff had been advised to look their best, and they were particularly on the lookout for troublesome parents who could walk into the building at an inopportune moment and mess everything up. She took her place at her desk, allowing herself plenty of time to prepare. It was still half an hour before the bell. She was ready for anything.

Except the mouse.

Rachel saw something twitch out of the corner of her eye, but the movement was higher up this time, at waist height, not on the floor. She jumped and emitted a small cry. Looking around to see if anyone had heard her, Rachel stood up to investigate the area where the movement had been, by some cupboards. Picking up a ruler from her desk, she

7

poked at the cupboard and removed a child's coat that had been left hanging limply from a door beside it. *Could a mouse climb that high? God, maybe it was a rat. It must have been a rat,* she thought. She made a decision to contact the maintenance department immediately after class and tell them about this. The movement had been quick and unmistakeable. *What else could it be?*

The classroom door flew open.

"Are you OK? Ready for another day of shits and giggles?" It was Sally Green, Rachel's closest friend in the school.

"Yeah, I guess," answered Rachel. "Where's the big boss?"

"Probably in his room, combing his 'tache; you know, doing something to *really* help the school pass the inspection." Sally smiled and walked into the classroom, noticing Rachel's uneasy bearing. "Are you OK, Rach?"

"No, I haven't been too well; the headaches, you know... Have you seen mice in here?"

"Mice? God, no... Have you?"

"I think so..." Rachel pointed to the cupboards. "A couple of times, I saw a movement by the cupboards. I think it was a mouse – or a rat – moving about."

"Ugh." Sally winced. "I don't want to be here if one of them comes out. Maybe we need a school cat; it'd be cheaper than exterminators. I'll suggest it to Mr Andrews. See you later." With that, she left.

Rachel watched Sally stride out of the classroom, closing the door behind her. Unexpectedly, she felt a small pain starting at her temple. It was just a tickle at first, but then it rapidly grew in intensity, accompanied by a wave of nausea. She thought the migraine had gone away. The very last thing she needed was it coming back now.

The bell went, prompting the school to begin to heave itself slowly into life, like a giant animal waking from a long slumber. Voices started to ring out from the corridors, and the clump of hundreds of feet shook the floor. Rachel watched the door fly open, followed by the customary torrent of schoolchildren flooding into the classroom. Her eyes began to water, and she felt dreadfully dizzy, so she sat down at her desk, hoping it would pass. A small-but-persistent well of panic overcame her, just briefly.

"Are you OK, miss?" asked Abbie, one of her pupils.

Rachel, determined not to make a fuss, simply replied, "Yes, I am fine."

Abbie looked both unconvinced and concerned in equal measure. She smiled weakly, and then walked to her desk and sat down.

Everyone was sitting down now, looking at Rachel, more quietly than usual.

It came with no real warning. Akin to a bolt of lightning, tearing through the sky and striking her, almost like a physical impact or whiplash in the world's worse car crash.

Bang!

A pain smashed through the back of her head, unlike anything she had ever experienced before. Rachel felt it pulsing through her body like a searing-hot knife. Her hand slapped instinctively to the back of her neck, and she closed her eyes against the agony. In a few nanoseconds, her brain tried to form coherent thoughts: *Has the migraine come back?*

Have I taken too many pills to stop it? But, as the pain grew from agony to indescribable torment, she stopped thinking and just reacted. She was vaguely aware that something was very, very wrong. She tried to speak; her mouth moved but nothing came out, and her tongue felt too large for her mouth. Panic started. Pain and panic. The torture was causing waves of nausea to wrack her body.

Please make it stop. God help me, she pleaded. Rachel tried to stand up, but she could barely move. Her legs would not take the weight of her body. In spite of her profound distress, she also felt an acute pang of embarrassment, as she was making a spectacle of herself in front of the children. That was the worst thing.

The children looked horrified.

I need to stand up and get help. The pain kept growing and growing, enveloping her. She felt tears forming in her eyes and then saw them spilling onto her desk. Her frazzled mind decided to put everything it had left into an immense effort to make her body stand up, so she did.

It was the last thing that she remembered.

CHAPTER 3

Light was everywhere. Bright light. Sounds and smells. *What's happening?* she thought. She tried to speak, but it was a wasted effort. Her brain and her mouth may as well have been in different time zones. *Where am I?*

There were more lights; so many lights. There was also dull pain now, in her head.

White light. Now she started remembering the torture she had experienced in the classroom.

Dead. Am I dead? Is this heaven? Rachel tried to make a noise again, but nothing happened.

Then came a face – a lady looking at her – but then the lady was gone.

Two nurses appeared at Rachel's bedside and checked the machines beside her. "She is awake," one of them said.

Rachel's mind drifted away. In her dreams, she revisited the people on the cliff again, but they were closer this time. They were still watching her. They looked more or less like regular people, except they were slightly faded and dark, as if they had been drawn with a charcoal pencil. She could hear the sound of people calling to her distantly. She looked over her shoulder and saw them on the opposing cliff that was bathed in light; she then looked back at the people in front of her. They remained in the shade. They remained silent.

★

Rachel spent seven days in the intensive care unit, drifting in and out of consciousness. Now she lay in her bed, in a general ward. She often found herself ruminating over how slowly time seemed to pass. Days felt like little eternities, just watching the patients come and go. What a mixed bunch they were. Just today, she had seen a soldier in a dated military uniform, bloodied and with bandages around his head, being guided around the ward by a comrade. He looked very seriously ill, and half of his arm was missing. Then there was the young boy with callipers on his legs. *Did people still wear those?* she wondered. He just stood in the corner of the ward, staring into space. She would ask the doctor about him; it wasn't right for a child to be left in a ward with seriously ill adults.

Rachel was somehow aware of her visitor before she saw him. She looked up and saw a man standing at the end of the bed, watching her closely. He was in his late forties to early fifties, slim and balding, but he still had a glint in his eye. He was very smartly dressed in pressed trousers, a slightly oversized shirt, a loose necktie, a jacket and a waistcoat, with a beard that lightly covered his chin. She knew beards had come back into fashion, but she had no idea why a doctor would sport one. He just stood there, looking at her. *This must be my doctor*, she presumed. *He's probably a surgeon; they're usually eccentric, aren't they? Why else would he wear a waistcoat and suit on a ward?*

"Doctor?" said Rachel. Her speech had returned, although her voice was raspy, and it was hard to get words out.

Her visitor looked surprised. "You can *see* me?" he said, coming closer.

"Yes, of course… My eyes… are a bit blurry, but yes. You are a doctor?"

"Yes… yes, I am."

"Shouldn't you be wearing gloves?" Rachel pointed weakly to his hands.

"I only wear gloves to the theatre; why would I wear gloves here?" He smiled again and sat down on the edge of the bed.

Oh no, a joker, thought Rachel before saying, "So what's wrong with me? What happened?"

"You can actually see me? Properly?" he said again, waving his hand to and fro in front of her face.

"Yes, my eyes are fine, thank you. Please, what happened to me? Can you tell me?"

"Oh, that." He paused for some time, deliberating over how best to tackle Rachel's question. "You had a bleed in your brain. It made you faint. They call it a subarachnoid haemorrhage; it's on your records there." He gestured towards her file at the foot of the bed. "They stopped it so you should feel much better now, thanks to the miracle of modern surgery, I would say."

Rachel was shocked. *Was that it?* She expected more from a surgeon; for instance, an account of what had happened in the operating theatre, as well as a clearer prognosis.

The lady in the bed opposite looked at her in an odd way, but said nothing.

Lowering her voice, Rachel queried, "I had a brain haemorrhage? What caused it?"

The doctor was still looking at her intently. "I don't know," he said. "Perhaps there was a problem with your humours or possibly the hemispheres were out of synchronicity. The people here are quite skilled at fixing that sort of problem." He got up from the bed and made to leave.

"That's it?" she enquired.

"For now," he replied, then he smiled and walked away.

Rachel watched him leave the ward.

Another doctor appeared, less than ten seconds after the last one had left. This one was in a blue theatre gown, with a paper mask hanging from his ear, and he was clutching papers. "Good afternoon, Miss Holloway; I am Dr Richard Brown," he said. "How are you feeling today?" He picked up the file from the end of her bed and started reading through her medical notes.

"A bit better," she responded. She decided that the last chap was most likely the doctor in charge of the ward, and this was the surgeon.

"You have been quite unwell," said Dr Brown, without looking up from her file. "Do you know what happened to you?"

Rachel sighed, hoping this man was better than the first doctor. "Yes, the other doctor told me. A suber-acker-nal haemorrhage or something? Bleeding in my brain?"

He looked up from his notes. "What doctor?"

"The doctor who was just here. He was old-fashioned-looking. So, is that what happened to me?"

"Yes, that is what happened, but there is no other doctor on duty on this ward." The doctor looked concerned.

Rachel noticed that the patient in the bed opposite hers was talking conspiratorially to one of the nurses. She pointed at Rachel in a fleeting, small way, probably hoping she wouldn't see her doing so.

"Well, he was here and he said that is what happened; I didn't make it up, did I? Anyway, what's going to happen to me?" questioned Rachel.

The doctor explained, "You will stay here for another week, then you will be able to go home. You've suffered a significant bleed to your brain – a subarachnoid haemorrhage – and you will need medications and monitoring to ensure the best outcome possible. We had to operate to stop the bleeding, so only time will tell how your recovery will go. Do you have any questions?"

Rachel had a few, but felt too exhausted. "No, that's fine for now, thank you," she said.

The doctor nodded and moved on to another patient in a neighbouring bed.

As Dr Brown left the ward, Rachel saw the nurse speak furtively to him on the way out. Rachel also noticed that the woman in the opposite bed was looking at her more intently than ever.

CHAPTER 4

Hospital life was quite boring, though interspersed with small distractions that helped pass the time. However, the increasing strangeness of the people on the ward began to distress her. A woman in odd clothes often hurried through, muttering to herself and clutching a bag. Rachel assumed that she was a relative of a patient. What was most concerning was that she always saw her entering the ward, striding to the far end and disappearing around the corner, where the toilet and wash room facilities were. Rachel never actually saw her leave the ward. Not once. And there was only one way out of the ward, which was also the only way in. *Maybe I fall asleep without realising. Maybe she leaves whilst I'm asleep. That's got to be why I don't see her,* she pondered.

The boy in the callipers still stood in the corner, watching her mournfully. However, she didn't see the horrifically injured soldier and his comrade again. *Maybe he had been at a fancy-dress party and had a terrible accident? I bet if this had been a private hospital, I wouldn't have had to share my space with such odd people.*

Rachel decided to try to think no more about it. The pain in her head was just a dull ache now, although the doctors had told her that the discomfort may never go away completely. They had shaved a chunk of her hair off to operate and advised it might be better if she cut her hair short till it grew back. Rachel decided against this; she loved her shoulder-length hair. *No, I'll just pin my hair over the bald spot for a while.*

Come what may, everything needed to get back to normal.

★

One month after 'the event', as Rachel called it, she was finally discharged from hospital. John was due to come at 2pm to collect her. She kept looking at her watch whilst sitting up in bed, with a plastic bag of belongings by her side that Sally had kindly gathered from her home. *Just another hour and I'm out of here…*

The eccentric doctor appeared again at the end of her bed; the one she had seen after she first woke up in hospital an eternity ago. "You are leaving us? That's a shame. I shall miss you," he declared.

Rachel regarded him cautiously. "They say I am well enough to go home now. I am sure there will be other patients to tend to."

"Not the same as you."

She felt uncomfortable. *Is this guy trying to chat me up?* She ignored him and tried to look forwards, so as not to catch his gaze. *This is awkward.* Time slowed down and oozed like treacle.

"Suit yourself," said the doctor.

Rachel turned towards him, but he was gone.

The same nurse who had tended to her most of the week walked to her bedside. Her face was set and grave. "Miss Holloway," she whispered, sitting on a chair by the bed. "Doctor has been concerned about you and about your recovery."

"You mean him?" Rachel gestured towards the curtain where the doctor had stood moments before. "Yes, he does seem concerned about me, doesn't he?"

"There is no one there, Miss Holloway."

"Yes, yes, I know that. He was there... He's gone now." Puzzled, she looked at the nurse.

"What else do you see, Miss Holloway?"

The nurse's repetition of her name, coupled with her authoritarian attitude, was starting to annoy her. "What are you getting at?"

"On the ward, around you, do you see anything worth mentioning? Anything unusual?"

Rachel paused, looked around, then pointed to the boy who was standing in his usual place in the far corner of the ward. "That's pretty unusual. He should be on a children's ward, and what's with the vintage leg braces? Have things really got that bad for the National Health Service?"

The nurse looked up, her face frozen. "Anything else?"

"The soldier... When I first came in, there was a soldier in here as well."

"Are you sure?"

"Yes, of course. He was wearing a dark-green uniform, and he looked like he was injured badly. Maybe it was fancy dress, but it looked pretty real to me."

"The doctor has said he wishes you to stay in a while longer, to see our other doctor, as your brain may have suff—" The nurse reconsidered her words. "Your brain may have undergone some changes that we have not taken into account." She stood up and began to walk away from Rachel's bedside.

"No. I want to leave. I am fine…" Rachel's mind started to churn over the information. "What changes? What do you mean?"

"The doctor will explain," answered the nurse over her shoulder, as she breezed out of the ward.

★

The following day, Rachel was taken to a doctor's room that was located a short distance along a corridor near the ward (the nurse had said that another 'health professional' would be caring for her for a while). She found herself in a brightly lit room, looking at a poster of Donald Duck and Mickey Mouse on the wall. Rachel didn't know why a doctor would have such a poster. *Maybe to entertain children?* she wondered.

As she waited, she saw a nurse come in through the door behind her, who was dressed in unusual clothes. Rachel could see she was a nurse, but she noticed that the lady was wearing a very old-fashioned uniform, which consisted of a starched, blue dress that hung past her knees; an apron; and a large, white, wimple-type hat. The nurse bustled in, went to the far corner of the room, appeared to be doing something (Rachel couldn't see what), and then walked past her and out.

As Rachel contemplated how rude it was that the nurse had ignored her, she heard a click as the door closed behind her. A man in a suit came in, who was about forty and very smartly dressed, with a bow tie on.

"Good afternoon, Miss Holloway," he said.

"Please call me Rachel," she offered.

"Rachel… Ah, yes." He sat down behind the desk, which took up most of the room, and opened a brown folder full of papers. "I am Mr Lunn; did the nurse tell you why you are seeing me?"

"No… just that I might have more damage to my head than you first thought. The nurse was very vague."

"Yes… possibly. Tell me, the nurse says you see *unusual* people in the ward, is that right?"

Unusual people? Her brain struggled with the question. "Oh, the boy with the things on his legs, and the woman who comes through the ward every day… Yeah, I guess they are unusual, but other patients aren't really my business."

"You… speak to them?"

"No, not really."

"Do they… er… speak to you?"

"No…"

"What about the 'doctor'?"

"What doctor?"

He sat back in his chair and folded his hands. "You seemed to be talking to someone you called 'doctor'. You did it on the morning when you first awoke; do you remember?"

"Which doctor? I saw two: the old-fashioned man and then the surgeon in the blue."

"The first one. We know about the second doctor; he is your surgeon. You saw a man by your bed and he said he was a doctor?"

She knew it. He was probably an imposter, someone who dresses up and pretends to be someone he isn't; she had read about cases such as that in the paper. "Yes, he did say he was; isn't he a doctor then?"

"No… no, he isn't. Miss Holloway, it is our opinion that the bleed to your brain appears to have caused you to begin to hallucinate, and this can mean a number of things."

"Hallucinate? What do you mean?"

"The doctor you speak of… There is no such doctor. No boy with 'things on his legs' or anything like that. Rachel, you are simply seeing things, things that are not there, and we need to find out why."

Her brain began to fog up again. She really didn't understand what this man was talking about. "What do you mean not there? Of course he was there. I saw him; I spoke to him."

"Yes, you were seen speaking, but to thin air; no one was there. You imagined this doctor, and chances are that it's also true of this boy in callipers, or whatever they were, and this other woman you say walks through the ward. You were seen by another patient – on more than one occasion, even today – talking to yourself. I am a psychiatrist, and I am here to help you, as there may have been something we missed when we first looked at your scan. More damage, for example, causing these hallucinations."

"I am not hallucinating…"

"They may seem very real, but they are not. We will be

discharging you, but you will be under the care of a mental health professional, and it will be put on your notes."

★

Half an hour later, Rachel was sitting on her bed again, waiting for John to pick her up. The boy in callipers had gone, at last. Nothing was amiss. Thoughts went round and round in her head, *Hallucinating? I couldn't have been; it all seemed so real. A mental health doctor... great. I'm not mad; they were there, and that doctor spoke to me.* To suggest she was mad was upsetting.

She lay back and closed her eyes. Maybe when she got home, things might get a little better. She had to keep positive; whatever happened, she didn't really have a choice.

CHAPTER 5

Andy knew he was different to most other people. He was 41 and had never really had a long-term girlfriend, or what people often referred to as a 'proper job', but he got by. Living as a lodger in his room with the elderly widow, Mrs Braithwaite, seemed an odd arrangement, but it suited him. When he got evicted from his last flat, Mrs Braithwaite – a friend of his deceased father – had said he could have her spare room. At first, he hesitated; at 85, he feared she may be a little intolerant of his lifestyle, but he need not have worried. She spent most days helping at the church and having tea in cafés; she was also mostly deaf, which was handy. The room was rented to him for next to nothing, and Andy helped her out with things around the house and doing the shopping. He felt at home now. Andy saw Mrs Braithwaite like a grandmother, as his own grandparents had died long ago.

Andy was not able to live with his mother; he had tried that, twice now, and both times had failed. People had asked why he struggled in this rented room when his mother lived three miles away in a large house with two large empty bedrooms. He didn't wish to explain, but would simply reply, "We don't get on," and leave it at that. Not getting on was an understatement, as Andy and his mother were like chalk and cheese. Once – at a Christmas luncheon, in fact – she had announced, to his then short-term girlfriend that, "I love Andy, as he is my son, but I do not like him." This kind of summed up the relationship they had suffered since Andy had passed puberty. Prior to that, she could control him, and she decided what he wore, said and did; however, after that – when he had started making up his mind about the world, the direction he had wanted to take and the kind of man he had wanted to be – she had begun to reject him.

She criticised him for being slightly overweight, his dress sense and the fact he insisted on wearing a small ponytail at the back of his head, although he was slightly balding. It was odd, he recalled, as when he reached forty, he had considered shaving off the ponytail, until his mother went into one of her rages about it and asked if he was gay. Then and there he decided it was staying.

This was why he lived at Mrs Braithwaite's.

Andy Horton wasn't sure what to call himself. When asked outright, "What do you do?", he would reply, "I'm an investigator"; people were inevitably impressed with the title, and asked if he worked with the police and tracked down missing people, till he let the cat out of the bag. He was an investigator all right, but a psychic one. He went to people's houses when they claimed they had hauntings or paranormal activity, and he would – using modern methods and ancient commands – try to find out what the problem was. He made enough money to get by doing this, but his income was topped up by benefits, or he would have been in trouble.

He had never confessed to anyone in the benefits office that he earned cash on the side, as he didn't like talking to people about what he did, unless they seemed open to the fact that spirits and ghosts did exist. He also thought they would probably take a very dim view of this and stop his benefits. Andy found the whole idea held by some that the paranormal world didn't exist to be quite hilarious, as he had seen numerous ghostly activities take place, some mundane and some horrifying.

The problem with ghosts, he always said to clients, was that they didn't know they were not supposed to exist, and people got haunted whether they believed in ghosts or not.

Work had dried up a little since it became more popular to look for paranormal activity in established groups. A lot of ghost hunting 'tours' in his area staged things, so when people attended the events, noises would inevitably be heard, lights seen, things found, tap once for yes and twice for no, etc. He did not subscribe to that; if people were foolish enough to be taken in by money-making tomfoolery, he didn't want them as a client…

At least, that was how he used to feel before his empty wallet managed his conscience out of a job. He needed to find more work. And soon.

★

Coming home had been more difficult than Rachel had thought. The school had signed her off with full pay, but John

25

still had to work, so she was alone in the flat most of the day. Her recovery had been slow. Well, she thought it was slow, but maybe it hadn't been; she didn't know many people who had suffered brain haemorrhages to compare herself with.

The doctors had told her that many people died after having a brain bleed, or were left with permanent disabilities. Rachel was still getting used to what she could and couldn't do, and she was still experiencing a few problems. Her main one was headaches; she had always suffered from headaches and lived on painkillers, but now they were worse. Every other day, she would have a bad throbbing head, which would inevitably end up morphing into a migraine. Pills helped, but she did have to take a lot of them. She was also constantly exhausted, but she was used to dealing with being tired in her job. It seemed that talking or thinking about complicated things was also difficult; the words would often get stuck, and she forgot what she had said. But, overall, things could have been a whole lot worse.

It was like being in a constant fight, akin to Moses commanding the sea, with her holding back her symptoms day and night, using nothing but the power of a concoction of pills. With every twinge of pain she felt, she also would feel panic flood through her, as she feared this might be the start of another haemorrhage. The twinge was always in the same place, at the top left of her skull. She wondered what was there that was causing the twinge and the pain. A person could go mad thinking that way…

She hoped she could go back to teaching in a couple of months. Rachel wanted to return, but she was worried how she would manage. Her job meant she would often have to speak most of the day and teach complicated things; she wasn't sure her mind was up to the job at the moment, but she was hopeful.

Rachel was more worried about John. He had become more distant recently; in fact, to be honest, he had been drifting away from her before this even happened. He'd been staying late at work, rowing with her more and saying things that were unkind. For the first time, she actually began thinking, *What if he left?*

She heaved herself off the sofa and walked to the window. Yawning, she pulled her curtain a little to one side and looked out onto the street; below her, she saw a lady walking along. This woman was wearing a long, black coat and hat, and she had about thirteen children around her, aged between four to twelve. In her arms, there were not one but two babies, both swaddled in cloth. How odd. Maybe it was a school thing, such as fancy dress? The children were all dressed up, some as urchins and others in regal-looking clothes, like lots of little King Henry VIIIs. One, a little girl, wore a pinafore and a bow in her hair. Rachel didn't think this looked good; the woman should have dressed them all the same if it was fancy dress. Also, why take the babies as well? They were real, she saw their hands clasping and moving. Whilst working as a teacher, Rachel had arranged many of these dressing-up events, and decided she would have dressed them as the Von Trapps or perhaps all as urchins. However, with all their different costumes, it looked mismatched.

As the woman drew level with Rachel, she slowly looked up and their eyes met. Rachel smiled; the woman looked

27

back at her, full of sadness, then walked on, her ragtag of children following her.

★

The following week, things were looking up; she felt a lot better, and so she had to do her first follow-up visit to the psychiatrist. As she stepped into the street, the sunlight burnt her eyes, and she fumbled for her dark glasses. A group of about fifty Orthodox Jewish men walked past, seeming to not notice her as she headed for the high street. Dressed in black, with their beards and big hats, they resembled a group of shadows, with half on the pavement, some in the road. They rushed past, talking in what she thought might be Hebrew. Where were they off to? She turned around; they had gone, probably into a shop. *Good luck to any shop owner dealing with them,* she mused.

She continued on her way and, once back at the hospital, she paused on the pavement opposite. Rachel hoped the doctor would have some good news for her, and there would be no more of this crap about her seeing things. She hadn't seen anything odd at all, and she would tell him so.

She crossed the road, entered the building and took the lift to the second floor (before the brain bleed, she would have bounded up the stairs). She quickly swallowed a painkiller before she got to the waiting room, then sat and waited for the doctor.

"Miss Holloway?" It was the same bow-tied doctor Rachel had seen before, the psychiatrist. He motioned that she should come into the room, which was Room 3.

She went in and sat down.

"How are we today? How has everything been going?" he asked.

"Fine. Well, I get very tired and find things hard to say at times, but I am getting there," Rachel confirmed.

"Your surgeon will talk to you about your physical symptoms; I am more concerned about your mental health. Have you seen anything unusual lately?"

"No, not at all. I am quite well in that department; I think I told you before that I am not hallucinating or anything like that."

"You have seen *nothing* odd at all recently then?"

"No, I have not."

"Good, good... We are going to discharge you from our mental health care today; however, should anything become amiss mentally that worries you, you must contact us at once. Do you understand, Rachel?"

Rachel said nothing, but then quickly nodded. Her attention had been snared by the nun in a full wimple and veil standing behind the doctor's half-closed cupboard door. Rachel could see the nun's hands – gnarled, veined and clasped together – and the nun was obviously no simple hallucination, as Rachel saw her chest slowly rise and fall, and heard the slow wheeze as air escaped her desiccated lungs. Rachel looked slowly up to her face, but where a face should have been, under the wimple, was just darkness – a never-ending abyss.

Rachel stood up, thanked the doctor and left.

Outside, standing too close to the door for her liking, was the old-fashioned doctor she had first seen in the ward. Today, he wore a long coat that was buttoned up almost to his neck, a crisp white shirt and cravat, and what appeared

29

to be a slightly larger than usual bowler hat on his head. She jumped when she saw him and walked past hurriedly.

"Rachel, my dear. I must speak with you," he stated.

"I am in a hurry," she replied.

"You need to talk to me."

His voice sounded like he was right behind her, but she had left him back by the psychiatrist's door. Obviously, he was fast on his feet.

"What?" She turned to find him right behind her. "Will you stop harassing me?"

He looked hurt. "Harassing… but…" He closed his mouth and looked at her. "I need to explain your situation to you; you've been seeing odd things, haven't you? Do you know why?"

"What odd things? I am perfectly OK." She looked at him more closely. "Why are you dressed in that way? Aren't you warm?" The afternoon was quite mild; he must be sweltering in that garb.

"I don't feel the heat or cold… You must understand that the woman in the ward, the child in callipers, the soldier, that nun back there… me… Why do you think you see us?"

"You're mad."

"No… I'm not mad, just very dead. Yet you see me; you see all of us… I am thinking perhaps this is a miracle sent to free us from our imprisonment here in purgatory."

"No, sorry, you really are mistaken." She turned and walked away.

"We are all dead, Rachel, yet you see us. You are *the answer*."

She turned to tell him to stop, but he had gone. With a growing sense of unease, she headed home.

CHAPTER 6

Rachel arrived home to find a letter waiting for her from the school. The headteacher wanted to see her next week, which was good news; he probably wanted to talk to her about returning to work.

John was there in the living room, watching TV, with the back of his chair facing her. He never seemed to ask how she was or anything anymore.

Rachel decided she would start the conversation. "I went to the doctor today."

"Oh… what did he say?" John didn't bother to look back; he just sat in his chair. His voice seemed to emanate from the folds of the cloth, as she couldn't see his face.

"Well, it wasn't the doctor I thought it would be. It was not the brain doctor, but a psychiatrist…" She walked round to the side of his chair. She could see him now; his face was intent on the flickering screen before him. Rachel continued, "It was a shrink; it's embarrassing to be honest. They think that the knock on my head made me see things that are not really there… They think I am a bit mad."

He looked at her slowly. "What do you mean see things that are not there? That sounds a bit psychotic. What things? Objects? People?" He began to frown.

"Er… mostly people, I think."

"That's crazy, man." He turned his gaze back to the screen.

"I know; I told them it isn't right. I am not seeing anything that isn't there."

"Why do they think you're seeing things? They wouldn't make it up… Oh, man." he put his hand up, a visible sign that the conversation was over. She walked away, feeling the pain of another headache coming on.

Leaving the living room, Rachel pondered how what the old-fashioned doctor had said about seeing dead people was ridiculous. Dead people didn't walk about; you didn't see them. That was quite the most stupid thing she had ever heard. Right, she would test this theory; the next time she saw someone unusual, she would pay more attention and maybe even speak to them. She would get to the bottom of this, one way or another.

This wasn't what was supposed to happen. Her life up to that point had been difficult, but one thing she had always relied on was that her health wouldn't fail her. She had too many plans for her future – children, maybe marriage, travelling abroad (she had never had enough money to do it up till now) – but a quiet, nagging feeling started in her gut that maybe she was kidding herself, none of this was ever going to happen, and she was an idiot to think so.

No, she thought, *I must keep the faith; everything will be OK. I'm not sure I believe it 100%, but I have to keep thinking that or…* She didn't want to contemplate the 'or', not right now. But it was getting even harder to fight the feelings of panic that kept engulfing her, rising like a tide of pins and needles, which started in her gut, then spread down her limbs, and left her dizzy and weak for hours. In her head, she wrestled with the fear of whether these were panic attacks or something physical, just waiting to consume her, similar to the brain haemorrhage. Rachel tried to brush the fears aside again, but it was growing harder and harder to do so.

★

He stood for a moment in front of the mirrored revolving doors that were placed inside the entrance to the hospital. He had never been so excited in his life, or death, and he hoped he hadn't scared her away. Dr William Maxwell looked at the mirror, which only reflected a couple of chairs and a poster that warned of the dangers of not washing one's hands.

A figure came slowly along the corridor. He walked with a stick, had a grotty bandage over one eye, and wore torn, filthy, old clothes. "'Ow do, Doc," he said.

"Hello Jeremy," greeted the doctor.

"What you be doing 'ere?"

"Where am I supposed to go?" He frowned, still looking in the mirror.

"Bain't no point peering in the looking glass, Doc, cos thee won't see thyself."

"I am aware of that; I am thinking."

Jeremy hobbled round and sat on one of the waiting-area chairs. He winced as his ulcerated leg twinged.

"Be no use to be thinking. Things are what they are, Doc."

"Perhaps not, Jeremy…" The doctor walked round and sat in the chair next to the beggar. He noticed a fly circling; surely it couldn't sense the spiritual putrefaction? "What if I were to tell you I know a woman who can see us… and hear us… clearly. I think she is *the answer*."

The old beggar took a battered metal flask from under his rags "T'would be false 'ope, doc…" He took a swig of whatever contents the flask held, winced, then put the cap back on. "People do see shadows sometimes, but they don't see us. Not for real."

"But she does." Dr Maxwell turned to him. "This young woman sees us, like we see each other, and hears us. My God, if this is salvation, I shall be the first in line."

"Don't you be liking it 'ere, Doc? There is probably worse places thee could go. Maybe the 'other place' ain't so good as some believe. I bide my time 'ere; at least it's what I know."

"How long have you been waiting, Jeremy?"

"I don't rightly know, but I did die just after the concubine was crowned."

"Who? What concubine? Don't speak in riddles, man."

"Anne Boleyn, sir, I died two days after she be crowned. I do know that much."

Dr Maxwell thought hard. "1533?"

"Mayhap…"

"My God, that's nearly 500 years."

"Been long time, sir; this I know."

"So, you more than anyone should want to find *the answer*."

34

Clearly tired of the conversation, Jeremy rose. He took his stick, and he put his full weight onto it. "No, Doc, you want *the answer*. Like I said, there's worse places than 'ere we can find ourselves in. I don't mind tarrying 'ere forever." With that, he hobbled off.

Dr Maxwell stared at the door. Automatic revolving doors; what was that about? What was wrong with a normal door that opened and shut? Newfangled ideas. He was going to find Rachel, as he needed to speak to her, but, God help him, he was not going to go through any revolving door to find her.

CHAPTER 7

Rachel stood, watching the school entrance from across the street. She was glad the headmaster had asked her to come in during lesson time, as the school would be quiet. No children or teachers would be rushing around, asking how she was. Although it was kind, she didn't want to talk about it, she just needed to put it all behind her and concentrate on getting back to work.

As she walked into the reception area, she noticed that the plant she always watered had wilted. No one else had bothered to water it. She took some water from the machine and poured it on the dry earth.

"You don't need to be worrying about that," said the receptionist, walking to greet her.

But Rachel was worried about the plant. She had spent years watering it, and she had only been away a relatively short amount of time, yet already it appeared to have been abandoned as no longer useful.

"Mr Andrews will be ready soon. Why don't you take a seat?" The receptionist gestured to one of the reception seats.

It seemed so odd returning to this school, where she had worked for over ten years, as just a visitor – an outsider – and being asked to sit and wait for entry, rather than just using her staff badge to swipe her way in. Mr Andrews had said she must not use her staff badge whilst off, but that she should come in via the reception and wait. It all seemed so formal. What was she, some kind of threat?

The old walls, which had seen children come and go since the mid-1800s, must have witnessed some drama. Rachel always likened a large school to a village; things were always happening and lives unfolding. People had affairs here or met their partners here, and two people had even died here in her time. One, a teacher, had a heart attack, and the caretaker had been found dead in his room. Arguments and fallings-out happened, as did gossip and even physical fights. Yes, everything happened in a school. She liked it there…

"Rachel, it's good to see you; harrumph." Mr Andrews appeared at her side. "Come with me… How are you?"

She had rehearsed the answer a million times. "I am fine, honestly. I'm just anxious to get things back to normal, really."

They left reception and soon arrived in his office. It was a muddled space, with an old, wooden desk, covered in files and papers; metal filing cabinets with plastic binders piled on top; various calendars pinned to the wall, some two years old; and a poster of the planets.

"Please do sit." He gestured to an old, wooden chair facing his seat.

Rachel sat, as Mr Andrews manoeuvred his bulk around the desk and plonked himself down heavily in his large leather chair, which had a bottom-shaped recess on the seat, probably from years of his ample posterior being placed upon it. Her eye was drawn to a drinks coaster on his desk, adorned with a picture of the Fonz from *Happy Days*. It was complemented with the slogan, 'Sit on it'. She had no idea what that meant.

Rachel started to feel the anxiety rise again. She had been in this office many times before, for meetings, and the mood had always been light, even jovial, though usually only until Mr Andrews had entered and installed his bulk onto the chair. But, now, the mood was different. Even the air in the room felt thicker, as if someone had infused some choking chemical into it; she was finding it hard to breathe.

"Miss Holloway... er... Rachel... we were very distressed when we found out what had happened to you, and on school premises during lesson time. It must have been a horrible experience."

"It was, but, to be honest, I am feeling much better now... It was just one of those things."

"Nonetheless, I would be failing in my duty if I were just to let this pass and put your health at risk by asking you to come back too soon. For this reason, I am going to ask you to remain away from school for the next three months, to see how your recovery goes."

Three months? What the hell? she thought. "Thank you, Mr Andrews, but I don't need three months. I am getting myself back on my feet, I have my medication, and the best thing I can do now is to keep myself busy."

"I have to think of the children."

"The children... What do you mean?"

"They cannot have a teacher who isn't able to… who isn't quite up to the high standards we expect at the school. You have been very unwell, Rachel, and it is going to take a while for your full faculties to return, if indeed they ever do. We cannot have a teacher who is dependent on strong medication to get through the day; that doesn't set the best example to our young people. No, we need to get you rested and well, and we will go from there…"

He stood up, signalling the end of the conversation, and started to leave the room. She also stood up and followed him silently out into reception. He was babbling away, saying something about keeping in touch and occupational health, but she wasn't listening.

As they neared the reception kiosk, a young man came into view, and she could hear his voice drifting over, he was clearly agitated. "So Mr Andrews doesn't want to give a statement. Well, that's fine; we are going to print in half an hour, so I will put it down as 'no comment'."

Behind him stood an elderly lady, in a long, brown coat, furry hat and gloves; she looked sadly and silently at him.

The receptionist stared hopefully as Mr Andrews came into view with Rachel behind him.

"Mr Andrews, good…" The receptionist projected her voice out the gap under the Perspex screen. "This is Luke Fairfax from the *Burwood Echo*; the reporter, remember?"

The reporter Mr Andrews had been trying to avoid all day. "Yes… harrumph… yes… How may I help you?"

"I am his grandmother," said the elderly lady, for no particular reason.

"The allegations made by one of your parents,

Mohammed Siddique, do you refute them? That his son was hit in class by one of your members of staff?" enquired Luke.

"He was not hit," blustered Mr Andrews. "He was restrained."

"He is a fiery, young man," continued the elderly lady. "He's just like his father, my son."

Rachel smiled at her, and then looked towards Mr Andrews, who had grown a bright shade of red.

"Talk to our press office, at the council; I have nothing to say," Mr Andrews continued. He then turned around and stalked off, leaving Rachel standing there.

"His father was an editor," the old lady went on. "He wants to be one too."

"That's good," said Rachel.

"Pardon?" Luke looked up, flustered.

"Oh… your grandmother… just said about you wanting to be an editor; that's good. I would hate to work in the media." She went to walk away.

"My… my what? Who?" He looked at her.

"Your grandmother; she said you wanted to be an editor like your father." She smiled at him then sat down, suddenly feeling very tired.

Luke came and sat beside her. "I am sorry; what are you talking about?"

"He can't see me, silly," said the lady. "You can; he can't."

"Why can't he?" replied Rachel.

"What?" asked Luke.

"You can see us… They can't…" She gestured to her grandson.

The words of the doctor came back. Rachel turned to Luke. "Your grandmother is dead?"

"Yes… a while back." He started to look fearful. "Did you know her?" He started to fumble in his rucksack. "Of course, you must have done; you said something about my father… the editor."

"Yes, I knew her…" Rachel looked at the grandmother, who was smiling broadly. "Blue eyes, greyish hair, always in a bun, and what was it with that brown hat with the red pin?" She fixed her eyes on the red pin secured firmly to the old lady's hat; the pin caught the light as she spoke.

"The pin… Oh yes." He took a pen out of his bag. "My grandfather bought it in Italy for her. I didn't like it; I thought it looked like an insect casing. My, you did know her well."

Rachel immediately felt very unwell. She did not know Luke or his grandmother, but she had to test what she thought she was seeing: a dead woman, a ghost, standing before her, large as life. Just as the doctor had said. Was she mad? But she wasn't hallucinating; this man had just confirmed that this was his grandmother.

"I wouldn't tell too many people you can see us, my dear," the grandmother suggested hurriedly. "They will think you are a lunatic." She smiled again.

A lunatic. Rachel was starting to realise something radical had happened to her brain when she had suffered that haemorrhage. But going mad? No, she didn't think that was what had happened at all.

"I need to go," she stated, then stood up. Her head started swimming.

"Don't go," said Luke, "It's nice to hear someone who knew my grandmother." He removed a mobile phone from his bag. "Tell you what, are you free later?"

"I think I may never work again," she declared unexpectedly. "This means I'll probably have a lot of free time now, so, yes, I suppose I am."

His grandmother had wandered over to a children's display of posters and was examining them intently.

What was it with dead people wearing coats, even when it is warm? Did they die in their coats? Or maybe being dead makes you cold? Rachel mused on what an odd prospect that was.

CHAPTER 8

The day had been booked months ago; she didn't really want to go, but decided that unless she was going to refund the two £30.00 tickets for her and Sally, she had better show up. It was originally Sally's idea to visit the old medieval castle, perched high on a hill, as part of some history project they were arranging for the children. Was this a pointless trip now? Rachel wasn't sure. At least it got her out of the flat she shared with John, who was becoming ever more distant.

The days of not having to go to work had started off fine, but they had started to merge one into another. Time no longer mattered; she looked at the clock less, but her mind began worrying about the future more. The school said that she would be on full pay for three months, but then she would be 'reviewed', whatever that meant. They didn't say she would be invited to come back to work or even to come back in to talk to Mr Andrews; no, it was to be 'reviewed'. Rachel had no family, and no one but herself to rely on; if she lost this job, who on earth would employ her with that kind of medical history?

Her mind began to race again as she walked up the path to the building. Pierrepoint Castle, it was called, and it sat atop a large hill, dark and grey-framed by the sky.

What if I lose my job and never work again?

What if I become homeless?

Where will I go—

"I wonder if they will have a loo outside?" Sally broke into Rachel's train of thought, "I need to go."

"I don't know." Rachel wasn't thinking.

"Are you sure you are up to this?"

"Yes, quite sure," she lied, "I needed to get out."

Talking about nothing in particular, they walked slowly up the path till they got to the outer courtyard; Sally rushed away, no doubt searching for a toilet, and Rachel was left outside. She looked at her reflection in a glass doorway; she thought she had aged. Rachel was slightly built, pale, with brown, shoulder-length hair, which she believed made her look like most other women. John once said to her that she had nothing that made her stand out from the crowd. Well, she didn't – hadn't – until now.

It couldn't be right. She cast her mind back to seeing the grandmother of the reporter and that doctor. They couldn't be dead; it was stupid. When you died, that was it – end game, finished. This idea that you floated about as a spirit, moaning to everyone and complaining about being dead, was the most ridiculous idea she had ever heard. She would have to find a doctor next time she went to the hospital and confess to seeing things again, so she could be done with it. Maybe there was some kind of pill she could take to stop it…

She jolted back to the present time.

An open, and very ancient, wooden door to the left bore the sign 'Ticket holders this way'. When Sally rejoined her, the pair walked in to sample Pierrepoint Castle's delights.

The castle itself was impressive. Huge in size and, from the looks of it, altered through the centuries by various owners. Standing with a group of visitors in the main foyer area – blown by a draught from the open doorway – Rachel stared at a dumpy, stern-looking, bespectacled woman, clutching a batch of papers, who was clearly one of the guides.

"The castle began with its roots in the 11th century, and it has seen many attacks and adaptations through the years," the woman explained. She had a dreary, monotonc voice that reverberated off the stone walls around them.

"I wonder if she's available for children's parties," Sally murmured to Rachel with a giggle.

The woman continued, "Owned by Sir Robert Earlsham, but lost during the battle of Bolsmoor in 1237, when Sir Robert died while fighting, it was then passed to his brother, Sir Phillip, who built a larger estate. It is believed that Sir Robert was killed by a rival lord, the Duke of Sudbury, who…"

Rachel wandered off. Another tour guide was talking about the Victorian small boys' room, which didn't sound very interesting; she could see Sally had been tempted away from the dumpy tour guide and into the gift area already. She told Sally she needed to go outside for some fresh air. Her head was playing up again; she had that now sadly familiar sensation that the psychiatrist told her was called 'depersonalisation', which meant she felt like her mind was in a different body, as if she had taken some hallucinogenic drug. Rachel hated that feeling, and she wondered if something else was wrong in her brain, perhaps another bleed they hadn't found.

Walking outside, she made a conscious effort to breathe slowly, to try to force herself back to reality. As she carried out her breathing exercise, she glanced back at the impressive building. It was huge, imposing and surrounded by several little outbuildings, with a café situated to the side. It appeared to shimmer slightly; once, twice, then it was like someone had placed a lens in front of her eyes. It reminded her of being at the opticians, and being asked to read the letter chart, while various lenses were placed in the uncomfortable trial frame that always pinched her nose. Her view changed. The surroundings of the castle and the outbuildings began to blur; the main castle seemed clear, but a little smaller and missing some windows. She rubbed her eyes. She didn't have a migraine again; was this an odd aura? *Oh, please God don't let me pass out,* she pleaded.

She closed her eyes tight, then looked up. The shimmer had gone, thank goodness. She turned and saw some people gathering by the side of the castle. It looked like men and horses, dressed in historical garb. It was obviously some kind of re-enactment getting ready for visitors. She walked towards them, interested in what was about to take place and whether you had to buy a ticket for it. She thought she had better get Sally, who would be angry if she missed this.

Rachel turned to the entrance again, to find that it looked strikingly different. The visitors were all gone, and the entrance signs were also missing. Turning back, she saw the castle had rapidly grown a huge outer wall, and – instead of standing outside the castle altogether – she was, in fact, standing within some kind of courtyard. Under her feet, rather than the flagstones she remembered walking over, was dirt. What the hell was this? Was she having some kind of psychotic episode?

"Oh shit," she heard herself saying. She closed her eyes again, then opened them. No, everything was the same.

Turning to the men, she saw there were hundreds – probably at least 300 – men of war; scarred, large fighting men, saddling and attending to even larger horses. The smell began to reach her – sweat, mud and another smell she couldn't place – as did the sounds: horses whiffling and neighing, and men talking in loud voices in a language she didn't really understand. An instant wave of silence rippled over the gathering, as two men on horseback approached them from the far end of the courtyard.

She looked more closely. Did these men see her? They didn't appear to, but, nonetheless, she decided to stand back, just in case; she didn't think it was a good idea for a woman to appear unexpectedly in front of all these men. That wouldn't be a good idea at all.

The two men rode slowly to the front of the group; they were clearly of a very different class to these other men. Both wore what she recognised as chainmail, from head to foot, and a kind of square helmet on their heads, with the visor up. Over the chainmail was something like a smock or a large vest, which came down to their knees and was yellow, with a kind of bird in red on the front. Both, she could see, carried large swords at their sides. Their horses too had been prepared. Both were adorned with the yellow-and-red livery under their saddles and bridles. The two impressively dressed men took up their position at the front.

"Oh, God help me." Rachel rushed away from the scene. She was now starting to realise this wasn't any kind of modern day re-enactment; it was probably another hallucination. She had to stop it. She sat with her back against the outer wall, pressed against a pillar, and rubbed her eyes. If this was a hallucination, it felt very real. The hard, spiky surface of the stone wall poked uncomfortably into her back; the stones were interspaced with lumps of green moss, growing in the shaded parts, which she could feel, soft and damp, against her.

"Stop... For God's sake, stop," she declared, but every time she took her hands from her eyes, the scene was still there.

The men began to advance, led by the two in front. She watched them come closer; all of them were in chain mail, with some bearing a coat of arms. They rode past her in a winding line, and she could see the men at the front clearly. The first, she guessed, was in his mid-thirties, with dark hair, a smart beard and heavy brows. The second was clearly younger – late twenties, she guessed; he had what she thought to be finer features, and was more delicately boned and smaller, but still with a beard. They had a similar face shape, so were maybe related.

She watched as a huge drawbridge in the outer wall began to lower, its old chains groaning. The drawbridge extended. The men rode out in a long line of grey, yellow and black, not speaking, but following the two men at the front.

Should she stay there? She looked around the courtyard.

48

Slowly, Rachel rose from her position and began to follow, just behind the men and horses walking unhurriedly along the huge path.

In front of her, she saw some small houses, which were off to the side in what looked like woodland. It only sort of looked like woodland because it was very hard to see. It was as if she could see it in her peripheral vision, but when she looked straight at it, the houses and trees seemed to fade. It was like looking at a dim star at night; if you looked straight at it, it couldn't be seen, but if you looked at it just off centre, you could see it clearly.

Then she saw them. Others, maybe 400 or so men, standing facing them, perhaps 500 yards away. It seemed the same kind of arrangement, with fighting men at the back, and this time there were three men at the front in a livery of some kind, in blue and white.

What was this about? Was it some kind of treaty? An argument? She stood rooted to the spot, watching this all play out, aware that everything she saw in front of her wasn't actually there. She didn't know why she knew it, but she did, and this didn't stop her seeing it, hearing it, smelling it and feeling the emotions of what was happening.

She carried on watching as the two groups of combatants grew closer and closer together. She felt the tension building in the air, and her temples began to tighten.

The men in the distance had almost met. They then stopped. The wind brought her sounds of speech: high, loud-pitched shouting. The two men with the yellow-and-red livery were speaking to the three in blue-and-white livery at the front of the opposing men.

She kept rubbing her eyes, and closing and opening them, willing the visitor information signs to come back. But nothing happened; the drawbridge was now closed, and there appeared to be a moat around the outer wall. There were no outhouses, cafés or anything.

All hell broke loose, so unexpectedly that she froze where she stood. The men on both sides had launched themselves at each other; all she saw was a mass of bodies and horses, and all she heard was screaming and horses crying out. Whatever discussions had been taking place had clearly failed. Rachel stood rooted to the spot, but then began to feel her legs crumbling as she saw throats cut, horses disembowelled, and men having their heads swept off with one strike of the sword.

From the side of the battlefield, she found herself walking towards the fighting. When the outer ring of the hostilities was about fifty feet away, she stopped. No one appeared to be aware of her presence. Her eyes were drawn to the two men in yellow: the two who had ridden from the castle, leading the rest of the men. They were on the edge of the fighting, and had both somehow been dismounted in battle. Protecting each other, they were turned back to back, fending off various others in the blue-and-white livery. She felt she was going to have to leave this place, to go anywhere but here till she…

Till I what? she wondered. *Wake up? Stop hallucinating?*

Then she saw it, quick and deliberate. If she had turned a second before, it would have been missed. Right in the middle of the madness, the smaller man – the one with the finer features – spun round and plunged his sword straight into the chest of his companion in yellow and red. From where she stood, she could see the expression on the face of the dying man: shock, horror and disbelief, as he fell lifeless to the ground. She doubted anyone had seen what had happened in the melee of battle. There were combatants from the blue-and-white group crowding around them, and then her view of the two men was swallowed up by the bloody chaos of it all.

What had happened there? Were they not on the same side? Abruptly, the fighting began to die away as the yellow-and-red-liveried men seemed to begin to gain the upper hand. The leaders of the blue-and-white group immediately rode away, and seeing that they had clearly been abandoned, this signalled to all the others on that side to scatter. All who were left were those in the yellow-and-red livery, picking up their dead and running a sword through any injured enemies on the ground.

She heard a wailing fill the air. The smaller man was screaming and cradling the older man with the beard; men came running. What the hell was that about? Whatever it was, she wanted no part of it. Rachel had spent what seemed like hours watching this play out, and realised unexpectedly that she was cold and shaking. She felt nauseous as she caught site of entrails, dead men, decapitated heads and slain horses strewn across the battlefield. She smelt blood and death. Turning instinctively towards the castle, she walked away, trying to stop herself from heaving.

Then she saw the shimmer again, and the castle in front of her shaking and changing. Gradually, it turned back to how she had remembered it.

An elderly lady stood outside the ticket hall, holding a

bundle of leaflets; as Rachel walked by, the lady looked at her. "You don't look well, dear," the lady stated.

Rachel didn't listen and walked back into the main foyer area, looking for Sally. She opened her bag and searched for her phone; when she found it, her hands were shaking so hard that she could barely dial the number. Frustrated, she closed her eyes and looked up.

There, in the main foyer, were both the men she had just seen. They were in a large painting on the wall, wearing outfits of black with what looked like gold woven into them. The older one, who stood at the front of the painting, wore some kind of green, velvet cape, fastened to his shoulder by a large, red gemstone; the younger one stood to his side with a cape of deepest purple. To their sides were swords, and that yellow-and-red livery was on a painted shield to their right.

Both of them were there. Standing together.

The plump lady who had started the tour came to her side. "It's an impressive picture isn't it? It shows both Sir Robert and Sir Phillip," she explained.

"Wha... what?" Rachel turned to look at the woman. "You... spoke about them earlier..."

"Yes, before you left the tour," the woman declared with a sniff.

Rachel turned back to the picture, her eyes glued to the image. "What..." She felt a growing sense of panic enveloping her. "What happened to them?"

"As explained on the tour, Sir Robert died in battle in 1237... He fought against the Duke of Sudbury, due to issues regarding the king's—"

"Who killed him?"

The woman looked at Rachel, slightly bemused by her sudden enthusiasm for local history. "Most accounts claim it was his main rival, the Duke of Sudbury; however, one monastic chronicle of the time suggests that it was the duke's son, Alexander, who was fighting alongside him."

"He was stabbed in the chest." Rachel shut her eyes.

"Possibly." The woman looked slightly annoyed. "However, the general consensus is that it was a blow to the stomach, and the neck."

Rachel looked up. "They didn't cut his neck. He was stabbed in the chest."

"As you wish."

"What happened afterwards?"

"Sir Phillip and the duke signed a treaty; they joined forces. Sir Robert would have been most against this, but, with him dead, the treaty went ahead, and Sir Phillip took over the castle and married the Lady Amersham, who had been handfasted with Sir Robert."

"Hang on… this is Sir Phillip? His brother?" Rachel pointed up to the younger man in the painting.

"Yes, that is so."

"So, Sir Robert being dead means Phillip gets the lot: the woman and the castle. And this duke guy, who was fighting them, he benefitted as well."

"It is a crude way of putting it."

"Phillip stabbed his own brother and killed him, probably for the position. You have got it wrong…"

The tour guide looked at her. "Some people have their own idea of history, madam, but—"

Rachel felt the anger rising. "Phillip killed his brother, probably to get his hands on the castle, and the duke had something to do with it; everyone benefitted with him gone, doesn't anyone see this?" Rachel clasped her hand to her mouth.

"I am afraid there is no evidence to support this; if you look on our history boards, you will see what happened." The guide walked away.

Rachel slumped to the floor and felt tears pouring from her eyes. She had just witnessed a murder; a murder that had taken place over 750 years ago. "He was bloody killed by his brother, you stupid people; they tricked him, made him go out there, then bloody killed him." Her eyes began to sting, and she was aware of a crowd building up around her. She could see Sally in the distance, hurrying towards her and pushing through the crowd of gawkers.

The tour guide returned, but this time with a security guard.

"It is clear, madam, that you do not know history," the woman declared.

Rachel stood up slowly and wiped her eyes with her hand. She began to sob and splutter, forcing the words from her parched lips, "No… no, you have got it all wrong… Yeah, OK, you supposedly *know* history, but *you know what?* I *see* history." Rachel accompanied this statement by vigorously jabbing a finger at the tour guide.

Everyone stood silently looking at her, including the two long-dead, painted brothers, who were frozen in time, with their faces fixed and emotionless.

CHAPTER 9

The walk to Rachel's flat seemed to take longer than she remembered it having ever taken before. The day's events had taken their toll, and, yet again, she began questioning her own sanity. Every single fibre of her body believed she had seen a true event in history and something that had actually happened, albeit a long time ago. There was no way it was a hallucination; she hadn't made it up. If she had made it up, she would have done it in a different way, she was sure. Her stomach began to lurch again, and she felt the gentle ebb of a panic attack begin at her extremities and work their way to her core.

She shivered, although she wasn't cold. What next? What would happen now? Rachel almost felt she was now constantly living in fear of the next... She didn't even know what to call it. Attack? Episode? Incident? She just wanted to get home, see John, and try to forget what had happened.

John. Oh Christ. What was she going to say to John? He didn't seem interested in what was happening. He had made his views very clear: she was still ill, she spoke about her problems too much, and they were mostly of her own making. He said she should ignore them, and they would go away.

A man hurried by her in the dusk. He was wearing a very sharp, grey suit, tie and hat; in his mouth bobbed a cigarette. He looked up at her as he passed. She noticed his feet were missing; she could only see him from the knees up, like he was in water and wading through the ground. Because of this, he appeared much shorter than he probably was. She stared ahead for a moment. What was all that about? She turned her head rapidly, looking at the road behind her. He was gone.

He was another ghost. Ghost; what a stupid word! It still conjured up pictures of a white-sheeted, chain clanking figure – but what else would she call them?

Rachel eventually arrived at her flat. Sally had offered to walk her home, clearly worried about her sanity, but this had been refused. Rachel wanted time for herself, to walk and reflect on where to go next. As she put the key in the door, she saw the lights were off, which was odd, as John should have been home by then. She was so glad to get home. She remembered the look on Sally's face back in the castle, and her horror when the security guard had asked them both to leave.

In front of the castle, Sally had seen shops, cars, roads and people going about their business, but Rachel kept thinking back to the world of over 750 years ago, with blood and guts spilt onto the dirt, and a betrayal. The murder of a man, committed by his own brother for gain, undiscovered for all these years, till she saw it. Why her? She was nothing special, and she never had been; why would she be able to see this?

The key was turned in the lock, the lock clicked, she pushed the door open, and the cold air inside hit her. John obviously wasn't home, but she called out anyway, "John?"

Rachel closed the door, and went into the bedroom. The first thing she saw was that his coat had gone from the back of the bedroom door. For some reason, she knew something was wrong and rushed to the large, old wardrobe in the spare room he had used to keep his clothes in. On tearing open the spare-room door, she saw that the wardrobe stood agape. It was empty.

John had gone.

His things were all missing: his wallet, his shoes – everything. Her mind began to spin as she sat heavily on the bed. Her mind rushed. *Where is he? Has he taken any of my stuff?*

She scrambled for her phone to call him, but there it was: a text message. She hadn't heard it come through, as she had been so highly charged whilst returning from the castle. It was simple. It was from John and said, 'Sorry, I can't take any more of this. I have gone to stay with a friend. Don't blame yourself.' That was it. Maybe he would come back? She rang him, but it went to voicemail; so she left a message, frantically asking him to call her back.

Rachel then lay back on the bed, her mind swimming. It would be so easy to just jump off a cliff and end it all. She closed her eyes again and was asleep before she knew it, dreaming of shadows and that damn rope bridge again, with the people in shadow calling to her. She woke at 3am to the beginnings of another migraine, and mused on how she got so many now; that familiar twinge of pain at her left temple seemed to take over her body as the hours ticked by. She took her medication and then said a small prayer – sometimes it worked, and sometimes it didn't. When it didn't work, it meant she would be wracked with agonising head pains for two days. *That's plenty of time to evaluate life,* she thought, through the mist of increasing pain.

★

The kettle had boiled, and Mrs Braithwaite poured hot water carefully into the cup for her guest, Miss Simpkin, who had turned up at her door, asking to speak to Andy urgently about a so-called haunting.

Mrs Braithwaite was used to random people turning up asking for Andy; however, she had noticed recently that fewer people had been calling. Many seemed to think Andy was psychic – which he wasn't, of course – and kept asking him to go to their homes, which they said had to be haunted, to either find out more about their unwanted spectral guest or to get rid of said guest. Such stories Andy had told her about his work! Often, the houses he visited either had an owner with mental health problems, bad plumbing (causing knocking pipes), or other very non-paranormal explanations. Very rarely indeed had he ever found a real haunting, as such.

Mrs Braithwaite took the cup and placed it with hers on a tray, then went into the living area. Although she was in her eighties, Mrs Braithwaite was still quite sprightly, and sharp as a tack. "I am sorry I took my time, dear; Andy won't be long."

Miss Simpkin looked about thirty, and was very slim, with clear skin and a short bob hairstyle. Well-dressed but in an old-fashioned kind of way, with an overly fussy pussy-bow blouse and black pencil skirt, she had keen eyes, which flashed around the living room, taking everything in. She watched as Mrs Braithwaite placed the cup slightly shakily on the coffee table before her. A small amount of tea slopped onto the saucer.

"I saw Mr Horton's ad online; I am hoping he can help with my problem," stated Miss Simpkin.

"What is your problem? A haunting?" Mrs Braithwaite lowered herself into her battered, old chair, which was always in the corner.

"It's something odd. At night, when I go to bed, I hear this banging noise, like tapping... banging. The neighbour hanged himself a while back, people tell me. I suspect it is him."

"Really?"

They both sat silently, sipping tea, as they heard the front door bang shut.

"Screw me... Jesus wept," could be heard from the hallway, followed by a loud bang, then slow and deliberate footfalls on the stairs as Andy went to his room.

Both ladies got up, and Mrs Braithwaite opened the door in the hallway, only to see a muddy pair of boots left sprawled on the front-door welcome mat. "Andy, you have a visitor here," she called.

"Jesus..." The word, although spoken softly, echoed gently down the stairs.

"No... a Miss Simpkin," said Mrs Braithwaite with a smile. "Where do you want her?"

He appeared at the top of the stairs. "My office, if you please…" He pointed to his door.

Miss Simpkin – although at first slightly perturbed at going into what appeared, to all intents and purposes, to be a bedroom – felt slightly more at ease after telling her story. This was the tale of a neighbour, who, according to people in her street, had hanged himself in the room adjoining her bedroom, in the house next door. The tapping came from there, though sometimes it was loud banging. She was convinced it was him.

"What makes you think that?" Andy queried, slurping from a tin of energy drink almost franticly.

"It makes sense, doesn't it? The flat next to mine is currently empty, so it isn't due to anyone living. Also, it is always, always about five minutes after I go to bed, no matter what time it is. I feel his presence; do you understand, Mr Horton?"

Andy looked at this quite attractive but oddly dressed lady. "I am happy to investigate, but I must charge a fee. I start at £50 for a callout and then charge £20 per hour afterwards."

"Mr Horton… if you can rid me of this ghost, I am prepared to pay £500," she said sharply, "Just do your thing and cleanse my home of this poor man's soul."

"Let's arrange a time for me to come and see you, and we can sort it all out," he replied, with £ signs floating in front of his eyes.

CHAPTER 10

Rachel had hardly slept properly for weeks now, since John had gone God knows where. She noted that, since he had left, her painkiller consumption had gone up; she was not only taking the medication from the doctor, but also copious amounts of strong codeine pills she had bought on the internet. It was the only thing that stopped the constant invasion of pain into her life. She didn't like to think about it.

When her doorbell rang one morning at 9am, she was still in bed. She debated ignoring it, but then worried it might be something to do with John, so she heaved herself out of bed, padded downstairs and answered the door.

On her doorstep was Luke Fairfax, the reporter she had seen before in the school. Thankfully, no ghost grandmother accompanied him this time.

"Miss Holloway... It is Miss Holloway? Remember me? I'm Luke Fairfax from the *Burwood Echo*," he explained.

"Yes, I remember you. May I help you? I don't work at the school at the moment, so it's no good asking me about that," Rachel responded.

"No, it isn't that… May I come in?"·

"You might as well." She signalled him into the main living area, which had its curtains half drawn and looked like some kind of riot had taken place.

"Excuse the mess; my boyfriend left me." She sat down heavily on a large beanbag in the corner.

Luke moved some magazines from a chair and sat down. "I am writing a piece for the paper about paranormal happenings round and about. You know, ghosts and stuff."

She carried on looking at him blankly.

He continued, "So, I er… thought I might be able to use your recent experience."

"What experience?" she enquired.

"At the castle; a number of people contacted us about some kind of incident at Pierrepoint… It seems you saw some ghosts outside."

When it was put like that it sounded awful. "I had an attack… I'd recently suffered a brain bleed, and it's left me a bit shaky. I'm taking a lot of medication, so I probably hallucinated."

"According to an eye witness at the castle, the theory you gave about one brother murdering another might not be quite as far-fetched as you think. I've done a little research of my own, been digging around, and discovered that some fresh evidence was recently stumbled upon that supports your theory. A small group of local historians have been keeping it to themselves for the moment, to give them time to cross check their information, so it hasn't been published yet. A layperson would never have known this."

"I would rather not think about what happened at the castle."

"I would like to write your story: a woman who has suffered a terrible health misfortune now gains second sight. It's a great story."

"I will sound like a nutter."

"I will write it sympathetically."

"I don't think so."

"You'll get £800 if it's published. More if the national papers pick it up."

Rachel had a think. She would be on half pay from next month, so the money might be useful. "Look, OK, but I don't want some loud, big piece; just a little story, OK?"

"Of course. I will come by tomorrow for the interview; how does that sound?"

"Fine."

She showed him out. Goodness, £800 just for a little interview. Maybe there was some money to be had in this. Nobody really read the local paper; it wasn't like TV news, was it? There was nothing to be lost by doing it, and, anyway, there was no story there really. She had a funny turn, and that was that. His editor would see it for what it was, and she would be £800 better off. She thought she may sleep a little easier that night.

★

Andy was all tooled up and ready to go. He was standing in Debbie Simpkin's flat at dusk, which he told her was the right time for ghosts, just as he always told everyone (although this

63

wasn't actually true, as some ghosts didn't like the dark and preferred daylight). He had rigged up his little closed-circuit television (CCTV) cameras that could see in low light, and he was now checking for electronic frequencies and making sure any surge wasn't due to a faulty electric socket. He removed his electronic voice phenomenon (EVP) box from his pocket and switched it on and off.

"Testing… yeah, testing… hum…" he said.

He played it back. The little machine whirred his voice back to him in a slightly shaky recording. He sniggered as he decided that the word 'hum' sounded like 'bum'.

"We are good to go," he said finally.

"What do I do now?" asked Debbie.

"I need you to do what you do when you go to bed; as much as possible, keep it real. Do everything as you would do normally, and I will watch."

"Watch?" She frowned.

"For the spirit to make an appearance."

Miss Simpkin didn't seem too convinced, but she was so desperate to get rid of this spirit that had been plaguing her that she agreed.

Whilst Andy sat in the living room, watching all the monitors, he heard her in the bathroom, water was running, then came a flush.

She came out. "I don't have to put on my pyjamas, do I?"

"Er, no, not for the moment. We will see if the spirit responds. Just get into your bed and turn the light off," he suggested.

"This had better work, Mr Horton." She went into her room and closed the door.

He heard the light snap off.

"I am in bed, Mr Horton," she called out.

"Please... call me Andy." He looked towards the bedroom. "That's the best offer I have had all week," he muttered to himself.

Nothing was happening. The CCTV cameras showed no movement, and there was no unusual electrical activity.

He sat down. He thought about it and wondered whether he might have to use some sort of 'conjuring' device to get the spirit out of its stupor. Then he heard it: tap, tap, tap. It was oh-so faint that it could barely be heard. TAP, TAP, TAP.

"Andy... it's coming!" he heard Miss Simpkin exclaim from the bedroom.

The taps grew louder, then became banging – loud, rhythmic banging.

Debbie Simpkin rushed from the bedroom. "Do you see, Mr Horton? *The spirit walks amongst us!*"

He went round checking the CCTV, but he could see nothing.

"I am afraid," whispered Debbie.

"Have you got a neighbour you can go to whilst I commune with the spirit? I would like you to leave, as this could be disturbing," Andy confirmed.

He didn't have to ask twice. She grabbed her coat, and, before he knew it, she had left the flat.

"Right." Andy went into the bedroom; the banging did indeed come from the wall between her flat and the empty one. He listened as, slowly but surely, the taps receded.

He went into the living area and proceeded to get out his

ultraviolet light and a Ouija board; then he stood up. From a small case, he took a Stetson; it had a crucifix tied to it with string, so that the crucifix sat at the front, resting on the brim. He shoved it on to his head roughly. Andy then switched on his EVP machine and set it down on the sofa.

"Speaketh, oh spirit; tell me your quest."

Nothing happened.

"Shit." Andy shifted position and went into Miss Simpkin's bedroom. It was a very pink, clearly female bedroom with a large floral duvet cover and an overlarge Hello Kitty stuffed toy on the bed.

He began to wave his arms back and forth, like a person guiding a plane down to land.

"Kum by yah… oh spirit… Speak to me."

Still nothing happened.

He removed his hat. "I need a piss," he said to himself, and he went into the bathroom. After relieving himself, he flushed the toilet and then went back into the living room to set up the Ouija board.

Just as he went to open the board, the tap, tap, tap started again.

An idea immediately came to him. He rushed to the sink in the kitchen area and looked underneath to see a pipe vibrating. "Screw me," he declared.

He then rushed to get a screwdriver. After hurriedly tightening some fittings that secured the pipe to the kitchen wall, he flushed the toilet again, and…

Silence.

Confident, he called her back.

As soon as she arrived, she asked, "What was it, Mr

Horton? A spectre? A demon?" She opened her purse, which was absolutely stuffed with large denomination notes.

He looked at the toilet, then slowly back to her. "It really was just a simple problem; I fixed it right away. It was just—"

"The *undead*? You dealt with it spectacularly, Andy; I feel peace running through my home... What was it?" There was a clear glint in her eye, and a smile played at her lips. Her fingers hovered over the bursting purse.

"It was a... er... phantasm."

"Not the hanged man?"

"No, but it's gone now. I... er... conjured it out with my Ouija board and... er... sent it off."

The EVP recorder was still humming away on the sofa, committing his lie to tape.

Miss Simpkin hugged him violently. "I absolutely cannot thank you enough for what you have done; you are my hero." She took out a handful of notes from her purse. "Here's £1,000 for you. I am so grateful."

"You said £500?"

"You have rid me of this phantasm, and I am grateful, as I can now sleep at night. God bless you, Mr Horton. I shall recommend you to everyone I know who has a ghost. You seem to have all the right equipment to track them down."

"Well, not quite everything." He smiled. "It would be cool if I could find some piece of equipment that could just sort of see ghosts and spirits, like I see you; that would make it all so much easier. Save on all this gear and shi— er, stuff."

"You would then be quite unstoppable, Andy."

With that, he packed up and left, with a delighted Debbie Simpkin waving him off. *Jesus, £1,000 for tightening a few screws,* he thought. He felt a little bad, but no one had lost out. Miss Simpkin could sleep well at night, and he could pay his bills now as well; it was a win-win situation as far as he was concerned.

CHAPTER 11

There were a lot of sleepers out in the park that night; some nights there seemed to be more than others, but, that night, the roads were lined with them. The clothed figures were lying down stiffly, some with eyes closed and some with eyes wide open, staring towards comfort and sleep that would never come.

Dr Maxwell wasn't a sleeper. Being a sleeper was fooling oneself. Some of those who were caught in this purgatory of being dead, and yet not redeemed to heaven, chose to remember being alive, and thus, every night, they would lie down – anywhere usually, but mostly down the sides of roads and beside buildings – to feign sleeping. But, of course, they could not sleep: they were dead. The dead could no more enter the state of sleep than a living person float unaided into the sky. But, still, every night, they did what they knew. They lay down as dusk began to settle and kept still until sun rose, when – like shuffling zombies – they would get up and begin to move again.

He stood in the light of a street lamp, pulling his great

coat around him – more in a habitual movement as, of course, he could feel neither heat nor chill – then cast a suspicious eye up to the electric-powered street light and sniffed. One day, they would discover that this electricity was damaging to people and the environment, as there was never a breakthrough without cost. He preferred the gas lamps of his time; yes, they could be dangerous, especially in houses and theatres, but they really used to put out the most wonderful glow, unlike these monstrous lights.

He turned away and stared again at the sleepers.

The dead were split into two camps: 'sleepers' and 'non-sleepers'. The sleepers, like those lying before him, chose to repeat the familiar pattern of lying down at night and rising in the morning. Non-sleepers, such as Dr Maxwell, lived during the night hours much as they passed the day: musing about things, walking around and thinking about *the question*: why, when they died, did they not ascend into heaven, descend to hell, or whatever? Why did they end up just aimlessly wandering the surface of the earth? Why did some souls, upon death, pass on, and some get stuck on earth? Sometimes they were stuck for centuries, walking amongst the living like faded shadows. This was *the question*.

The answer: now this was the big one. Those with religion claimed prayer and penance could bring ascension into heaven. This did seem to work at times. William knew a spirit nun he used to see at prayer every day on the church steps, but she disappeared one day, and never returned. Clearly, she had found *the answer* and had left this mortal place. Those who followed no god said hard work and reflecting on things one had done wrong in life brought *the answer*, but, again, he wasn't sure about that. He had seen both people pure of most sins, and those filthy and ridden with terrible deeds all caught here for years. Why some souls remained here and some departed was a complete mystery to him.

In life, William had been a man of science. He based his decisions and opinion on scientific facts that he had tested and found to be true or untrue, which is what had led him to become a doctor. He tried to do the same with his quest to find *the answer*, and this was why he was so excited about this lady he had met at the hospital, who could see the dead. He had seen others before in his lifetime and deathtime who claimed to see those who had passed on; some people could to a certain extent, but not like her. He was utterly convinced that she might be able to help him find out more about why some people remained and some went, but this meant he had to find her. She didn't go to the hospital anymore; he had waited there for many days, but she had not shown up. Besides, he thought she had probably been scared off by his approach last time, but he had been so excited.

No, somehow, he must find her again. And when he did, he must not scare her off but also must somehow utterly compel her to help him, and make her realise just how essential her ability was to assisting him and all the other lost souls stuck here in this eternal nothingness.

A woman lying on the path before him looked up. She had closed her eyes twice, but then they snapped open.

"You are a fool, madam," he bellowed. "You are as dead as yesterday's capon, so why you lie there as a vagrant is beyond me." He spun on his heels and walked into the shadows, leaving the woman remaining still, feigning the long lusted for state of sleep that would never overcome her again.

★

Rachel had cleaned up her flat as much as she could, and she watched nervously as Luke arrived and settled in. She had never been interviewed before; to be honest, she had never done anything interesting enough for someone to want to interview her. She watched as he got out a jotter, pen and a small voice recorder, which he tinkered with several times.

He looked up at her, his pen and jotter poised. She sat opposite him, her hands clenched tightly together.

"Are you ready, Rachel? Now, I explained most of this earlier. I am recording what you are saying, which will help me write this up later, if I miss anything…" He gestured towards the recorder. "If there are any questions you don't want to answer, say so, but I think your story is very interesting and should be told."

She smiled weakly. Talking about the haemorrhage was hard; she felt tears in her eyes and had to swallow heavily a few times. She heard herself saying it was one of those things and that life must go on, but she did not really believe it. It sounded good, so she said it. She brushed over John leaving her, saying it was a difficult time, and debated shaving a couple of years off her age when asked.

Rachel then recounted the day at the castle. She started off by sketching over the main facts, but, as she went on, she began to feel more and more compelled to say what she had seen. When finished, she sat back and looked at Luke. He

72

was just sitting there, looking back at her. She must appear completely mad.

Finally, he spoke: "So, the men you saw and the battle… You think you kind of travelled back in time and saw what really took place hundreds of years ago?"

"I don't know. I think so. I mean, I thought I had made it up in my head or dreamt it up, but I don't think so now," she clarified.

"Why not?"

"It's not how I would have done it… If I had imagined this, well, it wouldn't have been what I saw. I always thought the armies of important men in the past would have all been like knights – in armour, well dressed, etc. – but these men were not. They were like a ragtag of dirty everyday people, fighting for whoever paid them. They seemed to have no allegiance… Do you know what I mean? Also, how else would I have known about the theory that one brother killed another?"

"A lucky guess? Maybe you had overheard it somewhere. Being a teacher, you must have researched a lot of things, yourself."

"I don't think so. Also, I have seen others. One man with half his legs missing, just last week."

"Legs missing? Like he had been in an accident?" Luke was scribbling now.

"No, more like he was walking at a level lower than the street; do you know what I mean? I don't understand it." She had a thought. "Also there is a doctor who has spoken to me; I think he might be Victorian. I don't know his name. He keeps trying to speak to me, as he thinks I can help… them." She looked down. Her hands tensed again.

"Them?"

"The ghosts… but I don't think I can." She looked up. "I don't understand this myself, Luke; I am only just getting used to it, but I am starting to believe that I am not hallucinating. This is… something else…"

"You are psychic?"

"No. Well at least I don't feel that I am. I have been thinking about it, and, somehow, I wonder if the brain bleed has allowed me to see things differently. The dead are all around us, and not everyone can see them, but I can. I mean, there may be others in the world who can do this. I am sure I am not the only one."

"Ghosts… are they all around us?"

"Yes… you just can't see them usually, and it seems that they are not only in old castles and dark tunnels. They can be in the street in bright sunshine, in a park, an office or even in a toilet. Tell me, have you ever been in a bathroom where they have those automatic hand washers where you put your hand under the tap to turn the water on and off with a sensor?"

"Er… yes…" Luke had no idea where this was going.

"Have you ever been there alone, even in a cubicle perhaps, and the tap just came on, then went off, as if someone was there but no one actually was?"

"Yes."

"Ghosts do that." She sat back with a satisfied look on her face. "The spirit gets too close to the tap, and if the presence is strong, it turns the taps on… It makes them jump sometimes; I have seen it… Funny, isn't it?"

Luke put down his pen. "If you really can see them and

communicate with them, if this is true, you do realise that you are going to get a lot of them coming to you and asking you to help with issues they had when they were alive, to settle scores of the past?"

Rachel felt a tear prick at her eye, then she spread her hands. "I am very aware of this Luke. I am just hoping they are not all aware that I can see them, or that word doesn't spread about me, or they are all going to come to me, aren't they? Imagine being dead and knowing someone can see and hear you. It would open up all kinds of reasons for you to track down this person."

Imagine indeed. Luke raised one eyebrow, then looked down and carried on writing.

They spoke for nearly two hours, although it felt like less. By the time Luke left, Rachel felt like she had run a marathon, and her mouth was so dry that she could hardly speak. Before he left, he took a photo of her and said it would be used with the story.

Rachel went to bed, resolving that, the next day, she would check he had credited her bank account with the £800. She imagined for a moment selling more stories like this; people liked the paranormal, didn't they? She had heard of so-called psychics touring the circuit and making a mint, so maybe she could do that? Now the head pains were getting more predictable and painful, she worried if she could ever work a nine-to-five, permanent job again; this might be the answer.

Who was she kidding? The story may not even be published, and if it were, she would just be dismissed as a nutcase for a week or so, then, like yesterday's chip paper, her story would end up in local recycling bins everywhere. That was her fate. What a downfall.

She fell asleep. Her dreams were again bothered by the 'shadow people' as she called them, but this time it was a little different: she was off the bridge now and walking amongst these dark people in shadow. A little distance from her, she saw something amongst the people in her dreams, like a kind of animal; it looked a little like an ape, a chimpanzee, but a large one, sitting on its hind quarters in a clearing, just away from the others. As she looked its way, its mouth opened slightly, revealing rows of razor-sharp, pointed teeth. Then its eyes opened, but only to a slit, and were blood red. What on earth was it? Maybe it was an imp. Her friend, Sally, had told her about them; they were supposed to be mischievous, but harmless.

The dream then faded to black, and the rest of her night remained undisturbed.

CHAPTER 12

The benefits office was not one of Andy's favourite places. Every two weeks, he was summoned and told to prove he had applied for numerous jobs, so that he could carry on receiving benefits. Since being made redundant from his IT job two years ago, he had viewed getting the maximum amount of benefits as his new full-time job. Every week, he would apply online to a lot of vacancies, giving glib and superficial answers to any questions. Once, despite his best efforts, he had been called to an interview, but he soon scuppered that by turning up wearing Mrs Braithwaite's make-up, appearing as some kind of goth, and uttering monosyllabic responses to the interviewer. When he was asked his name, he even paused and grinned vacuously into thin air. He didn't get the job, which was fantastic; it ticked a box and ensured he got his full benefits the next week. It was good, this benefits gig; he could live with Mrs Braithwaite, do his ghost hunting and also get paid by the government. Sweet!

He had been warned this interview might not be so easy. Sitting at a desk opposite a grumpy-looking youth, he simply remained expressionless, trying to play it deadpan. This man looked too young to be an employee of the jobcentre, but, anyway, Andy remained resigned to having to listen to more nonsense. To Andy, it was like being strapped into a not-too-pleasant roller-coaster ride he had ridden many times before.

"Mr Horton…" The young man looked up from his computer screen and narrowed his eyes. "Despite applying for nearly 400 jobs and having one interview in the last five months, not one has been successful; why would you think this would be?"

Jobs? It was a laugh calling half of them jobs. Many paid the minimum wage but were miles away from where he lived. One, in a warehouse, demanded a 4am start, yet, as he was without a car, he had no idea how he was meant to get there on time. Another one, he recalled, had a five-hour travelling time to the job and back, and no help was offered with the train fare. Why had he not got these 'non-jobs' indeed? Because he didn't bloody want them, being as they were slave labour.

"I don't know," he heard himself replying. "I fill in the forms as best I can but nuffink comes of it." At these jobcentre interviews, he deliberately tried to come across as being a bit dense. It was this part of it that he found hardest; 'kidding he was daft', as Mrs Braithwaite put it.

"Well, as you know, it is our job to get people like you into employment…" droned on the young man.

People 'like him'? Andy made a mental note to ask what that meant.

"So, in order for us to do this, we are arranging a compulsory work placement for you, starting in two weeks' time," the young man confirmed.

A compulsory work placement; what the hell? "What's that?" Andy asked.

"That is where we arrange for you to attend a place of work, so that you can learn a skill. You work for benefits, if you like; the placement is over a thirty-hour week, Monday to Friday, 9.30am till approximately 5.00pm, in a retail environment."

Andy's mind raced. Monday to Friday, *all day? Every week?* How on earth would he run his ghost-hunting business? And, what's more, he relied on the benefit payments topped up by the cash he received from the ghost hunting; if he didn't get both lots of money in, he was going to be in the shit. OK, he had the weekends, but a lot of the wealthy spinster types who called him in wanted him during the weekdays; also, checking out hauntings in churches and so on was going to be impossible at weekends.

"What is this job, anyway?" Andy asked, again trying to sound as non-committal as he could.

"A produce-replenishment manager," stated the young man.

This sounded better than the usual fare Andy was offered at these interviews. "What does it entail?" He leant forwards.

"It's basically a shelf stacker in the local supermarket; think yourself lucky that you are not on the night shift." The jobcentre employee smiled.

"Right, so you want me shelf stacking to 'learn a trade', as you put it, but I don't get any more money for doing this?"

"That's right, but if you don't do it, you may well lose your benefits."

Andy's mind started clicking everything into place. OK, so this was basically about getting him off the dole queue, getting the stats down, with – let's be honest – no real chance of any job at the end of it, and he still got his benefits, so it didn't seem to save the taxpayer any money. "How much do these big supermarket chains pay you to get slave labour in for them?" he asked. As soon as the remark had left his lips, he regretted it; his observation pointed towards him not being as stupid as his earlier employment forms had made out.

"What do you mean, Mr Horton? This is a chance to learn valuable skills and get you signing up to a work ethic."

Work ethic? That was a bloody joke. His ghost-hunting business required that he keep detailed records of all his clients, payments, the details of the ghosts (real and fake) and how he got rid of them. He cross-checked these records weekly to see if any of the patterns tallied; in other words, if a ghost he had got rid of from one house reappeared in another. His 'job' needed excellent customer-services skills and utmost discretion. He had even got rid of a poltergeist for a famous soprano who lived locally last month; totally by accident, mind, but he had got rid of it, nonetheless. They didn't think this was more likely to instil a work ethic? But then, of course, they didn't know about this 'career' of his.

"Fine, when do I start?" Andy queried.

"On Monday 5th, 9am start, report here…" The youth handed over a slip of paper. "And, remember, if you fail to turn up to any of the days you are scheduled to work, without a doctor's certificate or valid reason, the benefits will stop."

Andy got up and walked slowly to the door that should have been signed 'EXIT', only someone had graffitied over it so it read 'EX-SHIT'; was that supposed to be funny? Andy walked down the stairs, out of the building and into the cold air outside. He sat down heavily on a nearby stone wall and watched the cars pass by on the high street.

"Bugger me," he muttered to himself. Now what was he going to do? His work had already taken a hit due to all the new, supposed ghost-hunting groups that had popped up recently; usually an assembly of attractive younger people, all wearing matching uniforms and boasting loads of technology. They always *guaranteed* they would find any ghost or spirit haunting a house. But Andy knew it wasn't like that, and it didn't work that way; you didn't really need a load of expensive equipment to find a ghost. Sometimes, he would walk into a house and find nothing, but people didn't like that – they wanted results, like Miss Simpkin – so he did what he could to provide a result for them, even if it was a bit faked. But now what? He would be sticking cans of bloody beans on shelves.

He put his head in his hands and actually felt a large wave of despair wash over him. He must not get depressed – that wasn't going to help – and he doubted Mrs Braithwaite would kick him out. But she was elderly. He loved her, but she wasn't going to be around all his life; if she died, he would be out of there in a flash, and then what?

A strong wind gusted up the street and hit him hard; he shivered. Now what was he going to bloody do?

"Crap." He had forgotten to ask the jobcentre employee what he had meant by saying 'people like you'. He would write it down when he got home so he didn't forget to mention it on his next visit.

CHAPTER 13

The van sped around, delivering the *Burwood Echo* to newsagents, government offices, supermarkets and shops. Gentle, flapping noises were heard all over town as the free local newspaper for the borough of Burwood dropped through letterboxes.

Flap. Rachel opened her eyes. She was lying in bed; she did a lot of that now, thinking about how there was only one month left before she had to return to school, to hear what Mr Andrews had to say. She thought he was going to get rid of her; then what? Her mind began to whirl. A teacher with a brain condition? As if work wasn't hard enough to come by if you were in perfect health.

Oh, yes, the letterbox… It might be the paper, she thought. She got up from the bed, pulled on her dressing gown, and then walked to the front door.

The paper, the *Burwood Echo*, was lying, slightly rumpled, on her doormat, next to three flyers that had probably been inside it; one she saw was advertising how to plan a funeral.

She picked up the paper and began to thumb through it; the headline was something about exam results being fiddled at a local school. Her eyes skimmed the text; it wasn't her school, so that didn't matter. On turning the page, her eyes flashed over pages two and three, but there was nothing about her. Slowly, she turned to page five, and there it was: a half-page piece with her photo, slightly discoloured with ink, and the headline 'I SEE THE DEAD – LOCAL WOMAN BECOMES PSYCHIC AFTER ACCIDENT'.

She heard the words, "Oh God!" come out of her mouth. She had told the reporter that she wasn't psychic, and it wasn't an accident, but more of an incident. Rachel sat on the stairs, staring at her photo, which was looking forlornly back at her. He had told her not to smile when he took it, explaining that the piece was meant to endear people to her. She thought she looked unhinged.

She placed the paper on the table by the front door, closed so she couldn't see the article.

The rest of the day was spent watching TV, only broken by a text message from Sally, asking 'Have u seen the local paper? U are in it!' which Rachel didn't reply to. Even though she never looked at the article again that day, she felt its presence in the flat. All she could wish for was that not many people read the local paper, and, hopefully, this would all be forgotten by next week.

★

The next day, Rachel got up and found herself feeling better about everything. She had forgotten, at least momentarily, about the newspaper article, and she was debating about maybe getting her life more in order, setting her flat straight and visiting the doctor to admit to the amount of pills she was taking (even today she had a muzzy head).

The silence was broken by a phone call from the school: Mr Andrews had asked Rachel to come in to discuss her working situation.

She felt hopeful. It was possibly the case that he had realised what a contribution Rachel made to the school and that he wanted her back quicker. This was fantastic news. For the first time since the incident, she really believed her life was shifting back on track.

★

Alice walked along the road with her usual assortment of children behind her. In her arms was a tiny baby, which remained silent and still. Wearing her long, black coat, small-heeled boots and dark pillbox hat, she made for a dour figure. The children behind her, ranging in ages from three years and up, were in various standards of clothing: some in rags and barefoot, and others in finest silk, rubbing their noses into lace handkerchiefs. She heard muttering from the back; no doubt it was Henry again, who was the oldest child and from the most privileged background.

"Henry, be silent," she said, whilst struggling with the baby and with her free hand tugging a three-year-old behind her.

"I am of an age when I no longer need the services of a nanny," Henry moaned. "I am almost a man, and as such should be free to make my own way in the world."

Her brow furrowed, but she walked on, throwing her voice back. "But you are not going to be a man, are you, Henry? You, as we all, must remain this age."

"But my knowledge grows, Nanny." He waved a lace handkerchief in a foppish manner about his face. "I wish to be free of having to follow children around. You choose to do this, Nanny, not me. I have things to do and see."

"Like what?" she turned to him. "If you walk away from us now, Henry, where would you go?"

He stared at her; his powdered wig sat at an angle on his head, making him look, Alice thought, ridiculous. But, no doubt, he was born a gentleman, and, in Henry's time, that was what young gentlemen wore.

Alice was what the spirit world called a 'nanny'. Usually women − although Alice had seen a man once − nannies were people who had adored children in life, and in death collected the souls of babies and children who had passed away. With older children, such as Henry, they gave them the confidence to try to strike out in the world of the dead alone. With babies, all they could do was pray for their salvation and carry the burden of their small souls, until the Lord came to take them. If, indeed, He ever did.

She herself had died aged 32. In life, she had been a housemaid and had become betrothed to one of the footmen who worked in the same grand house as her. As the date for their wedding was set, she had sickened and discovered that she carried his child. Something had gone wrong, Alice was not sure what, but she had awoken one night to soaked bed sheets. She firstly believed it to be her sweat as she had suffered fevers during the pregnancy, but, as she turned the candle to her covers, she saw it was, in fact, blood. Throbs of pain grew each minute as labour pains wracked her body. Alice remembered others fussing around her, trying to deliver the child. Then she instantly found herself standing outside the hall, in the kitchen garden, and unable to be seen by anyone, even her beloved Arthur, her betrothed. She had lost her child in life, and so she decided to help children who had passed, by being their nanny in death.

She had hoped to one day find her child amongst the babies, if indeed she would even recognise it, but she never did. It had obviously passed on. Alice did not even know if it was a girl or a boy. Some said it had gone to hell for being unbaptised and conceived out of wedlock, but Alice would not believe this. God would never turn an innocent away, would He? No, He wouldn't.

For over 97 years, Alice had walked the earth as a spirit, but she had known those who had been around for hundreds of years, caught in this way like a fly in a sticky web of time. She hoped this wouldn't happen to her, but that her Lord would send for her and she could glance upon the face of her child for the first time. Some nights she also prayed to see Arthur again; was it too much to hope one day that they would all be reunited?

She turned back from staring at Henry and carried on walking. Ahead, at a busy intersection, she saw Dr Maxwell, looking down at what looked like a crumpled piece of paper on the pavement. As she neared the junction, she said instinctively to the children, "Stay close to Nanny, as the road is dangerous."

"Horseless carriages cannot harm us, Nanny, being that

we are all as dead as an acorn in winter," Henry whined from the back of the group.

Giving the hand of the three-year-old to a little girl behind her, she walked over to where the doctor stood, staring at the cars and vans hurtling down the road at great speed.

"Good cheer to you, Dr Maxwell. How have you been these last days?" she enquired.

He turned slowly and smiled; he was fond of Nanny. "Very well, Nanny; I've no complaints. And you?"

She proffered the baby to him. "I have a newborn, who was just given to me last night; pray our Lord takes him soon."

"Indeed." He frowned, then looked back at the ground where a newspaper, damp from the night's rain, was fluttering in the wind, caused by the traffic. He looked up again. "Look at these objects of speed; an abomination made by man." He gestured to the cars and lorries speeding past. "There is no need to travel so quickly; one cannot take in the surroundings. It's all hurrying to get… goodness knows where."

Alice said nothing. Many were used to Dr Maxwell's complaints about modern contraptions and how he hated them all.

Seeing that she was not interested in this particular gripe, he gestured to the crumpled piece of paper near his feet. Unexpectedly, he pointed to it with his cane; the movement was so fast that Alice jumped slightly.

"Tell me, Nanny, can you think of a way to get a newspaper page to turn over? I can see half of a story on this page, but I can read no more without the page being turned back," he questioned.

Nanny looked at the rain-dampened sheet. She simply saw the headline 'I SEE THE DEAD'. "I cannot advise you, Dr Maxwell, but would only say that to believe in these tricksters will do you no good."

He tapped his cane at the newspaper harshly, but, of course, it never made contact; it just waved straight through. "No, Nanny, you don't understand. This is the woman I have been speaking about; she sees and hears us as if we lived. I met her at the hospital when I was there—"

"You should not visit places you knew in your lifetime; it only leads to heartache—"

"Never mind that… I came across her, and she sees us. Do you know how unusual that is? I believe it is a sign; she is *the answer*, and she will know how to help us crossover. Do you understand, Nanny? I need to find her and talk to her again, to make her realise just what a jewel she carries…"

Alice looked unimpressed. "It is quackery, Doctor, and false hope. The Lord will call us when He is ready."

Henry appeared abruptly by her side, immediately taking in the scene with his sharp, beady eyes. "What tarries here?" he said.

Dr Maxwell looked at him. "Who are you?"

Slightly annoyed, Henry turned to face him, opened his mouth to say something, reconsidered, and then said, "My name is Henry Swain of Cotterstokes House. I fell from my mount, and you are?"

"Dr William Maxwell, from East London, I…" He hesitated. "Perished in a fire."

Henry considered this, then looked at the newspaper,

damp and crumpled on the floor. "A living woman who sees the dead is a novelty indeed. You want to read this piece?"

"Yes, but the page is folded," responded the doctor.

"Then we shall unfold it, shan't we?" Henry walked away.

Dr Maxwell addressed Alice directly. "Who in all that is holy does that boy think he is?"

Alice stared after Henry as he took up a position about ten feet away from them, with his back turned. "He is from an incredibly high-born family of landowners and importers," she said. "He would have been some kind of lord or senior figure had he lived."

"Indeed." The doctor watched as Henry spun around to face them. The boy had a look of mild concentration on his face, his left hand on his hip and his right hand held aloft, the fingers of which he elegantly spun in the air, as if playing an imaginary harp.

The bent page flipped over in a sharp action, allowing the newspaper to be read.

"Sir, your page has now unfolded," stated Henry with a self-satisfied smile.

Alice looked at him. "Well done, Henry." She then turned to Dr Maxwell. "Henry has quite a talent for moving objects in the realm of the living."

Dr Maxwell was not listening; he was bent double, absolutely engrossed in reading the article still stuck to the pavement.

She then turned to her group of youngsters. "Come, Henry... children... it's time to go now, or we will all catch our deaths," she said.

CHAPTER 14

Hidden under the covers, Andy didn't want to move. In the days since he had visited the benefits office, his mind had been in a whirl. After the job at Miss Simpkin's flat, he had received two calls from anxious women, both saying they knew Debbie and would he please come and look at their presumed ghosts. Boldly, he had suggested a £500 fee for ridding them of the spirits, which was a complete change of tack from his usual cost of £50 callout and £20 an hour, but, after Miss Simpkin's financial gratitude, he felt emboldened to push up the cost.

Amazingly, both women had agreed, so he had been on cloud nine. What's more, both hauntings seemed to probably be the kind of thing Debbie had, like a loose pipe or a dodgy radiator. He would have been quids in, but then the benefits thing had happened. Andy had to give it all up to go and stack shelves. Why was life like this? It gave you a ladder, then a snake to slide down.

Goddammit. He had called both ladies to see if they could see him at the weekend, and both said that wasn't convenient. He kept going over and over how he could change his business hours, maybe tell some fib that ghosts were easier to catch on a Saturday or Sunday, which was a load of hogwash, or come up with some other bullshit to explain his restricted working hours, but he couldn't. Anyway, many of his customers, especially the elderly, liked him there in the daytime. What was he going to do? He lay there under his bed covers, depressed and hoping an answer would come, but all that did overwhelm him was immense fatigue.

Muffled through the covers, he heard a gentle tap at the door, and it slowly opening.

"Andy?" It was Mrs Braithwaite's quiet voice.

"I am resting…" he said, still hidden by the duvet.

"See what I have left you on the bed, as it might be helpful," she replied.

From where he lay he felt a slight weight as something was placed on his covers, then he heard the quiet click as the door closed again.

What on earth had Mrs Braithwaite brought him? Some sort of medicine or a book? He hoped it was not one of her bloody smelly candles again, which she said helped with stress. Whatever it was, he wasn't interested and fell asleep.

It wasn't until four hours later, when he climbed from his bed, that he saw the newspaper, folded open on page five.

A woman was frozen in print on the page, staring out at him and looking slightly manic, accompanied by the headline stating, 'I SEE THE DEAD – LOCAL WOMAN BECOMES PSYCHIC AFTER ACCIDENT'. God, another nutter. The first thing that sprang into Andy's mind was *What if this woman starts ghost hunting? She might take some of my customers.* The story had given her a prime position in the local paper, stating that she had the ability to actually see the dead and she could speak to them. This woman could be the ideal ghost hunter, and her 'career', if you like, had been launched by this piece, as an unpaid endorsement.

Why had Mrs Braithwaite given him this? To depress him further? He read the story again; within it, Rachel – as her name was – spoke about how some ghosts were seen knees or waist upwards, how they frequently only had banal things to say, and how there were just as likely to be ghosts around in daylight as at night time. Andy put the paper down. This confirmed what he already knew, and he started to wonder if she wasn't a fraud after all. There were so many misconceptions about spirits, most of them bandied about in books and films, yet she seemed to know quite a lot about the real thing.

With a smash, an idea fired into his brain like a bullet, and his own words from his visit to Miss Simpkin returned to haunt him: *"It would be cool if I could find some piece of equipment that could view ghosts and spirits, like I see you, which would make it all so much easier."*

He stared back at the paper, took note of the area she lived in from the article, and smiled to himself. "Ha… sweet," he muttered.

★

Rachel was back at school again, standing outside Mr Andrew's office. Although she had awoken feeling unwell, which was very normal now, she had tried to rally herself by saying to her inner mind that this meeting was probably to give her a date to return to teaching. So many thoughts had gone through her head that morning, such as how she would cope with the increased migraines and medication she now had to take, and whether she could just go back to teaching a junior class again. She was so full of self-doubt.

The same familiar walk to the school gates stirred her again. How many years she had walked down this street with its old-fashioned houses, where, every day as she passed them, she had speculated on what the family was like who lived within. Did they have as many problems as her or were their lives free from worry?

This morning, she had actually bothered to put her make-up on and had looked out her smart clothes. Again, hope began to rise as she checked in at the reception, and she smiled at the familiar faces as she walked the corridors to the headteacher's office.

As if he sensed her there as soon as she approached his door, Mr Andrews opened it and waved her in, and she sat, once again in the chair facing his battered, cluttered desk. Somewhere in the distance, she heard someone coughing, or was it choking? For a second, it filled her head and made her aware that panic had started to fill her body, making her arms and legs tingle. Quickly, she tried to gain control as he spoke.

"Rachel, I am glad you made time to come and see us today." His voice was low and clipped.

She didn't have anything to say, so she remained silent.

He picked up a folder of papers, glanced at them then looked up. "I have seen this week's paper; I assume you have as well. In it, you appear to have given an interview claiming to see… harrumph… dead people? Is this the case?"

Oh God, that interview; what should I say? The truth wasn't going to wash here, so she heard herself reply, "Oh… er… no, of course not. The man who interviewed me just wanted a story, and, as I was going to probably need some money soon, being on half pay, I thought that… er… that I could just make up an interesting story for him. It's all false, of course."

Mr Andrews's eyes narrowed. "So you made up a totally fake story and gave it to a paper, whilst on official sick leave, and took payment for it… cashing in on your illness? That sounds very poor form to me, Rachel."

"Oh, no, you don't understand; it wasn't like that. He needed a story and—"

"I am afraid I have heard enough. Your condition means you are very unlikely to return to teaching again, and I was considering if we would maybe be able to find you an admin job or a less challenging role in another school, but I am afraid this article has forced my hand. You have brought the school into disrepute, and I am going to have to dismiss you from our employment."

"What? No…" She stood up. "I have worked here for such a long time, and my friends are here."

He stood up to match her stance. "I am sorry, Rachel. We have already been receiving calls from parents about some kind of incident involving you at a castle, and now this. We cannot have a teacher who is hallucinating; it isn't right."

"*I am not hallucinating,*" she spat out, now furious. "I am not mad."

"Please do leave," he said, and he gestured to the door.

Rachel walked out, with tears stinging her eyes.

Behind her she heard his voice explaining, "We will ensure you are paid what you are owed, and we will send a letter outlining your position with regard to work and references."

But she wasn't listening; she had to get out of there. The familiar school walls, the polished floor and her plants – all so well known to her, and enveloping her in their normality – now appeared different and stark, with all urging her to leave. This had once been her second home, but, now, she felt nothing.

She walked the same familiar streets to get back home. On hurrying up the steps to her flat, she saw a man hanging about by the entrance. He was a slightly overweight gentleman, in his forties, wearing a battered bomber jacket and a cap with 'Roswell' printed on the front.

She stopped, looked at him and thought, *Oh God another reporter; I should have known more people would start contacting me after the story broke.*

He looked up, and she returned the glance.

"Miss Holloway?" Andy enquired.

"Yes, that's me," she replied miserably.

CHAPTER 15

They were both sitting in Rachel's flat, on the sofa.

Andy's eyes flicked over the slightly untidy surfaces and dusty ornaments. He thought he spotted a pile of clothes peeking out from behind her sofa. What the hell could he say about it? His bedroom was a mess, and if Mrs Braithwaite didn't remove his dirty clothes and plates as she did daily, it would end up in a similar state in no time. He eyed the coffee she had made him. It was too weak for his liking, but he wasn't there to drink coffee. He took a sip to appear polite, but then immediately wished he hadn't.

He began, "Er… Miss Holloway, I—"

"Rachel, please," she offered.

"Er… Rachel… OK. Look, I saw the thing in the paper, saying you can see ghosts; is it true? I need to know."

"Yes. Well, sort of. I had a brain bleed thing. Then, well, I sort of see them now." She looked at him, realising what she had just said must sound very odd to an ordinary person, but she continued anyway. "I don't know how it happened,

96

and I know they are there; I am not making it up… or hallucinating. They are everywhere, you see…"

"Everywhere?" His mouth had dropped open.

"They are everywhere, yes. I try to ignore them as they can be… intrusive…"

"You hear them as well?"

"Yes, I hear and see them, like I see and hear you."

He rubbed his hands together instinctively. "As I told you, I run a psychic-investigation company. Basically, when people have a ghost and it causes problems, I go in and help. I think that, with your ability, you would be an enormous help to me."

"How?"

"Well, you see them and you can talk to them, right? So I have this idea that, when I next get called to investigate something, you can come with me. You'll see the ghost, tell it it's dead, tell it to clear off, and, Bob's your uncle, we clean up."

"Er… they usually know they are dead… Besides, they might not want to go. I cannot command them to do anything; ghosts are simply living people who are dead… Some will do what you say; some will tell *you* to clear off."

He frowned. "You aren't winding me up. You really can see 'em?"

"Yes… unfortunately."

"Then next time I get a decent job, I will bring you along, to see how you go. If you are any good, you are on the payroll."

Payroll? Obviously, there was money involved in this. Rachel was unemployed now, so why not? This might be the answer to her prayers. Andy Horton and his dodgy-sounding ghost-hunting gig wasn't the best offer she had ever received in her life, but she was desperate right now and beggars could most certainly not be choosers.

★

It sat quietly in the corner of the train station. It was crouched down, waiting and looking for one certain person, who had not arrived yet. No one could see it, yet, as people walked by, they pulled their coats closer around themselves, glanced about as if expecting to see something, and held on tighter to their children. Although no eye could see it, many felt its presence.

It scratched at its flank, examined its claw afterwards and then looked around. This thing and its kind had moved around on earth ever since there was an earth. Untouched by age or evolution, they remained (rather like the louse), unchanged as everything else passed by. Its view of humans was a low one. Humans were physically weak, aged quickly and their actions were guided too much by their hearts, not by logic. They were no match for these creatures.

While inhabiting the bodies of humans, it had seen films and read books, showing the familiar fight between human and creature. Sometimes in these celluloid representations, the humans got the upper hand, by calling a priest or saying some words from a holy book. It smiled slowly, exposing its razor-sharp, little teeth. Why did humans think the creatures cared about holy words or priests, each of whom was, after all, just a mortal man in a dress? It was sheer stupidity.

It shifted from one foot to the other in its crouched position. Most people now didn't believe in anything paranormal or spiritual – they just trusted in what they could hear or see – and that suited it just fine. It meant that the creature could move amongst the living and the dead, relatively undiscovered and unspoken about. Like spies from the underworld, they came to this dimension, did what they had to do and then left. Most people didn't even believe in their existence, hardly anyone could see them, and, certainly, no mortal man – or woman – could stop them.

It grinned again when it saw its target. Following the smart-suited man along the platform, it began to move with a shuffle, with its hairy, ape-like limbs moving effortlessly to keep up, but it had to gather its speed as the man hopped onto the train. The railway announcement display flickered slightly as the creature passed, but, other than that, there was no indication it had ever been there.

CHAPTER 16

Andy walked up to the front door of the 19th-century property. It was a very simple house, with no front garden to speak of, just a small wall, and a two-foot gap between the frontage of the house and the street. It was well kept, whitewashed and had two windows to the front; it was a small terraced cottage.

He had received a call from the gentleman, a Ronald Easton, a week before; however, after meeting Rachel last night, he decided he needed to up his game. After about five minutes of thinking, Andy decided to visit all the potential clients he had put off investigating before now and explored the possibility that he could make a full-time living from ghost hunting, as there were only two weeks left before he had to start that blasted shelf-stacking job. In his mind, he had formulated some kind of plan in that if he could get through a few of the people on his list of customers, check that the haunting was legit (he didn't want Rachel seeing him fixing a knocking pipe and taking the cash), then return with her, he might be able to triple his income. He could then give the benefits office the finger and possibly become self-employed.

He wasn't sure what he made of Rachel; she was quite plain-looking with her slightly skinny build and brown hair, which hung down, hiding her face. He also wasn't struck by any kind of personality coming from her. There was no way he could leave her with clients, as you had to be a bit of a showman when visiting people's homes, and she looked so bored all the time. Andy would have to introduce her as being a psychic when he took her on jobs, then people would accept her oddness. You could be completely bonkers if you were labelled a psychic; in fact, people practically expected it. Maybe he should get her to wear some odd clothes, such as long, flowing dresses in bright colours, something crazy-looking, and maybe glasses too; everyone knew most psychics wore glasses.

He had chosen this case to visit first as it sounded more likely to be a real haunting. Mr Easton had explained that he had been bothered by a 'floating sailor', strange noises and a cold breeze coming through the room when nothing was there. The strange noises and cold breeze hadn't necessarily caught Andy's attention (people often felt that even in unhaunted homes), but the floating sailor? He was intrigued, so said he would stop by today.

Most of Andy's cases – in fact, he guessed about 98% of them – were nothing to do with the paranormal. After each 'investigation', he usually found a perfectly rational answer; this could include the person having mental health issues (such as paranoia), old houses making noises, people playing tricks, dodgy plumbing, tom cats yowling outside windows and even, on one occasion, a neighbour's radio being placed too near an old air brick, causing odd sounds to carry. All were explainable. Andy had started out by admitting the truth when he discovered it, showing homeowners the broken window the wind came through, getting them into the loft to see the knocking ballcock, etc., but he soon found that honesty was not the best policy. Confronted by the simplicity of the explanation, people would usually expect to not pay him, or only give him a small fee because he hadn't found a ghost. He had even received aggression on a couple of cases, where the person clearly felt foolish so took it out on him and, again, didn't pay.

So, now, whatever the problem, he pretended it was paranormal and that he had solved it. In the past, he also used to go in the house, snoop about, find the problem then confront the resident. Again, he had found this didn't work; people wanted a show for their money – calling out to the spirit, a rain dance to be done or some such – so Andy invented his own little performance. He had bought an old Stetson from a charity shop, and he had tied Mrs Braithwaite's crucifix to the front, which he would wear when he was 'in character'. He also made sure he used overblown, dramatic language: "Oh, come out ye spirit" and "Step forth." "Kum by yah" was also becoming a personal favourite; he told people this chant often revealed the dead, although, of course, this was a total pile of horseshit.

Over time, Andy became reliant on his own gimmick, in spite of being fully aware that it was complete bollocks. He found that the ritual itself not only helped him play for time, but also acted as a tuning fork that helped to sharpen his problem solving abilities, regardless of whether there was anything paranormal going on or not.

He had only ever met a handful of real spirits during his work, which had been enough, and a few things he couldn't explain. But now he had Rachel, well, maybe he could uncover some more real ghosts and make more cash.

Another trend that had emerged was that it tended to be wealthy, older people who called him in to get rid of paranormal activity. Andy wasn't sure why this was; did ghosts not bother the poor or the young? The person's age didn't bother him, but a rich customer was always good because he could charge more.

With the thought of £ signs floating before his eyes, he went up to the brightly painted, blue door and pressed the bell. A song played within; he recognised the melody but did not know what it was. Within moments, he heard footsteps, and then the door opened.

Mr Easton was in his sixties, Andy guessed, with neat, white hair, a small moustache and a beard.

"Mr Horton?" Mr Easton asked.

"Yup," confirmed Andy.

"Please do come in…" Mr Eastman waved Andy into a small but very clean living room.

It was furnished in a style favoured by older people, with a floral carpet and little doilies draped over the back of the chairs for headrests. As he sat, Andy noticed that cut-out, small pieces of carpet had been put by all the doors leading to and from the rooms, from the same roll of carpet that had been used in the main room, which was probably the worst tripping hazard ever invented. Mrs Braithwaite also used these ridiculously dangerous, curled, cut-out pieces of rug by the doors, presumably to save the main carpet. But they always looked tatty, and were probably dangerous in the home of an older person.

After the offer of some tea, which Andy gratefully received, Mr Easton sat down and began his story. "It started about a year ago, but has got much worse recently. My wife is particularly worried about it, especially after the… apparition."

"Tell me what happened. You said on the phone that you had felt uncomfortable for a while living here," ventured Andy.

"Yes, it was odd things; for example, we would be upstairs in bed and we would hear something moving around downstairs."

Andy groaned inwardly. It sounded like the 'spooky noise' thing; old houses often made noises, and also sound travelled from neighbour's homes quite easily. This was not compelling.

Mr Easton continued, "The cold breezes, I told you about. We would be standing in the kitchen, minding our own business, and we would feel a breeze, really cold, on our backs. It was only for a second mind, then gone, but no window or door was open. My wife also said something was watching us; she felt eyes on her."

Andy was bored. This was crap. A breeze and a noise; it was time to dig deeper. "The apparition, tell me about that."

Mr Easton leapt up. "Do you want to see where it happened?"

"No, just tell me."

Mr Easton sat down again, slightly disappointed. "My

wife and I were in bed when we saw a movement, like a mist, which drifted over our bed, then sort of disappeared. It was clearly a person; a sailor. It gave us a shock, and we thought we were imagining it."

"How did you know it was a sailor?"

Mr Easton looked surprised. "He had a beard and a naval uniform on: a big coat with stripes on the arms, and a cap with gold around the front of the brim. He was a captain, I think?"

Andy put his finished cup of tea down. "Did it speak?"

"No."

"Did he point to anything or make a gesture of any kind?"

"No, he just floated over the bed and disappeared."

Andy considered this. It did sound genuine. There was nothing spectacular about this sea-faring spirit; it uttered no well-worn phrases such as, "Get out," or "Avenge my death," nor did it point to any walls or floors, indicating secret passageways or hidden treasure, as shown in films.

"I would like to see your bedroom now, if I may?" Andy enquired.

"Of course; the wife has changed the quilt especially." Mr Easton jumped up again and led Andy up a small dog-leg staircase with ornamental plates on the walls, featuring Winston Churchill. At the top of the stairs, Mr Easton went straight into the room in front and ushered Andy in.

The bedroom was small and cottage-like, and, just like downstairs, it was neat, clean and twee. It had pictures of flowers on the wall, floral curtains and an old-fashioned wooden bed, which was pushed against one wall and had a sort of woven bedcover with yet more flowers on it.

Mr Easton hopped onto the right-hand side of the bed, lay down then pointed upwards. "It went from right to left, above the bed, then towards the window."

Andy looked about; he felt something was odd in the room, and he really felt the sensation of being watched – as if someone was by the window – but, of course, he could see nothing. "Show yourself," he said.

But there was nothing.

Andy frowned. "Thank you, Mr Easton. I will return with my psychic investigator and rid you of your ghost. Because there will be two of us, my fees must go up slightly, I am afraid."

Mr Easton sat up on the bed. "That is no problem at all, as long as you can get rid of it. My wife has been terribly worried about it, in case it comes down on her in bed."

"Ahem… yes…"

Andy looked at Mr Easton. Captain indeed; why the hell would a sailor float around a room in the middle of a city? This seemed likely to be some more crap, but something bothered him about the bedroom. Why not let Rachel loose on it and see what she could find?

CHAPTER 17

Rachel didn't know what was worse, the pain or the fatigue. She had never been a well person, not since childhood. Puberty had been hard; the hormonal changes had made her ill. She had always been prone to headaches and stomach upsets, often for no apparent reason, and she wasn't fit at all.

Since the haemorrhage, things had been a whole lot worse; every day, she had felt unwell in one way or another. Her problems ranged through extreme exhaustion no matter how much she slept, headaches and migraines, an upset stomach, problems with sleeping, and the constantly irritating 'brain fog'. The doctor said most of it was to do with the brain bleed, rather than stress or aging. She wasn't sure. All she knew was that she had grown tired of living half a life.

Things didn't hold much enjoyment for her anymore. As a child, she remembered becoming very excited as the family holiday loomed, watching her mother and father choose where they would go. Then, after they had booked it, she would take the old holiday brochure and keep it in bed with her, so if she felt nervous or had trouble at school, all she needed to do was turn to the page showing where they were going, and she felt better instantly. Looking at the brightly coloured pictures of parents and children on the beach and by the chalets – she loved it.

She remembered how she would select her best dolls and teddies to come with them on the trip, line them up and tell them all how fortunate they were to have this twice-yearly holiday. The day before they were due to set off, she wouldn't be able to sleep, so eager was she that her heart would race so it was fit to burst. She was so excited over this small thing, like an exquisite drug had been pumped into her veins. But nothing got her excited now; nothing. Not when she moved into the flat with John and not when she got a wage rise at work; nothing. It was as if her senses had been turned down or switched off. Was it depression? Who knew? But she wished something would thrill her now in the same way as she had been enthralled by holidays as a child.

Her parents had been killed in a car accident when she was nine; she didn't remember much about it. Rachel had been staying with her grandmother when it happened. All she could remember was her grandmother screaming in the living room, some policemen and that was it. Her memory from that time was very vague. She had later been told that her father had lost control on the motorway, and the car had flipped over, and they had died. That was it. She knew the story, and she had retold it many times, often in an emotionless way, to anyone who asked.

She was so jealous of people who had big families, brothers and sisters and those whose parents were still alive. Acquaintances would ask if she had any family, and she would say no. They would probe, asking if she had no parents, no siblings, and no aunts or uncles. All of which she answered no. Her grandmother was dead now too, so she had no one.

Since her brain haemorrhage, she had felt worse. Every day was an effort, particularly after losing her job, and this odd, newly acquired 'talent' of being seemingly able to see ghosts. Rachel looked up from the sofa and watched as a very large, old horse pulled a plough across her living room, followed by a man holding the plough share; they appeared from her doorway and vanished into the far corner. Again, the bottom of the horse's and man's legs were missing, as if below ground, so it looked like they were walking knee-high through the floor.

After watching them, she realised that some spirits seemed to have consciousness; they were aware she was there, and could speak to and see her, like a living person, such as that odd bloody doctor who had accosted her that time. But there were some who were more like 'recordings'; they would do something over and over again, as if in a film, but there would be no interaction, and you couldn't speak to them. The horse and ploughman seemed to be one of these occurrences. She knew they were recordings (as she called them) because they appeared slightly fainter than the other spirits.

All the while, in the back of her mind, she kept wondering if she was, in fact, mad; maybe the ghosts or whatever the hell they were – spirits or sprites – were not really there at all. Perhaps her mind was making them up, using information gleaned from her own years as a teacher to make them seem more real. If she actually was mad, she should keep a lid on it; she really didn't need idiots like Andy Horton running around, calling her a psychic. Rachel wanted to wind this all in, but she had a nagging feeling that this particular horse had bolted.

Her phone bleeped. Pulling it wearily from off her sofa, she saw a message from Andy. He had lined them up a job, which was something about a floating seaman; great. He would meet her at the house tomorrow (he only had a bicycle), and asked if she could make it there OK. She simply replied, "Yes", then put the phone down. Again, she wasn't sure about teaming up with Andy. Rachel had looked his company up on the internet, and, yes, it was there, listed as 'psychic investigators'. She recognised his mobile number, but no name was given, and she wondered if he was on benefits or something and trying to hide his earnings. Who knew? She didn't care.

She needed to look for another teaching job, but, in the meantime, she might as well cop some money from this caper to keep her going. Slowly, the exhaustion began taking over her again; her brain started slowing down, with the front of her head and her eyes feeling heavy. Within five minutes, she was asleep, her snuffles filling the room.

*

The morning seemed to come too soon. Rachel arranged to meet Andy in a small café, just down from Mr Easton's house, to discuss their tactics for the job. She found the café easily, which was a small greasy-spoon café, frequented by truckers. Ignoring the staring men sitting by the window, tea mugs in hand, she went in and looked for him. Seeing his overweight frame sitting in the corner and fiddling with a small, black box, she felt instant relief; the last thing she wanted was to be left sitting alone in this bloody awful café.

"Hello," she said, then sat down opposite him.

"I've had a bacon roll; do you want anything?" he replied, not looking up.

"Er… no. What's that?" She looked at the small, black box.

"It's me ghost box." He tapped it on the table, making his mug of strong tea vibrate.

"A what?"

He looked up. "A ghost box…" He tutted. "Like a radio, but this one makes white noise; you know, that 'shushing' noise you get on a radio between stations. Sometimes you hear the dead on it; they speak on it and say shit."

"Oh…" She didn't sound convinced.

She looked through the window at the street. Two spirit women, twins by the looks of it and dressed identically, stood staring in the café window, wearing outfits from the 1950s.

She tapped him. "There are two over there; can your radio thing pick them up?"

"Two what?" he asked.

"Ghosts… What else? Standing by the window, on the outside looking in; two women."

Andy looked at the window and saw nothing. "What are they doing?"

"Just looking in."

"If I went out there now and stood by 'em, would they do anything?"

"I don't know; they are like living people. If you stand next to that trucker in the corner, will he do something? The question is daft."

Andy brought a small suitcase out from under the table and popped the black box inside. He brought out another handheld box, this time with an array of colours at the top. "Hold on," he said, then he got up and hurried outside.

Rachel turned and watched as he walked out the café door and stood glaring in on the far side to where the women were standing.

"*Are they here?*" he shouted, causing all the truckers to turn and look at him suspiciously.

She shook her head and pointed to show that he needed to move to the right of the window.

He nodded, then went to the next window, within two feet of the women. He started waving the black box about. The women turned slowly to look at him, then returned to looking intently in the café.

He hurried back in, ignoring the odd looks from the café's patrons. "Me EMF meter says there's nothing outside."

She just stared at him.

He tutted. "This…" He pointed in an exaggerated fashion to the new box he was holding. "Is an electromagnetic field meter; it finds spikes in electrical activity. Where there are spirits, there is usually a surge in electrical activity."

"But you couldn't detect the ghosts outside…" She looked doubtful.

112

"Forget that," he said with a slight irritation in his voice. "Now, listen, about this job... we go in, you say *nothing* unless asked, and you do what I say... You make no sudden movements and no crazy statements. When I need you to do your... thing... I will say. Look about, see what ghosts are there, if any, and then tell me when the bloke is out of earshot. OK?"

She looked up. The two women were now standing silently right behind Andy, inches from him, and both were smiling.

"Are you sure you are not picking anything up, Andy?" she asked again.

CHAPTER 18

Mr Easton greeted Rachel and Andy with enthusiasm, and he wasted no time in ushering them to the bedroom. Remembering her instructions, Rachel said nothing as she entered, except a greeting, then watched as Andy put on his Stetson and started scanning the room with one or other of the black boxes, which squeaked loudly. Mr Easton stood for a moment by the bedroom door, gave a quick nod to them and then hurried away downstairs.

Rachel's attention was drawn to a cat sitting on the bed, watching her. It was a ghost cat, sleek and black, with a little white bib, just sitting there.

"Andy, shall I have a nose about?" she asked.

"Just in this room for the moment, nowhere else," Andy confirmed.

"There is nothing here…" She looked doubtfully at the cat. "Well, not a sailor anyway."

He turned off the machine and spun round. "You haven't looked properly; how do you know?"

"It's a small room; nothing is here."

"Goddammit," he said, then he picked up a walking stick that was propped by the bed, and started compulsively hitting the curtains with it, as if flushing out something hiding behind them.

She heard a bump in the next room and, without telling Andy, slipped outside onto the landing and eyed the closed door to the other bedroom.

"Kum by yah; oh spirit, show yourself," wailed Andy next door.

Slowly, she approached the door and opened it a little, then peeped in. The room was in darkness, with the curtains pulled closed; clearly, it was used as a storeroom, as stuff was in boxes everywhere, covered in sheets. In the corner, she saw a figure, a man, slightly silhouetted against the curtain. He wasn't moving; to the untrained eye, he could have been a coat thrown over a hat stand, but she knew it was a spirit. She was getting good at recognising them now.

She went in and closed the door. "Hello?" she said, "I see you there by the curtain."

The figure jumped visibly. "No one can see me, child," he said in a voice that was deep, male and with a kind of Cornish accent.

"I can. I hear you too."

He stepped forwards. Yes, he was indeed a sailor and a captain. He was about sixty, with grey hair, a beard and a full captain's uniform on. He doffed his cap. "Captain Anderson at your service... You see us? That is truly amazing."

"Yes, I see dead people," she sighed.

"Who is the loon next door?"

"He is looking for you; he is a psychic investigator."

"You really see us?" He waved his hand in front of her face. "Have you come to bring me salvation?"

"Er... no... The gentleman who owns this house said he saw you floating over the bed. He called us in."

"Floating? I wasn't..." he stopped. "This was my home, years ago in 1910; I lived here before I went to sea."

The door smashed open abruptly; it was Andy. "Rachel, I said to stay with me," he declared.

"He is here; the captain." She gestured to where the spirit stood silently.

Andy, as usual, saw nothing. "OK, great. Tell him to go, and hurry up." He shut the door.

"Go where?" the captain replied. "You can't bring me salvation? You aren't *the answer*?"

"I am sorry." She sat on a dusty seat. "I don't know what *the answer* is, but I would respectfully ask you not to haunt this poor gentleman and his wife who live here now. Are you not able to... I don't know... go elsewhere? Back to your ship perhaps?"

He looked mournful. "This is my home; I lived here before this couple. I died at sea, you know. My ship went down. I am not sure where else I can go. I am trapped here, you see, until God calls me home." He looked up again. "My ship is lost, and my shipmates are dead. All my friends are gone. This is the only place I can remain till I am taken up to heaven... or the other place." He looked slowly down at the floor.

Something began to dawn on Rachel. "What do you mean you are waiting to go to heaven? What's that all about?"

"*You don't know?* When you die, some people are taken

straight away. They go, presumably to heaven and to their maker. But some of us, for reasons we don't know, are stuck here on earth and made to wander, sometimes for years, waiting to be taken up. I pray a lot and ask God to help, but nothing happens. Maybe I am not yet good enough for heaven."

"So, some of you don't remain as... er... ghosts, but some do."

"Of course... If everyone and everything that died in the world became as we do, the earth would be pretty crowded, would it not? With every soul from goodness knows where wandering about wailing to their redeemer. You would see ethereal cavemen and ghost dinosaurs, but you don't, do you? No, some of us go upon death, and their souls are not seen, but we, the unlucky ones, remain. It comes to us all eventually, but some take longer than others to pass over, and no one – living or dead – knows for sure why this is."

Rachel felt the sadness coming from him. She felt pity. "Look, I can't help you; I just see you, and I don't know why I do. I think you should stay here, but make an effort so that the couple who live here now don't see you anymore; will you do that?"

The captain looked up. "Yes; yes, of course. I got excited one night and allowed myself to be seen. I never wanted to scare anyone."

"I suppose that will do. Look, I am going to tell the other man next door that I have asked you to leave. Please just don't bother the nice couple who live here again or they will only call us back."

"I wouldn't mind that. It is wonderful to find someone who sees us. Please do not go."

Rachel felt like she hadn't really solved anything here at all, but stood up and went to leave. "I'm sorry, I have to go," she said apologetically. "Please remember, don't get seen!" Without looking back, she went into the next room where Andy had resumed his assault on the curtains with the walking stick. The spectral cat had moved to a position on top of the wardrobe. She noticed a small, white splodge under its chin; she hadn't noticed that before. It was watching Andy intently.

"The spirit has… er… gone. Our work is finished here," she stated.

Andy stopped hitting the curtains "Gone? Gone where?"

"To another place… You asked me to tell him to leave, so I have. Captain Anderson was his name, and he died on a ship; he was lonely, so he came back to his home."

Andy couldn't believe his bloody luck. He had only been there twenty minutes, and they had found the spook and got rid of it. And it was a real spook to boot, not some wind-whistling-down-a-pipe nonsense.

"We'd better break the news to Mr Easton, eh?" he said, grinning, as he packed up the Stetson and his other bits and pieces into the case.

Downstairs, Mr Easton sat transfixed as Andy told him their findings. Mr Easton said he would research Captain Anderson and see who the man was, and he was very pleased to hear he had moved on. "To sea, no doubt," he finished.

Rachel smiled.

Andy happily took the fee. Rachel didn't see how much

it was, but it was a large wad of notes, maybe £1,000, and she wondered how much Andy was going to pay her. He then hurried out through the front door, leaving her behind in the hallway.

Rachel turned to face Mr Easton. "Oh, and by the way, your black cat, with the little white bib, is very happy in your room." She smiled then walked straight out, closing the door behind her.

Mr Easton felt a sudden wave of emotion come over him, tears pricked gently at his eyes and his legs felt a little weak, so he sat down on the heavily patterned sofa. "Toby cat," he said slowly. "You never left…"

CHAPTER 19

The young girl walked along, swaying through the trees; she had drunk far too much alcohol on her night out, but still she believed she knew the quickest way to get home. Her mother had said she must keep enough money for the taxi home from her friend's birthday party, but, of course, she had spent it on drink.

Walking through Darkfoot Wood was the quickest way home. Emboldened by her drunkenness, she didn't seem worried about who might see her; she just wanted to get back to bed and sleep it off. Thoughts crept into her mind about whether she would have to suffer a hangover tomorrow for this or whether she would get away with it. Her clothes didn't help her walking; she had a tight dress on, which she could hardly breathe in; a large coat; and, making everything worse, high heels she could barely walk on the pavement in, let alone on grass and mud.

She stumbled and fell on a fallen tree branch, gashing her leg. As she sat rubbing the wound, she swore she heard a sound behind her: a snapped twig, very loud, as if something or someone heavy had stood on it. A tiny flash of fear filled her mind, but only for a couple of seconds. The woods were full of animals and odd sounds, so worrying about one was stupid. She had used the torchlight from her phone to get this far, but the battery had died – probably from being overused at the party – so now she had to press on in semi-darkness.

She carried on wobbling through the wood, hoping that she was heading the right way. Some street lamps lit a road that ran alongside most of the way, and it was a full moon, so she could see her way forwards a little. But shapes and faces still seemed to leer out of the trunks of every tree and the branches of each bush, and little animal eyes shone in the darkness. Determined, she walked on towards Shore Moat.

Shore Moat sat in the middle of Darkfoot Wood; it had been there for centuries and maps from as early as the 13th century have it marked upon them. Some said it had once encircled a fortified building (ancient pottery, tiles, daggers and other artefacts had been dug up in excavations years ago), and this building, whatever it was, apparently had an underground dungeon with seven-foot-thick stone walls, with huge chains attached to them. This was all apparently discovered through amateur excavations in the past, before it had become a protected area. Whatever had been built on Shore Moat, it was not a peaceful home for a country squire; it was a place of war and death, that much was certain.

The water of the moat glowed slightly, with a green tint from the algae, giving it a kind of spooky, ethereal appearance. She stumbled on again, hoping this was the right way for the road; she had no idea of the time and was getting confused.

The thing sat crouched low beside the trunk of a large, old tree. It had placed one huge, hairy hand atop its head, mimicking what chimps often do in the sunlight, but the red of its eyes could be seen beneath. It watched the girl stumble past where it was sitting, and it remained still as she paused beside it, looked about with a worried frown on her face, then walked on. No human could ever see the thing, so it didn't matter. The creature watched as she staggered off into the distance, contemplating this as it brought its hand down and scratched its haunch. As the man silently walked past, following the path of the girl, again it didn't move. He paused right where the thing was, but, unlike the girl, he didn't look around, just stopped, made no movement, then walked on.

The thing stretched out, like a cat emerging from sleep, then silently, except for the odd crack of a twig, followed the man and the girl into the darkness, with its ape-like shuffle.

CHAPTER 20

Dr William Maxwell was now truly vexed. He had, after spending days wandering into the most unpleasant parts of town, tracked down the place where the lady who could see the dead lived. He absolutely had to speak to her without delay. Since he had died in a fire in 1852, which he strongly suspected was arson, he had spent most of his deathtime trying to solve the mystery of why he had ended up stuck on earth.

Had he not done enough to gain redemption? Fair enough, most of his life had been spent working in science and anatomy – he had little time for prayer or bowing his head to the altar – but then this might have been the problem. He also admitted that, in his earlier years, he had played court to rather a lot of women. Perhaps God was displeased, and thought this man of science liked the physical so much that he could remain on earth to repent. But now everything had changed. This lady who could see and commune with the dead was here. He needed to find her and tell her how important it was that she works with him to help all souls trapped in this state of limbo.

He had found details of where she worked in the newspaper article. After speaking to a ghost of a cleaner in her school, he had tracked down her street and now he just needed the house number where she lived.

William looked at the large townhouses, which were now split into flats, one of which no doubt Rachel lived in. Today, he wore a top hat and a large, black coat that flared at the bottom. These were accompanied, as usual, by his white shirt, simple shoes and a loose-fitting necktie. When dead, it wasn't hard to dress. All he needed to do was imagine the outfit he wanted to wear and it appeared on him. Well, that was the theory. Once, he had imagined his top hat but thought of it incorrectly, so it had materialised in a bright-red colour, which was very embarrassing. It had taken him the best part of an hour to reimagine the right colour. A friend had once appeared naked in front of others as a result of failing to imagine the appropriate attire. It could be problematic.

He stood staring up at the townhouses. He liked townhouses; in his lifetime, people used to occupy multiple floors, with whole families living together and often with servants in the basement. Now, they were flats, and only very few people had servants. Things had changed and not for the better in most cases.

A group of spirit Orthodox Jews gathered at the end of the street and eyed him suspiciously. There were nine of them in total; they remained in the middle of the road, and began swaying and calling out in Hebrew. The black-clad huddle of men, with white scarves about their necks, and the Torah in their hands, wailed and bobbed. What was all that in aid of? It wasn't even Friday.

He moved to a better position, where he could see all the houses clearly, and sat on a concrete bollard. He would remain there and wait as long as it took, as he had to talk to Rachel. Henry, the annoying young man Nanny had introduced him to, had said he wanted to accompany the doctor to help 'convince' Rachel. Dr Maxwell had thought differently; he couldn't see how Henry would make the situation any better, but could foresee numerous opportunities for him to make everything a thousand times worse. To appease the fervent fop, he had said he would return and teach Henry 'the ways of men' if Henry would just let him get on with this quest alone. It had seemed to satisfy Henry, who was apparently keen to leave the group of children that Nanny cared for.

William must have sat there for two hours, and he reminisced how time passed differently when you were dead. Time was almost nonexistent. You didn't age or die again, and nothing in particular happened if you failed to watch the clock. You didn't eat, sleep, use the bathroom or get sick, so, again, rituals that marked time were missing in the world of the dead. Time was meaningless.

He watched the Jews. The volume of their chants and the bobbing became more violent, almost like a slashing/ crushing movement. He then turned and saw Rachel, the whole reason he was there, hurrying along the street, no doubt returning to her flat.

Jesus be praised; at last. He leapt from his concrete seat and rushed after her. She had seen the Jews, as he saw a frown cross her face, but not him. As she passed them, the men began to bob ever more furiously, their ringlets flashing to and fro, and a word rising from their lips again and again, "*Shedim… shedim…*"

Ignoring their screeches, he rushed up behind her as she opened her front door; instinctively, he pushed his foot in the closing gap, then looked down as the closed door obscured half his foot, which was presumably in her hallway.

"Rachel… Rachel," he hissed through the closed letterbox. "It's me. The doctor from the hospital. I have to speak to you; it's really important."

"Go away," he heard from inside.

"I am afraid I cannot. I must speak to you about your gift, and make you realise how important it is." He started back as the door opened; she looked exhausted. "Rachel, I am sorry. Please, just give me ten minutes, and afterwards if you want me to go, I will."

The shouting men had dispersed now. She looked over his shoulder and watched them retreat.

"OK; look, come in. But ten minutes only, and no bullcrap, OK? I have had enough of that today," she stated.

Dr Maxwell was unsure what 'bullcrap' was, but he hoped he wouldn't say it without realising.

★

Rachel's flat was tidier than it had been in a while, but it still looked like it needed more attention. William remembered his lodgings in London, before he met his wife, and the chaos that ensued, especially when the gentlemen from the hospital came over with alcohol, so he chose not to judge.

Rachel appeared from the kitchen doorway, clutching a glass of water containing two dissolving effervescent pills. She sat down heavily in the armchair and lay back. William decided that it would be appropriate to sit in the large, lumpy sofa opposite. He made a slow and deliberate, almost theatrical, effort in doing this. When one happens to be dead, sitting or standing made no difference; but his memory of life often led him to sit when in the presence of others, especially ladies.

"Do you want a drink?" Rachel asked absentmindedly.

"Alas when you are dead, you lose the ability to drink," William mused. "This is especially frustrating if one happens to be haunting an alehouse."

"Oh, of course." She sat upright and gulped down a large mouthful of the fizzing liquid. "Yes, I know. I see you," she continued. "I see ghosts or whatever, but that doesn't mean anything." She sipped more of the fizzing drink, then blanched. "I am not a saint, nor a psychic, and I can't do anything to get you up to heaven or anything, so you must stop asking. What's your name by the way? I don't even know…"

"Dr Maxwell, William Maxwell, from London. I died in a fire."

She frowned. "Oh, I'm sorry about that."

He opened his hands. "My fate is my own. My dear, I have seen your article in the newspaper, and I really do believe that you are able to help us. You see, many people claim to be able to see the dead and talk to us, but you can actually do it. Whatever anyone says, this is a sign – a bridge between the living world and the dead. I cannot ignore it."

She held her head. "Look, I think I have another one of my migraines coming on… I have got so many worries right now: my boyfriend left me, I have lost my job, and, to be honest, people are reading the story in the paper and thinking I am nuts. My priority is to keep my head down and try to make enough cash to survive. That is all. I don't want to get involved in doing anything more than I need to."

"You have been given a gift; you have to use it."

"It's not a gift; it's a curse, believe me. I get it; if I can help dead people, then of course I will try to, but I cannot promise anything."

In the silence between them, the chanting of the Jews started up again, outside in the street.

"Will you go now, please?" asked Rachel "I really don't feel well with my head."

William stood up; he hadn't said half of what he had intended to, and he still didn't believe Rachel had a clue about how important she was; but he knew women, and if he pushed too much, she might not see him again. *Retreat, then return is in order here,* he thought.

"Very well, but I will return…" He looked out of her window and inclined his head to the street. "You have certainly shaken those fellows up."

"Wha… the Jews? Why? They are just doing their praying thing. They often do that out there; God knows why."

He turned to face her. "Their chant – you don't understand it, do you? The word, '*shedim*', you don't know what that means?"

"Of course not… Why would I?" She glared crossly at him.

"Jews argue as to its meaning, but most take it to mean…" he hesitated.

"God or angel… Meaning me; yeah, I get it. They were chanting it at me, at my bloody house, hoping I can help them go to their Jewish heaven as well."

He looked back out of the window, and then frowned.

"Look, whatever it means, I don't give a toss." She lay back in the chair again.

Dr Maxwell went to speak, but then thought better of it.

CHAPTER 21

Two weeks passed. Word was getting around town about how Andy's business had now received the instant boost of a real psychic who could see ghosts, and he was receiving more calls than ever from people wanting help and advice, including a local church, of all places. Someone had put a post on a social media site for local businesses that went on at length about the so-called powers of Andy's new sidekick. Some of the comments dismissed it as a hoax, but, interestingly, he had received five calls on the back of this post alone, all from paying customers wanting his services.

He had decided to sign off from the benefits and take a risk that he could now support himself, as he certainly didn't have time to stack shelves now. In one day, last week, he had made an astonishing £850. This was split between two jobs: one was a silly one (the bumping sound heard was a local tom cat, trying to get through a window to mate with the female cat that was owned by the lady who called him), but one was a real spook. It was a stable boy, who was trapped in a house conversion that was once a stable yard. As usual,

Rachel had spoken to him, and the ghost had decided not to haunt the outbuildings anymore. Whatever Rachel was saying to these spirits was working; they never bothered the people who lived in the house again.

He hadn't admitted to Rachel that he had charged for the tom-cat case (he always sent her out of the room before taking the cash), as he still wasn't sure what she would make of him charging people who didn't actually have a real ghost; but needs must, and he was skint. He would sound her out about that later.

The only fly in the ointment was that he was worried about an odd call he had received that morning from Mr Easton, the 'floating sailor' man; it sounded quite desperate, and said he had to see both Andy and Rachel as soon as possible, but down at the police station. Shit. What was that all about? Surely Mr Easton wouldn't lay some criminal charge at his door for what happened in his house? Andy had ripped a curtain slightly whilst hitting them, but surely this wasn't a police matter? As well as that, Mr Easton's ghost had been a real one, not a rip off. If Andy had pretended a knocking pipe was a spook, then, fair enough, he guessed that was earning money under false pretences. But this had been real.

Mr Easton had asked them to come today at 3pm, so Andy text messaged Rachel, who had just said, "OK" and not asked what it was about or anything. Thank goodness he was the one in charge of this outfit; she would never be a very good psychic investigator alone.

★

At 3pm, as asked, Rachel and Andy arrived at the police station. Rachel looked, as usual, slightly out of it; she claimed her medication made her sleepy at times. Andy just wanted to find out what the hell Mr Easton and the cops wanted with him, and then get out.

On arrival, they had been ushered from the bland station counter to what looked like an even blander interview room down a corridor. There was a recording system on the edge of the table, some hard plastic chairs and a poster stuck to the wall, simply saying, "Not a crime? Don't call 999" with a cartoon policeman shaking his finger. Andy noticed there were bars at the window. All sorts of things rushed through his mind, like maybe something had gone missing after they left the house and Mr Easton thought they were thieves. He suddenly felt very claustrophobic.

Rachel looked up at the woman standing in the corner of the room. She was holding a large book, and was dressed in an apron, an ankle-length brown dress and with a white coif on her head. Rachel guessed she must have been about 25 years old; or would have been if she was alive, of course. She wasn't. It was another ghost. She looked sad. She didn't look at Rachel, but just stared at the floor. Rachel looked away. She was getting used to seeing them everywhere now, so much so that she didn't even tell Andy anymore when they were nearby. She used to point them out, but did not bother anymore, as there were too many of them.

"Why do the police want to see us, did you ever find out?" Rachel asked, breaking the silence.

"Er, no… Mr Easton just said he had an important

matter he wanted to discuss, and it would be easier to do it here," clarified Andy.

She turned to him "And you didn't ask why? Maybe we are in trouble?"

"Why would we be in trouble?"

"I don't know; it might be that we have upset him in some way?"

The door opened abruptly and a middle-aged man walked in, wearing an ID badge and carrying some papers, closely followed by the familiar figure of Ronald Easton. The first man didn't look very happy or at all comfortable about being there. They sat down opposite Rachel and Andy.

"Are we in some kind of trouble?" Rachel asked.

"Trouble? I hope not, unless you know something we don't?" the policeman said grumpily. "I am Detective Inspector Derek Johnson, and this is, as you probably know, a colleague of ours, Ronald Easton. It was his idea to bring you both here." He frowned.

"Colleague?" asked Andy nervously; he didn't like dealing with the police at all if it could be avoided.

Ronald spoke up in a jovial tone, "I work with the police, on their lay committee, helping to make sure that officers deal fairly with suspects. It's a volunteer role, but one I am proud of…" He looked fleetingly at Johnson sitting next to him before continuing. "Anyway, after the experience at my house, I spoke to Derek here about a case he is working on at the moment. I think you might be able to help him, especially you, Rachel."

She jolted upright. "Me?"

"You said you can see… the undead?" queried Mr Easton.

"The dead, yes, sometimes… I know it sounds mad." (She always added that at the end.)

"Good." Mr Easton appeared completely unfazed. "Derek, show Rachel your information, please."

The policeman, still looking annoyed, opened up a buff-coloured file and took out a colour photo of a pretty, young girl, whom Rachel suspected was pouting at a camera phone; the girl wore a lot of make-up and had some cleavage on show. Andy stared at it, transfixed.

The policeman began, "This is Kayleigh Lovall." He gestured to the photo. "After a night out with friends two weeks ago, she went missing in Darkfoot Wood; do you know of it?"

"I have heard of it, but I've not been there." She kept looking at the photo.

"We found a shoe and her bag in the woods, and, worryingly, blood that matches Kayleigh's, but nothing else. We believe…" DI Johnson paused. "That… er… due to…" He stopped again. "Look, we think that, due to the amount of her blood that we found, she has been murdered."

"What has this got to do with me?" questioned Rachel.

"Our normal investigations are not casting any new light on this case. She was well liked, a respected student with good grades, and never in trouble, but we are drawing blanks here as to who is her killer or where her body might be. We, of course, will be carrying on with our own official investigation into what happened that night, but Mr Easton…" DI Johnson looked across at him with distain, "believes you might be able to help us in an unofficial capacity, as a psychic."

"I am not psychic. I cannot tell fortunes or what's going to happen to anyone; I just see dead people... Sometimes, I also see buildings as they were in the past, but that's it."

Andy coughed. "Is there any money in this if we find the body?"

Rachel turned to him angrily.

The policeman crumpled his nose slightly. "There has been a reward put up by her parents of £10,000, so, in theory, if your evidence leads us to the killer, who is then convicted successfully, then yes, you would be rewarded. Please also remember that during this investigation you cannot speak to anyone outside of this room, including the media, about what you are doing."

"Sweet! When do we start?" enquired Andy.

"Wait, I don't know about this," intervened Rachel. "I see spirits around me, but they just happen to be where they are, like in the street or in this room..." She was aware of the lady in the smock, walking backwards and forwards, still clinging on to her beloved book. "But I cannot conjure them up, like people on those psychic stage shows, who say, 'Is there anyone there?' I don't know if I could find this girl."

"Will you try? Her parents are desperate for news," said Mr Easton.

Rachel looked at the buff folder, which was now on the table; a photo had half slid out and all she could see was what looked like grass covered in red. "Look, give me some info on where she was last seen and a photo. I will give it a go, but I promise absolutely nothing."

The policeman, after pushing the red photo back into the folder hastily, pulled out two sheets and passed them over to Rachel, and, lastly, gave her a copy of the original pouting photo.

He declared, "I will be honest, Miss Holloway. I don't believe in all this psychic business, seeing ghosts, but Mr Easton has been... most insistent... that we try you, seeing as everything else is bringing no results. The only people who even know about us asking you are me, my immediate boss and Mr Easton." He paused, as if considering whether to say the next sentence or not. "I don't think I am the only one to say I don't believe in ghosts, and that's that."

"You're not alone," she said, looking at the photo again, with the young girl pouting back at her. "Some ghosts don't believe in ghosts; what about that? It's fine being alive and not thinking ghosts exist, but imagine being dead, being a ghost, and then still saying to yourself they don't exist, which is sometimes the case with religious people and scientists. It can get people into a bit of a spin."

The policeman looked back, unimpressed; Mr Easton was, inappropriately, beaming. Andy was just sitting there, thinking of the £10,000.

CHAPTER 22

Rachel had spent the weekend reading the notes about the short life of Kayleigh Lovall; she could only read it in small bursts of about an hour, due to her tiredness. The policeman had been right: Kayleigh had done well at school and was now at college; she had never been in trouble with the police; according to notes from her parents, there had never been any issues with her behaviour, and she had no boyfriend. Regarding her last evening alive, it was confirmed that she was at a friend's party; she had left at 11pm, and her friend, who was too drunk to notice, had not even seen she had gone. Apparently, Kayleigh was last seen on CCTV, heading into Darkfoot Wood, which looked like she was taking a shortcut to her home. If she had used the quickest route, she would have passed Shore Moat; the blood, shoe and bag (with nothing missing from it) had been found half a mile past the moat. That was it; that's all they knew.

Rachel had turned over in her mind what she was supposed to do. She had debated trying to ask the girl to appear to her, to try and conjure her up, so to speak, but that wasn't how it worked – she just saw spirits going about their daily business. So, in the end, she decided to go to Darkfoot Wood. She would have a look around there, especially down the route that the girl took through the area (the policeman had drawn a map for her), and if that wasn't fruitful, she would possibly visit Kayleigh's home, as she might be there.

Rachel had recently discovered, through speaking to spirits, that those grounded on the earth – the dead people she saw – usually had their own special reason for hanging around (or haunting) in the area they did. After death, some of them tried to make it back to their homes, but seeing their families in mourning often upset them too much; some went to workplaces they had known well, and others went to favourite areas in the locality. A spirit she had seen once explained that most of them could not just pop off to anywhere they wished – for example, to spend a week in Miami; many were 'grounded', usually within about ten miles of the spot where they died, although a small minority of them were able to travel longer distances. But then those who died far from home were sometimes able to haunt not only the area they died in but their home town as well; for example, those who died abroad. Most chose to come home. It was all somewhat random.

The ghost Rachel had spoken to also said he knew one spirit who had simply chosen to stand by the road where he had been killed, screaming at passers-by. Why ghosts stayed where they did was very individual to them. Would Kayleigh haunt the woods or her home? Or maybe she wasn't grounded, but was one of the lucky ones who didn't haunt anywhere and were whisked off to heaven, hell or wherever.

As soon as Rachel arrived at the edge of Darkfoot Wood, she began to think it was a stupid idea to be wandering about in the vain hope that this girl's ghost would just appear. The place itself was a well-known beauty spot, used by runners and dog walkers. It covered about 200 acres, and it was easy to get lost there. Clutching a folder of papers, given to her by D I Johnson, she went through the main entrance and walked to a grassy area further along, where Kayleigh had been seen going into the wood from the CCTV camera, positioned on the road. As Rachel passed the spot where the doomed girl had been, only a fortnight before, she looked back at the camera in the distance, which was watching everything from atop its pole, then she turned back and entered the wood.

She had heard of the place but had never been there; she had no reason to. Surrounded by high trees and the sound of the breeze, she walked on; she was passed about every ten minutes or so by a runner or a family out for the day. It wasn't scary at all. This must have been the path that Kayleigh had walked along, the policeman's map said so, and Rachel felt she would have seen something or had some kind of odd feeling by now, but there was nothing. Nothing came to her at all about the missing girl.

As she followed the path, she became aware of spirit people in the woods, standing in amongst the trees and working. Looking more closely, she could see they were mostly men, with a couple of youths, sawing and chopping at trees. Dressed in loose, stained shirts, tattered trousers and wearing battered, leather hats, they carried on sombrely at their task. One or two looked up, but the rest carried on, fervent in whatever work they were doing with the trees.

As she walked, she saw plenty of spirits – some men in Edwardian dress; a lady in what looked like 1960s clothing, with a small dog; and a stout man with a huge moustache, shouting at a spectral cat that was sitting high in one of the branches of an oak – but absolutely nothing that looked like it had anything to do with Kayleigh.

She hurried to Shore Moat; it was just past there that the blood and items had been found, so maybe she would have some more luck nearer to the murder scene. The moat in daytime, although lit by the sunlight filtering through the trees, had a slightly sinister air about it. She had read some information that the dark-green, sludgy water once encircled some kind of fortified building, hundreds of years ago. Now all that was left was the mainly oblong moat, about 300 feet across, and an island of land in the middle that could be accessed by a small causeway. The rest of the area was largely given up to the wild, although it was maintained now and again, so it was accessible.

Rachel stood about two feet from the water's edge. Being dark and uninviting, the moat had probably been much more well defined than this when it had guarded the building; but now, after centuries, nature had encroached and made it a slimy shadow of its former self, like a top athlete, withered by age and now unable to even move from a bed.

She looked about, saw nothing, and so sat down on a tree stump. The sound of voices caught her ear as she watched two girls, crossing the little causeway on to the island. Dressed in a slightly hippie fashion, they had ribbons in their hands.

Some of the trees around the moat had been decorated with little offerings and had ribbons tied to twigs. She wondered what that was all about.

Then Rachel saw her. Standing on the island, right by the edge of the water, and staring straight at her, was a young girl, who was wearing a large, dirty, white coat with fake leopard spots on it, and a tight, blue dress. She was just standing there, with her head to one side, her face pale, her hair stuck to her cheeks and forehead, and her eyes dark. And just staring. Rachel couldn't take her eyes off the girl. She tore them away to quickly scan the papers given to her, concerning what Kayleigh had been wearing when she had gone missing. Her finger turned the papers back and forth till she saw "Light coat with fake leopard-skin print, blue dress."

"Christ!" Rachel exclaimed.

She looked up again. Gone; the figure was gone. Scrambling up, she looked about, then she walked hurriedly along the causeway to the island where the figure had been. When she was standing right on the spot, there was nothing – even the girls with the ribbons had gone.

Unexpectedly, there in the woods, the figure reappeared again. This time, she was on the outer bank, across the water from Rachel, standing with half of her body behind a tree, again with her head inclined. Her skin was porcelain white and her eyes kohled, almost like a goth.

This time, Rachel fixed the girl in her sights before walking slowly back along the path; right now, she was a little afraid. Since her ability to see the dead had manifested, she had encountered lots of them and, to be honest, had felt no fear whatsoever; they were who they were – just ordinary people, albeit dead – but she had never felt under any kind of threat when seeing them. However, today was different. As she approached and got about fifteen feet away from the girl, the full horror began to reveal itself; she felt her heart thumping so fast that she began to find it hard to breathe.

"H-hello," Rachel uttered as she drew nearer.

The girl looked skeletally thin, and her cheek bones pressed out from what looked like a slightly puffed-up face. Her eyes remained unmoving. The girl then stepped behind the tree in a strangely jerky movement, and was gone.

Rachel stopped dead, now more scared than ever. She wondered if she should walk up and just look behind the tree, but then what would happen if the ghost – or whatever it was – came at her from behind? She didn't like this at all, and every part of her body screamed at her to get out of that place as fast as she could.

She walked closer, slowly; all her nerves were a-twitch for a movement or sound, but none came. Now at the tree, she peered behind it at a snail's pace, ready to attack or fight if whatever it was jumped out at her, but it had gone. It was not there anymore.

She sighed heavily and realised all of a sudden that she felt light headed. The feeling grew, like a gnawing sickness in her stomach; something was wrong – very wrong. She became aware of a pushing sensation bubbling into the back of her head. Slowly, she turned around to face what her soul was telling her to see, and there it was, for less than half a second, sitting in the branch of a large tree. The thing, the ape-like creature she had seen in her dreams, was sitting there, not only obscuring all light from behind but positively absorbing it into itself, forming a hairy, large blob of darkness. It shifted slightly, and reached up to a branch above with a huge, hairy arm, then it pulled itself out of sight in a flash.

What the hell was that? She took a step back, then felt the feeling of panic ebb away slowly.

It wasn't clear who was more surprised: Rachel on seeing the thing, whatever it was, or the creature itself, knowing it had been properly observed, for the first time in centuries, by a mortal.

CHAPTER 23

Andy pushed his way up the stairs to his room, carrying three large bags. The front-door key swung from between his teeth as he opened his bedroom door and, gratefully, put the bags on the bed. After removing his coat, he began to empty out the contents slowly. A new laptop in a box and some computer paraphernalia came out of one bag, a smart leather coat came from another, and a pair of designer trainers, ornately boxed up, came from the last.

"Sweet," he declared.

He rubbed his hands together, and reached instinctively for the laptop first, but then heard Mrs Braithwaite call him from downstairs.

"Andy... Andy, love..." Her voice sounded slightly faltering, so he knew something was wrong.

"Coming..." He frowned, opened up the box that contained the trainers, had a good look at them, grunted, put them back down on the bed and then descended the stairs.

Mrs Braithwaite was at the bottom, holding on to the

stair rail. "Your mother is here," she said simply, fiddling with her hearing aid as if turning it back up again.

"Jesus." He immediately felt his heart sink.

"No… just your mother," she replied. "I am going for some fresh air in the garden; will you be OK?" She touched his arm.

"Yeah, sure; you go." He thought it best that Mrs Braithwaite stayed out of this.

He took a deep breath and entered the living room.

His mother was standing, looking at the curtains closely. She was in her sixties, skinny, and with heavy make-up, thin red-painted lips, tight-fitting clothes, quite fashionable boots and a shock of blonde, permed hair. Mutton dressed as lamb, as Mrs Braithwaite always said.

Without looking up, she said, "God knows the last time these curtains were cleaned. They are filthy."

He just stood there, considering his answer, when she turned.

"I see that you have drawn some girl into this ghost nonsense that you do. I read it in the paper; you have got some woman, saying she can see dead people to line your pocket. It's shameful," she stated.

"She can see the dead. It's not a lie," Andy explained.

"Yes, of course." She sat down heavily in an armchair. "I haven't heard from you for weeks, not a word. I am your mother, Andrew, and the least you could do is pick up the phone to see how I am."

"You can always ring me; I have been busy." The truth was Andy didn't actually want to ring a person who would not only begin a row at the drop of a hat, but who would also unleash a whole torrent of abuse on him. He wasn't into masochism the last time he checked.

"Too busy to look in on your mother? That's disgusting." She got up and walked to the window. "So, I see you still haven't got a proper job yet. Dressed like that, it's no wonder employers don't want to know you."

"Was there a reason you came here?" Andy was growing tired of this now familiar charade.

"To see you and to find out why you still ponce off Mrs Braithwaite – living here, probably for free – when you could live with me; I have plenty of space."

"I pay rent and help out around the house. Besides, it's best we live apart."

"You only have a problem living under my roof because you fail to obey my simple rules."

"Like coming in by a certain time every night and not drinking? I am over-forty, Mum; I can pretty much stay out late and drink a beer if I want."

She picked up her coat and bag. "Remember I am your mother, Andrew; I won't always be here."

Slowly, she walked to the door and then paused. "You were such a good boy when you were younger, well behaved and polite, then you went to that secondary school and you became horrible. It killed your father, you know, the stress you put us through; it's why he had the heart attack so young. That's down to you, I am afraid."

He stood there silent and still. There was so much he could have said in response, but he instantly felt like he was a young child again, being scolded and told he wasn't good enough, and he just could not pluck up the courage to respond at all.

He hated feeling weak like this and wished he could give it to her with both barrels, but, of course, he never did.

"You could have been someone, Andrew, but no, you don't get a real job, you dress like a tramp and live here, badgering that dopey old bat Mrs Braithwaite, who is the only one stupid enough to take you in. Now, this crap about having a girl working with you who can see ghosts – what utter useless claptrap; by the looks of it, you have gone quite mad. But, to be honest, it's all I expect from you now." With that, she opened the door, walked out into the hallway and was gone.

He sat down. Her rules, her house; yes, he remembered those rules all too well; just a single step out of line and that was it. For some reason, an incident that occurred when he was about seven pushed itself forcibly back into his mind. He had been given a tank of stick insects from his school; they were funny things that looked like tree twigs, but they were easy to care for. His father had said he could have them, but, of course, his mother hated them. His father loved all animals, and he would go to great lengths to rescue a spider in the house or a worm, found on the path; but not his mother. *Squash, squash, squash* – she would kill anything she found that she didn't like. One day, a few of the insects escaped from the tank. He had only found out when he had returned from school for his mother to present to him their broken, crushed, dead bodies on a piece of newspaper. She had killed them all, saying they were horrible and she didn't want them in the house.

He had cried for a week after that, and learnt that it was pointless to have live animals in the house again. He was past forty, yet he still remembered that incident with stomach-churning accuracy. There were many, many other such incidents.

When Andy was seventeen, his father had died of a sudden heart attack; he was 51 years old. That was the tipping point for Andy. His father liked a drink, and he had been very stressed at work; now Andy was older, he could reflect on this and understand that these were probably the reasons his father had been ill, not because of him. But, after his father's death, his mother would always say Andy had caused the stress that had killed him, and Andy resented this. He had been a good person; as far as he could see, he had studied hard at school, never caused problems or hung out in gangs, didn't touch drugs, and got quite a few qualifications when he had left formal education, but nothing was ever good enough for his mother.

He had come to the conclusion that his mother had bounced a lot of her anger off his father – belittling him, rowing with him and moaning at him consistently – so when his father died, there was only one other person left there to take the shit: Andy. She started on Andy, and, unlike his father, he didn't have the time or patience to deal with it. Maybe that did make him a bad person, who knows? But he did know he had moved out of the family home as soon as he could, never, ever to return again. He had tried to return a couple of times in the past, but both times had been disastrous; the last time he left with her actually screaming at him in the street, throwing his clothes after him as he hurried down the road.

Screw that, he was never going back. Rachel had told him that her parents had died in an accident, so she had not had to deal with such issues most of her life. For a second, just one second, Andy imagined life without his mother, as if something had happened to her. The thought was broken as the door to the hallway opened and Mrs Braithwaite peeped in.

"Are you all right, love?" she asked.

"Yes, fine," replied Andy.

Unexpectedly, he felt his mobile phone buzz inside his pocket; it made him jump slightly. Fumbling, he fished it out and looked at the screen; it was a text from Rachel, which simply said 'I saw the girl at the park; we should go back there at some point'. He texted 'OK' in reply, then put the phone back.

"I am absolutely fine, Mrs Braithwaite," he said, and he hugged her lightly as he passed her in the doorway and walked up the stairs.

CHAPTER 24

A whole week passed before they could return to Darkfoot Wood. Rachel had caught a nasty cold, which had spread to her chest and lungs, making it difficult to breathe; her eyes were also swollen shut, which had made everything more difficult. This was the first time in years she had felt so bad. Why had she got so ill now? It had made her very depressed.

Her health had been, as usual, touch and go. It was easier now that she wasn't working as a teacher, as when she was sick previously, she would have had to muddle through at school, or call in sick and suffer the stress of having a review meeting with Mr Andrews. Now, she didn't have that, but she found not having a normal job was making her lazier and also more self-aware, which wasn't a good thing. Having very little to do each day left her more exhausted than when she knew she had things she had to get completed; maybe it was boredom or depression. She also worried about the work situation; there was no way doing this silly ghost investigation thing would give her enough money to pay her rent long term. Andy had told her that he had signed off the dole, so confident was he that a living could be made from it, but she wasn't so sure. Rachel had paid this month's rent, but all she had in the bank was one further month, then that was it; she would have to go to the benefits office and claim destitution.

Due to spending the week unwell, she had been given some time to think. Rachel had wanted to get back to the woods and take Andy with her, so he could bring his equipment or do whatever he wanted to do to locate Kayleigh. Maybe, by working together, they could find her remains or track down who had killed her.

Lying in bed, she had thought long and hard about all the possibilities. If she could see the dead and speak to them, which she knew she could, then, in theory, nothing could stop her from maybe looking into old, unsolved murder cases. Whilst browsing the internet, she had been surprised to discover that there were lots of unresolved murders worldwide. In theory, all she needed to do was establish contact with the dead person, then just ask them if they knew where their mortal remains had been dumped and who had killed them. It sounded so simple, but surely it wouldn't be that easy? She was also certain that she wasn't the first person in history who could see and speak to the dead with little issue. It was an exciting and certainly scary time. Could it really be as easy as that?

★

It was a Tuesday morning when she finally felt well enough to meet with Andy outside Darkfoot Wood, by the same entrance that was overseen by the CCTV camera that had captured Kayleigh's last fateful walk home on the night she was killed. He turned up – as usual, on his rusty bike – with a holdall swinging from the handlebars. After dismounting, he chained the bike to a metal fence and, without another word, they headed into the trees.

As they walked along, Andy pulled a strange contraption from his bag (Rachel noticed that he was a little quieter than usual and looked a bit paler, so thought maybe he had also been ill). The little machine resembled an old-fashioned tape recorder, attached by a length of wire to a handheld microphone. He pushed a button on the main part of the machine and replaced it in his bag, which he then slung over his shoulder. As they walked, he waved the microphone to and fro in the air, as if trying to capture something.

"I didn't see her here," said Rachel, wondering if he was trying to record a spirit. "It was further on in the woods."

"I know," he confirmed.

They walked on. The wood people, or whoever they were, could still be seen. Chopping and hewing in the shadows, dirty and crumpled with sweat-stained clothes; one lifted his hat in greeting as she walked past. She responded with a nod. Two boys in jackets and small caps pushed a go-cart past, with one sitting inside, pulling at the guide ropes, and one pushing; she heard their laughter before she even saw them. On this stretch of the path, she noticed that some people, such as the woodsmen, appeared from about the knee upwards; the boys with the go-cart appeared from the middle of their shins upwards. The go-cart had no wheels she could see; it was like it was buried in the earth, as if floating along the ground. Rachel supposed the earth on this path had built up over time; when the boys ran down this path, the earth level must have been a little lower, and when the woodsmen were here, even further back in time, it was clearly lower still.

It was as if the trees drifted past them as they walked, with some clearly centuries old; she wondered what they had witnessed in their lifetime: lovers meeting beneath their boughs, wars, ancient squabbles, entire empires being built up and destroyed. Trees, unlike the dead, always remained silent, with their long, spindly arms, showing the first buds of spring, reaching towards the sky as if in exclamation.

Andy stopped and raised his hand. "I hear something," was all he said as he dashed into the bushes, waving the mike franticly backwards and forwards.

She was left standing on the path. In front of her, as before, was the large man with the big moustache, shouting at the cat, which was apparently still stuck in the tree, although on a different branch this time.

She walked up to him and, just by using her power of thought (she had stopped using her voice now when speaking to the majority of the dead, as it brought her too much unwanted attention), she simply said, *"Hello."* Spirits understood this just as well as speaking out loud, but by utilising her mind, she could communicate with them far more discretely.

He spun round rapidly and, instead of showing alarm or fright (many spirits did when Rachel spoke to them), he swept his hat from his head and bowed. "Good day, lass." He had a countryside accent, though Rachel didn't know exactly where from. "You can see us?" he asked.

153

Rachel was used to this question. *"Yes, do you have a problem with your cat?"*

"Yes, indeed," he said, not seeming to notice her swift change of subject. He straightened up, beamed a smile and pointed upwards to a rather fat ginger cat, sitting upright in a stiff position, about ten feet above them, on one of the oak's broad branches. "This is Marmalade; he sits up in the tree and refuses to come down. It is a constant source of aggravation to me."

"How long has he been there for?"

"Oh, since about 1931 I think… May 1931, but forgive me, lass, I cannot remember the day."

She stared at the cat, which – if she hadn't known better – looked completely real and alive as the sun dappled its fur.

"He never comes down, and I am stuck here most days, trying to get him to descend, but he never does… Oh, my manners…" He whisked his hat off again. "I am Winston Mallory, from Kewstoke in Somerset; I had a heart attack."

"Oh, I am sorry to hear that," she said.

"What?"

"About your heart attack. You didn't have to tell me that, although it's interesting."

He frowned. "We always say that, don't you know?"

She looked puzzled.

"When a spirit greets another, whether living or dead, they should say their name, where they are from and why they died; it is politeness. Spirits will always do this; to not do so is rude."

"Oh." Rachel had never heard about this before. *"I guess it would be embarrassing if you died in an odd way, such as on the toilet, like Elvis… then I guess you wouldn't say…"*

Mr Mallory seemed unamused. Rachel looked over her shoulder and saw Andy had removed his Stetson with the crucifix from his bag, and now, with it firmly on his head, was doing an odd little jig in the glade, still waving the mike about.

"Is he unwell?" Winston asked, tapping the side of his head.

"Er no…" Rachel looked back. *"We are investigating the murder of a young woman, here in the woods, a couple of weeks back; did you hear about it?"*

"No, I have to say no; most of my time is spent here with Marmalade. Some of the spirits of the wood say that the day Marmalade comes down, we will all find *the answer* and ascend to heaven."

Rachel groaned inwardly at this *the answer* thing again; at least this gentleman didn't think *she* was his ticket to heaven, which most of them thought, including the Jewish men who had been bothering her more recently.

"I am probably stuck here due to this blasted cat." He looked back up in the branches again; the cat hadn't moved. "He was my companion for fifteen years, he died a year before me, and now we are reunited in death." Mr Mallory fixed her with a stare. "It's like a challenge, you see… I believe that if I can get him to come down out of the tree, it means I have done the task set for me and I get to go to heaven."

Rachel wasn't convinced. The dead all made an excuse for what they believed that they needed to do to move on and go to heaven, and they all had a reason why they were stuck on earth. Usually, it was associated with not being diligent enough with religion or not being good enough to people whilst alive, or the one supposedly bad thing they said they had done in their lifetime that they were ashamed of. Then they always set themselves a seemingly impossible task that, once completed, would guarantee their spirits would fade gently from earth and go to their maker (or wherever).

She had an idea. *"You say you talk to the spirits of the wood; do you see them often?"*

"Not often, no. The woods have sprites – they are like balls of energy, they never were people – but sometimes they speak to me."

Abruptly, Rachel felt the image of the dark, ape-like thing enter her mind; that was probably what it was: a woodland sprite, and harmless. It was only that it had taken her by surprise. *"What do they look like, these sprites?"*

Andy let out a loud moan in the bushes. Both Rachel and Winston turned to look at him. He stood there still for a moment, then – without warning – he started jigging about again.

Winston answered, "Nothing much, darkish shadows; they mean no harm."

"I think I have seen one, in the wood; it reminded me of a chimpanzee. I am sorry, I know that sounds silly, but it's the only way to describe it," explained Rachel.

Winston stopped looking in the direction of Andy and turned to her. "An ape? It looked like an ape?"

"Yes, that's right; it was dark, hairy and had pointy teeth."

He blanched a little; she could see it.

"Yes, well, I wish you luck with your search." He turned back to the tree.

156

Andy came up beside her, and she turned to him. "What did you find?" she enquired.

"Sod all. I stepped in some freshly laid dog shit, but that was it," he grumbled.

"Oh." She turned back to find Mr Mallory had gone, and so had Marmalade.

"We better get going; we need to find Kayleigh," urged Rachel.

With the Stetson and microphone packed safely in Andy's bag, they trudged on until they got to the edge of the moat.

As soon as Rachel saw the little causeway that led from the main forest to the island, she pointed in front of her. "This is where I saw her."

But, today, there was nothing.

Andy reached inside his bag again; this time, he drew out what looked like a small child's toy; a spinning, tiny umbrella attached to a box, which presumably had a motor in it. Rachel couldn't be bothered to ask what these gadgets were anymore, or whether they added any value to the hunt. He stretched, emitted a slight burp and then started walking around the moat, minus his Stetson this time.

There appeared to be no sign of anything spiritual there, except for a couple, who were having a picnic and dressed in what looked like 1920s clothing. She heard the gentle sound of music coming from where they sat; was it from a gramophone? She couldn't see one.

She sat down on a log again. "Show yourself," she said quietly, almost willing the soul of the girl to appear. Although ghosts appeared around her with growing regularity, she wasn't sure yet that she could actually compel them to appear; they just seemed to pop up when they wanted to. If she could actually invoke them to come, and choose who came, now that would be something. Personally, she would like to speak to some famous dead people – Kurt Cobain and Marilyn Monroe were at the top of the list – but then she began to wonder what if you didn't get a choice of who you spoke to? She could end up with Genghis Khan or Adolf Hitler. She blanched.

Rachel watched Andy in the distance; he was walking on the island of the moat, holding this spinning, little umbrella box in front of him like some kind of divining rod. It was odd that he hadn't asked her *exactly* where she had seen Kayleigh's spirit; that she had seen her in this vicinity seemed to be enough. She had decided a while ago to not question the way Andy worked, although it seemed a bit haphazard to her.

Snap.

She looked around. The wood was full of noises; yet, for some reason, this made her start. Her eyes darted amongst the bushes that ran around the outside of the moat area, and then she saw it; about twenty feet away, there was a small movement behind a bush. All of her senses came alive as she turned her body around to face the ape-like creature, slowly revealing itself.

Bloody thing. It must be the woodland sprite that Mr Mallory had referred to. It shifted unhurriedly from behind the bush, on its haunches, with only half of its body showing and the rest concealed by the bush. It looked at her and returned her gaze. Abruptly, it grinned – that nasty, pointed-toothy grin – and started waving its right arm back and forth. What was it doing? She felt the unease start up in her again. It looked like it was… Wait, was it gesturing she should come nearer?

She looked back towards the moat island. Andy was gone. Where on earth was he? She twisted back. The thing had gone back behind the bush; all that was showing was one ludicrously long, hairy, muscular arm, which was almost beckoning her. She got up slowly and walked towards the foliage. This time, she felt a little braver. Twenty feet, ten feet, nearer…

"Hello?" she called. Why did she always say that?

Then she saw it again; it had somehow moved from behind the bush and was now sitting on the path a little way off, in shadow. She narrowed her eyes and looked at it. The creature was so very black, its fur must be so thick, its head… She was looking closely at it now; the head was an odd shape, not human or ape-like at all, but much more rounded. As Rachel watched, it brought up a huge hand and rubbed its face, and she saw that it had enormous talons, claws or whatever they were, which were at least two inches long, and such spindly fingers, like a big, skeletal hand without flesh. It cocked its head to one side; blinked its bright-red, little eyes; gave a little wave; and shuffled off.

Where was it going? Was this a trap? Was she being lured to her own death? She debated following it, then somehow, deep inside her, she heard a voice (it wasn't loud but it was insistent), telling her that following the thing was the only way she would find Kayleigh. She pushed on, walking through twigs that smacked into her face and roots that tripped her.

Rachel could not always keep it in her line of vision, but somehow she found it impossible to lose in the woods, as if her senses always knew where it was. She could actually *feel* it.

Finally, she found herself in a small grove and stopped dead. The thing sat under an ancient tree, by a river, frantically scratching its flank and waiting for her to appear. When it was certain it had her full attention, in a grand gesture, it swept its large arm in an arc and pointed clearly to a spot under the tree with those evil-looking fingers. Its every move was over exaggerated, like an actor on stage that needs to be easily seen by people in the back row.

"Here," was all it said, and then it shuffled behind the tree. The voice was dark, rumbly, and without sex, accent or soul – *how was that even possible? A voice to be so soulless?*

Rachel hurried after the creature and, for some reason, started to feel brave. Slowly, she peered behind the tree, but there was nothing there. She then turned to the spot that the creature had pointed to, and with great care, she got to her knees and touched the ground with her hands. She jumped up; it was like an electric shock had leaped out from the ground and shook her entire body. Instinctively, she shook her hands, as if they had been burnt, and held them to her body in a defensive motion.

Then, almost on instinct, she ran as fast as she could from the spot; what direction she was running in she didn't know.

CHAPTER 25

She sat in the entrance to the hospital, watching the revolving doors, and people coming and going, obviously to appointments or to visit people. The first thing that struck Rachel was how well everyone looked; they marched in at a quick pace, with many fiddling with their mobiles, paying no attention to the 'Switch off your phone' signs everywhere. Did people even switch off phones anymore? Most people she knew simply muted them.

Rachel had come to the hospital in the hope of seeing Dr Maxwell again, as she needed advice from him urgently. As usual, there were some spirits standing around, most of whom looked perplexed. One, a man in his thirties, stood by the far wall, wearing a heavily bloodstained, green hospital gown and looking totally confused, as if he didn't know where he was. He looked at her for a moment, with sheer sorrow in his eyes, and then shuffled off. Her eye was then caught immediately by a stumbling figure making his way down the corridor; he looked as if he was straight out of some kind of medieval fancy-dress competition. Dressed in filthy clothes – a leather jerkin, ragged trousers and what looked like two big rags tied to his feet – she heard him coughing as he approached. The man carried a gnarled staff, which he was resting his weight on, and bore a disgusting, yellow-stained eye patch, which roughly covered one eye.

"*Hello,*" Rachel conveyed to him, intrigued by his appearance.

The man looked in her direction, squinting, with what was obviously his only functioning eye, and carried on towards her. "'Ow do," he said, half attempting to bow, but pulling himself up quickly enough when he looked like he was about to fall. "Would you be Rachel, mistress?"

She turned to him. "*Yes, do you know of me?*"

"Aye… the doctor be telling me about you. You is the woman what sees us." He sat heavily in one of the waiting-area chairs, removed a little flask from under his jacket, took a large swig of whatever the contents were, then replaced the flask with a wince. "I be Jeremy, from London, by the water; I passed with a contagion."

"*A what?*"

"A disease what rotted my skin and made me piss blood; bain't sure what it was, but I remember me passing to this day. Buggers burnt me corpse afterwards. Took me clothes, though." He sat back.

"*Oh, I am sorry to hear that; you look like you have been gone… a while?*"

He sat back in the plastic seat, eyes closed, and for a moment she thought he had gone to sleep, or passed out, till the good eye opened. "King 'Arry did reign when I passed; 'e be sickening when I died. I saw 'im once in Whitehall, when I was waiting for alms at the door. After all the rich 'ad finished eating, they used to throw their scraps out, like. One day, by Jesu', it was 'im – King 'Arry 'imself – at the door with an alms bowl. He probably did it to ease 'is soul and to get 'imself a place in 'eaven." He rubbed his arm with a filthy hand. "No matter why 'e did be there on that day, not many can say they 'ave seen 'Is Grace up close, eh?"

"Er no…"

"You wouldn't want to cross 'im; by Christ's blood, 'e 'ad the smallest eyes." He closed his own eye again and looked like he was drooping back into the chair.

"Jeremy, would you know where I might find Dr Maxwell?"

He didn't even stir.

"I need to speak with him."

The eye opened slowly again.

"Pah, there's no rest for poor, sick Jeremy, not in life nor death." With a slow heave, he pushed himself to his feet again, using the stained staff. "Follow me; 'e probably be walking the wards or sitting in the garden, thinking. Doc does too much thinking for 'is own good." With that, he limped off, with Rachel following, trying not to look too conspicuous due to walking at such a slow pace behind her invisible guide.

After what seemed like an age, they came to a bright, airy corridor, with large glass windows that opened out to a maintained garden area. As Rachel walked behind the coughing, stumbling Jeremy, she glanced out to see two nurses – clearly from long ago because they wore long skirts and white wimples, similar to nuns – playing with some children dressed in what looked like tweed hats and coats. She walked on till they got to the exit; Jeremy vanished through the closed door with a kind of falling motion. Rachel followed, opened the door carefully and walked out into the sunlight.

Straight away, she saw the by now familiar face of Dr Maxwell; he was sitting on a bench, staring at a sparrow that was pecking about in the grass. He looked up slowly, and, seeing Rachel, he leapt to his feet, as if being seen sitting and slouching in the presence of a lady was unforgiveable.

Jeremy had made some progress across the courtyard by the time Rachel emerged from the door. She saw him speaking to the doctor; he then sat down heavily on the bench, leaving Dr Maxwell to walk over to where Rachel stood.

"Rachel, I didn't expect to see you; you look a little cold… Oh, where are my manners?" He whisked his coat off and tried to put it around her shoulders to watch it fall straight through her to the ground. He looked sadly at her, and then bent to retrieve it. "Sorry, I often forget I am dead."

"I came to see you about an urgent matter; I wanted advice about something, and the only person I could think of to ask was you," she explained.

"Come, let's sit over there."

The two of them walked slowly to a second bench, which faced the glass corridor. After they both sat down, Rachel looked across at the nurses playing with the children; they had in their hands what looked like sticks with hoops on the end.

"How do you do that? I mean, sit on chairs and walk up stairs, and yet you can pass through doors. Either you can move through things or you can't; it's very confusing…" she declared.

"Not really; it just takes concentration. If you want to do

something like sit upon a chair, you have to think hard about the solidity of the seat before you sit down, or if you want to pass through something, such as a wall, you concentrate on what is beyond the wall – how unsolid it is, if you like – and then you pass through. It's all about focussing the mind." He paused. "However, doing these actions isn't without issue. A chap can find himself on his backside with his head poking out of the seat of a chair if he does not do it right."

Jeremy was smiling at a pretty young nurse, standing before him; she seemed to be offering to look under his eye bandage.

"Jeremy likes the ladies… Anyway, was that all you wanted to know? How we sit on chairs? Hardly the wonderings of a great mind."

"Er, no… I was just curious about that." She turned to look at him carefully. She noticed he had quite light-coloured, hazel eyes, and very long, blond eyelashes; she had not noticed this before. She looked away, as his stare had become too intense.

She continued, "I have been approached by the police to help solve the disappearance and possible murder of a young girl in some nearby woods. I went there and I saw the spirit of the girl, but I also saw something else; I just wanted your take on what this thing was."

"What did you see?" Dr Maxwell prompted.

"A spirit I met in the woods seemed to think it was a sprite; I think that's what he called it. It certainly wasn't human, it was covered in fur, and I wondered if you had ever come across anything like it?"

"A sprite, eh?" He rubbed his chin.

She could still feel him staring at the side of her face; the sun was getting warmer. Jeremy and the spirit nurse started laughing as he offered her the contents of his hip flask.

"Yes, there are such things as sprites, or whatever you want to call them. But are you sure it wasn't a ghost? Someone who was alive but is now dead? Or a residual memory; that is, something that happened in time and recorded in one place that repeats over and over again? Did you interact with it?" Dr Maxwell asked.

"Oh, yes; it spoke to me, it gestured, and I followed it. And, no, it certainly wasn't human at all," she confirmed.

"Then, yes, I suspect you met a sprite; did it say much?"

"No, just one word."

"Male or female voice?"

Rachel remembered the single word the thing had uttered. *"Neither; just... well, it was like a computer..."* She stopped and looked at the doctor; would he even know what a computer was? *"Er, it was like a robotic voice... I know that sounds silly, but it didn't really have a tone to it."*

He sat back on the bench. "I am sure you have heard of the word 'poltergeist'? Do you know what they are?"

"They haunt houses and throw stuff about?" She looked at him; he was smiling at her.

"No, not really. Poltergeists are like electrical energy; they have no consciousness and no free will, really. Think of them like a modern plug with electricity flowing through it; you cannot have a good or bad plug... It is innate; just energy. They usually attach to someone who is very stressed or troubled, and manifest around them. They repeat words they hear, like a parrot will do; they hold no meaning to the words, but they can say simple things. You said it was covered in fur?"

"Yes, definitely furry."

"That is the energy buzzing around it; I think, yes, you

do have a poltergeist."

Rachel was not convinced. She couldn't believe for a moment that the thing she had seen in the woods was an innate form of electrical energy; it seemed pretty much alive. She remembered feeling its presence near her, like when one looks over a cliff at a sheer drop, and feels pins and needles mixed with fear and excitement. That's what she felt with the creature. Maybe it was some kind of electrical pulse it gave off. But she didn't feel she could argue with Dr Maxwell; he had been dead a long time, so he should know.

"Is it harmless, this poltergeist/sprite thing?"

"It is neither harmful nor harmless. I told you, it's like a source of electricity; it can be used to light your home or electrocute you. It depends on how it is used, but it certainly has no agenda. You have been stressed recently, what with your illness, and losing your job and your intended. It's bound to upset a person."

She was amazed he had remembered this about her. *"Yes, I suppose I have been very stressed."* (She hated that word).

"There you have it, then. There are lots of entities that live in the world we inhabit: some good, some bad and some innate. You can obviously see them as well as us."

"So I shouldn't worry about it?"

"I would say not, no."

Rachel cast her mind back to the dark, shuffling thing. A poltergeist? A sprite? She still had this clinging, uneasy feeling, but, again, reassured herself that, as Dr Maxwell was dead, he should be an authority on these matters, so she had to trust him. She decided to change the subject, because the black creature had begun to fill her mind, like an ink drop contaminating a bowl of water. *"What about you? You were a doctor, so where did you live before you… er… died?"*

His face went slightly ashen, only for a moment, but then it passed. "What is there to know? I was born in East London, then moved to the city when I decided to become a doctor, and worked in St Bartholomew's Hospital; I assume you have heard of it?."

"Yes; yes, of course. It is still there now."

"It was very different in my day."

Jeremy had got off his bench and was walking towards the children now, accompanied by the pretty nurse.

"Did you have a family?" Rachel enquired.

"Yes. My wife and… " He turned to look at Jeremy again. "He's been around for a considerable time; did he tell you? He's seen King Henry VIII and all."

"That's who he was talking about?"

"Yes. He died of some kind of sweating sickness thing; apparently, his so-called friends stole his clothes after he died."

"Yes, he did tell me." Rachel was more interested in Dr Maxwell than Jeremy. *"What happened to your wife? It must have been hard after you died."*

His face closed down again. "She died. Just a little time after I did; the shock of me dying put her into…" He looked back at the birds, hopping on the grass. "It doesn't matter; it was all a long time ago now."

"You said you died in a fire…" Rachel didn't know how far she could push the doctor on this; she could see he wasn't happy speaking about it, but she was very interested in him and his life.

"Yes. I think it was set deliberately in my lodgings. The

door was locked so I couldn't get out, and I swallowed too much smoke."

"Oh. Your wife was hurt in the fire?"

He turned to her.

"My wife was out when the fire was set… Why do you ask me all these things? I try to forget them."

"Sorry." She could see he had become upset and agitated. No wonder, especially as the fire seemed to have been started deliberately.

Jeremy, who had paused momentarily when Dr Maxwell raised his voice, turned back to the nurses and children, then proceeded to do a quick jig, presumably for their entertainment. The children started laughing around him and clapping.

William got up. "I have things to attend to. Jeremy will see you out." Rubbing his eyes, he quickly walked away, then passed through the brick wall next to the glass door, and was gone.

Rachel sat there and felt a huge welling of sorrow. She had never meant to upset him; obviously, his death had been a horrible occurrence, and his wife's as well. She guessed most people's deaths were unpleasant at the very least, and some – such as dying in a fire that someone had started on purpose – were particularly horrible. She reflected on her own parents' demise; it had been sudden, and their doctor had told her that they had died instantly in the crash and knew nothing about it. Sometimes she wondered if he had been honest with her, and often contemplated on the accident in depth. What if one had died first, then had seen the other dead and smashed to bits before passing? It tormented her. Rachel was convinced she should have been with them and died too.

Why couldn't she see them? To see her parents one last time, even in the distance, to show her they were safe and together again would have been enough; but maybe they had moved on and not got stuck like the poor souls here, so she should be grateful. Perhaps they chose to not show themselves to her, knowing it may cause her upset. Who knew?

She had amazed herself by how accustomed she had become to seeing ghosts now. She could imagine some people would be freaked out at the prospect, but she had got used to them. At the end of the day, ghosts were just the spirits of people, and people – like ghosts – came in all shapes and sizes. Ghosts tended to be portrayed as scary, tormented spirits that floated around disused, old houses at night, but this really wasn't the case. They were everywhere, literally everywhere: in the street, in her flat and by the roadside, day and night. In fact, some spirits were scared of the dark, so tried to avoid night times. Some were evil and some kind, but they were all different, and most of them were searching for how to move on; she just wished she could help them more.

The sun had gone in, and she realised that Jeremy and the nurses were no longer there. She hadn't seen them go. Rachel realised that she was feeling cold; it was probably time she left as well.

CHAPTER 26

It took Rachel two days to return to the police station; she had asked Andy if he had wanted to come with her, but he said he was busy on a job. She wasn't sure what job it was; he always advertised he worked with a psychic now, who was her, so what kind of job he did alone, she didn't know. It was not her business, really.

Again, she found herself sitting by the bland police station counter. She had waited thirty minutes to be seen, as the person in front of her had spent ages shouting and screaming at the officer on the front desk about being wrongfully arrested. As Rachel sat waiting, more people began to build up: two youths who swore constantly, an African woman who spoke in a foreign accent on her phone and an elderly lady.

When it was Rachel's turn and she was signalled in, one of the waiting youths said, "You better not be too long in there lady; we're in a hurry."

She went into the counter area.

"Yes?" enquired a middle-aged woman. Although she

wore a uniform, a badge on her lapel simply said 'Police Volunteer'.

"I need to speak to Ronald Easton or DI Johnson," replied Rachel.

"Have you an appointment?"

"No, it is about the Kayleigh Lovall case."

Completely disinterested, the woman stood up and went to the back of the counter; Rachel saw her picking up a phone and speaking into it.

Rachel heard a loud bang behind her, which made her jump out of her skin, and she looked around to see the African lady had pushed one of the youths against the Perspex screen that separated the counter and the waiting area.

"They aren't here," said the volunteer blankly.

"My name is Rachel Holloway; please tell them that if they want to know where the body of Kayleigh Lovall is, they had best ring me."

Despite this revelation, the woman behind the counter continued to stare vacantly.

Rachel got up, feeling claustrophobic, and hurried through the door that led outside to the waiting area.

"*Skank!*" shouted the African woman as Rachel walked past.

Rachel turned to reply, but then immediately saw the whole waiting area shimmer, shake and change softly. The plastic chairs morphed into upholstered seating, black metal railings began to spring up outside the window like fast growing plants, and a blue police lantern appeared above the door. She was going back in time again, and she really didn't have time for this shit now.

172

"Whatever," she uttered under her breath, then walked out onto the street, narrowly dodging the metal gate that had sprung up before her.

★

The police phoned Rachel later that night, and she provided them with a detailed description of where the body could be found. She heard nothing more until the following day, when DI Johnson called her and explained that Kayleigh's remains had been discovered at the exact location she had described to them.

He had asked her the $1,000,000 question: how did she know the body was there?

She heard herself reply simply that Kayleigh's spirit had shown her. She didn't want to mention the poltergeist, sprite or whatever the hell it was. She had a nagging suspicion that the fewer people who knew about the horrible, furry, dark thing in the woods, the better.

★

Andy was having it large. The success of taking on Rachel had instantly made him a rather famous and increasingly wealthy man. He had been using Rachel on some of his bigger ghost-hunting jobs, which by now were flooding in, but he still decided to do the smaller jobs – ones he suspected of being fakery, or down to a rampant cat or loose plumbing – himself. That meant any fee paid would go to him alone.

However, he was grateful for Rachel and made sure that she had enough money to get by; Mrs Braithwaite had warned him that if he didn't give Rachel what she was owed or look after her, with her powers, she would go elsewhere, which was the last thing he wanted. Besides, he had changed his website and newspaper ads to say he was 'The only paranormal investigator in London to boast a real psychic'. If other investigators wanted to sue him, let them. He had also changed his company name; before, he was simply 'Andy Horton Paranormal Investigator', but he had changed it two weeks ago to 'Spirit of London Paranormal Investigations'. He thought it made the business sound like it was a larger concern, and was, in his opinion, a good play on words.

Andy had big plans. He had already met up with the curator of Howland Hall: a huge, local, stately home built in the early 1700s. They had struck a deal that, once every couple of months, he and Rachel would lead ghost hunts throughout the hall at £10 a ticket, then tempt thirsty ghost hunters to the bar around the back when it was finished. For this, Andy got 30% of the bar profits to share with Rachel, as well as 50% of ticket sales, which was, in his opinion, a very good deal indeed. He would help to sell the tickets through his website. The first event was due to take place in three weeks' time, so he thought he had better get his skates on and tell her about it.

His only issue was Rachel's flakiness; she often got severe headaches and migraines, and so would drop out of events at a moment's notice. After pondering the matter, he decided that it would only be vital for her to be at the first couple of tours. He would than ask her what spirits were there, and just say he could 'feel their presence' if he had to lead future events alone – being a showman came easily to him.

Andy had been amazed when Rachel told him she had actually discovered Kayleigh's body. He must remember to put this out in his marketing information for the Howland Hall tours; that would be a unique selling point for sure, as ghost hunts were ten a penny in London. He still wasn't totally sure what he believed about her powers. In the back of his mind, he often pondered whether she had some kind of delusion or mental illness, or whether it was perfectly true, and she could indeed see dead people. For the present moment, he didn't care, as long as fame and fortune remained on his doorstep.

When speaking to the curator, he had insisted on increasing participant numbers to 100 people per tour. The curator suggested a maximum of fifty, otherwise it would be too unwieldy, but Andy wouldn't have it – more people coming on the tours meant more cash for him. Sweet.

His dream was to make enough money to buy a decent car for himself, and some new curtains, furniture and carpets for Mrs Braithwaite, but who knew? If this celebrity status continued, he might even be able to buy a house of his own. Andy felt giddy and almost sick from the excitement. There would be no more damp, miserable, pointless ghost hunts that left him out of pocket, no siree; there was hard cash to be had finding spooks, and Andy was going to make sure he made as much as he could before the bubble burst, as it inevitably would.

CHAPTER 27

The spirit Jews were outside the flat again, but this time there were more of them. They stood silently this time, with no chanting, shouting or waving of hands. Standing in a dark circle, some bobbing gently, each of them holding the Torah, their lips moved wordlessly against the wind. From her position, they just looked like a small sea of large, black hats just standing there. Their ages varied from, she guessed, twenty to seventy plus.

Rachel watched them from her window; what did they want? She actually considered asking them, but shied away from it for some reason. They looked very angry and determined, something had clearly annoyed them, and, as they kept looking up towards her flat, she assumed it was probably something she had done that had offended them.

Her main thought was that they, as most spirits she met, thought that, because she could see them so clearly, she had the answers to how they could get to their heaven and meet their God. But, of course, she hadn't a clue. She also hated it when Andy put her down as being a psychic, as, in her view, she wasn't in any way a psychic – she could just see dead people and, occasionally, buildings, areas and events as they had appeared in the past. But she could not tell fortunes, look into people's minds or even summon spirits; they came if they wanted to but she certainly had no power over them.

As she was staring out of her window, a taxi pulled up outside, and the familiar figure of Andy got out. The chanting men didn't even look at him as he paid the driver and hurried up the steps to her door. It looked like he had a new jacket and trainers; he also had a brightly coloured sports bag over his arm. She went to the front door to let him in.

"Did you get my message?" he said, hurrying through the door.

"No, I haven't checked my phone. What's wrong?" Rachel queried.

"Nothing is wrong; everything is *right*!" Andy bustled into the living room and sat down, whilst fumbling in the sports bag. Triumphantly, he removed a small piece of paper with scribble on it.

"Victor Adeyemi... he called me! Well, texted me... saying he wants us to investigate some problems with spirits at his home." He looked at her for a reaction.

"Who is Victor Eye-yemo?"

"Victor Adeyemi! He's a premier-league football player with Flintock FC! He was the one who threw the Chinese lucky-cat sculpture at the photographer in Paris... remember?"

"Er... no."

177

He waved his hand back and forth. "No matter; he wants us, you and me, to come to his *massive* house in Hertfordshire and get rid of some ghosts."

"Get rid of them? Where?"

He lay back on the sofa with both his arms over the backrest behind him. "Tell 'em to stop haunting him or tell 'em to clear off; I don't care as long as we get rid of them. Oh yeah, and your mate, Luke Fairfax, the reporter, said he will cover the story in the paper if it's successful. Victor is up for that; he says it will be a boost to his profile with local people, so he's happy to have a photo with us and everything. It's bloody fantastic free advertising if we get in the paper, so I said yes; we've got to think about the pennies."

Rachel couldn't think of a situation that had more chance of going badly wrong than a famous premier-league footballer getting a paranormal investigation team into his house to get rid of ghosts, and willingly selling the dubious tale, and photos, to a newspaper. What was he hoping to achieve by it? It could go so horribly pear shaped. "Yes, about that," she said with a frown, "I think we need to sit down at some point and discuss remuneration – how much I get out of this."

Immediately, Andy sat up straight. "Are you unhappy with what I am paying you?"

"Er… well, I would rather it was put on a more formal footing; for example, I'd like to get a percentage rather than, well, what you think I should get each time."

"Charming. It's me who gets the jobs in and butters up the customers; you just go in and do your stuff. There's also a lot of preparation work to be done in this business, and a shit load of public relations and media," Andy complained.

"Without me, you wouldn't have the edge though, be honest. What was it... oh yes, 'The only paranormal investigator to have a real psychic'; I have seen your adverts, you know!"

"To *boast* a real psychic; get it right!"

"Whatever. I would like half of whatever you earn; it's only fair." Rachel stated.

"Fine, but you have to do half the donkey work then." He debated whether he should mention Howland Hall now. *Yeah, why not...* "I also got us a job doing regular ghost gigs at a local historical house, Howland Hall, every couple of months... We get a load of paying people turn up; you walk 'em round the hall, and tell 'em when you see ghosts and what they say. We will clean up."

Rachel wasn't sure. Andy still hadn't got the hang of what this was about. Ghosts didn't like to be told to clear off; they were also very likely to say quite offensive things, which might be difficult repeating out loud if children were present. Added to that, the idea of walking a load of random people around a large house, presumably in the dark, and jumping when someone farted, didn't appeal at all. But, as usual, she went along with it. "Fine, but I want half the money."

"Fair enough, but more work is coming your way if you want half the cash."

Rachel got up and looked out of the window. There were even more Jews now, facing her window and nearer now. One was standing on the bottom step to her flat; all were frowning.

"Do you know anything about the Jewish Orthodox faith, Andy?" she asked, not looking away.

Andy narrowed his eyes in concentration. "I don't think they eat burgers, do they? Or work on a Sunday? I also remember somefing about how they like taking chickens for walks wiv a piece of string. I don't know much else to be honest."

Great, she wouldn't get any help from him. That much was certain.

★

Henry had always known he was something special, right from an early age. The first thing he had noticed was just how huge and luxurious his family home was: the opulently furnished Cotterstokes House. There was nothing he could want for, as his father owned huge swathes of land, and imported fine things from overseas to sell. The Swains were an incredibly wealthy family.

Henry was an only child – this was unusual in his circle, as many of his peers had at least four siblings – but he liked it that way, as everything was done for him, and he didn't have to share with anyone. Though taught by a stern tutor, Henry enjoyed learning, especially science and numeracy. Being the sole heir of John Swain, he knew that, one day when his father passed, he would have sole charge of the house, lands and import business. Although he wished no ill will to his father, he believed he would make a success of this inheritance when he received it.

His mother referred to him as 'her kitten'; he was not sure why.

By the time he was eleven, he was already learning how things were done, the difficulties of running the land and dealing with the farmers who lived there. His eyes had been opened whilst helping his father, especially to the conditions some people lived in, and it had shocked him. Many of the farmers had no proper housing: often their cottages were very small and hard to heat in winter. Water was drawn from a well some distance away, and there appeared to be no obvious place for the householder to relieve themselves. He recalled once asking his father why this was, only to be told that, in this world, some are with and some without; it was the way of things. His father also reminded him that it was because of the generosity of their family that these farmers all lived so well; he only took a percentage of their crop and charged a fair rent for the land, so no one starved under the Swains.

Henry had always been well attired; both his parents had high regard for the latest fashions at home and abroad, and ensured that they bought the finest clothes. His father being an importer meant they could always get the best cloth or silks at a fraction of the price. This was one of the reasons why Henry was so concerned with his appearance.

He remembered the day of his death, it was 9th April 1711. Henry had decided to go out riding. He had ridden since he was three and was an accomplished horseman, so this was nothing unusual. Countless times he had mulled the incident over, as many of the dead did. They revisited their deaths again and again in their minds, forever replaying the day of their departure, to try to determine if they could have done something differently. Why them and why right at that particular time? But, of course, it was a wholly pointless exercise.

Henry only remembered that his mount was not his usual one; his horse had thrown a shoe and so he had ridden his father's horse instead, but it was broadly the same size and temperament as his own. He recalled galloping at speed across the fields attached to his home, and how happy he had been on that day; the weather had been fine and everything was good in the world.

Then it happened. The horse saw a fallen tree trunk in its way and leapt; Henry had been unprepared for the jump and remembered sliding from his saddle and falling heavily. The last thing he remembered in his lifetime was the sickening crack as his head hit a large stone by the roadside. That was it. He guessed he had smashed his skull or broken his neck.

The next thing he remembered was standing in the same lane, near where he had suffered the accident; just standing there. To him, it was only a second after the accident and so he had assumed at first that he had passed out, the horse had bolted and he simply needed to go home. But he had been wrong, he was dead, and, as he walked along the lane, he began to realise – simply by looking at those who passed him by – that something had changed.

After walking for some time, he arrived at Cotterstokes House, or, to be more precise, what was in its place. The home he remembered was gone, obliterated; instead, a completely different house stood there, all in stone and more modest. He kept going through it in his mind; was he lost? Had the knock on his head confused him more than he had originally thought? No, surely this was right. He remembered the large oak tree by the paddock; yes, this was indeed where his home had once stood.

He tried knocking on the door, but became alarmed when his hand passed straight through as if it was mist. He remembered crying and sitting on the ground, closing and opening his eyes, hoping it would go back to how things were, but, of course, it never did.

A spirit priest found him; it must have been hours later. He said he was from the local church and had died of a fit in 1815. After speaking to Henry, the priest told him what had happened, and worked out, broadly by Henry's recounting and clothing, that he must have died around the early 1700s. It had been the priest who had taken him to Nanny, and Nanny who had explained what sometimes happened when people died. Ever since then, he had followed her and her ragtag of dead children around, waiting for something or someone to compel him into action. He wasn't entirely sure what action he desired, but felt in his heart he absolutely needed to do *something.*

His interest had been sparked immediately by Dr Maxwell, a man of learning and science, and the doctor's quest to work out why they were all stuck on earth with, apparently, no way of moving on. This was of particular interest to Henry, as he had been thirteen years old when he had died, and had, somehow, been dead for over a century without being aware of it, before being returned to the earth in a ghostly form. If that wasn't going to interfere with a gentleman's train of thought, he didn't know what would.

CHAPTER 28

The visit to the home of Victor Adeyemi had to be postponed for a week because Rachel had taken ill again with some kind of virus. Andy had stopped asking how she was anymore, as she always appeared to be unwell; instead, he would explain to clients (unbeknownst to Rachel) that being psychic would often make her unstable and prone to eccentricity. He would then often add that it was worth bearing with her unreliability to get a real psychic. So far, most clients had swallowed this cock-and-bull story.

They were due to arrive at 10am; Rachel had turned up slightly earlier and was standing outside when Andy arrived, again on his old pushbike.

The house looked very modern; it was an impressively large, red-brick building, surrounded on all sides by a high, brick wall with sliding gates. There was an intercom outside that Andy used to buzz through, and the gates slowly drew open to let them pass.

As they walked to the front door, they glanced at a large fountain that was set in the main driveway. It was constructed in an ancient Greek style and featured the face of a young African man in the tiling around the side and on the base. Rachel assumed this must be Victor Adeyemi or, at the very least, a stylised version of him.

They stood at the front door, but no one came to open it. Andy frowned and pressed the loudly trilling doorbell till shuffling steps were heard, making their way towards them. The polished, wooden door opened slowly to reveal a heavily overweight, middle-aged African woman, wearing a pinafore with a scarf around her head.

"Yes?" she said.

"Andy Horton and Rachel Holloway to see Victor, please," confirmed Andy.

She looked them up and down slowly then closed the door completely. They heard her shuffling steps vanish within the house.

"He knows we are coming, doesn't he?" asked Rachel.

"Of course he bloody does. He asked us to come today; he probably has a butler or some shit to—" began Andy.

The front door was instantly torn open to reveal a tall, athletic man, who actually did look like the image on the fountain, dressed in a bright-purple suit. Beaming, he grasped their hands. "Andy, Rachel... cool... Come in..."

He led them through an opulent hallway, with brightly polished marble floors. The older lady who had answered the door, and was now standing on the steps, made a gentle sucking noise through her teeth as they passed her. Victor either did not notice or did not care, as he walked them through to a huge living area, all decorated in black and white, and again, with a highly polished marble floor.

He gestured towards a huge, black, leather sofa, and sat down in front of them in an oversized armchair. It had the initials 'VA' embossed in what looked like gold leaf on the wings of the headrest.

"Would you like something to drink? Auntie can bring something." He pointed to the older lady who now stood in the doorway to the living room.

Andy responded, "Er, yes; a coffee for me, black no sugar. Rachel?"

"Some water would be lovely," Rachel confirmed.

The lady muttered, then vanished back into the hallway.

Andy opened up the conversation. "Victor, I cannot tell you how excited I was to get your call the other day."

"You are a fan?" asked Victor.

"Oh, absolutely… And it is a pleasure to serve a local sportsman such as you with this, erm… delicate matter."

"Yes, about that—"

At that point, the lady returned unexpectedly quickly with the refreshments, and everyone sat in silence as cups were placed on coasters in front of them. Rachel noticed that on her coaster was yet another image of the footballer, this time it was a photograph of him doing a thumbs-up. She wondered why anyone would want their own visage emblazoned on items around them.

Victor began again. "Like I said, I have asked the local paper to cover the story, but I want to make sure it's handled right; know what I mean? I don't want anything printed saying Victor Adeyemi is a bit wacko, and sees ghosts and stuff; ya get me?"

Rachel frowned. "Are you sure you want to involve

the press, Mr Adeyemi? Once Luke has the story, you will have very little editorial control over how you, and we, are portrayed."

"Call me Victor, girl, and yeah, it's cool. After that thing with the photographer, when I lost ma cool in Paris – I'm sure Andy has told you – I need some positive PR, know what I mean?" Victor looked at both of them. "Also, I called a priest in last week, to see if he could help and send the ghost on, know what I mean? He waved some incense about and said some stuff from the Bible, but I am still getting grief. I hope you can help me?"

Andy had been writing notes all the while, and he looked up at this point. "Thanks for that, Victor; will you tell me a little more about the haunting? When and where it happens, and how long it's been going on for?"

Victor put his coffee down and looked solemn. "Yeah, cool, sure… I think it's a dude. He stands by the front window, over there…" He pointed to his bay window. It looked out onto the front driveway, and was ornately decorated with heavy, gold curtains that were tied back on either side. "But I think he also hangs about ma gym room upstairs… Ya get me? Also, I heard footsteps going up and down the stairs; Auntie said she saw a dark figure at the top of the stairs too. Once, she was so scared, she ran down them stairs so fast she nearly tripped."

"Did it say anything?"

"No… I've just seen movement, but it's getting worse. I was watching TV the other night and, out the corner of ma eye, I saw this dark shape, moving a bit by the window. It gave me the creeps."

"We will rid you of your ghost," said Andy. He opened the little suitcase he had brought with him and placed his now-customary crucifix-clad Stetson on his head, and then took out a small, black box, on which he turned a knob; it then began to emit a swooshing radio noise.

"I am going to check out the window, OK?" Andy got up and walked towards the window, waving the box back and forth. He frowned when it started to emit a screeching noise.

"I will check out the stairs," said Rachel. She got up and began to walk towards the hallway.

Victor jumped up. "I got two stairs; you want the one to the left, where the front door is, OK? Shall I stay here?"

"Yes, please," she requested.

He sat back down. Rachel passed from the living room, back out into the hallway again. In the distance, she heard quiet singing and the banging of pots; assuming this was Auntie, busy doing whatever it was Auntie did, she turned towards the staircase.

The stairs themselves were covered in a lush, black carpet that was pinned into each stair with a gold rail; the light-coloured wood of the stairs was highly polished. In fact, the whole house was spotless, but Rachel noticed that some mud had trailed in when she and Andy had entered. She began to climb the stairs, looking about, but could see nothing unusual.

At the top of the stairs, she found herself on a huge landing. She paused as her attention was abruptly drawn to a tutting noise from one of the rooms nearby. She went to check it out; after all, she told herself, she was supposed to be investigating! She approached a large door that led to the room she assumed the tutting was coming from; Rachel knocked and then pushed it cautiously open.

"Hello?" she enquired as she went into the room.

It was like a small gym area, with a treadmill in the corner, some weights on the floor and some sit-up benches. Sitting on a large bench press, by the window, was an older spirit man in Orthodox Jewish clothing, reading quietly. He looked up, saw her, then looked back down again. She guessed his age to be in the region of sixty to seventy. He wore a large beaver hat and top coat, and had a thick, grey beard; Rachel noticed that he had keen, small eyes that stared out from behind horn-rimmed glasses.

Switching to her inner voice she spoke to him. *"Hello? How are you?"*

He jumped up; the book fell to the floor with a bang, then it disappeared. Shuffling, he backed towards the wall, looking terrified. "You... you can see me?"

"Yes, I see dead people. The gentleman who owns the house you are in has seen you on the stairs and, apparently, by the front window. He has called in me and my colleague, to ask you to move on."

The man pulled himself away from the wall that he had pressed himself against and stood up straight. Taking a couple of steps forwards, he brought his hands together in front of him, which briefly emitted a pearlescent light that formed into the book he had just dropped a moment ago. "Thank you, madam, but I am happy here at the present moment; I do not wish to leave."

"You are in this gentleman's home, and it bothers him."

"Well, I am afraid, my dear, that isn't my concern. He already sent a priest in last week, did he tell you, to compel me to leave this place, as if I were some kind of evil being. Why would I obey the wishes of a Catholic priest, anyway?" He looked annoyed.

Rachel sat down on a facing bench press. *"My name is Rachel; the man downstairs, my friend, is called Andy. We go around, contacting spirits who cause problems for the living. What is your name?"*

The man crossed back to where he had been sitting before; he still looked rather annoyed at being questioned by this persistent woman. "Rabbi Joseph Lieberman. I am not leaving, nor am I causing problems, as you say."

She noticed straight away he didn't, as was spirit etiquette, say how or when he had died; maybe he was trying to be rude.

Andy's voice began to echo up the stairway. "Kum by yah… oh spirit… speak to me."

The rabbi looked disgusted. "I am going nowhere, miss; do you understand? I am here for a reason, and neither you nor your foolish friend down there will move me…" He got up and began to stride purposefully towards the adjoining wall. He then stopped and raised a hand to his face as if in thought; suddenly, he spun around and faced her, jabbing his finger in her direction. "*Feh!* You… you are the one… I didn't believe the boy." He groaned loudly.

The old rabbi rubbed his face with his hands. "I am such a schmuck; I didn't believe him… argh!" He grunted again. "My people know of you; we were warned you would come. The *shedim*… they work through you. Brothers have been gathering to pray for you to cleanse your spirit."

Judging by Andy's voice, he had gone into one of the bedrooms; he could be heard calling out random phrases.

"What do you mean?" The vision of the Jews outside her flat slammed into Rachel's mind.

"You. Using forces to communicate with us, which are powers from the *shedim*. You are invoking and awakening things, and you have no idea how to control them. You are shameful. Our community is strong; we will... deal with this problem." Rabbi Lieberman went to open his mouth again, his face reddening. But, instead, he turned on his heel again, his frock coat fluttering, and walked straight through the wall before him.

There was a knock at the door.

"Rachel?" Andy opened the door a crack and peered through; behind him was the inquisitive face of Victor Adeyemi. "You found the ghost? Has it gone?"

"Yes, he's gone," she said. How long for, Rachel didn't know, but – if only for the moment – the rabbi had indeed left the building, so in theory she wasn't lying.

CHAPTER 29

The news article appeared the following week in the *Burwood Echo*, entitled 'SPOOK KICKED INTO TOUCH FOR FAMOUS FOOTBALLER'; it was on page three. The piece featured a photo of Victor, posing with his Maserati in the front garden of his home, and another with him smiling, with one arm around Rachel and the other arm around Andy. Apparently, a similar article had also been reproduced in the *Flintock FC* fanzine.

The story seemed to have legs, as it quickly appeared online and on various social media platforms, prompting a flurry of phone calls to the Spirit of London's headquarters (Andy's mobile), which he was very happy to respond to. Copious letters were also being sent to Rachel, in a variety of languages. Many of the letters, which were now streaming through her letterbox, were simply addressed to 'Rachel Holloway, Psychic lady, Burwood Town, London'. Thanks to the diligence of the local postman, they all seemed to find their way to her.

They were an interesting read: some revealed the madness of their authors, with drawings of pyramids and eyes; some included photos and asked Rachel to reach out to dead relatives to ask them questions; and others begged for her and Andy's help with hauntings. Some were heartbreaking, with pages full of people's emotions at the death of babies and children, much-loved husbands or wives, and parents. The pile grew every day, so Rachel put them in a special large cabinet. Like a pop star with fan mail, she tried to read them all, but some days there were just too many, and they were too harrowing.

Some letters were horrible. They accused her of lying to make money, of fakery and taking advantage of the grieving for financial gain, and called her appalling names. She threw those away immediately, but felt somehow like they had tainted her. Some painted symbols that she didn't recognise appeared on, and around, her gateway outside – lines and stars; she suspected they were shapes meant to help or harm her.

Unlike Rachel, who was nervous about this sudden celebrity status, Andy seemed to thrive on the attention, almost like a flower stretching its petals towards the sun, and growing stronger and more vibrant with every ray. He had even gone to the trouble of getting some free copies of the *Burwood Echo* and brought them round to Rachel. She had told him that it was kind to bring so many copies to her door, but he should not have gone to all the bother.

He had replied that it was no bother now, because he had bought a car, so there would be no more trips on his rusty bike.

However, Rachel was beginning to feel troubled. Not only by the ghostly rabbi at Victor Adeyemi's house, who she was convinced would come back with a vengeance at some point in the future, but also about the wellbeing of Dr Maxwell. The last time they had parted, which was a while ago at the hospital, it was on bad terms, and she had clearly upset him, which she had never intended to do. She felt somehow that he had suffered much sorrow in his life, and she certainly did not want to cause him problems in his death. Rachel resolved to return to the hospital to see him again.

The murder investigation into the death of Kayleigh Lovall also continued. There were no tangible suspects thus far, in spite of the story being national news. The police had told her that people still visited the woods; it hadn't scared them away. In fact, it had done the opposite, as teens were now frequenting the Shore Moat area, probably to satisfy some morbid fascination.

The police had also repeatedly asked Rachel how she had known the body was there, and, each time they did, she simply told them that the spirit of Kayleigh guided her, which wasn't strictly true. DNA test results were inconclusive, and brought them no closer to the killer; however, the autopsy had revealed that, although there was no evidence of sexual assault, the person who killed the girl was almost certainly a man, not only due to how violently she had been stabbed, but also because of the force of the ligature marks on her throat. Andy had joked that if the fact that a man killed Kayleigh hadn't been proved, it might have been Rachel herself up on a murder charge.

It was only at this point that Rachel realised the importance of being careful as to whom she shared information with. If she went around finding the bodies of various murdered people, there would be a point when the police might start thinking that she had something to do with the crimes; perhaps that she was some kind of sick serial killer. She was too bloody innocent and trusting, that was her problem. Rachel had been handed a gift on the day her brain bled, but it could also be a poisoned chalice, depending on how she used it; she was definitely starting to see that now.

Rachel was in bed, thinking all of it over, with a small lamp at her side, gently illuminating the room. Around where she lay there were three spirits whom she could see. The first was an old woman, dressed in black widow's weeds with a hood covering her hair; she was sitting and sobbing gently on a chair in the corner. All Rachel could see from her bed was a gnarled hand, clutching a handkerchief to a wrinkled, large nose that protruded out from the lacy, dark head covering. The second was a young man, dressed in a dark-green, velvet coat with a fancy, ruffled, white shirt, and on his head was a large top hat; he also carried a cane, which reflected the light from Rachel's lamp on its shiny surface. By looking at his face, which was slim with pronounced cheekbones and not unhandsome, she would say he was about thirty. The last ghost in her room that evening was a middle-aged, slightly overweight man, wearing what looked like a white coat of the medical profession; his face was round and reddened, with small, gold-rimmed spectacles perched on his nose. He stood there silently, just staring at his watch, which was chipping away time with gentle ticks on his wrist.

Rachel looked at them all. *"I don't know what you want with me! Haven't you somewhere to go?"*

The sobbing woman did not look up, nor did the fatter man who was looking at his watch. The younger gentleman in the velvet coat cast his eyes slowly towards her, as if she was simply an annoyance, then turned them back to her window, which he had been looking keenly out of.

She didn't like having them in her room. In a normal life, people could be kept out of your house by locking doors and barring windows. If you didn't want anyone to come in, you could simply keep them out. Ghosts, on the other hand, could not be kept out: no wall and no door, regardless of whether it was made of steel, stone, wood or lead could keep them barred. They just walked on through it if they wanted to. One night, she had even awoken to a spirit man lying in bed next to her. His back had been turned, so she couldn't see his face; all she could hear was the gentle rasping of his uneven breathing, and she saw his side gently rising and falling with each breath. This had unnerved her terribly; slowly, she had got out of the bed, so as not to alert her unwelcome bed guest to her leaving, and slept on the sofa. Fortunately, whoever the hell it was had left by the morning.

She had no shield against them. There was nothing she could build or draw around herself that would stop the dead invading her world; she felt so naked and powerless.

As she often did now, she got out of bed, exhausted, with her head pounding as it always did, and walked in a drugged, sleepy state to the bathroom. Closing the toilet door behind her, she lowered herself onto the cold seat and relieved herself, her eyes closing as she tried to stop the whirr of thoughts tearing through her head.

Rachel wasn't overly frightened by the ghosts; maybe that was her problem. She should be bothered by them, but she wasn't. She had accepted them coming into her world now, and being part of her, almost like a cross between a disability and a gift. Some of them were odd, but most were fine; they were a little upset that they were dead, but she assumed that would probably upset most people.

Slowly, she became aware of something; it wasn't a sound, but more a feeling that she was being watched. Her head began to turn upwards to the ceiling, as if pulled by an invisible thread. There, sticking out of the top of her bathroom wall and the ceiling itself were two heads, both female, with paper-white skin, dark brown frizzy hair and rictus grins. They were just silently staring down at her. Frozen to the spot, she immediately shut her eyes and put her fingers in her ears.

But she still knew they were there, thanks to the one thing she couldn't muffle: her own mind.

CHAPTER 30

The night of the Howland Hall ghost hunt had arrived, and Rachel was very nervous about it. For one thing, she hadn't even been given the opportunity to familiarise herself with the layout of the house. First, she had been a little unwell, and then Andy had insisted that if she went to the house, he had to come with her, and he had been busy. Then they had gone there one afternoon to find it closed because of a water leak; it had been a catalogue of errors that seemed to have been designed to prevent them getting access before the night.

Andy was buoyant; he said it didn't matter that they had not given the place a decent recce, as they would 'play it by ear'. She hated that. Everything Andy ever did he played by ear; planning was not his strong point. Rachel had argued that she wanted to have some time alone to walk the corridors and stairs of the house, to find out what spirits it held, and decide which ones to feature for the tour, and which ones to ignore (not that all spirits took kindly to being ignored). But, no, he would not have a bar of it, and so, here they were, in his new car, drawing up outside a mere fifteen minutes before the event.

Rachel stared up at the magnificent stone building; it had been built strictly symmetrical, with a huge stairway leading up to the front of the house. The simple, white-painted windows, which interspaced the stone walls, twinkled in the floodlights that swept the whole front façade.

Behind her were crowds of people. She thought the 100 headcount limit had clearly been ignored; it looked like there must be 200 people there at least. Many carried battery powered torches, and were bundled up against the cold in thick coats and hats. She saw some people were in fancy dress, including one in a ridiculous skeleton costume and one dressed as a pirate (she had no idea why). There were also a few goths milling about.

Someone must have sold too many tickets. Who could possibly be so irresponsible? Rachel mused.

Andy bounded up. "*Wow!* Fab turnout, yeah? How many are here? About 130? Whoa, that's like £1,300, yeah? We get £650... Sweet."

"Of which I get £325..." reminded Rachel, wondering if Andy had deliberately under estimated how many people were there, or whether he had simply not seen them, being his eyesight was not the sharpest at times. Unless, of course, money was being counted out, then he appeared to have the eyesight of an eagle.

"Yeah, sure, whatever. Better get this show on the road, eh?"

They stood at the top of the entrance steps, squinting against the strong lights that burnt their eyes. Rachel listened as Andy welcomed everyone, introduced himself and then went on about health-and-safety rules. She looked out over the crowd; nervousness was creeping in, as she had never done anything this public before. What would happen if she became tongue tied or messed it up? She had made sure that her painkillers were topped up before leaving her flat, but she still felt her temple twitch slightly; she hoped it wouldn't turn into a migraine, not this evening.

As Andy's voice droned on about the Spirit of London Paranormal Investigations being on social media, she looked across the crowd. For every ten people, she estimated there was one spirit, standing amongst the living and watching on with equal interest. A tour for the living and the dead; that was a turn-up for the books. Why would a ghost want to join a ghost hunt? Maybe they were nosey? Ghosts were only living people who were dead, after all, and were just as varied and complicated as everyday people were.

"… and so may I introduce Miss Rachel Holloway, renowned psychic medium and necromancer, who will be leading tonight's tour," concluded Andy with a flourish.

What the hell? Rachel was horrified. *Renowned psychic medium?* And what the hell was a 'necromancer'? It sounded evil.

Andy had finished his spiel and was looking at her expectantly to say something.

All she could muster was, "I am delighted you have all come out here to find out more about what lives within Howland Hall." What she had said was crap, but they were not there for her public-speaking abilities.

The tour began. A nervous-looking teenager had already

introduced himself as their guide to the layout of the hall for the evening. His name was apparently 'Bim', although Andy called him 'Bin' in Rachel's earshot a few times. He was a tall, spotty youth, aged about nineteen, wearing a dark green peaked cap with 'Howlands' written on the front, and a cheap looking suit in the same colour.

At Andy's signal, the huge crowd of the living and the dead squeezed into the main entrance hall, all looking eagerly towards Rachel to speak. She noticed Andy had taken up a position to the back of the crowd, so he was going to be of limited use if something went wrong. Although the main hall lights were off (at Andy's request), the emergency low lights that lit stairs and doorways had been activated. Andy's original idea had been to have the walk in the pitch darkness, with people using torches, but the hall's owners refused, in case there was an accident and someone fell and then sued the hall. So emergency lights were all they had to lead the way.

The entrance hall was stone built, like the house, but it had a magnificent wooden stairway winding off to an upper floor. Disapproving glares were cast upon all participants from the huge portraits that were hung high on the walls, presumably people of note who had lived there at some point. Rachel wondered why they all looked so angry or miserable; presumably, they had been none too keen to sit for their portrait. Memories flooded back to her of the incident at the castle, and the painting of the two brothers, she quickly looked away.

Bim, who was almost like Rachel's shadow because he stayed so close to her, suggested that they start in the library. So, the solemn group, led by Bim and Rachel at the front, snaked up the grand, wooden stairs and through the ornately decorated corridors that were awash with paintings and tapestries, till they entered what was known as the Great Library. The library did not look as impressive as Rachel had been led to believe; it was nice, but certainly didn't take your breath away. Carved, wooden bookshelves, standing five rows high, lined the room. Lines of shiny, wooden tables and chairs ran down the centre, and large, yellow, glass lights hung low from the ceiling. There was also a musty smell coming from somewhere.

Rachel looked about; there were about five spirits in the room, and three of them turned to look when the group came in. She motioned to everyone to stand still by the door, then walked boldly up to a largish man who was wearing a red cape lined with white fur and a sloping, black beret on his head.

"Excuse me, sir, these people are here to see what spirits reside in Howland Hall. I wondered if I could ask your name?" On this occasion, instead of using her usual telepathic communication, Rachel instead spoke very quietly, only appearing to the tourists to be mouthing the words, so the crowd could see she was speaking, but without hearing what she was saying.

The spirit man glanced at her impassively. He was about sixty, with heavy whiskers on his reddened face; he reminded Rachel of a walrus. "Tell 'em to bugger off, that's what I say."

The crowd watched intently as Rachel stood, looking at an empty corner, her mouth moving noiselessly.

"She is communicating with the dead," reminded Andy loudly from the back.

"These good people have come to see what spirits live in Howland Hall. Couldn't you at least give me your name, sir?" Rachel asked the shirty spook. He turned back to her, with a snarl on his face. "Why would I speak to a whore like you? Begone from my house." He began walking off.

Rachel frowned. The dead had been getting a bit feistier lately; memories of Rabbi Lieberman returned to her mind. She called after him, "What year did you live here? Who was your master?"

He turned to her, then strode back; she thought for a moment he might strike her, but then concluded if he tried to do this his hand would simply whip through her. "I am not telling you anything. You and your kind come here to gawp at us like animals… You have no right!" he yelled into her face.

She looked up, but the other spirits, probably wanting to get away from the argument, had slipped through the walls. Rachel felt the crowd beginning to mutter behind her.

Andy's voice rose up again from the back of the group, like a flock of gulls, "Miss Holloway is communing with a ghost; she is now crossing the fragile tissue between life and death."

"Piss off," hissed the spirit man, and Rachel was left to watch as his body slowly slid down into the floor. His large frame, like mist, disappeared gradually downwards till only the top of his black beret could be seen; there was a little jolt, then he was gone completely.

Rachel looked up at the crowd, described the man she had seen, and remarked that he wasn't very cooperative.

Bim confirmed it sounded a lot like Sir Aloysius Hyde,

one of the owners of the house back in the late 1700s. Flicking through a large guide book that he had been carrying around, he showed her a picture of an oil painting of Sir Hyde. His fat, reddened jowls were unmistakable, as well as his emotionless eyes that stared out across the ages from the well-thumbed pages.

"Yes, that's him," sighed Rachel.

"How do we know you saw this bloke?" said someone in the crowd.

"Yeah, why can't we see 'im?" asked another man.

As people were becoming restless, Bim said it was best that everyone moved on to the North Tower, a place apparently well known for hauntings, strange noises and experiences. As they walked along, he told her how the mayor, on a recent visit, had felt something touch him repeatedly whilst in the tower. Rachel did not know how to respond.

Ascending the North Tower was going to be a difficult exercise, that much was clear when they all got to the small stone arch and battered, wooden door that guarded the spiral staircase. The door itself had thick, black hinges and a huge, ring door handle off to the right. A sign was affixed to the door that said, 'Do not pull the knocker'.

"What's the hold up?" asked the familiar voice of Andy from the back.

Rachel wasn't sure how safe it was for the 130 or more people to make their way up the narrow stairs, but, before she could say anything, Bim had pulled the door agape and called for people to follow him up the small steps. The tower itself, like much of the house, was made of ancient stone; the steps each had a small slope worn in the middle, where centuries of walking had eroded them away. Only a small piece of rope, attached to the spiralling wall, gave visitors anything to hold on to as they climbed the darkened, damp, twisting staircase.

Rachel got to the top to find that it opened into a circular room about fifteen feet in diameter; the domed roof echoed sound, distorting it and making it hard to hear. A small arrow-slit window let a tiny amount of light pierce the gloom, which was supplemented by a small, flickering, orange emergency light on the ceiling. Worried that not even one-third of the group would be able to stand in this enclosed space, Rachel stopped people from coming out from the stairway after about thirty people had passed her. The tiny room was already cramped; the 100 or so others would have to just wait on the stairs.

Where the hell was Andy?

Rachel's eyes caught a young spirit girl, aged about nineteen, in a long, white dress, sitting in the shadows. She had long hair, which was tied back, and it was clear she had also been crying.

"Who are you?" said the girl "What are you doing here?"

Rachel was surprised, because the dead usually let her speak first, as they often didn't know she could see them. If anything, they usually jumped when she spoke to them, so used were they to walking unseen amongst the living.

The crowd in the tower roof watched silently, resisting the gentle press from those caught on the stairway who couldn't see.

Again, Rachel appeared to be mouthing words to something that wasn't there; everyone watched intently.

205

"My name is Rachel, and I am able to see the dead. These people here are interested in the spirits that haunt this place; what is your name?" Rachel enquired in her normal speaking voice.

The girl removed a handkerchief from a pocket in her dress and wiped her nose. "My name is Becky. I died here; I threw myself from the tower." She said it with almost no waver in her voice. "Now I am stuck here forever as punishment for ending my life, and I'm caught here with my child."

Rachel couldn't see anyone else in the room.

"What happened?" she asked.

The girl looked towards the crowd, who were still watching silently. "I became with child, from the head valet of the house. He said he would not marry me; I had no parents and no support…" She sniffed. "So, one day, after drinking some of the Lord's wine, I cast myself from the top of this tower. Now I sit in purgatory, waiting for judgement."

"We can't see nuffink!" came a strangled cry from the middle of the stairs.

Becky's face darkened. "They come… to haunt me… Can you feel them? I must leave." And, with that, her apparition rapidly faded away.

Rachel was alone in the room.

"What did you see?" asked a middle-aged lady at the front of the queue.

Rachel went to answer when it happened. Out of the blue, the tower was filled with an ear-splitting, thunderous cry of what sounded like hundreds of babies. The wails spun around the circular room and hit those standing in the stairway full on. Then a series of ghostly screams began, ever closer and louder than the baby cries, compelling those at the top of the stairs to immediately turn around in a frenzied attempt to get away.

The screams and cries grew progressively louder and shriller, all competing against each other until Rachel thought her ears would burst. The tower began to rattle slightly, as if it had been struck by an earthquake; Rachel stumbled a little and fell to the floor with the vibrations. Shrieks and howls from the visitors now filled the stairway, and a scrum broke out as hundreds of bodies tried to squeeze back down the tower.

"*Demons!*" someone exclaimed.

"Help us," cried another elderly woman.

Rachel remembered calling out for Andy, but, as usual, he was nowhere to be seen.

★

Andy had decided not to snake his way up the tower with everyone else. He was at the back, so he had no chance of a decent view; besides, Rachel was the one who could see the spooks, so what could he do? No, he would wait here in the entrance hall for everyone to come back down. That was way more civilised.

A few feet away from him there was a large, red velvet, wingback armchair, with a small chain strung between both arms. A sign with 'DO NOT SIT' written on laminated card had been placed on the seat, together with a thistle, presumably to punish anyone who dared to sit on the chair.

Gingerly, he unclipped the chain, removed the sign and thistle, and then sat down.

Ah, peace… he thought.

He heard footsteps crossing the hard floor slowly. It was a latecomer, no doubt, which meant more cash for him. He turned his head to greet whoever it was who had bothered to turn up almost 45 minutes late, only to see his mother walking towards him.

Dressed like a teenager as usual – in tight, shiny trousers, fashionable boots and a fur coat – she came closer, her slim and slightly gaunt figure dwarfed by the largeness of the coat. Her face, as usual, was heavily lined, something no amount of make-up could disguise.

The taste of sick entered his mouth as he felt his heart almost jump in his chest. "Mother." He leapt up on his feet in an instant.

Her face broke into a sardonic grin. "Think you could have kept this little soiree from me, do you? Shame on you for not asking your poor, old mum to come and see your little performance…"

"What do you want?"

"Want?" she walked closer to him. "To congratulate my son on his unexpectedly successful business. I know it won't last; sooner or later, someone will expose it for the bloody sham it is. Using that poor, crazy lady who sees things, and pretending it's ghosts to make you rich, really is shameful."

Andy looked towards the crammed stairway; he could hear voices drifting down, mainly complaining they couldn't see. Where was Rachel when he needed her?

"Rachel really can see spirits; she had like an… ahem…

illness, and then started to be able to see them. It isn't a lie," he clarified.

She smiled again. "Now you're rich, I hope you'll remember your poor mother, who's left in poverty. All those years I did without to look after you, so maybe it's time you repay me. I mean, you are obviously raking it in… I saw you arrive in that nice car outside."

Andy was spooked. She must have been watching him for the entire evening if she saw them arrive; was she stalking him?

As they continued their conversation, Dr Maxwell drifted through the closed doors of the main entrance. He had seen a poster advertising this 'ghost walk', and he thought it was the ideal time to speak to Rachel. He was aware that they had parted on bad terms – it wasn't her fault, he was just touchy about his earlier life and didn't much like people asking about it – but she meant well. It was time he made amends; besides, he missed her in a way and also wanted to make sure she was becoming accustomed to her growing power. She could easily become unstuck if she weren't careful.

He looked around the hall and saw a man in front of him, about ten feet away, talking to an older, skinny woman. This must be the man Rachel was telling him about, the psychic investigator. *She has described Andy rather well,* he thought, smiling. He looked closely at the woman; there seemed to be a physical resemblance between her and the man, so he assumed they were related. He considered floating up the tower and finding Rachel, as he could hear her voice in the distance, echoing down the steps, but then his attention was drawn to the obvious tension between the pair.

Inquisitive, Dr Maxwell crept closer; they couldn't see him, so why not find out what was occurring?

"Your father would be here if not for you, Andy; I would have a husband, so you owe me…"

Andy was visibly shaking in front of this woman, so Dr Maxwell came closer still; he realised this must be Andy's mother.

"You wouldn't like this event mother; maybe its best you go," stated Andy.

"Let's say £100 to start; that will help me pay my heating bills, when I am left home alone and cold," she suggested.

Andy thought her boots alone must have cost more than that. He felt sickened. "You want money off me?" He frowned.

"You owe me!" Her voice became shriller, and her face twisted into a snarl, with her red lips resembling a slashed, bleeding wound.

Andy went to speak, but the words caught in his mouth.

Her voice began again, "You're bloody pathetic, you know that? If I hadn't pushed you out myself, I would have doubted you were anything to do with me." She came closer.

Dr Maxwell had seen enough; this woman was a bully, and he could see Andy struggling to respond. Slowly, he walked right up to her left ear as she stood there, still grinning at Andy, and roared with all his might, "*Get out, bitch!*"

Andy leapt two paces back. They had both heard it, clear as a bell, ringing around the hall. His mother froze momentarily, then, without a backward glance, she sprinted towards the main entrance. A terrified scream escaped her as she scrabbled at the large, iron handle on the door, breaking off several false nails in the process. She then fled into the night, leaving the ancient door to slowly close behind her with the help of a modern locking mechanism.

Andy turned deliberately from staring at the closed door to the source of the shout. In front of him, he could physically see nothing, but he could *feel* the presence of something there, merely inches from him. For that long moment, he and Dr Maxwell stood, just a foot apart, facing each other. The feeling that something or someone was in his personal space was becoming overpowering, but who or what?

The spell was broken as a huge seething mass of bodies poured from the staircase doorway, scrabbling, screaming and shouting.

Andy finally snapped his eyes away from the empty space as he thought, for the second time that night, *Where the hell is Rachel?*

CHAPTER 31

News of what happened during the tour of Howland Hall spread like wildfire. At first, Andy thought it had been an unmitigated disaster and a total flop. Health-and-safety legislation had been compromised by the storming of the staircase, and they had only encountered one (or two) definite spooks: the library man and the girl in the tower. Well, he had also heard the man's booming voice, but he alone was witness to that, so unfortunately it didn't count. But he was proved wrong.

People had been terrified by the tour, and news was spreading on social media that ghost hunts held by Spirit of London Paranormal Investigations were a must-see. Even Victor the footballer tweeted that he personally knew Andy and Rachel, who were the real deal. Andy could not have paid for PR like this. He was already planning the next hunt, which would be even bigger and better. He hadn't spoken to Rachel about it, but he knew she would be up for it.

★

Rachel found herself walking towards Shore Moat again. It was a windy morning, and a gentle rain was carried by the cold breeze that hit her face. She had been increasingly troubled by the thing she had seen during her last visit, and after struggling through a bad night, she had been woken up in the early hours by a terrible headache. Rachel had been halfway through another dream, in which she was moving among shadows and being pressed from all sides. Then thoughts of the moat came to her, telling her that that she should go there again.

She wasn't sure why she should return to that place. Kayleigh's body had been found, so what was left there to see? She didn't know, but she felt absolutely compelled to go there. Who knew, maybe she would see Winston again, trying to lure Marmalade from the tree; she liked him, as he gave off a good aura.

To be fair, she had nothing else on her agenda to do, so she had caught the bus and now found herself on the path leading right down to the moat. Everything smelt so fresh, gently damp, from the soft rain that was still falling like a light spray.

Winston wasn't there today; perhaps he had succeeded in coaxing Marmalade down, and they had both gone to a cat-loving heaven somewhere. She only saw one ghost, who looked like a Roman soldier marching up the hill a little way off from her; as she walked along, she pondered whether it was a real Roman soldier from history (she had never seen a ghost who had been dead 2,000 years) or someone dead who was just dressed as a Roman.

Rachel forgot this conundrum as soon as she entered the moat area. There it was again, that peculiar green space. It

213

was crowded with trees and plants that filled the void where there was once civilisation, dense enough to protect her from the wind and rain. She saw the little island ahead of her, surrounded by the green, algae-covered moat. The perfectly still water reflected countless tiny speckles of sunlight that had filtered through the canopy above. Slowly, Rachel walked across the narrow causeway that bridged the outer bank to the island. Just eleven steps were all it took for her to reach it. She then sat heavily on a large fallen tree trunk. *What now? There's nothing here.*

Rachel looked up and saw the tree across the water, on the mainland. It was the tree that the spirit of Kayleigh had first vanished behind. As her mind began to wander, she sensed a fluttering all around her; the trees and plants where she sat began to flicker and fade, and greyness descended like a dark veil falling from the sky. At first, she wondered whether she was having another brain seizure and felt the panic rise within her. She stood up and, without warning, saw grey walls and stone floors materialise around her. She could see them clearly, yet they had a glassy, translucent quality. Looking through them, she could still see the mainland across the moat. *What madness is this?*

Figures came into view. They were men. Perhaps fighting men. They were clad in dark cloth and leathers, their hands bound with rags as if to offer protection, and some wearing helmets. She walked straight through the translucent wall (thinking this must be what it was like for ghosts who passed through solid walls) and went to the edge of the island. Looking back, she could see the outline of a formidable, dark fort, looming against the sky. It reminded her of the castle she had seen before – shimmering, but clearly visible. More men now – mean, muscular men – milling about. They did not seem able to see her, as if they were a memory imprinted on the place. Rachel reflected how glad she was that she was unseen; men like this didn't look like they knew how to respect women.

She hated it when these transitions took place, and it still unnerved her when she saw these apparitions. As walls and people started forming and changing around her, she always felt the rise of panic, beginning like pins and needles in her hands and feet, then running like a cold, icy claw up her limbs and through her body to her head. Rachel did not like seeing these things, and often pondered why she had been chosen to have this sight. Every time her surroundings shifted like this, it felt increasingly uncomfortable to her, and brought all the horror back anew.

This must be the building that once stood on the island. It was made of dark stone, stretching to the sky, with small arrow-slit windows. It stole the light from the surrounding area, like a spreading oil stain. She looked again at the men. She could see them clearly, but could also tell they were not like ordinary ghosts, as she could not interact with them, or they with her; it was like watching a film playing.

Turning away, again feeling relieved that these intimidating men could not see her, she walked along the little causeway, towards the outer bank, feeling herself pulled towards the tree. Then her mind was full of Kayleigh, remembering the photos showing a beautiful, young woman full of life. Rachel sat down on a tree stump, avoiding the damp part, and looked up; the fort had almost vanished, like it had never been there. The men were fading slowly from the banks of the moat. Rachel rubbed her eyes; blasted visions.

Her mind kept going back to that thought. Kayleigh should be remembered. This place should recognise the death of this young woman; maybe it should be turned into a place of remembrance or even a shrine that people could go to. Yes, that was it. As soon as her mind fixated on the thought, she felt better; yes, a shrine should be set up to mark the death of this promising local girl. She would speak to the reporter, Luke Fairfax, about it as soon as she could; maybe he knew some sponsors. Yes, this was a good idea.

The wind began to blow cold, and spray from the rain hit her face. The fort was now totally gone. Rachel rose and began her walk home, resolute in her determination to get her latest project off the ground: a proper place to remember Kayleigh. She would have to speak to Andy about it, but she knew he would agree, as he would no doubt see it as yet another money-making venture.

CHAPTER 32

Dr Maxwell stood on the corner of the high street, with Henry behind him. In the last three weeks, Henry had attached himself more to the doctor and was spending less time with Nanny. He said he wanted to learn more about what it was like to be a 'proper spirit' and how, as a dead teenager, he was meant to make his way in the world.

William was unconvinced that he could help. He had never been a father, knew little about teenage boys (except from his own experience), and did not want this flamboyant hanger-on. He also had a concern that, as a spirit, Henry was never going to get any older, mature or grow into a man. So, unlike a living person, who would pass through the teenage phase over several years, Henry was likely to be struggling with it permanently, unless God took his soul. Guiding him through this eternal turbulence did not appeal to Dr Maxwell at all.

Henry had asked him whether he was pally with Rachel again. William didn't know. He had only spoken to her briefly after the business at Howland Hall, as he could see she had been shaken by the whole thing, so he had just said hello, asked how she was, then said goodbye. Had they made their peace with each other? He wasn't sure.

At the moment, he was preoccupied with a front page headline on a pile of free newspapers outside a shop: 'LOCAL MAN QUESTIONED OVER KAYLEIGH LOVALL MURDER'. The article didn't give a name or much information, he assumed this was in the event that it should prejudice the case, but William had heard two women gossiping about it outside. They had said that the person arrested was a man with a history of being violent, who lived just five streets from Kayleigh. They also said he had been seen near the area where she was killed only a week before. Interesting.

"Dr Maxwell, are you concerned about that lady, Rachel... the one who sees us?" enquired Henry.

The doctor started. He had forgotten about his new shadow. "Me? A little, yes... She seems to have taken on this new mantle of being able to see the dead very well, but I am still not convinced she is as aware as she should be about the things that exist in our realm."

"Those from the underworld?"

"Yes, but also, as news of her power spreads, I fear she will enter turbulent times. The living will become dismayed that she cannot conjure up at will news of their loved ones who have passed, and spirits will become disgruntled as she cannot deliver *the answer* as they wish. Basically, the living and the dead will despise her."

"You think it will be as serious as that?"

"Yes. She holds within her grasp a great power. I don't think she understands it. She just thinks she sees ghosts, and that's that; she has no idea what this means for our kind. Spirits may rally against her, questioning the origins of this power. Darker forces may also begin to open their minds to the possibility of exploitation; we must be on our guard and watch out for her."

Henry frowned. "What of this Andy Horton? Does he not have her welfare in mind? After all, she is the reason that his business thrives."

Dr William Maxwell had no doubt as to Mr Horton's primary goal. "No, Henry, I don't think he does. He only has one priority, and that is to fill his coffers with gold, to the devil with what souls he distresses on the way."

Henry looked closely at the newspaper poster. "I wonder if he did it? This man they speak of here."

"Who knows? We have to simply have faith that the justice system will out the guilty."

"You have more belief in our legal process than I do, Doctor. Many innocent men have gone to the fire and the gallows."

"Indeed."

Dr Maxwell decided he would try to find out more about the arrested man, and, more importantly, whether Rachel had given any input into these latest happenings. Perhaps the dead girl had made contact with her.

These were exciting times, but also worrying. Thanks to Rachel, the thin tissue that separated the living from the dead had almost been removed altogether. Dr Maxwell was pleased Rachel could see him, but he could not help but feel some fear; ghosts remained unseen to the majority of the living for a reason, but now, as the two worlds began to collide through Rachel, he did muse over what would become of it.

★

Rachel sat on the Tube train heading into central London. As the gentle clacking of the rails lulled her senses, she thought about the last two weeks. They had been insane. Andy had reported being inundated with requests for help with paranormal problems, all fuelled by the 'Howland Hall event'. Luke Fairfax, their new pet reporter, had also published a piece in the local paper about what had happened in the hall, referencing Victor Adeyemi, and that was all it took; it was like a media bomb had gone off.

For some reason, most of the attention seemed to be gravitating towards Andy this time, rather than her; not that this was necessarily a bad thing. The begging letters – which, up till now, had been pushed regularly through her letterbox – had slowed a little. Andy was making some personal appearances at local fetes, events and business seminars, and had also set up his own social media pages. To be honest, if she really looked inside herself, this suited her well enough, as her stress levels had been through the roof recently. Andy seemed to thrive on the attention, like some plants flourished in bright sunlight; she on the other hand merely wilted and withered into a pulp.

She was on her way to central London to meet Sheikh Mohammad bin al-Rahman. Andy had described him as a 'rich, Saudi Arabian dude' who lived in a £8,000,000 mansion right in the centre of town. Apparently, he had

220

made his fortune in real estate and luxury hotels in the Middle East, but had contacted Andy on quite another matter.

According to Sheikh al-Rahman, his palatial home, including his numerous wives, were being haunted by something terrible. He reported dark shapes, whispering voices and some of the wives being touched by something whilst in bed. Andy had told Rachel that the sheikh had called in Spirit of London Paranormal Investigations because he needed complete confidentiality. The sheikh also claimed that, as they had dealt with a Premier League footballer incredibly successfully, this also confirmed in his mind that they could help him. Rachel still wasn't honestly sure if they had helped Victor Adeyemi at all. Rabbi Lieberman was still probably hanging around in the house, more furious than ever. She expected a phone call at any moment, bringing news of the haunting starting again with a vengeance.

Andy had already gone to the sheikh's house a day ago and reported back that it boasted a splendid swimming pool and spa, which he seemed more enthusiastic to check out than any ghostly goings on. He told her that, so far, he hadn't seen anything untoward, but that he wanted Rachel to come and give the house the once-over.

So, there she was, off to this big house in Belgravia.

It was 4pm when she alighted from the Tube. Not surprisingly, she felt a migraine coming on; she got them daily now, which was very depressing. Oddly enough, even though they were a regular occurrence, she forgot about them until about the time when they always started to come on. Leaning by a wall, she took one of her pain pills with a swig of water. *Please God, this will kill it off. Right, where is this place?*

After consulting the map given to her by Andy, she turned down a side alley. As she walked down it, ghostly shapes began to form around her, like steam. Two figures could be seen collapsed on a wall as she passed, their faces disfigured through being covered in boils. A man, dressed in ragged clothing, with blood running from his mouth, screamed to the sky. She realised she was stepping back in time again and seeing events of the past, but from when?

She recoiled as a wooden cart pulled by a shabby horse rumbled by, piled high with bodies, some in a state of decay, bobbing around with the cart's side to side movement, and all covered in blistered boils. The man leading the way was himself dressed in brown sackcloth, with a twist of the coarse material covering his nose and mouth. For just one second, as they passed, she smelt it: the stench of decay and putrefaction. Holding her mouth, she hurried down the street, only to be confronted by a priest, hurrying by and clutching a large book.

"Oh Christ," she said aloud. *Where was this bloody house?*

There were more bodies appearing on the ground now: some dead and some dying. Children could be heard crying in the distance. She started to feel increasingly unwell. A sharp pain pulsed in her temple.

Picking up the pace, she saw the name of the road she needed, but how would she know which house it was? She need not have worried, as the mews only had two houses in it, and the first was whitewashed, with golden gates. It had no number, name or sign, but Andy had told her to look out for the 'really white gaff', so she assumed this must be it. After walking up to the gates, she pressed the intercom.

A voice with a foreign accent responded, saying something incomprehensible.

"Er… Rachel Holloway here to see Sheikh al-Rahman?" she offered.

More foreign sounding words came, then a click when the person hung up.

Rachel then saw a movement out of the corner of her eye. A tall man – or, at least, she assumed it was a man – dressed in a long, black robe walked slowly towards her. He wore a wide-brimmed hat and his face was hidden by a dark, shiny, bird-like mask, complete with a large, hooked beak. In his hands, he carried a long cane.

The golden gates began to open noiselessly before her, and she hurried in. As she turned, she watched them close slowly behind her, stopping just short of the hooded figure. She saw his body jerk slowly up and down, then she realised why: he was laughing.

CHAPTER 33

Andy and Rachel sat in Sheikh al-Rahman's front room, or they assumed it was his front room. It was the size of what looked like a quarter of a football pitch. Heavily themed in red and gold, with thick carpets on the floor, it must have cost a fortune to decorate. It was not to Andy's taste though. A huge picture of the sheikh hung on the wall, in the pop art style of Andy Warhol.

The sheikh himself looked in his mid-sixties. Dressed modestly in the traditional dress of spotless, flowing, white robes and a headscarf, he stared at them, expressionless, from the high-backed, golden chair he sat upon. His face revealed a man who liked his food, as he was a little overweight; he had keen, small eyes and a very neat but clearly greying moustache.

Andy shifted about on the hard chair that he had been offered to sit on. The back and legs were gold (Was it real? Certainly, it was at least gold leaf.). The backrest and seat cushion were sumptuous, red velvet. He would have, however, preferred to sit on a massive sofa like Victor had offered them. His backside was starting to go numb.

"Prince al Mohammad, I am so pleased you asked us here to your beautiful home," Andy stated. "I do hope we can help you with your problems. This is Rachel Holloway, ghost hunter and gifted psychic. She can see the spirit world and will be able to see what ails your palace."

The sheikh frowned. He said, in perfect English, but with a slight accent, "Please address me as sheikh, if you would."

Rachel realised Andy had pronounced his name incorrectly and called him prince. That wasn't the best start.

Andy looked at Rachel, then back at the sheikh. "Er... Mr Sheikh, would you please tell us what has been happening here, to whom and in what room? Any detail, however small, would be very helpful."

Sheikh al-Rahman frowned again. He went to speak, stopped and then began again. "I have lived here with my wives for a year and a half now. The house was purpose built to my instructions, and I do believe an old house was in this position previously; this may have a bearing on what has happened. It all began very suddenly, about four months ago, when some of my wives said they had seen what they described as a 'dark figure', usually in the corner of a room, like a shadow, but moving as if alive."

Andy was rummaging in his suitcase; he took out his Stetson with the crucifix on it.

The sheikh looked at it doubtfully. "We are Muslim here, sir."

Andy sat up. "You are, but maybe the ghosts aren't; we cannot be too careful."

Again, the sheikh went to say something, but clearly thought better of it. He looked at Rachel, who smiled back.

The sheikh continued, "Anyway... er... yes, the shapes. Dark shapes were appearing in corners, but then noises started; loud whispering could be heard in darkened rooms and at night. My wives ignored it at first, wondering if it was possibly sound carrying, but then the touching started."

"What happened?" asked Rachel.

"In bed, they said they felt hands... on their bodies... where hands should not go; do you understand?" He began to flush. "One wife, Laya, said that it was a man's hand, on her leg and breast. She was alone in the room at the time; she screamed and it went away."

Andy looked unconvinced. "She was not dreaming, was she?"

"No, there was a bruise on her leg the next day where whatever it was gripped her tightly," the sheikh confirmed. He then abruptly stood up. "My wives," he said, and he waved his hand to gesture behind them.

Andy turned to see a line of dark shapes – about forty women in long, black robes and face veils, appearing to be almost floating – passing silently through the doorway and beginning to stand, side by side, like a bizarre police line-up. One by one, the black robed figures – who were a mixture of fat and thin, short and tall – glided to their positions next to the woman in front of them. Some had niqabs, showing only their eyes, and others simply covered hair with hijabs, revealing ages between approximately mid-twenties to mid-sixties. Once they were all in a formation they stood silent and still, as if waiting for further instructions.

"Please," began the sheikh, "ask them anything you would like."

"If I may," said Rachel, "would I be able to borrow someone please, to show me the places in your house where the haunting took place, especially the bed?"

Sheikh al-Rahman nodded. "The women cannot go anywhere with your friend unaccompanied, but with you, yes, certainly… Laya…"

A slim, black robed figure with a full face veil stepped forwards.

"Please show Miss Holloway where the trouble has been happening," requested the sheikh.

The figure inclined her head slightly and gestured that Rachel should follow her. The two women left the room, and as Rachel walked behind her dark guide, the voice of Andy could be heard in the distance, obviously asking more questions. Rachel preferred to simply go to where the trouble was and see who or what could be found lurking, that was usually the quickest option.

Quietly, Rachel was led up two flights of sumptuous stairs by the cloaked wife. Laya then turned to her right and, with a gloved hand, opened a large door within a carved, golden frame. Rachel wondered how hot it must be to wear robes all the time, especially in Saudi Arabia where the sheikh was from; she decided there and then that she was glad she didn't also have to wear this attire.

They both entered a large bedroom, bedecked in gold and red, with a huge four-poster bed in the centre of the room. Laya turned the lock on her door, and removed her veil, revealing a very beautiful woman of about 25, with dark hair and eyes, full lips and a flawless face, which was, surprisingly to Rachel, adorned with make-up.

"Please sit down." Laya gestured to another one of the hard-backed chairs the house seemed to be festooned with.

Rachel sat whilst Laya remained standing; her accent was unusual, a mix of Arabic and English, but again with perfect pronunciation.

"You see spirits, they tell me; is this true?" Laya sat on the bed facing her.

Rachel wasn't ready for such direct questioning. "Er... yes... I had... er... something happen to my brain, and from then on I could see spirits, just like everyday people see living people."

"This... gift... how do you feel about it?"

"Er... I'm not sure. It's good to be a liaison between the worlds of the living and dead, and I have met such lovely people in the spirit world, but... well, some can be troublesome."

"Troublesome? How?"

"Oh, in the same way as living people, being argumentative and difficult to deal with." Rachel glanced around whilst she was speaking, but saw nothing untoward.

Laya looked up at her. "I will be blunt if you will permit me. I had no idea my husband would actually get a real psychic to come here; I expected a fraud, so I think it's best I simply tell you what spirits lie here, and you can then, how shall we say, deal with them as appropriate?"

Rachel sat stock still, slightly stunned.

The wife stood and walked slowly to the window, and her voice drifted back to where Rachel was still sitting. "There is a woman who walks from the hallway and through the wall into our back kitchen area; she probably causes the voices the wives hear, and she follows the layout of the house that was here before. She isn't a spirit as such; I believe it is simply residual energy... You understand this?"

No, Rachel didn't. This was ghost speak that Andy understood, not her. "You have seen this lady? Walking in the hallway? What do you mean she is 'residual energy'? No, I don't know what that is."

Laya frowned. "Residual energy is like when something has happened a while ago, and the imprint of it plays out like a recording. You know it's that and not an active haunting, because the person does the same thing time and again, like walking a certain route through a house or saying the same thing... You cannot interact with residual energy like you can a real spirit."

Rachel was stunned. "You obviously have read up on this."

Laya returned to her position on the bed. "I will tell you something now, but you must tell no one; I think you are probably a good person to confide in, being as you are, well, saddled with the same supposed gift. I see them too, you see – spirits and... other things that exist; I have from a child. My mother had second sight and, now, so do I, but we do not speak of it, as it is *haram*. This means forbidden."

"So, let me get this straight; you claim you can see ghosts as well? But what do you mean by har... er... forbidden? Forbidden by whom?"

"Yes, I see them... Why are you surprised? You see them... but it is forbidden by my culture and my religion. If I confessed to seeing the undead, I would most likely be cast out."

"I don't think that would happen…"

"What would you know of my life? *My existence?* Yes, I would be sent from here in shame. To see those that should be passed… Where do you think this so-called power comes from?" She had clearly become slightly angry.

Rachel looked sheepish. "God?"

"I don't want to debate religion. Anyway, you should be concerned with the other entity that lives here; the old lady is nothing, a faded memory of the past, but this… *thing*… that's something else entirely."

"Entity?" Rachel didn't like the sound of that.

"What it is, I do not know. It is some wandering force, dark and malevolent; it is that which grabbed me under the bedclothes. Its face was not human. It frequents everywhere; it goes where it pleases. I am sure that if you remain in the house long enough, you will see it as well."

"How do I get rid of it?"

Laya pursed her lips. "You are the psychic; you tell me. My husband has called you here to solve the problem, and, trust me, I know my husband; he will not pay you a riyal until this spirit is gone from our house. The old lady, she is just an annoyance, and you cannot remove residual energy anyway… but the other spirit… good luck with that."

The voice of Andy rose up in the hallway "Kum by yah… oh spirit… speak to me…"

Laya looked towards the sound, then returned her gaze back to Rachel as she reattached her niqab. "You asked me if this power to see comes from God; well, to answer you, foolish sister, it comes from the evil one." Coming closer, she pointed to her bright, brown eyes, visible through the slit in

the face veil. "Malevolent forces give us the eyes to see…
When you think of it like that, it makes it clearer, does it
not?"

Laya then walked over to her door, unbolted it and was
gone. Rachel was left in the silent, spookless room with the
sound of Andy calling nonsense which reverberated around
the house. It hadn't made it clearer at all; in fact, she was
more confused than ever. Up till now, she had been under
the impression that she had been touched by God, and given
a spiritual power, but that was all now in question – and she
didn't like it at all.

CHAPTER 34

The thing sat alone on a burnt-out car shell; being solitary was really what it was all about. Its kind avoided others of the same ilk, in the same way that spiders avoided their fellows. If they should meet, they either fought, or one had to leave the other's space; that was how it was and how it always will be. But the thing did what it could to avoid battles, as – even if it won – it would take a lot of effort to recover, and besides, fighting its own kind took up valuable resources that were better spent elsewhere.

It had been told that if it took the most souls, it would get to do what hardly any of its kind had ever done: see the supreme leader. It had remained unconvinced about this, wondering whether it was an untruth told to it by its superior to reap more souls, but – considering that the thing enjoyed capturing souls – it had agreed.

It shifted its position slightly; it was crouched, as usual, surveying its surroundings. There was a dark, red sky, with a hot wind blowing that rustled its fur. Here, it was twice the size it was on earth, and it could move more quickly. Burnt-out cars from every era littered the dark desert road, stretching off in a scorched, higgledy-piggledy line. The road was flanked on both sides by the shells of ruined buildings, interspersed with parched, lifeless trees. Its eyes followed the road off into the distance. The air was thick with the familiar acrid sulphur smell, mixed with the heavy stench of burning matter; it sniffed the hot air through its nostrils with delight, as one would enjoy a strongly fragrant flower.

Many of its kind simply possessed the bodies of the living, then killed them and claimed their souls that way. At times, they would use the body of a mortal to carry out a task, then simply leave it and move on without taking the life, depending on their purpose.

But possessions were sometimes troublesome, particularly on the rare occasions when the soul fought back, which could drain the creature's energy. A failed inhabitation could be disastrous, as the struggle could cause the beast to make mistakes whilst mimicking the mortal, which could lead to detection. Their mission was to enter the physical body of the living, use it as a tool to do what they had to do, then leave undetected.

While it enjoyed the silky thrill of taking over a body, it had grown to find the process slightly distasteful. Entering the meat sack that was the mortal body, then merging with the minds of these pathetically weak and backward humans was beneath it. The creature was more than capable of possessing a person if it chose to, but it had, in its cleverness, devised another, more elegant method of carrying out the task; but without the danger of detection, or anyone

233

thinking anything was amiss. There was far more potential in manipulation, and using the stupidity and evilness of man against itself.

It was a smart plan, one expertly hatched and that had already worked with that girl, Kayleigh, but…

It leapt down from the car onto the boiling sand. Heat didn't bother it; in fact, in the fire was where it was created and where it drew its power from.

Picking at its ear absent-mindedly, its thoughts went back to that psychic girl in the woods. Who or what was she? She had seen it clearly, it was sure. It had seen the surprise in her eyes when their gazes met in that place; it had leapt out of the way, but perhaps too late. It had felt her eyes scraping along its form as it jumped. What should it do about her? There were hardly any mortals who had the power to see its form; very, very few. It sensed this girl was dangerous; it would have to keep a watch on her and perhaps reap her soul in time.

It wasn't too bothered at this stage. There was too much out there she would have to deal with first: the ghosts of dead mortals were the least threat to her; possibly, an entity would get her first or another one of its kind. She seemed naïve and unsure of herself, which was dangerous for one who would now come into contact with darker forces on a regular basis.

It smiled, with its pointy, little teeth reflecting the glow of the swirling sky. Its eyes, small and red, stared off into the distance. It twitched and, instinctively, its long, dark fingers scratched at its flank in a desperate motion, just like an ape or monkey when bitten by a flea. But this was no primate; it was not born of earth, blood, bone or seed. To compare it to anything on earth was akin to comparing an earthbound spark to the fires of hell.

★

Rachel had woken at 7.30am after a night full of dreams. There were dark shapes coming and going like smoke down walls and through floorboards, and the furry ape-like thing she had seen in the woods was there as well. For some reason, it was sitting on a scorched, burnt-out car, just smiling at her. What the hell was that about?

Her second thought after the dreams was the pain. The niggling, small migraine that had started yesterday when she had alighted from the Tube, that had begun like a small mouse nibbling gently at a piece of cheese in her brain, was now like a pneumatic drill piercing her skull. The moment she opened her eyes, she felt the sick realisation and panic flood through her that she was going to be out for the count for at least two days. Goddammit.

Two days were thus spent moving from the bed, to the chair and to the bathroom to be sick when the agony in her exploding head made her stomach retch. It was a hellish two days, made worse by the fact that the sheikh had requested she and Andy spend a few days at his house to address the problem, so she wasn't even in the relative peace of her own home. During this time, she was assisted by two women that Sheikh al-Rahman had kindly provided. Rachel gathered that these were normally handmaidens to the wives, but the sheikh – presumably wanting to make sure she didn't ruin his room, and trying to ensure that she actually got some work done whilst they were there – thought the assistants might help.

On the third day of her sickness, Andy appeared at her door; he only opened it a crack, as if she was struck down with some terrible contagious disease. He asked her when she would be fit to begin investigations at the house; she replied that it would be tomorrow. He then went away. Goodness knows what excuses he had made to the sheikh about this, but, according to the women helping, he had made full use of the home's pool and spa complex, even bothering Sheikh al-Rahman for the hospitality of the luxurious 30-seat cinema he had in the basement, to watch heaven knows what.

On the fourth day, she got up and dressed, ready to investigate whatever had been occurring in the palatial house. She was not exactly fully recovered, however, because a point of pain – like the tip of a nail stuck in her skull – still remained; she was also a little weak from the sleepless nights. Nevertheless, in a determined mood, she decided to make a trip to see for herself the residual energy Laya had spoken of. Rachel hadn't seen Laya since their discussion in the bedroom; well, she thought she hadn't, but there were black-robed wives floating gently around everywhere, so maybe Laya was one of them; but if so, surely she would have acknowledged her?

Rachel had arranged to meet Andy in the main hallway. As she descended the magnificent stairway, she saw him bending over some equipment on the floor: the little box with the mike attached and the music box/mirror thing. Sitting on a side table, she saw a small video-recording set; the little, green light was blinking, so it appeared to be recording. Attached to the recording unit was a small speaker.

He looked up. "Are you OK now? What brought that on, eh?"

"I don't know why they come; I feel a bit washed out, but the pain has mostly gone," Rachel confirmed.

He stood up and shook the box-and-mike contraption gently. "Prince al-Rahman told me about the ghostly old woman that walks here; this is probably the main issue he has, so I have set up a recording to catch her if she walks past. I am thinking that if we get her, you can tell her to leave, like you did that rabbi, and then, Bob's your uncle, we can get the cash and scoot."

Rachel frowned. "Did he tell you about... er... any other ghosts here?"

"No, why? Have you seen any?"

"Well, no..."

"Good." Andy seemed satisfied at this. He rubbed his hands together, then bent down and picked up the little contraptions on the floor, and put them in his holdall. "Right, I am off." He began to walk away.

"Where are you going? Aren't you going to wait for the old lady?"

"She could be ages... and, besides, I have a hot date with a *Red Dwarf* Blu-ray in the sheikh's cinema. If the camera records anything spooky, a tune will play to alert us, so don't worry." With a slightly jaunty step, he vanished down the hallway.

Brilliant, now what? Rachel had got out of bed for nothing it seemed. To kill some time, she decided to go outside into the garden area and wait for something to happen. This was the last day here, so if nothing happened, Andy would have to front up to the sheikh, who looked like a man who meant business.

The gardens attached to the house were magnificent, as was everything else. A bleached, white, stone path, bedecked by fragrant, bee-covered flowers, wound its way to a round island encircled by trickling water and hedges cut into square shapes. On one side of this beautiful area was an empty bench; on the other side was a seat with two robed wives sitting on it. Well, at least Rachel *thought* they were wives; she had been assuming every woman in a burqa was a wife, but maybe they were handmaidens to the wives.

She sat down and mused how she would be glad to leave this house, for all its luxury, and decided she would try to see Dr Maxwell. She kept thinking of him, where he was and what he was doing. He probably didn't give any thought to her from one day to the next. Her mind began to wander.

The two wives, or whoever they were, sat silently, looking forwards at the fountain, which gushed water lit by a myriad of bright-coloured lights. Like two dark chess pieces against the sunlit background, with every inch of them covered, they looked slightly sinister. Again, Rachel thought about what life must be like in this place, with such opulence, and everything anyone could want materially and more, but something was missing. She wondered about all these young (and older) women being married to this one elderly man. Did he sleep with them all? Or was it marriage in name only? She could see no evidence of hordes of children; maybe they were all packed off to a nursery or private school somewhere.

Then she heard it: an odd tune that didn't seem to fit in with the surroundings, drifting on the breeze…

She turned round to the source of the music and recognised it as being *Eye of the Tiger*. She couldn't imagine the sheikh listening to such a song. As she turned back, she noticed the wives were gone.

"Rachel!" It was Andy, shouting from the house. "The spook is here."

She jumped up and hurried to the doorway; rushing through, she entered a scene of chaos. The video player that Andy had set up was now whirring away, and, oddly enough, playing the offending tune simultaneously, at quite a loud volume from its deceptively small speaker.

Andy was standing there with a *Red Dwarf* T-shirt on, pointing in an animated fashion to the kitchen doorway. "Look, look the ghost! It's sprung the video."

She whirled around to see just the last glimpse of the smoky figure of an elderly woman hastening down the corridor and through the wall, next to the kitchen doorway. She could only be seen from the knees up; below that just a small cloud of mist. But it was clearly an old woman; Rachel could see this from the shapeless cardigan and fluffy bubble perm.

"What you waiting for? Jesus Christ." He immediately grabbed the camera and speaker, then set off in hot pursuit, with the theme tune following him.

The sheikh appeared, as if by magic, from a gold-framed door. As usual, he was wearing his white robes, but this time he was holding a smoking pipe.

"What is this commotion? And music… music of a Western persuasion is forbidden in my house!"

Rachel looked around, but Andy had gone. From behind the sheikh, Laya stepped out; she knew it was her from those brown eyes, burning out from the niqab.

"I… er," began Rachel, as she and Laya stood there, eyes locked.

"*Speak!*" bellowed the sheikh.

"Er… An— Mr Horton has found a spirit." It was all Rachel could think of saying. She pointed feebly to the kitchen door. From somewhere in the house, Andy's bellowing voice could be clearly heard over the music as he chanted, "Begone from this house, oh spirit, and leave Mr Rahman in peace. Namaste… Namaste…"

Instead of being relieved, Sheikh al-Rahman looked furious. "He dare speak heathen words in my home!" He swiftly passed his pipe to Laya and hurried down the corridor in the direction of Andy's voice, his robes flapping.

Rachel went to speak. Then she saw it. Thinking back she had seen it seconds earlier from the corner of her eye but hadn't noticed it properly till then. It was a black speck on the clear, white wall at the top of the stairs, growing larger and larger, and spreading in a roughly circular shape. It looked as if someone was blasting the darkest ink through the wall from behind and it was staining through.

By the time Rachel turned to it, the stain was about four feet across and growing. Instinctively, she began to walk up the stairs.

Laya warned, "Don't…"

But Rachel wasn't listening. She went up, up with each step, nearer and nearer.

Whatever it was remained silent; there was no sound or

smell, just a large, inky blackness growing and growing.

Two steps away now, Rachel stopped, watching the blackness creep up across the ceiling, down the walls, around and behind her.

"Rachel... no..." Laya was now on the second step up.

Rachel dragged her gaze from the spectacle and turned to face her. She could see that Laya was terrified, just by looking at her eyes. She looked back towards the wall.

The face – it had a face! She could see it, in the blackness, eyes and a mouth had formed. She felt no fear or alarm, just wonderment.

Rachel could feel it, whatever it was, pushing towards her like heat. It was as if it emitted a bass vibration, yet, to her ears, it was silent.

In the distance, like a man calling from a cliff, she could hear the sheikh shouting and Andy complaining. Laya was still on the second step up, looking straight at the darkness.

Then it happened, in less than a second, a moment within a second, the darkness sucked back within itself, like sand haemorrhaging from a timer, and it was gone. Rachel felt the force of it leaving, like a rush of wind, but instead of the wind pulling away from her, she felt it blow scorching hot into her body and face.

Then there was nothing.

Rachel turned, shaking slightly, to see Laya collapsed by the handrail; the sheikh was near the foot of the stairs with his back to them, apparently oblivious to what had just happened. He was gesticulating and screaming at Andy about 'dark forces', who responded by desperately trying to turn off the music, which was still playing. The sheikh's smoking pipe lay abandoned on the floor where Laya had dropped it. Rachel saw that a small amount of tobacco had fallen out, and had soiled the immaculate carpet. "Did you see that?" she said.

No one responded, so she tried again, this time louder. "Andy... did you see it?"

Looking up the stairs, he yelled, "*Yes, of course I bloody did; I went after her, but she vanished. Where the hell were you? Jesus.*" He stormed off.

"No, I mean..." She looked back to the wall.

Laya stood up slowly; shook her head, whether in despair or anger Rachel wasn't sure, and then left.

Only the sheikh remained, looking up at her. "Why do you stand there, foolish woman?" he said, "The ghost has gone." He raised a hand and pointed to the kitchen. Cursing, he bent to pick his pipe from the floor, and then strode off.

Rachel realised that neither Andy nor the sheikh had seen the thing on the stairs at all, so engrossed they had been with the old lady's apparition. But Laya had; she had seen it.

CHAPTER 35

It had taken two months to arrange for the shrine to Kayleigh to be built, which was no time at all. Once Rachel had mentioned the idea to Luke Fairfax, he had gone straight to the girl's parents. Surprisingly, they had agreed, saying it was a wonderful idea to remember their bright and happy daughter, and were honoured that Rachel – the person who had found her remains, someone so moved by her spirit – had suggested it.

They also felt that a memorial would help bring them a small degree of comfort, particularly since the police had released the man they were questioning for Kayleigh's murder. The local oddball they had arrested had insufficient evidence against him, which meant that whoever murdered their daughter was still out there somewhere.

Luke had run a piece in the *Burwood Echo*, and a local business had come forward with most of the money needed to set the memorial up, and after Kayleigh's parents had also chipped in there was enough to build a half-decent shrine.

It was basically a memorial bench, a plaque with

Kayleigh's name and face on it (her parents had chosen the 'pouting' picture Rachel had first seen in the crime file), plus a little, stone memorial in the shape of a teddy bear (Rachel had been told the dead girl had a thing for teddy bears). Around the area of her murder, bunches of flowers, in various states of decay, were tied to trees.

On the morning of the day of the memorial event, Rachel had woken up feeling a little sick, but, strangely enough, she had no customary pounding headache, which she thought was a good omen for the day. The shrine was to be opened by Victor Adeyemi (which had been Andy's idea), the boss of a local butchers who had donated a majority of the funds, (Morris's Meats) and, of course, Kayleigh's parents.

On arrival at Darkfoot Wood, Rachel was surprised to see that about 150 people had showed up to witness its opening. She was quite proud of its construction; it was only small, but she felt it was absolutely the right thing to do.

At the allotted time, Victor, dressed in a bright-white suit and purple shirt, stepped up to the podium and mike to address the crowd. He said he was delighted to have been asked to open this beautiful shrine, dedicated to the memory of a much-loved local girl. Then was the turn of John Morris, of Morris's Meats, who spoke at length about the eighty years his company had traded in the local area and how he had been happy to support the campaign. Lastly, Kayleigh's father stepped up, and, for a while he could not speak; in the end he simply waved his hand slightly and thanked everyone for coming, then he stepped down tearfully.

All that remained was for Victor to step forth and cut the yellow ribbon, which had been tied across the bench seat, and declare it open.

As Rachel stood off to one side, she looked around at the crowd. It was then that she saw her, a dark-robed figure standing just to the side of one of the trees, flanked by a tall, muscular, white-robed Arab man with dark sunglasses; perhaps a bodyguard? The woman looked like Laya. Rachel could tell by the way she stood and her build. What on earth was she doing here?

Then she felt him, seconds before he spoke, as a kind of heat behind her.

"I am glad you came here, I thought I'd stop by on the off chance."

Looking around, she saw Dr Maxwell, standing right behind her and smiling, with those familiar light-hazel eyes looking straight at her.

Rachel moved back a step so she could stand next to him and began to speak silently in her mind in reply. *"It's nice to see you here; I meant to come to the hospital, but so much has been happening…"*

"So I see."

Victor had cut the ribbon to loud applause.

"How have you been?" she asked.

"As usual, not a great deal happens when one is dead. Time just passes; you remain the same." He smiled at her again.

She decided to bite the bullet. *"I am sorry if I upset you last time; I really didn't mean to…"*

"Don't worry; it is water under the bridge. I don't like to

245

speak about my family and what happened to them… So… who is that lady then?" He inclined his head towards Laya, who had not moved a muscle throughout the ceremony.

"Oh, she's one of the wives of Sheikh Mohammad bin al-Rahman, an Arab gentleman who asked us to investigate his haunted house."

"You solved the problem?"

"No, not really. My partner, Andy, just reassured him that the spirit haunting his home was harmless, just a repeating imprint of a person and nothing to be concerned about, and that the house was safe."

"So it was a memory ghost, that's what we call them, you know; the ones that play out the same movements every time?"

"Yes, that's it."

"So it seems all is well."

Rachel frowned and was about to speak when Andy bounded up.

"I have handed out loads of cards for the business; lots of people are right interested in what we do, so we are going to clean up today," Andy explained, and with that, he hurried over to where Victor was standing, surrounded by photographers. Shaking hands and proffering a Spirit of London Paranormal Investigations business card in front of the lenses, the assembled photographers snapped away.

Rachel turned to William, but he had gone. Instead, a skinny, teenage boy with a powdered wig, velvet jacket and hose stood in his place. She took a visible step back; it was as if Dr Maxwell had shape shifted.

"Dr Maxwell has left; you have bored him," declared the boy. He then turned and left himself.

Rachel was dumbstruck for a moment, and then

looked back; Laya, and the man who was presumably her bodyguard, had also gone.

Andy still held court; this time, he was having his photo taken with the meat company man, both of them doing a thumbs-up.

Rachel felt that, in spite of all the difficulties that she had been experiencing lately, at least Kayleigh's shrine was now open and could be visited. That had been the whole aim of the exercise, and she had made it happen.

★

Mia pushed her way through the trees; she was so excited. Despite dusk having fallen half an hour ago, she could still find her way towards the memorial using the street lights from a nearby road to gently illuminate her way.

She had been devastated when her friend Kayleigh had been murdered. One minute, Mia was spending all her free time with Kayleigh, doing girlie things such as trying on clothes in her room and going out to parties, then came the news that she had been brutally killed; stabbed, it was said. She couldn't believe it. Mia didn't know what to do. Kayleigh had lent her a bangle a week before she died, and Mia had slept with it under her pillow from that day as a way to remember her friend. But then Mia had read about the memorial.

A psychic lady had apparently found the body whilst walking in the woods; when pressed, the woman (she thought her name was Raquel) had said Kayleigh had pointed to the ground where her remains had been buried. This had seemingly compelled this Raquel to set up the memorial.

Until her friend had died, she always known where to go when she was feeling down – Kayleigh's house – but now the memorial would have to do. She had brought a bottle of wine, and was planning to sit on the bench and remember her friend.

Mia reached the moat, glittering green out of the corner of her eye, and then the memorial. Numerous teddy bears had been placed on the bench, in different sizes and stages of wear. She walked slowly towards it and sat down. After rummaging in her bag, she took the wine bottle out and unscrewed the lid. Slowly, she brought the bottle to her lips and took two long gulps.

The whole thing was over in less than a minute. The first thing she felt was the ligature thrown around her throat from behind and pulled tight. The bottle fell to the floor, spilling its contents in a pulsing motion onto the damp grass.

Mia's hands flew to her throat, tugging, pulling and trying to free herself from whatever had caught her. Thoughts spun through her confused mind – maybe a bush had snagged on her or someone had left a rope on the trees – but, as it pulled tighter and tighter, she knew she was being attacked.

Before her crazed mind had time to think further, he struck, the blade swiped through the air as the attacker's arm arched from behind, and punched through her chest into her heart, stopping it within three beats. With a swish, the blade was sucked out from her chest and the ligature was loosened.

The man walked around the bench to survey what he had done. Hastily, he threw a dark tarpaulin over the body and wrapped it around her, securing it closed with string. Grabbing her feet, he pulled the lifeless corpse from the bench; her head banged against the seat as the full dead weight landed on the floor.

Gripping her ankles tightly, he pulled Mia into the undergrowth. As the bushes closed behind them, there was hardly any trace she had ever been there, except for the discarded bottle and spilt wine. There was also some blood remaining on the bench slats and the ground, and where it had mingled with the wine; it was beginning to congeal, leaving a sticky, dark-red stain on the grass.

The thing lay back, reclining slightly against a nearby tree; it had watched the whole scene play out. Its whole body was throbbing and aglow with the magnitude of what it had just witnessed; so much so that it could hardly think. The idea, which the creature had itself doubted would work at first, was turning out to be more successful than any of its kind could have imagined.

The supreme leader, when it heard, would be pleased. The creature would then perhaps be able to meet the great one and learn from its infinite wisdom. But it should not rest on its laurels, as more still had to be done.

The raptures had passed, exhausting the creature. It took an enormous effort for it to get to its feet and stumble off, with every part of its being still tingling with what it had just observed.

CHAPTER 36

Rachel's day had turned out to be very eventful, to say the least. Everything started when she received a phone call in the morning, and not from the police. It was from Ronald Easton. He told her that it looked like another girl had been attacked in the woods. The police suspected the same person had committed both crimes, and a man was already being questioned who was clearly in the frame. Rachel remembered being lost for words as he reeled off the information.

Mr Easton went on to explain that he could not say much about the suspect, other than he was a local oddball who was into the dark arts and violence. He added that, no doubt, the police would contact her in due course. Sniffer dogs and forensic teams had been sent to the wood and moat, and although the girl (whose name he wouldn't tell her) had clearly suffered trauma there, they could not find a body. He concluded by advising that even though no body had been found, evidence at the scene did indeed indicate that the girl was dead.

She wondered if the police would call her and ask her to help again, given that she had managed to locate Kayleigh, but then again maybe they wouldn't. Rachel had the distinct impression that the police thought she was a nutcase, and it had only been Ronald's insistence that brought her in on the case in the first place.

The day had also been marked by her receiving a text message from John, her ex; it said he was sorry he had walked out, he had been having trouble at work, he had seen her in the paper a few times, and it seemed she was doing well for herself. Just seeing his name flash up on her phone was enough to pull at her heart. She hadn't heard a word from him since he walked out and now he was contacting her.

She still felt something for John, so seeing the message had dredged it all up again, feelings she thought had been washed away, but the way the text was written triggered the intervention of her head rather than her heart. His mentioning that she had done well for herself particularly interested her; he probably thought she was rich now, which was far from the case. Rachel had enough money to get by, to pay the rent and bills, but not to buy expensive clothes or take holidays; she was bringing in just enough to cover living expenses only. Deep down, she knew that she and John were not compatible, he was an uncaring, hard person, but it still hurt.

She was sitting down in her flat when she heard the familiar voice of Dr Maxwell by the front door.

"Rachel? Rachel? Are you there?" he enquired.

As soon as she heard his voice, her heart leapt to her throat; she buzzed into life as if she had instantly been infused with some kind of amphetamine. Standing up, she remembered she was wearing her cat-print onesie. Oh God, she didn't have time to change.

"Rachel?" His voice was closer now.

She glanced out of the window. The Jews were there again; this time, there was more of them, maybe 100, all gathered around, silently facing the flat. A dark mass of overlarge, black hats and heavy coats, completely out of place in the mild weather, stood but five feet from her gate. An older man of about sixty stood at the front, holding a large, black book; he appeared to be reading from it for the benefit of the crowd. Some nodded and bobbed along to it, and others remained stock still.

A little way off, Rachel saw that the boy with the wig she had seen at the shrine was sitting on a concrete traffic bollard, looking like he was whittling a stick. She could see the little blade flashing in the light and the stick bobbing about with each flick of the knife. Now and again, the boy paused and looked at the Jews, then continued.

Dr Maxwell appeared at her living-room doorway.

"Rachel, I called out, but you didn't respond." His eyes looked up and down at the onesie, but said nothing.

"Sorry, you caught me unawares. The Jews are back; can you see them? I don't know what they want from me..." she stated.

"Indeed." he frowned.

They sat on the sofa; both were silent for a while. Rachel searched her mind for something to say. *"Did you hear that another girl has been killed at the moat? The man who works with the police told me."*

"Have they found her remains?"

"No; apparently, police dogs have been taken there, but found nothing…"

"That probably means she isn't in the woods then."

"No. I guess not. They haven't asked me to intervene, so I won't till I am approached. Maybe they think I am mental; I have a feeling it was Mr Easton's doing that I was even involved with the last girl's case."

"Yes, but you helped them find her body; why would they not ask you about it?"

"Who knows? Like I said, if they don't want my help, I am certainly not volunteering it."

Dr Maxwell decided to change the topic of conversation: "How are you? I have been worried about you; that's why I came…" He rubbed his hands together slowly.

Her mind filled with the – whatever it was – that had appeared at the top of the stairs at the sheikh's house. Last night, she had walked past her kitchen and swore she saw the same dark stain in a corner of her ceiling; she hadn't paid it much heed as, since the brain bleed, her eyesight for the realm of the living hadn't been what it was. It was probably a floater in her eye or something. Rachel remembered she had walked on to the living area and settled down to watch a film, but, in the back of her mind, she could almost feel the force from whatever it was.

Annoyed, Rachel had got up, walked to the kitchen and snapped on the fluorescent light in defiance. As the tube flickered into life, strange shadows appeared on the walls. The ghost of an old milkman in an apron and hat, clutching a rack of bottles, was standing by the washing machine, but there was no sign of the dark stain.

She had turned the light off, and had thought no more about it until she went to sleep and began to dream of it sliding up and down inside the walls of her house, covering everywhere, like some messed-up cavity wall insulation. She had awoken briefly in the night to, again, what she thought was a stain on the wall, but had gone to sleep almost moments afterwards.

She turned to the doctor. *"I think I am OK… Tell me, in your… er… world… are there things other than ghosts?"*

He looked up. "What things?"

"Like…er… dark-shaped things, dark forces… Things that are not human or the ghosts of dead people. Scary looking things…"

His face looked even paler than it usually did. Having ginger hair and a redhead's pale complexion, Dr Maxwell had always looked washed out during his lifetime. Fortunately, he had lived during an era when the paler you were, the better. It was said that those whose skin became burnished gold by the sun were the lower classes in society, such as those who worked the fields or in the outdoors to make a living. Professionals such as him, and ladies, were pale by nature as their work or pastimes kept them within doors. It marked him out – rather like one's wardrobe, shoes or method of travel – as being a gentleman. Nowadays, it appeared people liked to be brown and even sprayed a dark substance on their skin to dye it. He couldn't understand why.

The Jews began calling out in the street; she could hear them distantly. The older man was shouting something in a foreign language. She tried to ignore them.

William swallowed then began. "Yes; yes, we do have such things in our realm. Those who were never carried in a woman, never born or died; inhuman things." He hoped that would suffice; he didn't like talking about these things,

254

as if just mentioning their existence would conjure them up before him, like magicians drew rabbits from hats.

She wouldn't let it drop. *"What are they? Where do they come from?"*

He frowned again; slowly, he picked at his nails. His colleagues had told him a gentleman should have clean, neat nails, but he picked at his, and so they had never been neat his whole life. His wife also used to mention it; she used to say his picked-at nails spoilt his appearance.

"There are many different things that are not ghosts. There is energy, which just comes from the earth. It is benign, but does sometimes cause chaos in your world; men often refer to it as a poltergeist. Then there are sprites, which, again, were never born of a human; they are most mysterious. There is residual energy, or memory ghosts, which are an imprint of a person who lived but who is not there now. And there are… er… others…"

"What others?" Rachel had a feeling this was what she was really after.

He shifted a little in his seat. "We do not like to speak of them; they come from somewhere else."

"Evil things?" she asked.

"Yes… darker forces, entities and… others…"

"What do entities look like?"

He began to look uncomfortable. "Entities are like dark shadows or masses; they are like the foot soldiers of the underworld… They are there to drain joy, bring sadness and melancholy, or illness… to whomever they haunt."

Rachel frowned; this sounded like the stain. *"What about the others?"*

255

"You won't see them; they are invisible to mortals unless they inhabit the body of a host… You don't need to even think about them. Why are you asking about this?"

"I think I have an entity in my house. A little while ago, Andy and I went to the home of a rich gentleman, a sheikh; you saw one of his wives when we last met. I saw this thing, like a dark stain on the stairs. I felt its power and its heat. It kind of rushed towards me and was gone. I now feel it is here."

Dr Maxwell became annoyed. "You should not be interfering with dark forces; you are mortal and have no idea what you are dealing with."

"I didn't ask to bring it home, but I think it's here. I am going to ask Andy if he can exorcise it and get rid of it."

The Jews' chanting became more aggressive outside.

Rachel stood up and peered out of the window. *"Blasted people. I can't help them. I think they want me to do something to get them into their Jewish heaven, but I can't. I think I might tell them so."*

"I wouldn't if I were you…" Dr Maxwell looked worried. "I am not sure that's why they are there."

She sat down again. *"Then why are they bloody well out there? I am fed up with spirits asking me about 'the outcome' or whatever it is."*

"The answer," he corrected.

"Well, I don't know the answer, or the question or whatever else…"

He could see she was agitated, and he felt he needed to try to reassure her. He reached out to put his hand on top of hers, but, of course, it sailed straight through.

However, even though their skin had not connected, she had felt him. Slowly, she looked up and went to speak. It seemed like their eyes were locked for hours, but it must have been seconds only.

"William…"

Everyone jumped as Henry unexpectedly appeared around the doorframe, his wig, as usual, awry.

Dr Maxwell withdrew his hand rapidly and stood up, clearly alarmed. *"What in God's name do you want, Henry?"* he bellowed.

"Sorry… I…" He looked at the doctor's now flushed face and Rachel's onesie. He swallowed then continued, "I thought you might want to know that the gentlemen outside are becoming somewhat aggressive." He looked at Rachel. "I do not think they like you very much."

"They probably want me to tell them how to get to heaven, but I can't," she suggested.

"I do not think that is what they are saying… They are saying—"

"Henry!" William snapped again. He turned to Rachel. "Henry and I will do our best to get rid of them; you stay in here and, whatever you do, do not invite them in or speak to them."

In a flash, Henry and Dr Maxwell were gone.

She looked out of her window and watched them speaking to the older man with the black book. Voices were raised between them, but she could not hear the words as a strong wind was blowing. Whatever they said did the trick as the older man made a hand signal and they all hurried away, following their leader.

Dr Maxwell turned back to look at her, framed in the window. She raised her hand in a little wave and thought he might reciprocate, but he didn't; instead, he just turned with Henry and vanished slowly in front of her eyes.

CHAPTER 37

Four days had passed since Dr Maxwell had visited Rachel. In the meantime, she had not heard from him or that annoying youth Henry, but to not hear from the latter was a relief; she didn't really like Henry, as he was too snobbish.

Rachel rarely went out of her flat now. She often suffered from panic attacks when she was out, being scared of when her head would start pounding and how she would get home; it was a vicious cycle. When she got migraines and headaches, she was in agony, and on the odd occasions when she wasn't experiencing pain she was instead suffering from panic symptoms, as her brain raced along, envisioning all kind of horrors for her future. Her mind filled with visions of terror, such as she was going to have another haemorrhage or a stroke, or that she would end up living alone, sitting in a wheelchair. As the weeks passed, going out in public became more of a chore. She would feel the fear rise as soon as she was a certain distance from her flat, like waves engulfing her, and certain situations made her particularly unwell, such as large crowds, heat or loud noises.

She had meant to stay in her flat that day and watch some tedious TV documentaries to distract her troubled mind, but then Andy had texted her, saying he needed to go over a few things. She wished Dr Maxwell could ring or text her, she would welcome his messages, but there were obvious issues with this. Firstly, she doubted a ghost could even hold a phone, and a Victorian gentleman was hardly likely to know what a text message was, let alone send one.

At 1pm that day, Andy arrived in his new car. She watched him park outside and hurry up the steps. There had been no Jews outside since Dr Maxwell's visit. Goodness knows what he had told them, but she didn't care; they were gone and that was good enough.

Rachel led Andy to the small balcony that could be reached from her spare bedroom. A tiny, circular table and two iron chairs had been set up there. On the table there were two glass cups, a bottle of lemonade, two teacups (one chipped) and a teapot. There were no cakes or biscuits, only hot and cold drinks. Andy was disappointed.

He pushed his slightly overweight frame around the table and sat on one of the uncomfortable iron chairs, looking out over the back gardens. In the distance, a large block of flats dominated the skyline with the name 'Shangri-La House' displayed across its facade.

"You wanted to see me, Andy?" Rachel sat down opposite him with an overlarge, dark cardigan pulled round her shoulders.

"Er… yes." Not having been offered a drink, he poured himself some lemonade, didn't offer any to Rachel, and continued. "I just wanted you to know that the business is going really well. Bookings are coming in thick and fast. As you know, I am dealing with the smaller ones…"

Yeah, you get all the money, that's why, thought Rachel.

"But, with the larger, high-profile jobbies, we need to go in as a team." He gulped the lemonade down, lifted the lid of the teapot and sniffed the tea. Wrinkling his nose, he replaced the lid. "Even though I thought it was a total clusterfuck at Howland Hall, as you know, the feedback we got from it was really positive, and they want to do more, bigger hunts, not only in the house but in the grounds. Some dude hung himself in a tree in the gardens once, so maybe his ghost is floating about."

"Hanged, not hung."

"That's what I said. Anyway, it's all good. I spoke to Luke, the reporter bloke, about us maybe doing some column thing in the paper, every couple of months or so. People could email in with stuff like problems with spooks, and then we can offer advice."

She looked back at him, but said nothing. Somewhere off in the distance, a magpie called out.

"Anyway… another idea of mine was that we could maybe speak to your ghost mate Dr Mantell and ask him about what it is like being dead, what happens when you die… shit like that. We can write about that as well," Andy explained.

Rachel frowned. "It's Dr Maxwell. Look, I don't think you are taking this seriously, Andy. For you, it's all about making money, putting on some kind of show, and trying to explain something that is very difficult and complicated in an easy way; it can't be done. And all this talk about getting rid of ghosts… They don't want to go most of the time. For example, the rabbi in Victor's house hasn't gone anywhere; we will probably get a call any day now saying things are worse than ever."

"You're a bloody pessimist, that's your problem," grumbled Andy. "You've got this great gift to see dead people and all you do is mope about. We have this unique chance to really make a difference."

"Make you money, you mean. What about pondering the meaning of life? Asking why do some people pass straight on when they die, and why some get stuck as ghosts on earth? That's the big issue. If we solved that, could you imagine the enormity of it?"

Andy was pouring himself more lemonade. His phone went off. Like lightning, he snatched it up and walked off into the hallway to answer. Rachel frowned.

His voice, although lowered, could be clearly heard. "I told you to wait till I rang you… Yes, yes, I know… I was going to ring…"

Getting up, she walked slowly to the kitchen to see if she had any food to offer Andy.

Then she saw it. It was the middle of the afternoon, and her kitchen was well lit – not dark or shadowy – but there it was: the entire far-left corner of her kitchen was in dark, seeping shadow. The stain, entity or whatever the hell it was, as first seen in the sheikh's house, had returned. It looked so out of place against the bright room, but the sunlight, streaming in from the window, did not touch the enveloping darkness.

It appeared to have been in the process of spreading throughout the room until she walked in, then it abruptly stopped, as if caught out. She stopped, and it stopped. For a second, her mind went blank. What should she do or say to it? Then she saw it was moving slowly again as its quest to cover the kitchen continued. Her sink, worktops and cupboards were gradually being hidden behind an unrelenting, thick, silky blackness. On the back wall, where it appeared to have started, that face began to form again, with eyes first, then mouth…

"Andy?" She looked back nervously.

The eyes began to take a slanted shape, and a smaller circle within the eye started opening. The mouth began to gape. She felt a force again coming from it; the feeling was like the silent bass from a speaker, and there was an icy coldness in the air, like a door to Alaska had been opened. She stepped back.

"Andy… *Andy!*" she screamed louder now.

"All right… for fuck's sake…"

She heard his footsteps coming.

Almost the second he entered the room, she felt the rush of whatever it was sucking back into the wall, sliding and whooshing, back to wherever it came from.

"Is there any grub going?" he asked.

"Did… did you see it? By the wall… on the wall? I think you scared it off!" declared Rachel.

Andy had indeed seen something, but he was unsure what it was. When he walked in, he saw half of the kitchen kind of get a little hazy in front of him. He had wondered for a moment if it was due to the magic mushroom he had sniffed in the hippie shop during the week. But it seemed as though Rachel had seen it too.

She hurried towards him and grabbed his arm. He stood back; he wasn't overly keen on physical displays of affection or touching.

"What was I meant to have seen?" Andy enquired.

She stood back from him, fixing him with her gaze. "You never saw it, did you? The black thing on the wall."

"No." He decided that she was seeing something frightening due to her migraine attacks; didn't people see zigzag lines or something when they were coming on? Or maybe she was just bloody barking mad; all those pills she popped couldn't be good for the mind.

"Jesus; God." She walked over to the sink and leant on it heavily.

"Look, I had better go now, but I am glad we had that catch up. The business is doing better than ever, keep up the… er… good work…" With that, he left.

Rachel sat in her kitchen, staring at the now ordinary looking room. It was clear that whatever she had seen in the sheikh's house had come back to haunt her instead, but what was she to do about it? She felt very tired and ever so slightly sick.

★

It was 11.30pm, and Andy was sitting in his special captain's chair, fashioned to look like the chair Captain Kirk sat in while commanding the *Starship Enterprise* through its various adventures. In front of him was his new computer; the only thing out of place was the old writing desk the laptop sat on. It had been his father's. His mother wanted to throw it

263

out when his dad had died, but Andy had saved it by asking a friend to tie it to the top of his Land Rover and take it to Mrs Braithwaite's. This was before he had officially moved in, but she had still kindly stored the writing desk for him without qualm or complaint. He honestly didn't know what he would have done without Mrs Braithwaite. She was like a friend, mother and grandmother in one, and he often had low moments wondering what he would do when she passed.

He was in the middle of writing a press release for Luke Fairfax, to introduce their new newspaper column, which was due to start in two weeks' time. Called simply 'Ghost Stories' it was going to be an agony-aunt-type page for people thinking they may have a paranormal problem. Readers would email the paper with their issues, experiences and, hopefully, photos, and then Andy and Rachel would answer them, giving advice as to what type of haunting they may be experiencing. They would also be heavily plugging Spirit of London Paranormal Investigations if the haunting seemed troublesome. Andy rubbed his hands together with the thought of the new income stream this would generate.

He then felt it, caressing his body coldly like a kind of mild panic attack. It raised thoughts of Rachel, the kitchen and the ethereal haze he had seen there. He rubbed his face, and once again blamed his time spent in the hippie shop. He must have inhaled something he shouldn't have.

Andy looked back at the screen, with the words sitting there, impotent, in front of him. He couldn't get the piece to sound the way he wanted, or spooky or interesting enough. In his head it sounded good, exciting, edgy and a sure hit with the public. On screen, it looked like crap.

"Fuck it…" he muttered. Let Luke rewrite it. It was the reporter's job to make it sound more interesting, not his; he was not a writer, nor did he want to be one.

As Andy stood up, his head began to slowly fill with intrusive thoughts of Rachel, curled up in a ball on the floor, with blackness everywhere. He walked to the bed and frowned. Picking up his phone, he decided to call her; he wasn't sure why, but he felt he needed to check in. It rang for a moment, and then the dial tone changed; the sound reminded him of an overseas call. There was a long purr then a click, a long purr then a click. He started to feel uneasy, but carried on waiting. After a loud click at the end, he heard rasping breathing.

"Rachel? Rachel? Is that you? It's Andy… Are you OK?" He was starting to panic. There was nothing good about the sound coming from the other end of the line. The breathing became quieter, followed by a long, feeble moan. "Rachel? Are you ill? Shit!" He didn't know what to do. Maybe she had experienced another brain bleed; he needed to see if she was OK.

High-pitched laughter erupted from the earpiece, like a crazed, chattering primate…

Andy hung up, grabbed his keys and swiftly left the house. Something was wrong. He knew it. After jumping into his car, he sped off towards Rachel's flat, with his heart racing and the sick taste of bile burning the back of his throat as he drove. The road seemed more empty than usual; the street sounds were quieter and muffled, similar to when heavy snow had fallen.

Within twenty minutes, he pulled up outside her flat. It

was in darkness. He got out of the car, hopped up the steps and knocked on the door.

"Rachel? Rachel?" he called frantically.

Even though he was sure the door was locked closed, when he knocked again, he noticed it was open an inch. After pushing it gently, he entered the darkness of the hallway.

"Rachel? Are you OK? Jesus…" He had visions of her dead in bed or on the floor somewhere. When his father had died, he had been urged to go and see him lying in the chapel of rest, but Andy had refused. He had only been a young man at the time, but he had known for certain that he wanted the last mental image of his father to be one of him alive and laughing, not waxen-faced, cold and dead in a coffin.

Ahead, he saw the kitchen; an odd, purple haze was coming out of the door in wisps. Slowly, he crept towards it, his mind racing. Had she killed herself with some odd fumes or something?

Looking around the doorframe, he saw her. Just as in his mind's eye, back in his room, she was on the floor on her knees, with her head lowered as if in a yoga prayer position. Above her was a swirling, thick, black mist, as dark as ink and totally impenetrable, with an outer layer of what looked like softly glowing, purple dry ice.

He just stood there, stunned. He had never seen anything like this. What the hell was it? Had Rachel been pissing about with Ouija boards or something? He wasn't scared, because he didn't fully understand what he was looking at, but it seemed to have some control over her. It was clearly some kind of paranormal thing, that much was for sure.

He took a deep breath and bellowed, "*Step forth ye spirit…*" but held off asking it to show itself, as it was apparent that it was actually showing itself enough already; any more showing of itself might be a very bad idea indeed.

The dark black and purple mist that was enveloping Rachel seemed to freeze in mid-air. He heard Rachel gasp gently as she was engulfed by the smog.

"Begone, vengeful spook. Leaveth this place," he commanded as he edged his way towards Rachel, his head filled with the thought that he should have brought his special Stetson. As he got closer to the mist, every bone in his body started to ache, and it was as if time was slowing down. It felt like minutes passed before he managed to get to Rachel's limp body, though it must have been only seconds. He grabbed her around the waist and pulled her towards the kitchen door.

Andy thought the mist would somehow stop him, but it didn't seem to. He dragged her out the door and along the hallway. As he neared the front door, he had visions of it being stuck shut, as often seen in horror films, but it opened easily enough, and they got out into the street.

Once out into the colder air, Rachel began to revive. He sat her on the steps and propped her up against the handrail, to prevent her from slumping onto his shoulder in an overly intimate fashion.

Coughing, she opened her eyes slowly. "Wha… what happened?"

"I don't know; some kind of entity is in your flat… At least, that's what I think it is," Andy confirmed.

"Oh God."

"Are you OK? What happened?"

267

"I can't remember. I went to the kitchen to get a drink, and I… I remember feeling faint. I fell to the floor, then the face… it was over me…" She turned to look at him.

He could see she had a bruise on her cheek, probably from falling.

"Can you get rid of it?" asked Rachel. "You are a paranormal expert, after all."

A paranormal expert Andy was not. He bit his lip a little. Most of the so-called hauntings he visited were either in the mind of the person who called him, which accounted for 85% of his visits, or were caused by something very normal like a knocking pipe, an inquisitive magpie or buildings just making the normal creaking noises that they do; they were not paranormal in nature at all. He had experienced a couple of cases where, to be honest, there was an element of paranormal behaviour about them, but he had resolved them more through luck than proper investigation or exorcism. He wouldn't have a bloody clue what to say to the mist, entity or whatever it was.

"Andy… can you get rid of it?"

"Why do you think it's haunting you?" Andy questioned.

She wiped her nose with her sleeve. "I first saw the thing in the sheikh's house, at the top of his stairs; I think it kind of followed me home. Can entities do that?"

"I guess they can do what they want. Maybe it felt drawn to you or something…"

"Oh God." She buried her face in her hands, and then looked up. "You can get rid of it, can't you?"

"At least you managed to get to the phone when I called you, thank God."

"The phone? What phone? What do you mean?"

"I just thought you were in a bad way, I don't know why, so I rang you… You answered, remember? But your breathing sounded a bit dodgy. I thought maybe you were having a bit of a funny turn, because you started laughing."

Rachel looked at him. "I didn't answer anything; my phone is on charge in the bedroom. I don't have any family and no kids, so there's no need to have it to hand; no one would ring me… I didn't answer any phone. I went into the kitchen, and the thing was there."

What the hell had answered the phone then? Andy peered back through the crack of the open front door. Whatever the entity thing was, it appeared to have gone now, from what he could see. The mist certainly wasn't present anymore.

Silently, just below where Andy and Rachel were sitting, behind the steps and shrouded by darkness, stood Dr Maxwell. It was unusual for a ghost to worry about being out of sight – being seen wasn't much of a problem for a spirit, as most people couldn't see him – but he knew Rachel could, so he kept down low.

He often watched her house at night, being as he never slept. He thought about her in there, alone; how he wanted to go up the steps, slide through the door and see her. But he never did. He was also quite worried about the Jewish men who gathered regularly outside her house. He had managed to fob them off last time, saying there were not enough of them in their crowd to have much effect. The rabbi appeared to take it to heart and left; maybe, upon reflection, this had been without enough argument for his liking. As far as Dr Maxwell was concerned, there surely weren't enough dead

Orthodox Jews in the area to make the group much larger, so there was hardly a great risk of them returning with double the number. It hadn't been the greatest idea he'd had for dispersing the chanting men, but it seemed to have worked, at least for now.

Tonight, he had been standing in the street as usual, watching the sleepers curling up on the pavement or going in nearby houses, pretending to enter the embrace of slumber, like fools. But then he had seen Andy turn up and rush to Rachel's front door. He wanted to follow Andy in, but decided it might be more prudent to stay outside. He didn't like to interfere with the lives of the living; it wasn't his place. But, in Rachel's case, he would sometimes make an exception. After all, she was interfering with the lives of the dead.

He had heard their entire conversation afterwards. It appeared that an entity had now lodged in Rachel's flat, and had clearly followed her from somewhere that she and that blasted Andy had visited; what did she say, a sheikh's house? His face darkened a little; this was the price to pay for interfering in what did not concern them.

Dr Maxwell had never been interested in the Middle East. He had known of fellow doctors travelling to the land of scalding sand and blazing sun, to seek out cures and do research. But, in his view, the hard way of life, dangerous infections and terrible heat in that part of the world (he hated heat) had convinced him to not follow in their footsteps. He had never met a sheikh, nor did he want to.

He briskly walked away, hoping Rachel would not look up and see him; it was clear that Andy could handle the situation, and it did look like the entity had run out of steam. Rachel obviously needed help; her power was going to get her in trouble if she wasn't careful. Perhaps this entity was what she was alluding to when they spoke together on the hospital benches. He had been stupid and played it down, confirming it was a sprite, but this was no sprite. At least there was something good in this: an entity wasn't good news, but there were things far, far worse than that in the underworld. If Rachel had an entity attached to her, she would be able, somehow, to get rid of it. There were things that simply couldn't be destroyed or got rid of. Things could be worse indeed.

He had heard Rachel mention the name of the sheikh once before: Sheikh Mohammad bin al-Rahman, he believed his name was. There couldn't be many men called that in London, so he would ask Henry to help him find the address. Then what? He hadn't thought that far ahead.

Henry was a nuisance most times, but, in finding out information in the world of the living, he had become very useful indeed. Henry had become especially taken by the new invention of the internet. William did not understand the internet at all; many ghosts were afraid of it, what with its magical powers of connecting those all over the world at great speed, the amount of information it held and how it was accessed by using a machine called a computer, or other similar contraption. William had looked at a computer once, trying to work out how the steam that powered it entered the system; he had seen a small plastic string attached to it, and had assumed the steam somehow went through that. But Henry enjoyed finding out how it worked; he even once foretold how one day it might be possible for spirits to merge with the internet and become as one.

Ghosts in the machine indeed. It was not to Dr Maxwell's taste at all. Give him a pretty young woman singing at a piano any day; blasted modern inventions.

CHAPTER 38

It had taken Henry just one day to find the address of the sheikh. He had told Dr Maxwell he had used the internet and discovered a story about a big celebration that had been held at the sheikh's house to mark the acquisition of an important racehorse. The street name had been in the piece and, after that, the residence had been easy to find.

Henry had insisted forcefully on accompanying William to the palatial home, and, at first, due to misjudgement, the pair had manifested in the gents' toilet of a nearby downmarket public house. A quick adjustment later, and they reappeared in the magnificent courtyard.

Henry tugged at his wig. Today, as always, he was – in Dr Maxwell's opinion – dressed garishly. Wearing a fancy, large, red coat, trimmed with gold edging, white hose on his legs, and large, black buckled shoes, he looked quite the dandy. William even fancied he saw a trace of lip stain at his mouth.

The doctor thought about remarking that Henry looked more like a maid than a boy, but then decided against it.

"So, what are your plans whilst here, Doctor?" Henry asked.

"I am unsure. I am going to go into the house, see if I can find out any more about the entity that has attacked Rachel, and then go. I do not plan to stay for long," Dr Maxwell explained.

"I will accompany you."

Abruptly, William's eyes went round with silent alarm.

"Er… no; no, Henry you are best placed to stay here. Keep a watch on the courtyard, so as to see who comes and goes."

Unconvinced, Henry sat on a small stone lion under a weeping willow tree; he didn't look happy.

"Very well. I will remain here, but if you are longer than the turn of an hour, I will come for you."

"Indeed," muttered Dr Maxwell. William was unsure how Henry, who, if he remembered correctly, was from the 1700s, could possibly know when an hour had passed. Did they have watches back then? If so, did Henry come back in spirit form with his own timepiece? William remembered in life that he had a fine golden pocket watch that had been presented to him from the College of Surgeons. When he died and came back in spirit, it seemed the watch had not returned with him. For some reason, known only to God, William walked the land of the dead with only two remnants of his old life; these were an old handkerchief and a miniature of his mother-in-law. But no pocket watch. No matter how hard he tried to imagine it, the watch would not appear. The last thing he would have wanted to take into the spirit realm was any memory of his mother in law, perhaps God was trying to prove some kind of point.

Leaving Henry to the now familiar whittling stick, Dr Maxwell slipped silently through the main doorway. He looked about at the opulent hallway and staircase. Walking slowly down the entrance hall, he turned his head into the living area, and then walked in unhurriedly.

He had visited some exquisite houses of wealth in his lifetime, the homes of important surgeons and heads of state, but this was by far the most splendid modern living space he had ever seen. Large, framed paintings adorned the walls, thick carpets and polished floors were underfoot, and there was gold everywhere, like the inside of a mythical palace from a storybook.

In the corner of the enormous room sat a smallish, older, Saudi Arabian man, dressed in a flowing, white robe and headpiece. Around him, were five younger men, again Saudi Arabian, dressed in the now familiar identikit robes. William drew closer and watched the older man as he waved some papers in the faces of the others – this was probably Sheikh al-Rahman – and he appeared slightly angry. Speaking in quick, fluent Arabic, one of the other men tapped at an iPad and held it up, pointing to a graph displayed on the screen, which was presumably meant to appease the sheikh. Instead, Sheikh al-Rahman's voice rose to a chattering crescendo as he threw some of the papers on the lap of one of the other men and began waving his hands about.

Bored, William left the living room and looked down the hallway. Slowly, his interest was drawn to the sweeping, large staircase; after pausing to glance back at the shouting sheikhs, he ascended the stairs.

On the landing, he stopped and looked towards the spotlessly clean wall that faced him. Touching it with his fingers, he recoiled; something paranormal had been here, perhaps the entity, but maybe something else. Before his mind could follow this train of thought for too long, his interest was gently tugged by a large, gold-framed door to his right.

Slipping through the door, he found himself in what was clearly an important person's bedchamber; looking around, he saw the usual colour scheme of gold and red covering just about every surface: the floor, walls, chairs, etc. As he went to walk further into the room, he saw her.

She was an exquisitely beautiful woman in her mid-to-late twenties, with long, thick, brown hair tumbling down her back, and was wearing a small vest top and loose-fitting, black, silk drawstring trousers. With pale skin and bright, brown eyes, she was half sitting, half lying on the bed, reading a thick, bound book.

At that very moment, he saw her, and she looked up and saw him. Both started, with William stepping back and the girl visibly jumping, causing her book to smack onto the floor.

It took a good ten seconds for William to realise she could see him. Recovering swiftly, he reached for his hat to lift it by way of introduction and apology, realised he had not put a hat on that day, and slowly dropped his hand to his side.

"Mistress, my apologies. I am not used to being visible to the living," he offered.

"So I see," she said aloud.

"My name is Dr William Maxwell, from East London; I died in a fire."

She sat up unhurriedly and signalled that he should sit in a large chair in front of her. As he sat, she said, "I am sorry to hear that. I am Laya, wife of Sheikh al-Rahman..." She paused, her eyes unfocussed for a second. "Well... *one* of the many wives of Sheikh al-Rahman. You haven't come here to see me I suspect..."

"No, madam... no... Unfortunately not... I have a... friend... I believe she came here. Her name is Rachel Holloway; she sees the dead..." He was still contemplating being in the presence of another living person who could see him. He wasn't sure whether he liked it or not. Dr Maxwell always preferred to be in the shadows, and anonymous, both during his lifetime and deathtime.

"Like me." She smiled at him.

He was taken by her beauty, and her dark-brown eyes were like small pools; a man could find himself falling in if he weren't careful. "Indeed... ahem... yes. She came here a while ago with a nincompoop called Andy Horton; do you remember them?"

"The paranormal investigators? Yes, indeed I do. I didn't think much of them, and, to be honest, whilst they were here, most of what they did revolved around insulting my husband and our home."

He sat forwards, genuinely interested. "How in God's name did they do that?"

"Oh, Andy did, by playing Western music and using forbidden words within these walls."

"I suspect that would have struck a low note."

"To be honest, I am surprised that Andy did not get struck himself, by my husband. But anyway, all was forgiven in the end. He did what others failed to do: he removed the entity. It's gone, and my husband is delighted." She frowned.

"That is the problem, my lady. Rachel somehow transported the entity back to her house; it is haunting her."

"So you are here to try to help her?"

"Yes, by finding out about the entity and how to get rid of it. Can you assist me?"

She got up and walked to her bureau, where a jug of water was sitting; she poured herself a glass. He couldn't stop his eyes being drawn to her figure as she stood with her back to him. After turning around, she stood there, still smiling and glass in hand. He quickly averted his gaze.

"I'm not sure that I can. I can only tell you the entity is bad but not evil. I would say that there are worse things Ms Holloway could invoke. A good medium could be rid of it. I could command it, I suspect," she explained.

He looked at her. "You? But your husband called someone else to banish it from your house; why did you not just remove it yourself if you didn't want it here?"

"I didn't want it to go. It gave me something to occupy my mind; it used to visit me at night, in bed… unlike my husband."

Dr Maxwell felt embarrassed, and most certainly did not wish to pursue that particular angle any further. "I er… see…"

"I liked it… It paid me attention. I made the mistake one night of shouting out when it came to me. My husband interpreted it as a scream of fear… I screamed out, but it wasn't fear. He called in various people to get rid of it; they all failed, until your friend." Her mouth turned down unexpectedly in a look of disappointment.

She drank deeply from the water again and put the glass

down. "This Andy Horton man, he claims to be a psychic, so can't he get rid of it and send it back here perhaps?"

"Madam, I do suspect Mr Horton could not remove a wasp from a window. In any case, I am worried as the entity appears to have tried to attack Miss Holloway."

"Then it clearly doesn't like her. It never attacked me."

He stood up. "Dear lady, if you would be so kind, may I reserve the right to call upon you again if you permit?"

"You are leaving so soon, Dr Maxwell? Why not stay longer?"

He went to doff his hat again, and remembered once more that he had no hat. "I am afraid not, my lady. I fear for Miss Holloway and need to try to help her; not only to get rid of this spirit but to try to protect her from the dangers of the underworld. She is, in my view, somewhat naïve to the ways of men and spirits."

She walked from her position by the bureau and stood across the closed door to her room, barring the exit. "You are in love with this woman, yes?"

He stared at her. "Love? I am dead, a spirit, mere ether… How can I love a living woman? I could not touch her, kiss her, hold her…"

"You have not denied it."

He cast his gaze downwards. "I am married; my wife…" His eyes closed a little. "She died just after me."

"In the fire?"

"No. Afterwards… When I died in the fire she found me and it brought on…" He looked up at her, his eyes glistening. "That doesn't matter anymore, but I believe that I could have possibly prevented it."

"In answer to your question, William, you are always very welcome here in my room; you do not have to ask…"

He wiped his eyes and stood in front of her. Her beauty was captivating. He couldn't fathom why on God's earth her husband paid her no attention; he certainly would if she were his wife. "Madam, I must bid you good day. If you would step away from the door."

"You can move through doors, walls or anything else if you wish to; but if you want to leave you need to pass through me." She smiled captivatingly at him and gave a little laugh.

They both heard a loud male voice, shouting in Arabic, coming from somewhere outside the room. Someone was bounding up the stairs; it sounded like a heavyset man.

Understanding her request, Dr Maxwell said, "Farewell, my lady," and, within a second, he passed straight through her and out of the door.

As their souls met for a second, she closed her eyes with the quick rush of bliss that pulsed through her body.

For a moment, he remained on the landing, savouring his first emotional contact with a woman for over a century, but it was not to last. Standing at the top of the stairs, William witnessed a particularly well built bodyguard (the same one who had been at the shrine opening) hurrying up the stairs, his robes flapping. When he reached the landing, the bodyguard began to push heavily on Laya's bedroom door, shouting in Arabic, presumably demanding entry. With a smash, the door gave way, and William heard Laya scream.

Dashing for her bureau, she snatched up a veil lying on the top and held it roughly to her face. "*Idiot!*" she shouted at him, "*I am not in my niqab!*"

"*What is happening up there?*" roared Sheikh al-Rahman from the entrance hall.

William stayed rooted to the spot, slightly amused.

The bodyguard, with aviator sunglasses stuck to his swarthy face, shouted back. "Your wife was talking to someone in her room; I heard her!"

"Which wife?" inquired Sheikh al-Rahman.

Laya carried on shouting, struggling to cover her body with a black shapeless robe that had been lying on her bed. "*Fool! If I had anyone in this room, where has he gone? He would have to be invisible, yes?*"

Smiling, William walked down the stairs, straight past the furious sheikh, through the front door and out into the bright sunlight.

Outside, another scene of chaos greeted him. Two equally burly bodyguards were yelling at each other in Arabic and pointing to a wide, low-slung sports car that was hovering gently, several inches off the ground.

Standing nearby was Henry, laughing and pointing. "Greetings, Dr Maxwell; did you find what you sought within?"

"Er… yes… What are you doing, Henry?"

"Isn't it a mirthful sight? I have made their motorised horseless carriage levitate… It is a new trick."

The Lamborghini started to float smoothly towards where they were standing, as if some invisible breeze were pushing it. Meanwhile, the bodyguards were calling out to the skies, and the sheikh appeared in his doorway. "What evil is this?" he exclaimed.

"I think it is time to go, Henry; put that contraption

down, please. I think we have caused enough mayhem in this place today."

The supercar fell slowly to the ground with a gentle bump, and Dr Maxwell and Henry vanished.

William's last two thoughts as he disappeared were, firstly, about Laya, and then a wish that they did not reappear in the stinking public house latrine on the way back. He had experienced more than enough excitement that day, and revisiting a noisome pisser – even in spirit form – was certainly not welcomed.

CHAPTER 39

Rachel had seen the entity three more times during the week since the first incident, in which Andy had come to rescue her. It had not attacked her again, so to speak, but she felt strongly that it was trying to force itself on her in some way. The first time it appeared in her living room, again manifesting from the top corner of her room downwards, with no face, just darkness. The second time was in her bedroom; this time the face was there as it slid from under her bed like a black fog. The third time it appeared from the ceiling of her bathroom, together with the eerie, white-faced women. Not only did the women poke their heads through the ceiling, but just to add to the horror, had started whispering as well.

Every time the entity appeared, she experienced the silent-bass vibration emanating from it, which made her feel like her head had been placed in a vibrating vice that was crushing down on the plates of her skull bones. The first time it had gone into her, in the sheikh's house, she had felt heat. Now, when it was around, all she felt was intense cold – icy, freezing cold.

She wondered, firstly, what this thing was and, secondly and most importantly, could Andy get rid of it? She had asked him about it a few times, but he had been very non-committal. This lack of answers was beginning to worry her.

It was a Friday afternoon, and Rachel was lying in bed even though it was only 2pm. That past week, she had felt no urge whatsoever to rise (was she depressed?) and a migraine was coming on, yet again. The gentle pulse of pain began like a lover's hand touching the side of her head, but then grew in intensity over the hours until it was like a drill tearing through bone and sinew into her brain. She had taken her meds, just like the doctor had told her to, but, as was the typical case now, they didn't seem to be working as well as they used to.

She felt the pain pulsing, not only through her skull but seeping into her consciousness. What if this was all she had left now? As each week passed, the pain of her headaches and migraines grew worse and more frequent. She had spoken to neurologists, who just kept trying her on new pills, which either made her gain weight or become tired. She felt exhausted enough as it was. Every spirit she saw took a little more of her energy and hope away each time she laid eyes on them, to lose more energy now was a disaster.

Rachel picked up the local paper she had laid on her bed earlier. Her vision was quite blurred now; she would need glasses soon. The headline read 'POLICE STILL SEARCHING FOR BABES-IN-THE-WOOD KILLER'. She wrinkled her nose at the title. Since the death of the second girl, a local paper had christened the murdered girls the 'Babes in the Wood' and it had caught on. She mulled it over in her mind: *So who the hell killed those two poor girls?*

She must have fallen asleep for a couple of hours after that, as, upon wakening, she first felt the throb – crushing all the left-hand side of her face and head, like a powerful neuralgia – then heard the noise. What was it? Rachel lifted her pounding head from the pillow to hear it more clearly.

There were male voices – a lot of voices – in a foreign language, seemingly coming from her living area. She closed her eyes and let her head fall back onto her pillow. Should she move and investigate it, or leave it be? It was probably more spirits come to torment her.

With a grunt, she forced herself up from the bed and walked slowly towards the deep drones that seemed to be coming from the living room. She didn't suspect burglars; it was obviously some spooks who had worked themselves up, or perhaps the entity was speaking with many tongues. *God help me.*

Stopping by the door to her living room, she gave her head and temples a final rub before entering; the pain had been made worse by her moving. The sight before her made her gasp aloud. In her living room – rocking, praying and calling to the heavens – stood about fifty Orthodox Jewish men. Pressed together, they knocked against each other in an aggressive fashion as they bobbed to and fro, clasping their religious texts to the ends of their noses. Some wore over large black hats, and others, smaller skull caps.

She felt acute annoyance, which turned to mild anger when she saw her old acquaintance, Rabbi Lieberman, two rows in, bobbing back and forth, yelling very aggressive sounding words and, presumably, praying with the others.

Summoning up additional courage to grapple with the pain which threatened to blind her, she spoke out loud from her position just inside the doorway. "Look, I don't know what you want, but I cannot help you get to heaven, OK?" Her voice was low and weak. At first, she thought no one would hear her against the chanting, wailing and loud astral shuffling caused by the numerous sets of spiritual heavy boots on her floor, but hear her they did.

As soon as her first word was uttered, they stopped and became silent, as if a plug had been pulled from each one of them; like puppets with their strings cut, they stood motionless, staring at her as if she were a circus oddity.

"Look, fine, I know. I see the dead. But I *don't* know how you can move on to God and heaven, OK? If I did, I would tell you, but I don't bloody know... You are all stuck here being ghosts, and I am sorry, but I really can't help you. So standing outside my flat doing this..." She waved her hand in their direction. "And praying to me and stuff won't help your cause."

A middle-aged man, dressed in the usual uniform of black frock coat and a white shirt and hat, came forwards. He also wore a white shawl around his neck with two blue Stars of David on the end pieces.

He walked towards her and stopped only a foot away. He looked her up and down. "My name is Rabbi Shapiro. I do not know why you believe we come here seeking salvation, for this is the last thing we would want from you. You have no power to grant it, nor would we taint ourselves by courting your favour.

"We have, in fact, been congregating to tackle the immense

286

evil that is being spread by your folly and necromancy, as it was foretold would come to pass by the boy child."

He turned to face the silent men who were hanging on to his every word, then looked straight back at Rachel. "As you seem completely in the dark about this, I will enlighten you. During your brush with death, evil forces touched you and granted you the eyes to see the departed. Instead of turning your back on this and praying for the cleansing of your soul, you seek fame and money with this so-called power. This is *yetzer hara*, and we are here to stop it. Your bridge to the world of the dead has opened up a way into the world of the living for the darkest and most malevolent creatures, so they can create havoc in our world. You stand there as an innocent, but you are not."

Rachel was struck speechless by Rabbi Shapiro's words. For a silent moment, they just gazed at one another.

"Your dabbling with the darkness was foretold by a boy whose family is touched with the ability to be able to see what will come to pass," continued the rabbi. "Brothers were told that if we did not tackle this problem, devote to putting an end to what you are doing, then evil would reign upon this world." He stood there frowning.

"A boy?" Rachel responded. *You are here because of what some boy said?* "Look, I didn't ask to be able to see the dead. Every night I go to sleep and pray that when I wake in the morning this... power... will be gone. But it isn't, and it grows stronger."

Rabbi Shapiro seemed unmoved. "At least you confess that you pray, but I doubt even that can close the diabolical gate that has been opened. As I have stated here before my brothers, the deepest, darkest evil stalks you now, and – like the man standing in a clear lake who drips ink into the water – you are tainting us all with eternal blackness. We are here to stop you being used as a tool for the *shedim*."

"*Shed... him?* What's that?" She was getting worried now at the urgency and harshness of his tone.

Four men walked forwards, all with the white scarves on and black books in their hands, which she assumed were their holy books. Rabbi Shapiro held up his hand in front of her face and began to recite more words loudly, she assumed in Hebrew.

The rest of the crowd remained silent, standing, watching...

The four men encircled her, then began speaking the same words as Rabbi Shapiro: harsh, sharp, ancient Hebrew words that she felt were forming an invisible verbal ring around her very soul.

Enough of this, who did they think she was? Feeling like her head was about to explode, she went to walk away. Her aim was to call Andy, to tell him to come over and help her. But she couldn't move; she was rooted to the spot. She felt panic rise up within her, making her extremities tingle with fear.

Rabbi Shapiro's hand was only inches from her face; she could see the wrinkled palm moving in front of her transfixed eyes. Then the entire crowd of men joined in, bobbing, shouting, casting incantations towards her. Was this some kind of exorcism? She felt the pain in her head pulse along to the chants, making her feel waves of nausea and dizziness.

Please God help me... She tried to close her eyes, but they

288

would not shut. Was this some kind of panic attack, or had the rabbi cast a spell on her? Would she die here? Condemned, like those she saw every day, to wander the earth seeking *the answer* or trying to find peace with their maker?

How long she was standing there, with the throbbing voices rising over her she didn't know.

Then it happened. Like a giant hell-bound Cheshire Cat, the entity – the thing that had been wafting around the walls of her home – appeared in the far corner of the living area. She saw the mouth first, then the eyes formed, slanting upwards. It then crept out along the walls and ceiling, its black and purple mist intertwined, behind the shouting men.

Her frozen eyes remained unblinking as she stared at it, her pupils immobile as it now covered one-third of her living room wall and ceiling in impenetrable, light-draining blackness. Her body screamed contradictions; Rachel so desperately wanted to move – to run away as far as she could, from the men and this evil entity – but she was frozen completely, like a statue, facing this horror.

Then the silent bass started, the almost inaudible pulsing that came from the entity, driving her back yet compelling her forward towards the darkness.

One of the men, right at the back, must have felt the entity's throbbing, as he stopped chanting and spun round, then turned back and began screaming something, again in a foreign language. More men turned now, some didn't make a sound, some vanished and others simply fled through the doorway.

"Stop and face the *shedim!*" commanded Rabbi Shapiro.

As he turned to face them, Rachel felt the incantation's grip loosen from her body. This was her chance. She sucked up every molecule of strength in her ruined limbs and ran from the room, rushing to the front door and scrabbling at the lock.

Of all people, it was Rabbi Lieberman she saw next, his furious little eyes and face floating through the front door panel, towards where she stood, fumbling with her door key.

"*Just bloody leave me alone, won't you?*" she yelled.

Finally, the door crashed open, and she felt herself half running, half falling down her front steps.

"Piss off! Go away! I am not a devil… *I never asked for this!*" Rachel yelled, as she sat half sprawled on the pavement, frantically waving her hands about as if batting away a swarm of wasps.

As she remained on the street, she saw the spirit Jewish men making their escape in all directions as the blackness engulfed the entire expanse of her flat, just stopping at the front door. Rachel looked up from where she sat, feeling her bottom beginning to numb from the cold, hard concrete beneath her, and remembering that she was still wearing her old house clothes in broad daylight.

Rabbi Shapiro loomed up abruptly before her. "You may have set your familiars on us, necromancer, and some brothers have faltered when faced with pure evil, but this is not the end. We will return even stronger to defeat the rotten, putrefied flesh within you." With that, he was gone.

At the sight of two more Jewish men running from her house and down the street, she began screaming again.

Slowly, she became aware of the crowd of people who

290

had formed around her in the street; she heard the words 'nutter', 'ambulance' and 'mental' float out from their number as her bloodshot eyes met their concerned, amused and frightened faces.

A policeman walked up, seemingly out of nowhere. Rachel found this particularly annoying as she recalled never being able to get a police officer to turn up in the past when she had been the victim of a crime. "Now, now, miss; it looks like you need some help here," he said in a pitying tone.

Angrily, she leapt to her feet. Everyone in the crowd took a step backwards.

"Look, I don't need any more bloody ghosts haunting me and calling me the devil... so you can piss off as well... See my house; look at it! An entity has taken it over, I have Jews wanting to kill me, and..." She looked back; her house – which, just seconds ago, had been covered in thick blackness, like a dark whipped cream poured on a pudding – was now just as it was before. There was nothing unusual at all.

"There's no need for anti-Semitism, miss," said the policeman calmly.

Rubbing her eyes, she realised that the policeman in front of her was not a ghost at all, but a real, living officer of the law who someone, probably from the gawking crowd, had called over to assist.

Oh Jesus Christ. Now what? Rachel had never been arrested before. She wondered if she was arrested, whether she would get the one phone call she saw people being offered in films. She wanted to call Dr Maxwell, but that was pointless, being as he was a ghost and didn't like phones anyway. For a second, she thought about calling John, but why would she do that? He didn't give a shit about her really.

All that was left was Andy. Like the last broken sweet in the bag or the tiny crisp always found hiding in a fold at the bottom of an eaten packet, she had to choose him, as there was no one else alive left in the world for her now.

CHAPTER 40

The three of them gathered in Andy's small bedroom. Andy was sitting stiffly on his Captain Kirk *Star Trek* chair, Rachel was seated on the bed, and Dr Maxwell stood in the corner by the window, where he had a good view of the street. Rachel always wondered why so many ghosts looked out of street-facing windows and liked standing by them; she resolved to ask him later at a more opportune time.

Andy began in a brisk tone, "Right, so we have convened here today to discuss the most recent incident that has happened at Rachel's flat, where she was attacked spiritually, and to review the future of Spirit of London Paranormal Investigations."

He glanced around the room.

"Obviously, Rachel you are here…" He gestured towards her. "And Dr Mantell is also… er… apparently here." He gestured towards the doorway; the complete opposite place to where William was standing.

"The man is a buffoon," muttered Dr Maxwell from his corner.

"Andy... Dr Maxwell is by the window, in the corner," confirmed Rachel.

"Yes, yes... right..." Andy put on a large, black-framed pair of spectacles, glanced at a tatty piece of paper with writing on it, removed the glasses and put the paper down. "This is where we are. The company, Spirit of London Paranormal Investigations, is doing very well. I have been on numerous visits to people who have experienced hauntings and have, in all cases, resolved the problem. The website is getting fifty-odd hits a day, and money is rolling in... On paper, it's all tickety-boo, to be honest."

Dr Maxwell made a small huffing noise of dismissal.

Andy continued, "But... we now have some problems that need to be resolved for us to move forward. Namely Rachel, who is back under the care of the psychiatric unit, thanks to last week's alleged episode with the Jews, and the entity which we believe came from Prince von Rahman's house."

"Those men *were* there! They were trying to exorcise me or something. I didn't make it up!" exclaimed Rachel.

"I never said you did. But, whatever you say, the company is fending off a lot of negative PR thanks to your very public breakdown. Our Twitter feed is alight with talk of you having mental issues... It's not good," declared Andy.

Dr Maxwell interjected, "All he cares about is his blasted pocket and how much he can fill it with coins; he cares not one jot about you."

Rachel looked at William then back at Andy, who threw his hands in the air.

"*Did he speak? The doctor?* You will have to tell me what he said; this won't bloody work unless you tell me what the dude says," complained Andy.

"Dude? What is a 'dude'?" asked William.

Rachel sighed. "Dr Maxwell just wants to know if you intend to do anything about it. For example, getting rid of the entity would be a good start. It's the entity that caused all of this; the Jewish gentlemen think I am in league with it in some way. That's why they tried to exorcise me."

"Yes, yes... I was going to comment on that," stated Dr Maxwell. "In truth, I am very worried about your Jewish visitors. They appeared very aggressive before."

Rachel angrily turned her head towards the window. "You think?"

Andy looked at Rachel, towards the window and then frowned. It was easier said than done having a three way conversation when one of your group was as dead as a doornail. He cleared his throat. "I am going to have a hard think about this whole situation, but, to recap, the main problems we have are the entity and the Jewish guys; to be honest, they are probably targeting you because of the entity. So we are going around in circles."

"I saw them out the front of my flat way before the entity took up residence," she confirmed.

"Yes, I know, but they never actually *attacked* you until the entity came into the frame. I think they believe they are saving the world from what they assume to be an evil person who sees demons," Andy observed.

"Me? You mean me?" Rachel was shocked.

"I don't actually feel the entity is a demon," interjected

Dr Maxwell. "I believe it is just, well, a certain kind of evil spirit."

Rachel rubbed her face. "Look, I have to be honest; there is something else I am worrying about…"

Andy shifted position. "What's that? As if we don't have enough to deal with…"

"The poltergeist/sprite thing… that I saw in the woods. I told you about it." she looked towards Dr Maxwell. "I have a terrible feeling it's not good and—"

Andy cut in, "OK, in all likelihood, the hairy woodland-ghost thing is probably linked to the entity. As if the entity has split itself into two things: the ink-blot shit that came out of the wall and this sprite monkey thing that you see in the woods. I am confident that if we deal with the entity, then any offshoot manifestation will also perish."

Rachel rubbed her eyes with exhaustion. "I am not so sure. Look, I told a bit of a lie to the police, to everyone in fact, about the first girl's remains."

"What lie?" asked Dr Maxwell.

"What do you mean lie?" said Andy, almost at the same time.

She looked at both of them, bit her lip, then continued. "Firstly, when I found the girl's body, it wasn't her spirit who showed me where it was. I said it was to the police, but that was only because I couldn't comprehend what actually *had* shown me where the remains were."

"Did the hairy poltergeist show you?" asked Andy, reaching for his spectacles again.

"Yes. It actually pointed to where the body was," Rachel confirmed.

"So you never saw an apparition of the girl?" Andy enquired, popping his glasses on his nose, making him resemble a rather fat, bemused owl.

"Yes; yes, I did, but she was odd. She didn't look normal, like normal ghosts look…" she explained.

"What do you mean?" asked Dr Maxwell.

Rachel answered, "She was pale – really pale, like she had stage make-up on – and her eyes were black, sort of dark rimmed. And there was something wrong about how she moved: it wasn't normal; it was jerky. I mean, I know ghosts are people who are dead, but when they walk, they still move like the living do. This was way different; something was wrong, I could tell."

"Did she tell you to build the shrine?" asked Dr Maxwell.

"No, no… That came to me kind of organically while I was in the area. She seemed unable to speak," she concluded.

Dr Maxwell walked from the window; he looked gravely concerned.

"What? Tell me what you are thinking," Rachel demanded.

"Did he say something?" asked Andy gesturing to where Dr Maxwell had been standing, but wasn't anymore. "This isn't going to work if whatever the blasted doctor says isn't relayed to me."

"Be quiet, Andy; Dr Maxwell is going to speak," commanded Rachel.

"Oh, I will just shut up then," Andy grumbled.

William stopped in the middle of the room and looked at Rachel. "The girl you said you saw; Kayleigh wasn't it? You said she was pale, that her movements were… inhuman… to your eyes?"

"Yes... Why? What does that mean?" Rachel questioned.

"It means she might be in, for want of a more appropriate word, hell. Her soul may well be trapped in the underworld, where the dark ones live; her soul has been taken. But we should also ponder on whether the hairy ape thing, the entity in your abode and the so-called spirit of the girl are one and the same evil force, just appearing differently. But truly, before——"

A gentle tap came at the door.

"Andy? Andy, can you come down for a moment?" It was Mrs Braithwaite.

"We don't want any tea or Battenberg cake, Mrs Braithwaite," Andy called out in a slightly irritated tone, clearly trying to get out of answering the door.

"No... I, um, need you downstairs," Mrs Braithwaite replied.

"For fuck's sake," Andy moaned, heaving his frame out of the captain's chair. "Don't you two be speaking without me, you hear?" he said before leaving the room.

They heard Andy's footsteps stomp down the stairs, and the gentle lilt of Mrs Braithwaite's voice as he descended.

Rachel looked at William. Glad to give her voice a rest, she spoke to him psychically: *"Go on, what were you saying about hell?"*

Dr Maxwell sat down beside her on the bed. He had visibly eased since Andy had left the conversation. "Mortals trapped in hell – well, that's what you may call it – or the underworld, sometimes manage to manifest in your world, but they always appear strange, inhuman and affected... Imagine, if you will, that I took you to a room next to where someone is sitting, separated by a window of frosted glass. You want to communicate with your friend in the other room, who is sitting on the other side of the glass. You shout and call, and try to press your face to the window. She can see you, but your features are distorted; she can hear *something*, but not your voice clearly, and certainly not the words that you are saying." He stood up and walked back to the window, glanced outside, then turned around to face her.

"Hell, the underworld, is like this," Dr Maxwell continued. "The person's soul – damned eternally – appears distorted in this world, but can still often be seen in some form. But, like I said, this is assuming this is this girl's hell bound spirit, not a visual trick, devised by the entity."

"I don't accept the idea of a hell; it's a Christian construct, and it doesn't actually exist," stated Rachel.

"Well, I might not believe in your modern day internet, but that does not stop it from existing. Hell is unconcerned whether you believe in it or not. In fact, the evil ones prefer that mortals do *not* believe in them, as it allows them to move amongst your kind with more ease. If you do not think that something exists, you are certainly not going to be looking out for it, or guarding against it."

A frown appeared on Dr Maxell's face as he continued: "My view is that this thought you had, to build the shrine, was placed in your mind by the entity, but I am still confused; this is more the work of a…" He coughed. "A demon than an entity…"

"Maybe the furry thing is a demon?" Rachel asked.

"No… no, it couldn't be." He crossed his arms, deep in thought. "Mortals, for the most part, cannot perceive demons. If they can see them in some form, and happen to glance upon them for any length of time, they become ill and perish, so it cannot be a demon." He seemed certain.

"Look, I see dead people, walking around, day and night, and now I am seeing entities; why would I not be able to see a demon as well?"

He turned to her sharply, clearly irritated. *"You just couldn't!"* Probably less than one in a million are capable of seeing them, and if you could, and it chose to manifest before your eyes, you would sicken and die, because your physical body could not withstand such a diabolical onslaught. A demon has the power to steal the mind of its victim, in order to use the living body as a puppet to act out its will. No, this is merely an entity; albeit an evil one that has manifested as the mist in your flat and as the furry beast you saw in the woods. Entities can still be dangerous and do hover on the peripheries of hell."

"Maybe I am the less than one in a million?" she ventured.

"It has used you; don't you see? It relished the death of the first girl, so it placed an idea into your mind to build a shrine that would be visited by other youngsters, which it can also prey on. Like I said, entities can also be evil in nature. Basically, you have been used."

"That's crap; sorry, but it is. How could a hairy entity kill someone, especially if it isn't actually a demon? And, how would you know the difference between an entity and a demon in the first place? They don't exactly wear name badges do they?"

"It has used someone else to do the deed for them; a mortal, someone vulnerable and already nursing a grudge."

"That sounds more demonic to me…" she said slowly.

Raised voices were heard downstairs, Andy's and a woman's, clearly arguing.

"Woman, *I have told you a hundred times! It is not a demon*! It cannot be!" exclaimed Dr Maxwell. "Look… look… tell me what happened when Icarus flew too close to the sun?"

Groan, another analogy. "What has Greek mythology got to do with this?"

"Tell me what happened!" he demanded.

Rachel sighed in resignation. "The wax that held his wings together melted, then he fell out of the sky, and into the sea, and drowned."

"*Precisely!* If you had gazed upon a demon, your fate would have been like that of Icarus, you would have perished, overcome by the sheer force of evil before you. Only very rare people, such as religious scholars or learned monks can gaze upon a demon and remain untouched, with their mind unturned, and their body unaffected. Why can you not just believe me?"

"Fine; you are the expert. So, basically, you are saying that this entity has used me to help it succeed in its evil plan to attack humankind, to be part of a plot to assist it in luring other young girls into hell?"

"Yes, that is essentially what I am saying. Your own power has been used against you."

Rachel immediately jumped to her feet. "Screw you! No really. Screw you to hell!" She yelled out loud. "Yeah, great; because of me, this second girl is dead, and probably more are going to go to the shrine, get murdered and burn in hell. Brilliant…" Tears welled in her eyes. "I didn't ask for this. *Do I look that stupid?* I didn't ask to see ghosts and devils everywhere. I hope the Jews come back and kill me, and then all this can be over!"

A woman's loud scream was heard downstairs, then Andy shouting again. They both paused at the sound.

"I have to get some air," muttered Rachel as she rushed out of the door.

William heard her footsteps as she ran down the stairs. He was sorry he had upset her, but, bizarre though his idea was, he was so very sure that he was right.

★

"Don't you two be speaking without me, you hear?" said Andy to Rachel and Dr Maxwell. Irritated at the interruption, he left the room, closed the door behind him, and then stared at Mrs Braithwaite. She was standing on the landing, rubbing her hands together gently; she always did that when she was nervous.

"What is it? You know you shouldn't really disturb me when I am in the middle of a business conflab," moaned Andy, worried that he was probably going to miss something interesting between Rachel and Dr Maxwell. He suspected some kind of romance thing was going on between them, but how one could do anything remotely romantic with a ghost was beyond him.

Mrs Braithwaite began to descend the stairs, with Andy behind.

"Your mother… has called again. She is downstairs and wants to speak to you," Mrs Braithwaite explained. She stopped midway down and looked back at him; he could see worry in her eyes. "I wish she wouldn't come here, Andy; really I do…"

He put a hand on her shoulder; she touched it briefly. "I am sorry, Mrs Braithwaite; I wish she wouldn't come here too. I don't know what I would have done if I couldn't have come and lived with you... There was nowhere else I could have gone," Andy declared.

"Well, you are here now, and all is well. I am just saying that if there is anything you can do to stop her... er... visiting, it would be appreciated."

As they continued down the stairs, both took care to avoid Andy's extensive collection of *Star Trek* action figures that had been left on the bottom steps, pushed against the wall. Andy had brought them down to clean them earlier, but had not yet bothered to take them back to his room.

"Andy, I have told you about leaving things on the stairs; it's dangerous, and someone could get hurt with them..." Mrs Braithwaite remonstrated.

"I am sorry; yes, I will take them up after I have dealt with this," he agreed.

A door clicked open. From their position, standing on the third step up, they saw Andy's mother enter the hallway from the living room, where she had obviously been stashed to keep her out of the way.

"Ah, Andrew... there you are..." She stared hard at Mrs Braithwaite, who walked calmly down the last steps and off into the kitchen.

"What do you want now?" he frowned.

As usual, his mother was dressed inappropriately for her age. She wore leggings, or perhaps pyjama bottoms, that looked a size too small; a tight T-shirt with a big, pink cat logo on the front; and her oversized, suede boots. Her face seemed more lined than ever, with the deep crevices highlighted by the light streaming in through the front-door glass. She had always been a heavy drinker and smoked like a trooper; Andy guessed his mother's unhealthy lifestyle was finally catching up with her.

She walked a couple of steps closer; he got a gentle whiff of booze from her breath.

"I don't know how you did what you did last time, getting that bloody voice to shout at me. I assume it was some kind of recording you hid somewhere in that hall to scare your customers. But calling your mother a bitch is low, even for you, Andrew."

He walked down the last few steps and stood there facing her, as if he had reverted back to being a frightened child, standing still, pretending to be a statue and waiting for the tirade to end. God, he wished something would happen to her to wipe her from the face of the earth and out of his life. "It wasn't a recording; it was a ghost... Someone who clearly wasn't too pleased with the way you were banging on."

Her face darkened. "Yes, of course, it was... My God, you must think I am as gullible as that thick little tart you have got upstairs. Managed to screw her yet, have you? Would be the first time ever if you did."

He plucked up as much courage as he could muster. "I would like you to leave now, and if possible, please do not return again; it upsets me and Mrs Braithwaite. You have nothing sensible to say, so I cannot see why you continue this charade."

She looked at him quizzically. He could see she didn't know what the word 'charade' meant.

"I told you before, and I will tell you again. If you want me to go, you are going to have to pay me. My husband died because of the stress you put him through, poor sod, and you owe me now," she declared.

"I owe you absolutely nothing." Andy felt his eyes getting wet with tears. "My father died through stress, and, to be honest, it was probably caused by you—"

She made a swipe at his face, and he instantly stepped back.

"Look, just bloody go, OK?" he shouted.

Mrs Braithwaite appeared quietly around the kitchen door. Her old eyes surveyed the scene: that horrible woman, Andy, and then, just to her right, standing in the hallway with his back to her, was a teenage boy, dressed in what looked like red velvet pantaloons and jacket; a very flamboyant, white, frilled shirt; and on top of his head was a powdered wig, slightly off to one side. He was staring at Andy and his mother intently. Even with her old eyes, she could see him clearly; he just looked like he had a sheet of tracing paper over him, as though he was faded out, but only slightly.

Walking two steps so she stood directly beside him, she whispered quietly, "What I wouldn't give to have that woman out of my house." She turned her head and smiled at him.

Henry started a little. He was still getting used to Rachel being able to see him, but now someone else? Being dead didn't hold the same anonymity it used to. "You see me?" he replied.

"Oh yes," she said under her breath.

Andy's mother ripped her glance away from Andy and stared at the elderly figure, who appeared to be smiling at the wall. "Jesus Christ, you have lost it, you silly, dried-up, old hag... Why the hell Andrew would—"

"Oh Cheryl, surely you can do better than that," interrupted Mrs Braithwaite.

Abruptly, the ghostly boy walked down the hallway, past Mrs Horton and Andy, and stopped in the far corner where the front door was. Sticking his tongue out with concentration, Mrs Braithwaite saw him lift up both hands in the air straight out in front of him, his fingers outstretched. Then he jerked his hands towards the ceiling.

At exactly the same time, the *Star Trek* figures, which had been sitting on the stairs, flew into the air and hung there, unmoving, as if in zero gravity.

Alerted by the sudden movement, Andy looked behind him. Seeing the figurines simply hovering in the air gave him a start. "Oh bollocks… me figures!" He went towards them and lifted his hands to scoop them from the air. But it was too late.

From his position in the corner, Henry threw both his arms down and forwards in a violent motion. In less than a second, every single figure that had been suspended in mid-air all shot forwards, like bullets fired from a gun. Whizzing past the shouting Andy, they struck Cheryl Horton, in her face, hair and chest. One poked her in the eye, and another grazed her cheek with its sharp edges.

Her hands began trying to bat them away as if she were being attacked by a swarm of wasps, her screams then filled the house as she tore at the front door and, as if being followed by a cloud of bats, ran up the path and down the street, still yelling and clawing at her hair and face.

"*My figures; my precious figures! Stop, stop!*" shrieked Andy as he scrambled to pick up the little plastic pieces from the floor, and where they had ended up caught in the folds of the assorted coats and jackets hanging on the nearby coat hooks.

It was at that moment when Andy heard Rachel tearfully storming out of the bedroom door above them and speedily running down the stairs. His eyes flew to the prone figure of Mr Spock, right in the middle of the second stair from the bottom. "*Noooooo!*" was all he could yell as Rachel stood directly on the figure, snapping the head from the body in an audible crack, before she vanished out of the door and took off down the road in the same direction as his mother seconds before.

Sitting on the step, he cradled the ruined body of Spock. "I blame the fucking doctor for this," he said sadly, inclining his head up the stairs.

Looking at Henry – who remained in position by the front door, with a small figure of Sulu by his feet – Mrs Braithwaite replied, "Blaming this on a ghost... Wouldn't your Dr Spock say that was illogical?"

Holding the broken, little figurine in his hand, Andy stared back. "*Mr* Spock... And, no, I am beginning to see how much bloody trouble spirits can be."

Dr Maxwell, seeing the scene below and that Henry was clearly something to do with it, decided against going down the stairs, and instead floated quietly upwards through the roof and out of sight. He had encountered more than enough chaos for one day.

CHAPTER 41

The creature sat on a rock in the searing heat of its world, with its mind turning over what had been happening. It frowned slowly, its hairy, prominent eyebrows eclipsing the little red eyes beneath. It was clear the plan had begun to fail, and it felt the plot strings lengthening then snapping one by one. The idea to capture souls, using the compelling pull of the shrine, and that idiot Sean, had seemed an excellent idea to start with, but it had one big Achilles heel in that it relied on mortals to succeed. Relying on meat sacks to do what they were supposed to do was inefficient; that had been proved throughout time, both by other mortals and its own kind. Young flesh, the very thing it needed to frequent the shrine, had dried up. The creature had thought the murders might cause a crowd of youngsters to visit the woods, their interest piqued by the macabre and paranormal, thus luring even more to their doom; however, it had not counted on people becoming afraid instead and staying away.

It had been lucky with Kayleigh and Mia, with them both knowing each other, and being able to use Sean against them. Two souls had been bagged with relatively little effort, but, now, relying on lone teens to visit the shrine seemed more futile as each day passed.

But it had another idea. At first, when it had seen Rachel, it was amazed to encounter a mortal who could not only see it clearly, but who didn't wither in its gaze. It had hardly ever witnessed anything like this before, not in all the millennia it had walked the earth. Its first thought was that she was a clear threat – sent, perhaps, from the place of light, to destroy it – and it had been ready to do the unthinkable: to join forces with others of its kind to get rid of her. But, then, it had reconsidered, as it often did, and decided that – far from being a threat – this girl, Rachel, could in fact be the biggest and best weapon in its armoury thus far.

Like a structure between two continents that could withstand both heat and ice without bowing or rusting, Rachel stood between the mortal world and the underworld. She was just like a human bridge, which could be used not only to lure souls from the light to the gloom, but also to bring forth evil from the darkness. It felt its skin and fur bristle with the concept. It rubbed its long, spindly hands together; then finished with one of its customary clawing scratches to its flank.

The supreme leader had, according to its gatekeeper, been interested in the creature's bold claim that it could bring forth more souls than any other. The gauntlet had been thrown down; for a basketful of souls, the creature could gaze upon the supreme leader and drink in its wisdom. Proudly, the creature had promised more than a basketful, it had pledged a whole chasm of souls, enough to fill the deepest pit.

But now its boasting was at an end, and it actually had to do what had been promised, otherwise it would likely end up finding itself roasting in the fiery pit, alongside its own victims.

Like a lumberjack, it was getting ready to fell the largest trees in the forest of souls, and Rachel would be its willing axe.

★

Rachel felt cast adrift, like a small boat thrown into the roughest sea. Her whole life had been a difficult journey of sorts: losing her parents, working a part-time job whilst training to be a teacher, the brain haemorrhage, losing the teaching career she adored, John walking out, and of course, the small issue of being able to see the dead. Some people lived an easy, charmed life, and she knew friends whose life had been simple, such as her friend Sally. Sally had gone to school, had trained at university, had become a teacher, had married her childhood sweetheart, and had a son who was now doing well in college; her parents were alive and well, and they all enjoyed family holidays together. She had no financial worries, no one hated her, and she had no specific problems to overcome. Life for her had been uncomplicated; an easy ride, like you would find in a children's fairground.

Rachel's life, on the other hand, had been marred by unwanted changes, illness, death, desertion and now this. How many people in the world suffered a near-death experience and then, unexpectedly, started seeing ghosts? She bet not many, but she did; oh yes, she did all right.

She had felt betrayed by Dr Maxwell. Before the meeting, she had believed he was on her side and that he cared about her, but, since their last conversation, she didn't know what to think. To accuse her of being as gullible as to allow an entity to manipulate her thoughts – her most intimate thoughts – to compel her to construct some kind of trap that it could use to capture souls. The whole idea was horrible and ridiculous. The theory relied on a person believing in evil entities, that they walk among us, and the idea that entities could manipulate the very minds and actions of mortals, not to mention the existence of hell. It was quite the most absurd thing she had ever heard.

However, even though it was a far-fetched notion, she decided that – much like the atheist who occasionally prays for help – she must hedge her bets and set her mind on getting the shrine removed. Then, if the projection of the entity – the hairy, ape-like thing – *was* using the shrine to lure victims, it would put a stop to its plans.

She had been walking through Darkfoot Wood and thinking at the same time. She hoped the ape thing would appear in front of her, as part of her was actually very angry, and she wondered if there was any value in confronting it. As if waking from a dream, she looked up to see the shrine in front of her; it appeared to have fallen into slight disrepair since its opening. Long weeds were growing around the bench, and thistles had started to pop through the ground. Clearly, no maintenance people had been around to tidy it up. Stopping dead, Rachel saw, sitting on the bench, the spirit of a young girl, who was between fifteen and seventeen years of age. Dressed in tight jeans and a large woollen jumper, she seemed to not notice Rachel at all. Her hair was a mousy blonde and — straight away, even from that distance — her large, blue eyes, round and innocent, were obvious.

Blast. Rachel wanted to be on her own. There was no way the hairy, ape-like thing would come out with someone here, even if the someone was a spirit. Now what was she to do?

Looking up, the girl immediately noticed her, and her face lit up with a beaming smile. "Hello," she said brightly, "I knew you would come."

"*Really?*" Rachel drew closer. "*Why is that?*"

"The spirits of the woods have told me about you, and how you made this shrine to my friend, Kayleigh. I came here one night to be closer to her, but a horrible man murdered me." She delicately wiped away a tear.

Intrigued, Rachel sat down. The eyes of the memorial teddy bear remained fixed, staring at her, as if making some kind of accusation. Ignoring the staring stone bear, she turned back to the girl; she was very pretty in a naïve-looking way.

"*Mia? You are Mia, aren't you?*" enquired Rachel.

"Yes, that's right." The girl beamed again. "And you are the woman who sees the dead; everyone is speaking about you, saying you have *the answer*. Is this true?"

Rachel looked at the ground. "*I am afraid I don't have any answer…*"

"But you see us… clearly… That is unusual, yes?" Mia shifted her position to be closer to Rachel; she held her gaze quite firmly. "To be able to see us… to speak to us… Not many people can do that."

"I am sure I am not the only person in the world who can see ghosts."

Mia smiled. "You are one of a kind, Rachel; believe me when I tell you that. You have a power that you should use for the benefit of everyone."

"It doesn't feel like a gift, more like a curse. What use is seeing dead people?"

"The police have used you, haven't they? To find the remains of the deceased?"

Rachel thought Mia had a precocious way of speaking. She was about sixteen but spoke like someone much older; 'the remains of the deceased' was an odd thing for a young person to say, why not, 'dead bodies'? But then she reminded herself that she did not know the kind of person Mia was.

"Yes, with Kayleigh," said Rachel, *"but they didn't ask about you, I am afraid. Not that I could help them. I don't feel your remains are here in the woods anyway."*

Mia sat up straight. "That's because they are not here. He shoved me in a water tank in the old Mountain View Hotel; do you know it? It's the abandoned hotel, just on Birkbank Lane."

"That's… that's where your body is… now?"

"Yes. It's best you tell the police."

Taking a deep breath, Rachel asked the obvious question. *"Do you know your murderer, Mia?"*

"That depends…"

"On what?"

"Do you have a spirit guide? Someone to help you locate the dead, like a go-between?"

Rachel thought hard. *"Well, there was this one man… a doctor, but I don't think he is too keen on helping me anymore."*

Mia began to play with a loose bit of hair by her ear. "You need a spirit guide; every psychic person has one. Maybe I can be your guide and your helper... What do you think?"

"I am not psychic. I just see dead people. I don't know if people will win the lottery or meet a tall, dark handsome stranger. I have no clue how people will die or when. I just see ghosts, and I am not sure how someone who is a ghost themselves can help with this."

"Think of how your powers could be used. Those who have been murdered can speak through you to identify their killer. People can be apprehended for terrible acts they thought they would have got away with."

"Yeah, providing the ghost knows their killer, and assuming that they are stuck here and haven't floated off to heaven."

"Or elsewhere," stated Mia with a smile.

"Do you believe in a hell?"

"If that's what you want to call it, then yes. To believe in heaven means one must believe in hell; to believe in God, then one has to believe in the supre—" she stopped, pulled an odd face, then continued. "Satan."

Rachel considered. *"Look, Mia, I do want to help your remains to be found, and if you want to help me, of course, I am very grateful..."* She paused. *"I do have to say that, for a young person who was brutally murdered, you seem to have a very positive outlook."*

"Some ghosts enjoy being ghosts... I mean what is not to enjoy? There's no sickness, tiredness, having to study or work, no worries about money, or fears of growing old and dying horribly... You can go where you want and see what you want. It's probably the closest you can get to being omnipotent. Being a ghost is great. It's better than floating off to heaven or wherever. No one survives to come back to tell the tale once they have gone there; it might be awful."

"So ghosts conjured up by mediums, and the spooks people see floating about, real ones, are only those who are stuck here, not ghosts who have gone to heaven… or wherever?"

"Correct. Once you've gone, you've gone. Like a hair in a flame, there's no coming back. When spirits pass to heaven, when they find *the answer*, they become incommunicado." She smiled again.

"So why do ghosts seek the answer, if no one knows what heaven is like?"

"Some mortals seek death when they don't really know what it is like; same difference."

Rachel seemed unconvinced. *"Well, will you tell me who killed you?"*

"May I be your spirit guide?"

"I suppose… well, yes, if you want to help me, I cannot see a problem with that."

"We can work together to help the dead, and the living…"

"Yes, OK; fine."

Mia seemed satisfied. "It was Kayleigh's stepbrother, Sean. He wanted Kayleigh sexually… Oh, don't get me wrong − they were not blood related − but she still didn't feel it was right, so she refused him, and then he killed her. I found out about what was happening, confronted him, and then he killed me. That's what you get for poking your nose in." Mia sat back and grinned.

Rachel looked stunned, and ignored the smile on her

face, which seemed quite inappropriate. *"So he killed both of you?"*

"Yes."

"Just like that?"

Mia frowned. "Passion makes people do the most violent and desperate things. Anyway, take this as me helping you to solve a crime. Tell the police where the… my body is, and that Kayleigh's stepbrother, Sean, did both murders. I'm sure they will be very grateful for your help."

"Or they will think I am nuts, or that I did it."

"He strangled me with such force that he crushed my windpipe; you wouldn't have had the strength to do that." She smiled again, as if speaking about buttercups and puppies.

Rachel stood up. *"Well, I had better get this news to the police, hadn't I?"* She went to hurry off, then stopped. *"How do I find you again Mia, should I need you?"*

"Come here and call me, and I will come."

"Er… okay. Look, tell me, what made you come to the shrine in the first place, when you were alive, I mean… Did you feel compelled to… forced to? Have you ever seen a hairy, big thing that looks like a slightly gormless ape? Like a macaque?"

Mia jolted visibly. *A gormless ape?* She composed herself, and fought the urge to wreak havoc on the pathetic piece of shit right then and there. "I believe a macaque is a monkey, not an ape! But in answer to your question, I'm afraid no, no… I haven't seen anything like that. Sean suggested I come here; he said it might be a good thing for me to be closer to Kayleigh." She forced a sickly smile.

Rachel frowned. *"A macaque is an ape, because it is big, monkeys are smaller. Anyway, are you sure that it was Sean who told you? That nothing supernatural contacted you? You didn't feel... like something odd was luring you here?"*

Mia looked at Rachel. *Fuck me, this cretinous meat sack is supposed to be a teacher.* "A macaque is a monkey, it has a tail, apes do not have tails, and no – there was nothing that lured me here."

"That's a relief. Thank you, Mia." Rachel wished she had not gone on about macaques, but what was done was done. *"I had best get to the police station then, to report your body."*

"Yes, you do that."

Rachel walked away.

'Mia' sat on the bench until totally satisfied that Rachel had left the area. Scratching its side frantically, it mulled over the conversation that had just taken place. Gormless ape? The creature had been described as a gormless ape. Foolish, stupid girl. If it hadn't needed her, it would have destroyed her with one glance, and made her suffer and writhe in agonies till she perished with prayer gushing from her lips. It would get its revenge somehow.

It quickly turned as its attention was engaged by something.

Walking slowly towards the bench came a little spirit boy, aged about four. Gingerly, he was holding a ghostly flower in his hands; it looked like a large daisy. With a happy laugh, he walked towards the creature, clearly seeing a pretty teenage girl.

Nanny rounded the corner. "Percival... where are you? You mustn't pick—" She stopped.

Both looking up, the creature and Nanny faced each other; Percival was oblivious, stooping to pick another spirit flower just ten feet from the beast, still in the form of Mia.

317

Nanny thrust her hand out to stop the gaggle of children behind her from advancing further.

"Stay here," she barked at them. "P-Percy... come back to Nanny now."

As she watched, the 'girl' smiled, and 'her' mouth split wider and wider to her ears, revealing rows of fine, needle-like teeth.

"Percy!" Nanny's voice raised in urgency. "*Please come back to Nanny, now!*" she shouted, her call shrill and high, quavering with desperation.

The creature stood and took one step towards the stooping child. The smile had closed shut. "Have you a little flower for me, Percy?" It took another step.

"Yes, pretty flower for you," said the child, as he walked towards the creature.

Nanny had no option. Thrusting the swaddled baby she had been carrying in her arms to the youth behind her, she ran towards the darkness, with every step she took seeming to push her four steps back in the opposite direction. "Look away, look away!" she screamed to the children behind her.

Calling and calling the child's name, she ran and ran, feeling her long coat flap in the breeze and the hair pins holding her hat on working loose, one by one. Every fibre of her spirit compelled her to stop and run the opposite way, but she was a nanny, and her job was to save the souls of the innocents, even if she perished in the fire doing so.

Then she was there. In a swift tackle, she grabbed Percy and hugged him close to her in a huddled position on the ground, just inches from the diabolical thing. As the child struggled, she held him tighter, and a prayer escaped from her lips in a soundless motion.

The creature bent down and extended a spindly hand towards her, then stopped. Hanging loosely from her neck, Nanny's cross glinted in the light; like a bright moon casting radiance on the darkest night, it blinded the beast temporarily.

Turning, it moved away in revulsion, as a human might react to a fresh pile of vomit. Enraged, it then swung back around to take them both. It gazed upon the female, saw the faith, wisdom and resoluteness of her soul, and knew that it had been recognised for what it was, even while masquerading as the dead girl.

The creature hesitated.

The struggle involved with taking a soul as strong as this would drain its energy; energy that it needed to carry out its plan. It could not allow itself to be distracted. Besides, the souls of the dead were not nearly as coveted as the souls of the living.

The beast took a step back and turned away from them. As it began its walk away along the path, it started off as a young woman, walking with ease, but, with each step, its gait began to jerk and move more erratically till it sank to ground level, as if its legs were made of ice and had melted on a hot day. Abruptly, the arms pushed out of their sockets and lengthened to support the hunched torso.

Nanny glanced up and turned away in horror at what she saw, barely holding on to the complaining, protesting child. As she turned her eyes to the creature again, she saw a quick shuffle into the trees and a fleeting, grasping, upward movement, as the thing propelled itself into the tree canopy and was gone.

Loosening the child from her grip, she wiped his tears with her ever present handkerchief.

"Look, Nanny, flower dead," Percy said, proffering a rotten, black flower towards her.

She saw her charges standing back with a look of horror on their faces, as all around the living woods where she sat, the grass had turned to blanched straw, and every flower and bud had blackened, wilted and rotted.

"Nasty lady killed the flower," complained Percival as he ran back to the group, crushing the remnants of the spirit flower beneath his feet as he ran. Nanny remained on the ground in shock; thank goodness she wasn't still mortal as the site of such an abomination would have left her sick, blind, or even dead.

With her hand to her breast, Nanny stood up. "Come on, children, let's find another place to walk; it isn't safe here."

No one disagreed as they walked away, in the opposite direction to the creature, and in complete silence.

CHAPTER 42

At first, the police had not really taken it in when Rachel told them that Kayleigh's stepbrother should be questioned about both her murder and Mia's. Especially, as up to that point, Mia's body had not been found, so the crime was recorded as a missing person case, not a homicide investigation. As part of the original inquiry, Kayleigh's entire family had been called in, but Sean's interview, like all the others, had passed without note. He had no criminal record and no history of violence, so they did not detain him further. It was only when Rachel told them where the body was to be found, and insisted he be questioned again, that they seemed to sit up and take note.

She wondered if, as she hadn't been asked about Mia's murder during the investigation, the police actually had no faith in her predictions, and this most recent information, plus their knowledge of the Jewish incident would simply confirm their own suspicions that she was mentally unstable. Part of her hoped that no remains would be found, as she wondered deep down if the spirit she saw in the woods really was Mia, and, who knew, she might still be alive somewhere. But, by the same token, she thought if a body *was* found, this would not only prove the spirit was Mia and bring the killer to justice, but also prove she wasn't insane. Rachel was scared that if things kept happening to her, she might end up being taken by force in to some kind of mental institution for treatment; she really did not want that at all.

Well, it was up to the police now. It was best to leave it to them.

★

It took a whole week to get a forensic team out to the derelict Mountain View Hotel. People had driven by the place many times, as it stood on a main road, but no one really acknowledged it, as it had been empty for some five years. Taking into account its broken windows, rotten roof and driveway that was overgrown with weeds, it sat as a sad, rotting reminder of the area's past. A few months ago, rumours had passed around that it had been bought by a private owner to turn into a private clinic, but nothing had happened since. No one even knew why the abandoned hotel bore the name it did, as it did not look on to any mountains, just a main road and the houses opposite.

The police were not sure what to make of Rachel's 'insight' that the body of the dead girl could be found in the water tank. To be so exact as to not only name the building, but give *where* the remains could be found was quite extraordinary, and it had only been due to Ronald Easton's insistence that made them take it seriously.

The hotel boasted two enormous, cylindrical water tanks on a raised platform behind the main building, and both were only accessible by climbing a long ladder, breaking through some padlocks and shifting the huge, heavy lids. Upon arrival, and after examining the tanks from the outside and seeing no disturbance to the immediate area, Detective Sergeant Milton – the officer in charge – contemplated that they should just return to the station. The most compelling evidence that Mia's body was not inside one of the tanks was that no single person could have lifted one of the lids alone. In his estimation, the strength of, at the very least, six very powerful men would have been needed to remove the lid from each tank. Rachel had apparently been adamant in her statement that it was the stepbrother working alone. Three large padlocks stood guard on each tank, preventing anyone moving the lids; they were covered in dust and looked to have been undisturbed for some time.

But something niggled at the detective sergeant, and, in the end, he made the decision to open the tanks. It took almost two hours to cut through the locks and, with the help of six of their strongest officers, force the two weighty lids aside. They found nothing untoward inside the first tank they selected. It had clearly not been drained when the hotel was closed down, so was still almost completely full. When they managed to shift the lid on the second tank, Milton immediately peered inside the opening, using a torch to illuminate its contents.

The first thing that struck him was the overpowering, sweet, rotten stench of decay, and the second was the bloated, ashen, white head of a young girl that was bobbing half submerged in the water.

His next decision was whether to throw up in front of his colleagues, or try to hold it down until he could be alone.

CHAPTER 43

It had been two whole weeks since Mia's swollen, waterlogged and half-rotten corpse was found. Rachel thought she would get some kind of satisfaction out of helping find the body, allowing the culprit to be arrested and Mia to be buried decently. But when news reached her that the teen had been retrieved from the water tank, she only felt deep sadness.

Rachel had heard, via Mr Easton, that the stepbrother – Sean Lovall – had been arrested and charged with the murders of Kayleigh Lovall and Mia Logan. Andy had been delighted by the news. Rachel suspected that his elation was less to do with them being a step closer to justice being done, than it was to do with them being a step closer to the £10,000 reward that had been put forward by Kayleigh's parents.

During all this time, the entity in her home had become more and more troublesome. Since the Jewish incident, although it had not outright attacked her again, it was still being a nuisance, filling the kitchen with darkness every night, which made Rachel afraid to go in there. It was also setting off lots of electrical equipment after dark, and turning on the TV and radio in the early hours. She also had a suspicion that it was growing in strength; the light it emanated seemed to be brighter, and its silent-bass noise louder.

It had also started activating an old, cloth talking doll that Rachel had kept since childhood, which her mother had given to her when she was eight. By pulling the worn string in its back, the doll would cry, "Mama," again and again; however, about fifteen years ago, it had stopped working, until now. Every night, at about midnight, Rachel would hear its eerie call echo around the flat, with its faltering voice calling to an unknown lost mother.

She had tried shouting at the entity, asking what it wanted, and tried closing her eyes under her bed covers and asking subconsciously why it had decided to attach itself to her, but there was nothing and no answers, only more problems. She had tried ignoring it, but it still grew more powerful.

Her only hope was Andy, and, because of this, she had begged him to do an exorcism on the flat. He had swerved her requests a few times, until last week when he said he would be prepared to rid her flat of the problem, but on two clear conditions. Firstly, that his new girlfriend, Debbie Simpkin, would be allowed to take photos of the whole affair, and, secondly, that he could send a write-up to the press about how he had 'triumphed over evil'.

Tired of the whole business, she had agreed, and the date for the entity removal had been set for an unremarkable Wednesday evening. The entity always manifested in her kitchen at about 11pm every night, so at 11.15pm on Wednesday it was going to happen, for better or worse.

326

Rachel prayed for the best, but feared the worst; that was the only way to be with Andy.

★

Rabbi Lieberman sat on the bench beside a bus stop, watching the cars whizz by on the busy high street. There were so many cars now, going so fast. He had died in 1952 and remembered, at the time, coveting a car owned by a neighbour: a Morris Oxford. Cars in those days had personality, not like today's vehicles, which all looked the same for the most part. The rabbi liked cars and had enjoyed riding in them during his lifetime. Now, in his deathtime, he found it hard to remain inside a car in spirit form, especially fast cars, as when they drove off, his spirit usually ended up floating in mid-air long after the car had disappeared down the street.

A Jewish brother he knew, Joshua, spent most of his time frequenting a petrol station beside a busy thoroughfare. When cars stopped to take on fuel, he was known to sit in the back seat and enjoy the ride for a few miles, before returning back to the station to ride somewhere else in another car. Joseph Lieberman could not condone this action, as it seemed to be done only for the fellow's sheer delight and took him away from religious study, which could not be encouraged. But he did envy Joshua for being able to keep his spirit inside the car when it was going fast, rather than ending up floating out as the rabbi had done. He also wondered what would happen if a mortal who could see the dead was driving and happened to glance in his rear-view mirror, only to see a Jewish gentleman in the back seat. It would cause an accident one day, he was sure.

As he looked up, he saw Nanny coming around the corner. Today, she had a small number of children with her and no babies. Rabbi Lieberman was glad; he didn't much like babies. In his lifetime, newborns had been brought for him to bless and welcome into the faith. However, this was a task which he held very little love for; babies always screamed and often smelt horrendous.

His old eyes watched as Nanny turned and spoke to the oldest child at the front of the ragtag bunch of urchins. The girl she was speaking to was aged about twelve and dressed in clothes that looked quite modern to his eye, not that he was really a follower of fashion.

Nanny left them and slowly walked towards him. He saw the children check she was not looking their way, and then, when they seemed satisfied her attention was focussed elsewhere, they hurried into a nearby shop.

She sat on the other end of the bench and considered him. Joseph had never met Nanny before, but he had heard of her and her tireless work to guard the souls of babies and children still seeking *the answer*. As a man of faith, he had often wondered how babies and children coped with being dead, considering they had barely lived. Regarding Nanny again he noticed that her face was pale, even for a ghost, she was slim and, although not classically beautiful, she held a plain serenity that was attractive in itself.

"Good day, madam." He inclined his head towards her.

She went to shake his hand, but he politely waved her away.

"You are Rabbi Joseph Lieberman?" she enquired.

"Yes, indeed," replied the rabbi.

"I understand you wanted to speak to me? What have I done?" She looked concerned.

"Apparently, you faced the *shedim*, the evil one, and lived to tell the tale, so to speak."

Her memory returned to the fateful day in Darkfoot Wood, when she had seen the 'girl' turn into a demon. She shivered as if someone had walked on her grave. "I did not choose to face it. It was threatening one of the children. It had appeared as a young girl, but I knew right away what it was."

The old man removed his glasses and began cleaning them on his coat; he did not meet her gaze. "The girl... Rachel... she was there as well?" he asked.

"Yes, I think the demon had spoken to her before I got there. I don't think she knows the difference to be honest."

He replaced his glasses, and she noticed one of his ears was slightly higher than the other one, and that the arms of his spectacles had been bent slightly to compensate.

"Knows the difference? What do you mean, child?" he enquired.

"Rachel. I heard something happened to her head, some kind of accident, and then, suddenly, she could see us all. She sees us through her eyes, but I don't think she sees us in her mind. She doesn't understand the difference between spirits, such as you and I, and... well, the other things that lurk in the underworld. She sees them as simple ghosts as well."

"Really?"

Alice rubbed at her forehead, then pulled two pins from the top of her hat and removed it, placing it on the bench beside her. She then remembered she was in the presence of an older Orthodox Jewish man. "You don't mind me… removing my hat?"

"As you wish." He waved a dismissive hand.

"It's just so nice, sitting here in the sun. I remember when I was alive I used to—"

"We tried to cleanse the soul of this girl and remove the influence of the *shedim*… the demon. Some brothers and I went to Rachel's home, but we were stopped; they took fright and ran away because something was there already."

Nanny frowned at the way she had been interrupted, but guessed this was just the rabbi's way of doing things. "Something? What something, another demon?"

"No, it was troublesome, but I did not feel evil coming from it… It was an entity, you might say. The woman is a *putz* and one of these days— anyway that is not why I asked you here."

A bus stopped right by them, and the pair watched as a group of people slowly pushed their way out through the automatic doors as they whooshed open. A small boy, led by his mother, smiled at Nanny; she responded with a small wave, and the mother, seeing her son wave at an empty bench, tugged him gently away into the crowd.

The rabbi continued, "The girl, Rachel, has become a danger to the living and the dead. She appears to have the power to be in the presence of the evil one, but not wither, die nor turn mad."

"Isn't this to be welcomed? Many say she will bring *the answer* and allow us salvation to seek our Lord."

"I think the opposite. She is being manipulated by the

evil ones. Oh, don't get me wrong, I do not believe she intends evil in her heart, far from it. But she is too naïve; she is allowing herself to be used for their ends."

"What ends?"

"I do not know for sure, but I believe it is something to do with bringing souls from the light to the dark, increasing the influence of the evil ones in not only the mortal world but in the spirit world."

"How do you know all of this?"

The old rabbi closed his eyes, opened them slowly, then spoke as if it required extra effort. "There is a boy, in our community; his name is Adam."

"A child?"

"Yes, he is nine. He has been born from a line of…" He paused and waved his hand. "Divine seers. Those who can see the future of mankind… of our dark fate or salvation. His grandfather foresaw terrible things for our people, and all that he said came to pass. Adam approached me one day to speak of the coming of this woman, whom I now know is this Rachel, and how it would be up to me and other Jewish brothers to stop her."

"From doing what?"

"From being used by the *shed*— demons… to bring a terrible darkness to our world. I must confess that I was both honoured and afraid to be entrusted with such an enormous task, but now I am under obligation to gather other members of the righteous together, to stop this spread of evil.

"Although our faith cautions against contact with the dead, and instructs believers to reject those who claim to be a seer in any form, Adam is very, how do I put this? He is unusual. This is why his warnings have been considered very seriously." He coughed lightly.

They both sat silently on the bench. The rabbi saw one of Nanny's spirit children leave the shop they had entered and float gently upwards, to the laughter of the others.

"I must go soon, Mr Lieberman. What is it you want of me?" Nanny asked.

"Your vow, dear lady, that when the time comes – the day of reckoning – you will stand alongside my Jewish brothers and I, and those of all other faiths that champion the light, to defeat the demon."

"Why me? There must be someone better than me – stronger or more pious… I do not think I am your best choice to help defeat something as utterly evil as you say."

"You have been chosen because you have put your eyes upon it, have witnessed its malevolence, and can attest to the fact that if it remains in this realm unhindered, such regrettable things will occur. Someone without this conviction would wither in its gaze."

Alice looked at her feet. "I was afraid, sir, when I saw it; I thought at first that I would collapse upon the ground in a faint. I do not think you need someone like me; you need someone braver…"

His faded eyes turned to her. "But you did not faint, nor back down; you took heart."

She looked up. "The children… I am here to protect the children, even if it is at my own peril. I feared the thing would hurt them, so I had to do what was right."

"And you will do this again? When called on to do so?"

"To save the children, yes, of course, without hesitation. That is why God put me here I believe…"

Rabbi Lieberman watched a spirit pigeon walk slowly past the bench, bobbing its head this way and that, with the sunlight picking out the green and purple feathers that dotted its breast.

He nodded towards it. "Why do you think our Creator allows such a simple creature to cheat death and return in spirit? What can it add to the world? I will tell you why: it is because, no matter how humble we are, we all have a reason to be here – a task we must fulfil – even this bird."

Alice looked doubtful.

Joseph continued, "So, Nanny, I can rely on your support in this matter?"

"Yes, to save the children from the evil one, I'll do anything."

The rabbi stood to leave. "My lady, I fear the next time we face the *shedim*, it will not be just to save the children, but to save us all." He bowed his head towards her and then left, causing the pigeon to briefly stop pecking the ground to watch him go.

A chill spiritual wind blew Nanny's hat from the bench, and she realised the sun had gone in, hidden by some ominous black clouds gathering overhead that had cut off its warmth and light. She shivered, re-pinned her hat to her head and sought to gather up the children from wherever they had scattered to.

CHAPTER 44

The evening of the exorcism had arrived, and Rachel, Andy and Debbie had gathered in Rachel's living area. It had just turned 11pm.

As usual, Andy had brought a box of paranormal articles: his Stetson, some kind of radio transmitter and the by now familiar music-box-with-mirror device he used. Rachel didn't know why he brought this; the entity could clearly be seen already, lapping gently out from the kitchen into the darkened hallway, so no mirror would be needed to view it, just a pair of eyes.

Debbie Simpkin stood there, dressed in a pale maxi-dress, a long necklace with very large orange beads clasped around her neck, and her bobbed hair, as usual, fastened on one side with a simple hair clip. What had possessed Debbie to date Andy, Rachel didn't know, as they seemed very different people to her, but, obviously, since Andy had visited her flat, something must have happened to gel them together as an item.

"I rigged up a video link in the kitchen earlier; look, it's working," said Andy, pointing to a small TV screen he had set up beside the sofa

Rachel could just see her kitchen, in black and white, with a mist-like object pulsing gently in the middle.

"Right, are we all ready? Debs?" he queried.

"Yes, Andy," she said enthusiastically, waving a camera at him.

"Rachel?" Andy asked.

"Yes, whatever. What do you want me to do?" Rachel replied.

He put his Stetson on, fiddled with the crucifix on the front so it was straight, and then took up the radio transmitter. "Right, you walk into the kitchen, and I will follow. The idea is that the purple spook thing will try to possess you, and then I will drive it back with ancient words."

"What ancient words?"

"That's my business. Are you OK with that?"

"Er, not really, but as long as it works… You have to get rid of it, Andy."

"Debs will be taking photos throughout, so that we will have a visual record whatever happens. Also, the video link is recording, so nothing bad can happen, and, well, if it does, again we have hard evidence."

"If you say so."

He positioned Rachel just down from the kitchen door opening. She saw a bright-violet smoky haze leak out from the doorway, as if a large, purple disco strobe was pulsing within.

Staring ahead, Rachel thought it was a bit like being on one of those talent shows on TV. The stage curtains

335

suddenly part, and the performer is shoved forward to face the audience and scorching lights.

"Right, in you go," Andy declared.

"Now?" She actually felt scared; all the memories of the Jewish incident had returned in a pins-and-needles-like attack on her whole body, and she was starting to feel sick.

"Yes, NOW… come on…"

With a quick push from Andy, Rachel was inside the doorway.

In front of her, she saw the entity. It had no features, but was just a purple-and-black haze in the top left-hand corner of her kitchen. The silent-bass sensation could be felt, but only weakly, as it gently throbbed away to itself like a cat, purring in its sleep.

Andy stood to her right, and then, without warning, he bellowed, "Kum by yah… oh spirit… speak to me!"

There was nothing. No reaction and no change.

Taking two steps towards it, he began waving the radio transmitter back and forth. Gentle hissing emanated from the small speaker in the device. "Thine immortal spirit, have cometh here without welcome. The fair maid here wanteth you to leaveth."

Behind them, Rachel heard the gentle snapping of the camera wielded by Debbie.

Again, there was nothing.

"Maybe it's asleep?" hissed Rachel.

Andy took another step closer and then continued, "Thee spirit, thou dost abide in this domain without invitation and must leaveth back to whence thee…"

In an instant, the by now familiar face of the entity began

to form, with the eyes and mouth slowly becoming visible in the swirling mist. To Rachel's perception, the purple haze seemed brighter.

"It's smiling," offered Debbie hopefully.

Nobody knew quite what happened next. But, within the blink of an eye, the entity – which had been lingering peacefully in the top corner of Rachel's kitchen, like a giant cobweb – immediately lunged forwards like a trap door spider springing towards its prey. It enveloped Rachel and, in a throbbing and pulsating motion, curled around and around her, like a winding slug, crushing her within its constricting hold.

Clearly taken aback, Andy dropped his radio. "Rachel? Can you hear me?"

"Andy…" Her voice was unclear. He could just make out her body, standing there stiffly, her arms pinned to her sides within the translucent entity's coils. "Help me… I can't move…"

"Do something," called Debbie from somewhere in the room; the snapping sound of the camera could still be heard, so she was clearly focussed enough to keep taking photos.

Determined, Andy pushed his Stetson back and strode towards the entity, which had totally encircled Rachel's body, surrounding her within its mass. He stopped within inches of the pulsating shape and, in an attempt to rescue her, he reached out with both of his hands towards the purple-and-black mist.

Instantly, he was screaming on the floor as a wispy tentacle snaked out from the entity and began, like a slick python, to curl around Andy's arm, tugging him into the mass to join Rachel.

The thing grew in size, spinning slowly around and around like a huge spiral, with its eyes and mouth appearing randomly within its curls. Rachel seemed to be suffocating inside as her eyes were rolling and her mouth agape. Andy, meanwhile, remained on the floor, tugging and kicking the tight, unyielding appendage that pulled him unhurriedly towards the entity.

Debbie knew it was up to her. Looking around in desperation, she spotted a fire extinguisher affixed to the far wall. Hurrying over, she snatched it from its fixings, tugged the safety pin off and unleashed a shower of foam on to the entity. Although clearly not losing its grip on either Rachel or Andy, it howled, and the spinning motion ceased for a moment.

"Let them go, you bastard," Debbie screamed, but then she fled when a large octopus-like tentacle snaked out, searching to drag her into the whirling, purple hell.

Running for all she was worth, she tore up the hallway, with her beads smacking against her face. Tugging at the front door, she threw herself into the street. "*Help! Help me!*" She looked left and right. There was no one to be seen, just the odd twitching curtain.

After the Jewish incident, it was clear no one in the street was prepared to help; they were probably thinking that Rachel had suffered yet another nervous breakdown.

Hidden by the shadows, Dr Maxwell looked up. Most nights, he stood there, just below Rachel's entrance staircase, watching and waiting, just to catch a glimpse of her, to check that she was well.

Debbie snapped her gaze down to where he stood, and, for a second, they locked eyes. "We need help," she uttered. Rubbing her face, she raced back into the flat.

William felt a lurch in his chest; had she seen him or just felt his presence? Walking up the stairs to the open front door, he saw the wisps of smoke and purple light filling the hallway.

Inside, he could hear Debbie screaming. He lifted a foot to enter and then stopped. What in God's name could he do to stop this thing? Nothing. He couldn't even touch anyone or move anything. If only Henry were here, maybe he could levitate the entity or something.

Jesus Christ.

"*Rachel!*" he shouted.

There was only silence.

He took two more steps down the hallway; Debbie's screams had stopped now. "Rachel? *What's happening?*" he yelled, aware that, being a ghost, only Rachel could hear him, so if she was unconscious, or dead, his efforts would be hopeless.

What the hell could he do? The purple smog got thicker and thicker, and began to completely fill the hallway. He felt like it was stopping him from advancing any further, and forcing him back. Who could do something? That blithering idiot Andy had clearly made matters worse.

After rushing outside, he stood in the street and closed his eyes. He wished for her, thought of her face, her lips, her eyes (brown and clear), her touch and her smell. He was willing himself and hoping to get closer to her, to be with her. He couldn't do anything, but he believed she could.

Feeling himself sucked through space, Dr Maxwell found himself in her room. Standing on a chair, of all places. "Laya?" He prayed she was there. "Please God…"

"William… you scared me." A light snapped on in the corner of the magnificent, golden room, revealing the large bed with red, silken bedsheets. She sat up in the bed, smiling. "What would you want this time of night?"

Leaping from the chair, he hurled himself onto the bed, kneeling almost on top of her. "Laya, dear lady, you have to come. Rachel is in trouble; the thing that attacked her before has got her again, and I am powerless to stop it, but you… you can help?"

She frowned. "Ah, Rachel; you are here for her, of course. Please close the spiritual door on your way out." She nestled under her covers.

"She will die; all at the hands of that nincompoop Andy, who has been messing with things he doesn't understand."

"It's not my problem. She should have left the entity here – it amused me – but, no, she compelled it to return with her; and now it's gone wrong, I am meant to bail her out?"

Angrily, she sat up in the bed again. He saw she wore a loose black T-shirt, and her hair tumbled down to her waist in messy tangles. In his lifetime and youth, he probably would have been inside the covers by now, joining her in the bed, but not this time. More important things than lust were at hand.

Dr Maxwell became desperate. "Look, I do not believe she compelled it to do anything, it sort of attached itself to her whilst she was here, and now it will kill her if we do nothing."

"I am not a powerful psychic; I cannot help deal with any entity that Rachel has got herself tangled up with. Call the police or something."

"I can't call any police; I can't use telephones or anything." He waved his hands back and forth through her torso to prove a point. "Please help me, Laya; I don't know what else to do…"

Muttering, she climbed slowly out of bed and rubbed her eyes; under the T-shirt, she wore small shorts, which showed off her tanned, slim legs. He found himself staring at them as she stood before him, lit gently by her small bedroom lamp.

"How am I supposed to get to her house? It will probably all be over by the time we get there," she stated.

"You have a chauffeur, don't you? He can drive fast?" the doctor suggested.

"What do I get for this? I am not risking my life for nothing. The driver will want a big payout for this as well, to keep his mouth shut."

Putting his hand to his face, Dr Maxwell looked desperate. "If you can get rid of the entity, I will come here and stay with you; forever, if you want. I will do anything. Please, Laya; you can see them, which means you can compel them."

Muttering something under her breath in Arabic, she walked to her wardrobe and removed one of her many flowing, long, black robes and struggled to get it over her head. After adjusting the dark folds, she pulled black, satin gloves over her hands, and reached for the niqab and lifted it over her face.

"I can see spirits, but I do not know how good I will be at removing them," she explained.

"But you will come and… try to help? I cannot do this alone," the doctor stated.

"For you, yes. But if I die…?"

"You will not."

"You probably didn't think you would die when you did, Dr Maxwell."

"You have a point, madam."

"Where does she live?"

"14C Rainton Avenue, Burwood."

"My driver will find it. Now go," commanded Laya.

Drawing his mind back to Rachel, frightened and strangled in the hold of the entity, he found himself transported back to her open doorway. By now, the purple fog had completely blocked the hallway. He made a couple of attempts to fight his way through, but was constantly driven back. Even though he was a spirit, and did not have real lungs to speak of, the mist seemed to fill him with a hot and cloying ash, weakening him at each step and forcing him to remain outside.

It seemed like he waited on Rachel's doorstep for hours until Laya appeared. A supercar – a silver Bugatti – purred silently to a stop outside the house. A very well-built Saudi Arabian man in robes and headdress leapt from the driver's seat and rushed round to help her out. Some words in Arabic were exchanged by the roadside, then he nodded, got back into the car and quietly drove away.

"This has cost me dearly, William," she complained as he hurried towards her. "I have had to pay my driver, Ahmed, and one of my sisters, Maryam, to pretend to be me in my bedchamber, in case my husband visits."

"Wouldn't he know it wasn't you?" he asked.

Laya frowned. "Probably not," she said, and inclined her head towards the open door. "They are in there?"

"Yes," confirmed the doctor.

Taking a deep breath, she walked up to the front door, which was still encased in fog. Turning back, she looked at William, who smiled at her weakly; she then faced the door again and was swallowed by the deep mass.

Dr Maxwell went as far as he could into the hallway, as if to follow her, but was driven back again. Standing outside doing nothing made him feel as useful as an umbrella at the opera, so he decided he would go and try to find Henry, who could possibly do something to move the mist so he could enter. Yes, that was it. Willing himself elsewhere, he vanished, hoping to find Henry, wherever he might be.

CHAPTER 45

Laya put her hands to the veil covering her mouth, and pressed on down the hallway. Although not like physical smoke, the entity felt thick and heavy about her person; it was like walking in water when it was up to the neck. She felt the force of its presence all around her.

Ahead of her, to her left, she saw the kitchen door, and at the bottom of it was a shadow, rounded, with an uneven surface; was it perhaps fur? Then two little, bright-red eyes popped open at the top of the figure, which was like a dreadful, hirsute dwarf.

For a moment, Laya and the creature looked at each other. She felt no fear or horror, just curiosity as to what the thing was.

Then it spoke. "You have come to help, yes? That saves me doing anything." Its monotone voice, like something generated artificially, had no accent and gave no clue as to sex.

A spindly, long, dark, clawed hand pointed to the room. "Go on then…"

What was this thing? It looked like a large, scruffy cat, or some kind of tatty, miniature caveman. Was it one of Rachel's friends, caught up in this madness, dressed in a costume? But slowly, as the hairs on her arms began to stand on end, she realised what it really was, rotten and evil to the core.

"I cannot compel entities," she said.

"You can now," it uttered, giving a deceitful smile that swiftly turned into a grimace, as pointy teeth immediately became visible amidst its obsidian coloured fur.

She glanced sideways and saw horror. The entire kitchen was now a swirling, pumping, purple-and-black mass. Like a translucent snake that had swallowed its prey, she could see Rachel and Andy crushed together at the centre of its vortex. Both were either dead or had lost consciousness.

"Go," the thing hissed, "Rachel cannot die."

Stepping into the room, Laya looked around her; she had no idea what she was meant to do. In her house, the entity had been like a slightly aggressive friend, whom she had welcomed into her life as a distraction from the monotony. But it had only ever appeared in a smaller form, not like this; not as powerful as this. Something in Rachel's house must have caused it to grow in size and strength.

"Remember me?" she called out to the fog. "You left my home to come here. Please… let them go."

She expected it to stop turning, to shrink back perhaps or to at least acknowledge her, but nothing happened.

She stepped forward. "*Stop!*" she called out. "Please release them."

She watched as the entity began to constrict. Tighter and tighter, she witnessed invisible tentacles press against

Rachel and Andy's bodies, squeezing every last bit of air from their lungs. Andy's eyes popped open and his tongue began to protrude.

In helplessness, she turned back to the creature, who had stepped out into the light. It now looked more like a grotesque chimpanzee, with a stocky, hunched, muscular body; short, bent hind legs; and strong, long arms which rested on the floor. Its head was small and human like, but covered in the darkest, thickest fur, and with little ears, like a cat's, slicked back on its head.

Its tiny red eyes turned to her. Saying nothing, it lifted both its spindly hands out in front of its face as if pushing back. "Compel it to leave," it hissed. "Like this."

Turning back to the swirling, dark hurricane before her, Laya lifted both of her arms, at first uncertain, spreading out her gloved hands as the creature demanded. All at once, she felt as if invisible gauntlets had been placed on her, from her shoulders to the tips of her fingers, holding them firm and resolute. Closing her eyes, she started to concentrate.

The mist stopped swirling, and its face formed before her again, almost filling the room.

Opening her eyes, Laya willed it gone and, out of the blue, was shaken by a force ripping from both palms of her hands. Out of the corner of her eye, she could see the creature was now behind her, in the same position as her, with its claws outstretched, but its eyes were clearly tightly shut.

Like a firefighter struggling with a high-pressure hose, she could barely maintain her footing as the energy streamed from her hands and smashed into the entity. For a moment, it screamed and whirled, and then, with an ear-splitting scraping noise, like nails tearing at a blackboard, it was gone.

Rachel and Andy dropped over three feet to the floor. They both appeared to be lifeless.

Debbie appeared from a corner, dragging herself along the ground, and sporting a heavily bruised eye and split lip. Taking almost no notice of Rachel, who was pale and prone on the linoleum, she dragged herself to Andy's side. Taking him in her arms, she began to weep. Laya heard Andy emit a small cough, and his arm moved. He would be fine.

Rachel.

Laya hurried across the room. Debbie started at first on seeing the dark-robed figure rush past her, thinking it was another evil force, come to wreak havoc; then, on seeing it was a woman, she smiled weakly.

Laya fell to her knees and looked at Rachel. Her lips were blue; her face pale as snow. Putting her ear to Rachel's mouth, Laya stayed quiet, but heard nothing; she wasn't breathing. She placed a gloved finger to the pulse point on Rachel's neck, and felt nothing. Rachel really was lifeless.

The furry thing appeared by her side.

"She is dead," whispered Laya.

Without hesitation, the creature took Laya's hands in its own and pressed them to Rachel's stomach. She felt the burning heat of its claws pressing down on her fingers, which, in turn, touched Rachel. Laya almost felt compelled to look away from the beast, fearing that looking straight at it would burn through her eyes into her soul; strangely though, she felt no urge to pull away, or fight it off.

Andy was retching, and as Debbie cradled his wounded body, she looked up to see Laya, on her knees over Rachel, appearing to do some kind of chest compressions. Rachel was clearly not breathing; Debbie could see that much from where she was sitting. "Please help her," she cried.

The creature frowned at Debbie momentarily, then looked straight at Rachel's body on the floor and muttered something. Laya didn't know what it was; it was in a foreign language or dialect, but not one she had ever heard before.

Rachel began to transform. Colour swept from her neck and across her face, and her lips began to turn pink. Laya was relieved to see she was now breathing on her own.

The thing removed its hands, freeing Laya, and sat back on its haunches. The creature looked satisfied, but then frowned. It moved nearer to Rachel, squinting closely at her left temple.

Chattering gently to itself, again in an odd dialect, it placed its hands on Rachel's head. Closing its eyes again, it muttered some more words, gave her head a little pat then sat back. "All done," it proclaimed; and, with that, it frantically scratched its flank (making Laya jump) as if it had been bitten by a flea. It then flashed a terrifying smile, filling one-third of its face with pin-sharp, thin teeth, swivelled around on its long arms, then scuttled away through the kitchen door.

Laya looked up to see Debbie by her side, weeping.

"You have saved her; she is alive…" Debbie wailed.

"How is Andy?" Laya replied.

"He is shocked but he will be fine, I think." She looked over to where Andy had sat up by himself and was holding on to a kitchen chair.

"I am Laya, by the way. I met Andy and Rachel when they got rid of this... er... problematic spirit I had."

"I guessed you were... Andy told me about you. You are a heroine."

Just as Laya went to leave, two policemen hurried through into the hallway, although, at that point, both the dark creature and the purple entity had long gone. Whether that was a good or bad thing, Laya didn't know.

CHAPTER 46

Rachel lay in the hospital bed. She had absolutely no recollection of what had happened to her three days before, with her last memory being of Andy pushing her into the kitchen; that was it. She remembered nothing more, except coming to in an immodest, blue hospital gown, lying in a bed once again.

She had asked the doctors if she had suffered another brain haemorrhage. The doctors had said no, just crush injuries, and it had looked like her heart had stopped. She had been told how Laya had somehow appeared in her kitchen and performed cardiopulmonary resuscitation (CPR) on her, which had saved her life; all witnessed by Debbie.

There had been bad news, though. In the scans taken when she was admitted, it appeared that the site where she had suffered the original brain bleed had a bulging artery or something, which would need further surgery to prevent it bursting. She had been told that, providing she didn't take part in any violent sports or bungee jumping, she would be OK for the moment, as the bulge – despite being present – didn't pose an imminent risk. Rachel would need surgery soon though, and had been asked to think about it, whatever that meant.

Debbie had kindly brought some women's magazines in for her to read, about famous singers and z-list celebrities having affairs and taking their clothes off. This reading material was not to Rachel's taste, but it was better than having nothing to do at all.

Debbie had also kindly delivered the local paper, the *Burwood Echo*, which had a story about Rachel (this time on page three), entitled 'LOCAL PSYCHIC INJURED IN PARANORMAL BATTLE'. There was the old library photo of her – the mental-looking one that it had used last time – to accompany the story. The text informed readers how Andy Horton had done battle with a poltergeist that had attached itself to Rachel, and how, thanks to the speed and efficiency of his response, she was going to be OK. The last line carried the Spirit of London Paranormal Investigations' phone number and website details.

She had been told by Andy that, after checking the digital SLR camera that Debbie had been taking photos with all evening, not a single shot came out. Every single one was completely blank, as if taken in a dark room with the flash disabled. The video link recording on the night had also apparently failed, showing nothing but static, so not a jot of evidence remained that anything supernatural had occurred at all that evening.

At least there was no mention of Laya; Rachel thought it was probably best that her husband didn't know that she took to the streets at night, like some robed crusader, fighting dark forces.

But there was no doubt who had fed this story to the press. Andy looked like a hero, and she, as usual, looked like a crazy fool. This had further dampened her spirits.

Since awaking in the hospital, she had also suffered a constant, dull headache, which came and went in severity on a whim; this was interspaced with severe stabbing pains in her temple. Whether this was stress, a normal headache or this bulging artery, she had no clue.

Whilst pondering this, Rachel saw a movement at the end of her bed. It was Dr Maxwell. She had seen him at her bedside a couple of times in the past day or so, but couldn't remember much about it. Rubbing her sore head, she propped herself up.

He broke the silence. "Hospitals have changed significantly since my day… They're more disordered now…" He looked about nervously. "How are you anyway?" William continued. "I heard the doctors saying you had another problem with your head?"

"Yes, a bulging artery or something. It's lucky they caught it when I came in here, or I would have been walking about with it and not known. They say it might have burst, but it seems stable for the moment," she told him.

"Where is it?" He came closer.

"Where the original bleed was." She pointed to her left temple. *"It's a bit sore."*

"Oh, I see. You need surgery?"

"Yes."

"Or…?"

"Or I die."

"Would that be so bad?"

352

"Pardon?" Frowning, Rachel put her magazine to one side. *"I don't really want to die, so yes…"*

William looked sheepish. After removing his pocket watch, he gave it a bit of a polish before returning it to his waistcoat. Shortly after playing his part in saving Rachel's life, he discovered that he was finally able to manifest his treasured gold pocket watch, gifted from the College of Surgeons. He was at a loss as to why he was suddenly able to make it appear with ease, after spending his entire deathtime trying to do so without success. He wondered if it was perhaps a sign that, in finding his watch, he was beginning to find himself. "If you died we could… well… be together…"

Rachel sat silently for a long moment, slightly embarrassed. *"I am sure I don't know what you mean."*

"Yes, you do. We could court, perhaps?" He looked doubtful.

"But you are a ghost."

"Yes, and if you died, *you* would be a ghost as well."

"What if I got sucked up to heaven, and you stayed stuck here? Then we couldn't."

"No… perhaps not."

Silence.

Rachel decided to change the subject. *"I was taking my medicines and everything, so I don't know why this would come back again."* She tapped her head.

"It's probably because of what you do. Perhaps you moving between the living and the dead is how you can see us, and why spirits are drawn to you: because you yourself sit between these two worlds… alive but seconds from death with your aneurysm. You cannot get into spiritual water without getting wet, if you understand my meaning…"

"Thank you, Doctor, you have lifted my spirits no end…"

Another change of subject was needed.

"Laya. Remember that Saudi Arabian lady in the veil? Debbie said she saved my life. Apparently, when it all went tits up, and Andy and I got trapped by the entity, she got rid of it and then saved my life as I wasn't breathing. She performed chest compressions on me and got me breathing again… Debs said she was sure I was dead, but Laya brought me back; impressive, huh?" recalled Rachel.

"Laya is certainly special…" he confirmed.

She saw him look away. *"Have you seen her since?"*

"No, but she has asked me to drop in from time to time. I think her life, with all the wives and the sheikh, is a lonely existence."

"Then you should go to visit her."

"Really?" He turned back to her. "You… wouldn't mind me going to see her?"

"Why would I? It's nothing to do with me what you do."

He went to open his mouth, looked down, then sniffed. "No, I don't suppose it is…"

A nurse walked by, looked at Rachel, frowned and walked on. Although she was speaking to Dr Maxwell in her mind she needed to be more careful of her facial expressions, as she didn't want to end up in the psychiatric ward again.

"At least the entity and the furry ape thing have gone. Laya sorted them out," said Rachel.

"The ape… thing?"

"Yes, the physical manifestation of the entity or whatever you call it.

354

I don't mind seeing ghosts, normal dead people who used to be alive, but I certainly want nothing more to do with evil stuff. Andy said that, now the entity has gone, the furry ape-like thing cannot bother me anymore, being as they were one and the same thing."

"Andy has been here? I thought he was injured as well?"

"You know Andy..." She looked down at the bed. *"He wants to know how his investment is doing... Without me, there wouldn't be a Spirit of London Paranormal Investigations team. Apparently, his phone is red hot with jobs. Someone even offered us a piece on a digital channel, talking about ghosts."*

"'Dig-it-all' channel? What in Jesus' name is that?"

"It's on TV... television..."

"Oh, the moving-screen thing with the people inside... yes, I see."

Again, there was silence.

He stood up abruptly, looking crushingly sad. "I will be off then."

"Yes, thank you for coming."

He did a little bow and left.

Rachel didn't know why she felt down. There was nothing between her and Dr Maxwell. He was too old for her, and too dead. How could one date a ghost, especially a ghost from another era? She would consider a young man who had died in the 1960s, but a Victorian? That was ridiculous; it would be all penny-farthing rides, hat doffing and corset wearing. No thanks. Besides, where was he when she was dying on the floor of her kitchen? He was probably somewhere polishing his pocket watch. It was a good job Laya had turned up when she did; perhaps Andy had somehow managed to get word to her. Maybe she owed Andy a debt of gratitude, as it was probably right what the paper had said, that he had helped her out; she had probably been too harsh on him by far.

Rachel lay down on her side, pressing her head into the scratchy, hard hospital pillow. She felt a gentle throb, as if her artery was saying, "Hey, look at me; I am still here." Closing her eyes, part of her hoped William would come back, say he didn't want to go to Laya and that he wanted to be with her. It was sheer stupidity, but…

She felt the weight of someone sitting on the end of her bed. It brought a smile to her face as she sat up, expecting to see the familiar face of Dr Maxwell at her side, forgetting, of course, that a ghost does not usually carry weight. But it wasn't William. The man sitting there was about forty, smallish in stature, with short, dark hair, a cheap suit, a shiny briefcase and piercing, brown eyes.

"Miss Holloway?" He leapt up from the bed as she sat up, blinking. "I am so sorry; I thought you were sleeping… I was about to leave a card." Like a magician, he flipped his hand up for a business card to appear, which he then offered to her. As their fingers touched, she felt that his were ice cold.

Rachel looked at the card through blurred eyes. It said 'Rennison Wright – Publicist' and included his contact details.

"Sorry… What do you want?" She propped herself up.

He shook her hand briskly. "You are becoming very famous, Miss Holloway; there's talk of your psychic ability, of being able to see ghosts, and how you defeated some kind of dark force in your home. You need to protect yourself."

"From ghosts?"

"No, Miss Holloway, from unscrupulous newspaper

articles such as this one…" He drew a copy of the *Burwood Echo* from his briefcase and flipped it in front of her, helpfully opened to the page she featured on. "I will also guide you through TV appearances and shield you from cranks demanding your help. I would like to meet you, perhaps for coffee, to discuss how we could enter into a mutually beneficial professional relationship."

"I don't have much money, Mr Wright. I live from hand to mouth nowadays."

"Don't you worry about that; you are hot property right now… Goodness, you are modest." He leant forward and smiled at her, showing slightly uneven teeth; his brown eyes flashed again. "Promise that you will give me a ring when you get out?"

"Why pick you? I mean, there are lots of media people out there… I would have to see what they offered first."

"They are not like me."

"I am sure."

He bobbed his head towards the exit door. "I saw him too you know… the vintage-looking guy who was here a moment ago; he had a pocket watch, right? Took it out and put it back?"

She looked up, stunned.

"The girl over there…" He nodded towards a spirit girl, standing in the corner. "About eight years old, wearing a white petticoat and with a large bow in her hair… you see her?"

Yes, of course she saw her.

"I see 'em too… You aren't the only one, you know."

What had she to lose? Dr Maxwell had obviously cooled towards her, and it was clear that Andy was only in it for the money and his own self-promotion. "Yes, sure, but I need to rest."

"Of course." He leapt up and clutched his briefcase to his chest. "Don't go making any media deals without speaking to me first, though, OK?"

"Yes, OK." She smiled weakly.

The same nurse who had frowned earlier appeared at Rachel's bedside. "Are you family, sir?" she quizzed him. "Only family is allowed in here."

"I am her brother, can't you tell?" he said, winking. Lying obviously came easily to him. He flashed another quick smile, and then disappeared behind the plastic curtain.

The nurse walked away, leaving Rachel to examine the card he had left. "'Rennison Wright'," she said aloud, reading from the neatly printed text, "'Get the Wright deal for you and your business'; Jesus God."

A psychic publicist; could things get any odder?

She lay down again, her mind filling with Dr Maxwell and Rennison Wright. She never dreamt for a moment that she was the only living person who could see ghosts (why would she be?), but it still jolted her to speak to someone who could do it with the same apparent ease that she could.

Slowly, she fell into a slumber, and, for once, her dreams were not haunted by visions of dark figures, only William and Rennison, standing either side of what looked like a never-ending fence, just staring at each other.

CHAPTER 47

Rachel found herself, once again, in a police interview room. A week had passed since she had been discharged from hospital. She had only been into her second day back at home when she received the initial phone call from the police. They said that they wanted to speak to her regarding the murder case. She had tried to put them off, but they had proved to be quite persistent over the days that followed, and had phoned her numerous times in an attempt to coax her into helping them with some 'further enquiries'.

So, here she was, back on familiar territory, except that, this time, she was waiting alone because she didn't want Andy butting in. In fact, Rachel had told him nothing about this visit to 'the feds', as he would probably refer to them. She sat in the same kind of drab room as before, dominated by one large, charcoal-coloured table in the exact centre of the floor space, with recording equipment placed on the side of it. A barred, tiny window allowed in a pointlessly small degree of sunlight, like a half-hearted afterthought.

Above Rachel's head, a yellowed light fitting cast a defined circle of luminescence on the table's surface in front of her. A single poster on the wall depicted an old-fashioned cartoon police constable, blowing a whistle, with the slogan:

If you want to report a crime,
don't ask a policeman,
do it online!

A website address was included beneath the slogan.

As Rachel pondered over the poster, a sharp click from the door latch broke the silence, and a strikingly handsome man entered the room. She guessed he was mid-thirties, with a lean, muscular physique, bright-blue eyes and short, mid-brown hair. To Rachel, he looked more like a catwalk model than a police officer.

"Miss Holloway," he said with a radiant smile.

"You can call me Rachel, if you like." *Did that sound flirtatious?*

He sat opposite her. "Rachel…" He opened a folder and placed a couple of papers straight onto the table in front of him.

She strained to see if she could make out any words on them, but the font was too small. She saw a photo of what looked like a large water tank. It made her shudder.

"I am Detective Sergeant Jack Milton, and I have invited you in to tell you what has happened regarding the case of Kayleigh Lovall and Mia Logan." He looked up from his papers to meet her gaze. "You are no doubt aware that Kayleigh's brother, Sean, has been charged with both murders, so it seems that you were correct in implicating him. He is currently remanded in custody until he goes to Crown Court. It looks like we have our man."

He smelt vaguely of sandalwood. Rachel always had a thing about the smell of sandalwood.

"Do you have enough evidence to condemn him?" she asked.

Milton smiled at her again. "Absolutely. Thanks to your tip-off, we organised a second, more-thorough search of Sean's room and belongings. The first time, he wasn't really in the frame, but this second sweep gave us a shoe, with both Kayleigh's blood *and* mud from Shore Moat on it. All it took was a little push under questioning, and he admitted his guilt for both murders. We got a result."

"Oh… right," Rachel mumbled. *He really is bloody handsome, and he has no wedding ring.* "Did he say why he killed them?" She reflected his smile back. "I'm just being nosey."

"Lust." He paused fleetingly. "It was lust, apparently. Sean felt strongly for Kayleigh in a sexual way. Remember, they weren't blood relatives; Kayleigh was his stepsister. It often happens, but, on this occasion, Kayleigh didn't feel the same way. She told him nothing would come of it, so… he killed her."

"But how did he lure her to the moat?"

"He didn't. He had been stalking her for quite some time up to that point. But when she walked through the wood to get home that night, he struck. It was pretty straightforward, really."

"And Mia? What of her?"

"Apparently, Kayleigh had told her about Sean stalking and bothering her, so when Kayleigh was killed, Mia confronted him and rightfully accused him of murdering her. He told us he couldn't risk her mouthing off about him, so, one evening, whilst following Mia, he attacked her when she was paying her respects at Kayleigh's memorial."

"It almost sounds too easy… You give the impression that there was no real planning behind what he did. That he just struck almost randomly, when he felt like it."

"Yeah. Murders are often unplanned. In fact, most are done on the spur of the moment."

"Yes, but *two*…?" Rachel mulled it over for a moment. "If you don't mind me asking, Sean didn't mention anything about paranormal influences, demons or entities, did he?"

Milton looked into Rachel's eyes. "No, he confessed that the only thing that drove him was lust and anger, nothing ghostly."

"I see." She gathered her thoughts again, them having been scrambled by Milton's gaze. "Did he mention anything at all about Kayleigh's shrine and why he chose to kill Mia there?"

"Why do you ask?"

"I feel… You see, it was *my* idea to build a memorial for Kayleigh. It makes me think I am somehow responsible."

Milton placed his hand on hers. "Rachel, your actions have done nothing but help our investigation and assist in giving those girls a proper funeral. You had absolutely nothing to do with the murders; this was all down to the evil of one man."

Rachel smiled, but she did not remove her hand. Her eyes fell to the photograph on the table. "So you found Mia in the water tower. Did he explain how he managed to get her body in there?"

He removed his hand and sat back. "I'm afraid we haven't got that out of him yet. Sometimes, though, when people are aroused in anger or passion, they can have superhuman strength. I've seen some pretty crazy things over the years. Anyway, he gave a full confession, so that's that."

"That's that," Rachel echoed. "So, I guess I'd better be going then. Nice talking to you." She started to stand up.

"Rachel, before you go." Milton's hand shot out again and touched her forearm gently. "We have another case. A missing boy…"

Rachel reluctantly sat down again as the detective sergeant fumbled with some papers in his folder. Eventually, he handed her a photograph of a young boy with blond hair, who was wearing a red jumper. It was slightly blurred and very obviously a family snapshot. "His name is Oliver. He is seven years old and went missing two days ago. His father thinks someone may have kidnapped him, and the usual leads have gone cold. Can you help us find him?"

She looked sadly at the photo. "I'm afraid I can't. Not if he's still alive. But, if he… isn't alive, well, then perhaps I can find out more."

"Have you a spirit guide to help you? Is that how it works?"

Rachel put the photo down onto the table. *What an odd question.* Then she thought of Mia. "Yes. I might do."

"Well, if you do, now might be a good time to… er… have a word with him… her… it."

She tried to remember if she had ever met a police officer before who believed in ghosts. *Aren't they only supposed to deal in hard facts? The provable? This was a refreshing change.* "I

363

feel I should tell you at this stage that… I am not very well at the moment." She looked up from the photo on the table. "I have a problem with my head. I will need an operation, and I don't know how it will turn out."

Jack Milton sat back in his chair and beamed again. "Rachel, I am positive you will be absolutely fine. So you'll help us with the case, yes?"

"I suppose so."

"Fantastic." He scribbled something down on a police business card. "Here's my card, with my *personal* number, should you ever wish to call me at any time of the day or night." Their fingers touched briefly as he handed it to her.

The business card felt slightly warm in her hand. It somehow made her feel better. *He* somehow made her feel better, too. *Yes, I'll call him.*

CHAPTER 48

Sheikh Mohammad bin al-Rahman was furious. Ever since that fool, Andy Horton, had been in his house, there had been unrest. Although the spiritual whispering had stopped, and he seemed to have removed the odd thing that lingered on the stairs, this had been replaced with general unease amongst his staff, his wives and especially Laya, who was quieter than usual.

Very soon after Andy had left the sheikh's home, he had been informed of two issues by his staff. Firstly, in the room that Andy had stayed in, an empty miniature whiskey bottle had been found at the back of the wardrobe, proving he had been drinking alcohol. He had been very clearly informed that alcohol consumption was strictly forbidden in the sheikh's house. Secondly, and more worryingly, a gold bust of the sheikh, which had been cast by the famous Saudi Arabian artist, Rashid, had gone missing from the sun lounge on the same day that Andy had left.

Sheikh Mohammed had held an important meeting that same day with some influential Saudi men, hoping to get their support for a new hotel that he wished to build in Sardinia. It was, of course, possible that one of his brothers could have stolen the bust, but he doubted it. He was sure that Andy was the culprit. Over time, it troubled him more and more, and during a recent business trip to Dubai, he found it difficult to think about anything else. He considered arranging for Horton to suffer a 'misfortune', but then quickly banished the idea from his mind. The fool was not worth the aggravation of such a deed, and besides, if he was dead, the whereabouts of the bust would never be discovered.

So, when the sheikh woke up that morning, he came to the conclusion that something absolutely had to be done. His assistant had offered to report the crime to Scotland Yard, but the sheikh believed that if he reported it to the local police station, in person, in the same area where Andy and Rachel lived, more might be done. After all, Andy Horton was well known now. In Sheikh Mohammed's view, the police would find the idea of investigating this so-called 'local celebrity' interesting, so might put more effort into finding the bust.

The sheikh was at the police counter, ranting at the clerk, flanked by two burly bodyguards. In the waiting area nearby, four of his wives sat in a dark line, in complete silence, like a row of crows. Laya sat watching from the end of the row, as her furious husband continued his tirade at the older man behind the counter.

"The man disrespected my home, my wives and my customs! Now it seems he has also robbed me of this most important possession! I want his house searched and I want him arrested!" ranted the sheikh.

Laya's head turned at the sound of a familiar voice. *That sounds like Rachel.* She lifted part of her veil, in order to see more clearly. It *was* Rachel. She had come out of a side room and was talking to a young man. Laya watched as Rachel shook his hand and, smiling, walked out through the revolving doors onto the street, clutching a folder.

Laya glanced back at the young man. *There's something oddly familiar...* She felt her eyes being drawn towards him as surely as if fishing hooks had been lodged in them, and his very presence was reeling them in. He stood there, concentrating on the door to the street. Then he absent-mindedly scratched his side, as if bitten by something. His eyes turned to meet hers, unswerving, as if he had always been aware that she had been looking at him. There they both remained, locked in each other's sight as the seconds thudded by.

Then he smiled, revealing rows of pin-sharp teeth crowding his mouth. It was like a shark's mouth. Laya could clearly see them from across the room. Like a toothy vortex, they drew her into a blackness far emptier than the vacuum of space and more dreadful than dread itself.

Each tooth became a step. A flight of winding steps.

A spiral staircase of bone. The steps were cold. Laya knew the steps were cold because her bare feet were upon them. She looked down and realised that she was completely naked, but was untroubled by it. Taking a deep breath, she thought that she could smell blood. There was just enough light to perceive a narrow space, and as her eyes adjusted, she began to make out a circular wall around her of skinless, gristly pink and red flesh, interlaced with bone. Laya sensed that she was standing within the tower of a castle. A castle of flesh and bone.

She looked back to see the bone steps curve around the inner wall and out of sight above her, towards an unknown source of grey light. Turning, she looked down at the steps, curving to her right, into the shadows beneath her. She began to descend, away from the light, one hesitant step at a time. A thought entered her mind: something about castles; a fact that she had read as a child, about spiral staircases in old castles. *They always spiral upwards in a clockwise direction*. She remembered it was something to do with making it difficult for an invader to wield his sword while climbing the stairs, because his right arm, usually being the sword arm, would be hindered by the interior curve of the wall. The defender, coming down the stairs to fight the invader, would have the advantage because his sword arm would most likely be next to the curve of the outside wall, giving him room to swing. It then occurred to her that this staircase descended clockwise. *These steps are wrong… They are supposed to descend anticlockwise. This is all wrong.*

As Laya descended, she wondered how long she had been there. Perhaps just a moment, a year, a lifetime. The coldness of the steps on her feet sucked the very essence of who she was out of her. The darkness increased with each tentative footfall, and a disturbed, uncomfortable feeling began to weigh her down. She became aware of the smell of putrefying meat, becoming more intense as she advanced further into the depths of the fortress of flesh. She wondered why she hadn't climbed upwards, towards the light, then realised it was because she could feel that something below was drawing her closer, silently calling to her.

The darkness continued to envelop her, until it was absolute. Her eyes may as well have been gouged from her skull for all the use they were. Unable to see in the pitch blackness, she instinctively reached out a hand for support, and felt the cold, wet, rotting meat of the outer wall. Snatching her hand back in revulsion, she hesitated before continuing her descent, one careful step at a time.

Finally, the steps seemed to come to an end. Blind and suspicious of her own senses, she carefully edged forward, her numbed feet cautiously feeling around the continuously flat surface. Her arms outstretched, she advanced a half step, then another. She took a full step forward, then another, and immediately became aware of a presence. She could not see it, or hear it, but every cell in her body screamed at her that it was there.

Laya knew it was in front of her, and she knew what it was going to feel like before she had touched it. Her hands reached out and made contact with *something*. It felt like the gnarly, wet bark of a tree trunk, but instead of curving around in the familiar way a tree would, this was more like a wall. Her senses knew immediately that it was vast; a thousand miles high and a thousand miles wide, neither truly alive nor dead, and yet infinitely powerful and abysmal.

As she blindly felt around the bark wall, a sudden, terrible realisation hit her that it was moving around her, closing in. Panic swept over her, as it became apparent that she was completely surrounded, as if being trapped at the bottom of the deepest and darkest well. She started to struggle as the wall continued to contract, but it was too late; it completely enveloped her, leaving her unable to move, unable to breathe, unable to scream.

As the diabolical bark gradually began to press into her body, tear her flesh and break her bones, she wondered if she was being digested. She was not entirely sure. The only thing she was certain of was that there was no way out. She had no sense of how long she had been engulfed by the presence, and as she wished for the simple luxury of being able to feel her own tears upon her face, she found herself on a plateau of endless despair and hopelessness.

Eternal

Sulphurous

Agonising

As she started to feel her soul being peeled from her dying body, she perceived a sudden jolt, a tear, a rip, a gash forming, as the police station began to reassemble. The shock of being sledgehammered back to her senses was almost too much to bear. It was followed by a brief, sinking sensation that reminded her of how air turbulence felt on an aircraft. Finally, the banality of the front counter room of the police station settled around her.

Shaking and sweating, she gazed upon the creature. It winked at her.

Continuing with his tirade, Sheikh Mohammed looked around to check on his wives. "If it costs to investigate this, then so be it, name your price and I am sure..." He saw Laya, her hands clasped tightly together in her gloves, sweat marks lightly spotting the outside of her niqab, with her head turned at a ninety-degree angle, clearly enthralled by something across the room. His gaze followed her line of vision to rest upon a young man – a very handsome young man, with perfect white teeth. He was smiling broadly at his wife, and then he winked at her. *The audacity!* His rage exploded. "*Laya!*"

Laya jumped out of her skin, as if awoken from a trance. She stared, wide-eyed, back at her husband. The sheikh scowled at her then turned back to the counter. "You have all my details. I want this Andy Horton arrested and my bust returned, or I will ensure a diplomatic incident will follow with the leaders of your government."

Striding away from the counter, robes flapping, the sheikh signalled with a flip of his hand that the four women should follow. They responded immediately, in single file, shuffling silently after him until they reached his limousine outside.

A muscular Saudi Arabian man, in robes and a headdress, bowed and opened the front passenger door to the sheikh, who immediately climbed in. He then opened up the back doors, allowing the wives to silently shuffle into place on the sumptuous leather seats. Once they were all settled, the chauffeur drove off.

As the car purred gently out of the police station car park, Laya stared out of the window. Still in shock, she felt the bile rising in her throat. Moments ago, as she had followed her husband out of the police station, she had glanced back to see if she could catch a glimpse of the creature, just one more time, but it was gone.

As the limo turned out of the main street, she saw the ghosts of about twenty Orthodox Jewish men, dressed head to toe in black, much like herself. They were gathered together in a group, praying and chanting. As the car drove past, one of the men looked up. He was older, with a thick, grey beard, and wearing – like many of the others – a large beaver hat and a long, black coat. She also noticed that he wore old-fashioned horn-rimmed glasses.

Laya turned away and looked at her hands, which were still shaking.

The sheikh spoke without turning around to address the car's occupants. "*Insha'allah*, let this be an end to all this nonsense and vexation that has been felt in my house."

There was no reply from the robed figures in the back seat. The first three had remained silent because they had nothing in particular to say. The fourth remained silent because she knew that her husband was as wrong about this situation as anyone could possibly be.

The troubles had only just begun.